Critical Praise for Laurie Loewenstein

for *Death of a Rainmaker*

- Finalist for the 2019 Oklahoma Book Awards, Fiction
- A *Library Journal* Best Book of 2018 (Crime Fiction)
- An NPR "One of the Best Books of 2018"
- A *Publishers Weekly* Pick of the Week

"Loewenstein movingly describes the events and the people, from farm eviction auctions and hobo villages to Dish Nights at the movies. She vividly brings to life a town filled with believable characters, from a young woman learning her own worth to the deputy sheriff figuring out where his loyalties lie. This warm and evocative novel captures a time and place, with well-researched details shown through the lives and circumstances of one American town."
                                                                    —*Kirkus Reviews*

"The plot is compelling, the character development effective, and the setting carefully and accurately designed . . . I have lived in the panhandles of Texas and Oklahoma; I know about wind and dust . . . Combining a well created plot with an accurate, albeit imagined, setting and characters that 'speak' clearly off of the page make *Death of a Rainmaker* a pleasant adventure in reading."
                                                                    —*The Oklahoman*

"Set in an Oklahoma small town during the Great Depression, this launch of a promising new series is as vivid as the stark photographs of Dorothea Lange."
                —*South Florida*, One of Oline Cogdill's Best Mystery Novels of 2018

"After a visiting con artist is murdered during a dust storm, a small-town sheriff and his wife pursue justice in 1930s Oklahoma. A vivid evocation of life during the Dust Bowl; you might need a glass of water at hand while reading Loewenstein's novel."
                                                —*Milwaukee Journal Sentinel*, Editor's Pick

"Laurie Loewenstein's new mystery novel . . . expertly evokes the Dust Bowl and the Great Depression . . . Loewenstein's novel sometimes reads like a combination of a Western and a mystery. But that genre mishmash works."   —*Washington City Paper*

"The plot is solid in *Death of a Rainmaker*, but what makes Loewenstein's novel so outstanding is the cast of characters she has assembled . . . *Death of a Rainmaker* is a superb book, one that sets the reader right down amid some of the hardest times our country has faced, and lets us feel those hopeful farmers' despair as they witness their dreams turning to dust."   —*Mystery Scene Magazine*

"*Death of a Rainmaker* is far more than a murder mystery set in the Dust Bowl of the 1930s. It is a poignant recollection of the desperation of farmers whose land, livestock, and household are in foreclosure, a stunning description of a dust storm that leaves imaginary specks of dirt on the reader's neck, a sensitive rendering of tough times and their toll on the psyche. Some books have such fine character detail . . . and complex, nuanced storylines that the reader naturally slows down to savor the experience. This is one of them."

—*Historical Novel Society*, Editors' Choice Selection

"Readers will be completely absorbed in the lives of Loewenstein's characters who epitomize the extraordinary resilience of small-town folks caught in the throes of the Great Depression . . . Loewenstein manages to connect an enticing murder mystery with riveting historical fiction that places the reader directly in the dusty shoes of her characters."

—*Reviewing the Evidence*

"Loewenstein is establishing herself as a master of nuanced historical fiction, especially when it comes to the political infighting and swirl of intrigue around small communities in the early half of the 20th century. Loewenstein is a talented researcher with an eye for the historical detail, but also a gifted storyteller capable of breathing life into a wide cast of characters. For historical fiction readers, this is an author to watch."

—*CrimeReads*, One of Fall's Best Sophomore Crime Fiction selections

"A portrait of Depression-era America so searingly authentic that the topsoil practically blows off each page." —Louis Bayard, author of *Courting Mr. Lincoln*

"As if the black blizzards of the Dust Bowl weren't worrisome enough for an Oklahoma sheriff and his spunky wife, Laurie Loewenstein piles on even more troubles . . . Like the storms themselves, the plot powers its way across the landscape and seeps into everything it encounters." —Dayton Duncan, coauthor of *The Dust Bowl*

"It's odd for a story about a murder to be gentle and generous, but this one is . . . Laurie Loewenstein has a knack for writing the early twentieth century. I sure hope this is a series, because I'm smitten." —Robin Oliveira, author of *Winter Sisters*

"A lovingly and eloquently told murder mystery. It is not only the unfolding plot and the metaphorical obscuring of truth by dust, but Loewenstein's masterful prose—with its tender language and skillful resonance—that will captivate readers and keep them enthralled." —Leslie Schwartz, author of *The Lost Chapters*

"When the wind comes sweeping down the plain in *Death of a Rainmaker*, Laurie Loewenstein takes your breath away. Her haunting and vivid prose deftly describes the opening chords of a dust storm that left families sick with dust pneumonia or dead broke. In this gripping tale of a sheriff searching for a killer in a dying town, Loewenstein rounds up characters with true grit, cunning, and kindness."

—Mary Kay Zuravleff, author of *Man Alive!*

"A jewel of a novel. The scenes and characters are so vivid and alive that you forget that the Internet and interstate roads haven't been around forever. Loewenstein is a born storyteller . . . It's a read you won't forget."

—John Bowers, author of *Love in Tennessee*

for *Unmentionables*

"*Unmentionables* transports the reader to a time not that long ago—when women were not allowed to vote and racial prejudice was commonplace—when so much was different, but human nature was so much the same. Treating us to a captivating narrative that illuminates as it entertains, Loewenstein reminds us that it is the courage and integrity of individual people that changes the world."

—Beverly Donofrio, author of *Astonished*

"I loved this beautiful book . . . Loewenstein's ability to create a moment in history is authoritative and accurate. I was lost in that world, believed every word of it, and loved and wept with the delicately drawn characters. Love, fear, shame, regret, hope, and independence intertwine as the story moves from farm country to war-torn France and big-city Chicago, replete with anarchists and artists, suffragettes, freethinkers, and the working poor. This is a perfect book club pick, dealing with real history, real issues that are still relevant today, and real and unforgettable characters."

—Taylor M. Polites, author of *The Rebel Wife*

Laurie Loewenstein is the author of the best-selling novel *Unmentionables*. An Ohio native, she currently lives in Columbia, Maryland.

DEATH OF A
RAINMAKER

A DUST BOWL MYSTERY

LAURIE LOEWENSTEIN

KAYLIE JONES BOOKS

This is a work of historical fiction. All names, characters, places, and incidents are either a product of the author's imagination or are used fictitiously. Any resemblance to real events or persons, living or dead, is entirely coincidental.

Published by Akashic Books
©2018 Laurie Loewenstein

Paperback ISBN: 978-1-61775-665-8
Hardcocver ISBN: 978-1-61775-679-5
Library of Congress Control Number: 2018931312

Kaylie Jones Books
www.kayliejonesbooks.com

Akashic Books
Brooklyn, New York, USA
Ballydehob, Co. Cork, Ireland
Twitter: @AkashicBooks
Facebook: AkashicBooks
E-mail: info@akashicbooks.com
Website: www.akashicbooks.com

ALSO AVAILABLE FROM KAYLIE JONES BOOKS

Unmentionables by Laurie Loewenstein

Sing in the Morning, Cry at Night by Barbara J. Taylor

All Waiting Is Long by Barbara J. Taylor

City Mouse by Stacey Lender

Some Go Hungry by J. Patrick Redmond

The Year of Needy Girls by Patricia A. Smith

Starve the Vulture by Jason Carney

The Love Book by Nina Solomon

Little Beasts by Matthew McGevna

Flying Jenny by Theasa Tuohy

Foamers by Justin Kassab

Strays by Justin Kassab

We Are All Crew by Bill Landauer

Angel of the Underground by David Andreas

The Kaleidoscope Sisters by Ronnie K. Stevens

For Nathaniel, my greatest joy,
and for Steve, the love of my life

CHAPTER ONE

THERE IS NO MAN MORE HOPEFUL THAN A FARMER, who wakes each morning to the vagaries of a heifer gone off her feed, seed that doesn't take, a late spring, an early autumn, too much rain, or, worst of all, no rain at all, and still climbs out of bed and pulls up his overalls. And so it would seem that a fellow who swears he can cure this agrarian heartache, who swears he can make it rain, would be clinched to the bosom of every farm family from here to kingdom come.

And that was pretty much the case in the county of Jackson, in the state of Oklahoma, in the bull's-eye of the Dust Bowl, on August 2nd in the heart of the 1930s. As evening fell, farm and townsfolk loaded up their children and climbed into their jalopies. Strung out in a gap-toothed cortege, they motored a ways outside of town. The procession then turned sharply off the road and into a field. This particular field had once been fertile soil, etched into deep furrows. Now it was nothing more than hardpan—as impenetrable and unforgiving as granite. The last speck of loamy topsoil had blown across Oklahoma's borders into Arkansas years back, leaving behind compacted dirt, its individual particles bound together so tightly that even a drop of water couldn't wiggle through. But that made no matter because there was no water. Not an iota of rain had dribbled into the parched mouth of Jackson County for 240 days.

In silent choreography, the folk parked alongside one another and debarked. As they gathered, billowing dust settled wherever it chose. Pastor Coxey stepped into the semicircle to bless the crowd and the rainmaker's efforts. A woman commenced coughing but quieted when a stranger with rolled shirtsleeves stepped into the headlights' silver shafts. Roland Coombs was tall, with an open, easy face. He grinned and a bit of dental work glinted far back. He'd driven into Vermillion, the county seat of Jackson, just that morning with wooden crates of TNT and blasting powder roped down in the back of an open truck. Tucked within the pocket of his store-bought jacket had been a sheaf of testimonials from drought-stricken towns across four states. Vermillion's Commercial Club had hired him on the spot.

Now Roland was studying the ground, cupping his fist to his chest, as if a pitcher contemplating an opening throw. When he spoke, the words sluiced easily over his lips: "Thank you, Reverend. We are surely in need of the good Lord's blessing."

Several amens resonated from the crowd.

"I am here to tell you that He has placed in my hands the tools with which to bring rain to your parched fields. Nothing complicated. Just this little old matchstick and a load of TNT."

A skiff of dirt blew up, skimming the hardpan and whipping against the bare legs of little girls in short dresses. Several of them set to bawling and had to be comforted.

Roland didn't pause. "You see, I was a munitions man during the war. Shoveling shells into howitzers and blowing the Huns to kingdom come. One afternoon it came to me that every time we'd deliver a good old dose of TNT, we'd get a thunderstorm sure as shootin'. Seemed like the explosions would give the skies a healthy kick in the drawers and down came the rain. Blam if I know why, but it happened all the same."

Roland grinned wide. A good number of the crowd chuckled, relaxing into his river of words. Some, mostly farmers and their wives, retained a stiff reserve. Their hearts had been broken too many times. Yet still they wanted to hope.

Roland cocked a finger at the crowd. "But I recognize some doubters out there. And that's for the good. Because seeing is believing. Tonight I'm going to pepper your skies with TNT and see if you don't get rain by tomorrow afternoon. Maybe not a soaker, but at least a shower to prime the pump. How about that for a guarantee? And I'll keep at it for the next three weeks to make sure the heavier rains follow."

He rubbed his hands together. "So, let's get the ball rolling. Mamas, hold your little ones tight." Switching on a heavy flashlight, he trotted to the launch area he'd set up earlier that day. Twenty shells packed with TNT were pointed nose up toward the stars. Roland squatted to inspect the charges, then began delicately linking each fuse to the detonator. He inhaled. Nothing sweeter than the scent of explosives. For this launch, he'd arranged the shells in two concentric circles. The same pattern had

produced rain before and it was worth trying again. It was all about the
timing and the pattern. If he found the right combination and summoned
up a healthy dousing, the whole Oklahoma Panhandle—hell, the entire
High Plains—would be his gravy train. He'd had a couple of miffs. Been
escorted to several county lines. But he knew, in his heart of hearts, that
he was close to nailing it down. Striking the match, he studied the blue
flame. It jiggled like that girlie show dancer he'd seen in Kansas City,
who'd shimmied while he and the rest of the audience panted—thumping
away under the newspapers covering their unbuttoned flies. He lit the
fuse and hustled back to the gathered crowd.

"Ladies, cover your ears. It's a-coming!" he shouted as the rockets
shot upward with high-pitched screams. A series of thudding concussions
shook the sky and shot vibrations deep into the hardpan. It was as if the
millions of buffalo, slaughtered sixty years back, had risen from the dead
and were stampeding again. And with the concussions came explosions
of harsh white light. Flashes revealing all, then plunging the spectators
into darkness, then stripping them naked again. Over and over. The loose
blankets of dust on the road, on the fence posts, on the cars, and on the
people, rippled and settled time and again.

Some of the folks, including Reverend Coxey, fled to their vehicles.
But most, like Jess Fuller whose farm was scheduled for foreclosure the
next day, stayed put, with heads cocked back and hands keeping their
hats in place. As each explosion burst, Jess pumped his fist, shouting,
"You go, you go!" as if cheering on Dizzy Dean rounding the bases.
Despite years of toil in the sun and wind, Jess still had a smooth boyish
face. Beneath the brim of his woven hat, his eyes were as blue as penny
marbles. Hours before, ever since he'd heard about the rainmaker, Jess's
ruminations had spun around one thought: *Just one good soaking. Justa
one.* He figured a single cloudburst could salvage the kitchen garden and
the remaining cattle, at least enough to hold off foreclosure. *Justa one,
Lordie.*

His wife Hazel stood alongside him in her old-fashioned hat, under
which her thoughts spun in a different direction. She was wrung dry. She
couldn't squeeze out any more tears for the plot they'd dreamed about
as newlyweds in Indiana, the plot they'd scrimped for and bought and
tilled and sweet-talked for the past eight years. For the house, in whose
single window she'd hung lace curtains. Tomorrow it was all going on the
auction block and good riddance. The sooner they got back to Indiana,

the sooner they'd get back on their feet. If this rainmaker brought down just a single drop, she knew that Jess would dig in his heels. He'd take it as a sign that the rains would be back, that the green sea of sprouting wheat would again lap at their doorstep. But she understood that the life they'd had in the good years had withered and blown away. With each explosion, she watched mournfully as Jess's face brightened in the white light. The smell of explosives thickened the air. Hazel felt a sprinkling across her hat and for a second she froze. Rain? Already? But when she held out her hand only grains of dirt, tossed by the explosions, spattered into her palm. She smiled.

Then, as suddenly as the clamor had begun, it broke off, leaving behind only an echoing hum that beat against the eardrums of those gathered like moths. Soon, a few jalopies started up, lights from their headlamps thick with swirling soil.

"Show's over!" Roland shouted. "But I'll be here every night for three weeks, so stop on by. I could use the company."

That got a few laughs.

"And set those washtubs out when you get home. The rain's coming, sure as shooting."

Most of the crowd cleared out. A few lingered, including John Hodge, Vermillion's most prominent attorney, and, trailing two steps behind, his wife Florence.

"Impressive show," Hodge said, extending his palm.

Roland pumped the man's hand. "Glad to meet you."

Hodge continued: "Hope your method does the job. Matter of fact, I'm an amateur chemist myself. I was wondering about the explosive compounds you use."

The rainmaker reached for Florence's hand, bending as if to kiss it. "And this must be your lovely . . ." he said, then paused and surveyed her face. He cocked his head to one side, narrowed his eyes. Florence's pasty complexion turned to chalk. She yanked her hand away.

"Say, you look familiar." Roland slowly shook a finger at her.

Florence quickly pressed a hankie over her nose and mouth. "Is it all right if I go back to the car? I'm not well," she said to her husband.

"Stay where you be." Then, turning to Roland, Hodge grabbed the man's arm, his fingers pressing hard enough to bruise. "Don't you ever touch my wife again."

Roland raised his hands in surrender. "No harm intended."

"Just so we're clear on that. Right?"

"Absolutely."

Hodge went on: "I've got some questions about your operation. And keep in mind I kicked in a fifty toward your fee."

Roland smiled tightly. "I appreciate that and I'm glad to give you the low-down on my system."

"That's more like it. What I'm wanting to know is how the materials are packed into the tubes. What goes in first?"

As Roland answered the lawyer's questions, keeping back a couple of trade secrets, his eyes shifted to the thin pale woman half-hidden behind her husband's broad back. When Hodge's inquiry ran out of gas, he gruffly thanked Roland, snatched his wife's arm, and stomped off toward the cluster of parked cars. Roland watched as the fellow's sedan backed up with a jolt and accelerated toward the road. He dipped his head in thought, then trotted out to the detonation site. The beam of his flashlight illuminated the blackened squibs. As Roland collected the rocket launchers, three teenagers in baggy denim uniforms approached.

"That was the aces," said the shortest kid. He had the clipped accent of a city boy.

Roland studied the youth's wide-legged stance, the brim of his hat rolled back over wavy dark hair. "Where you boys from?"

"CCC camp, just west of town," the kid said.

Roland finger-snapped the patch on the boy's sleeve. "Civilian Conservation Corp. I've heard of that. So FDR's tree army has set up shop in Jackson County?"

The kid nodded. "I'm Carmine. This is Chet and Gordie." He jerked a thumb toward his two sandy-haired companions, who had the gangly appearance of Midwestern farm boys.

"We was thinking it would be swell if you'd come out to the camp one of these days and talk to the fellows about your setup."

"Be glad to."

From across the way came the slow crunch of tires on gravel as the last of the spectators departed.

"How you boys getting back to town?" Roland asked.

Carmine shrugged. "Hoofing it, I guess."

"How about you three help me load my equipment? I'll give you a ride and throw in a round of beers."

"You bet!"

After the crates were loaded under a canvas tarp, the boys scrambled on top. The truck had bumped along a mile or so when its lamps shone on a stooped figure tromping toward town.

"Want a lift?" Roland called out, tugging on the brakes.

The man, wearing a shapeless fedora, wordlessly waved Roland off without lifting his head.

"Suit yourself, old-timer," Roland said, releasing the clutch and applying the gas.

From his perch in the back, Carmine watched the man diminish in size until he was no more than a blurred gray shape before he disappeared altogether. "Nuts to youz, grandpops," he yelled, leaning back against the covered crates and stretching out his legs. "More room for us."

The truck putt-putted toward town, a dark mourning veil of dust in its wake. Shuffling along the berm, the bent traveler coughed and spat. After that, the quiet of the prairie was restored and the only sounds were the creak of his boots, the arid susurrations of the dead stalks, and the prayers of the people.

CHAPTER TWO

SUNRISE THE NEXT DAY, dozens of farm wives rushed outside to peer into their washtubs and basins, expecting to see at least a puddle. But instead found only a few trapped weevils flopping in the dust.

And in town, the owner of the Jewel Movie House also noted the lack of rain. Sniffing the dry air, Chester Benton immediately sensed that the rainmaker's promises of the evening before were nothing but false gold. He congratulated himself for refusing to hand over a single penny to the Commercial Club's rash backing of that hustler. But with the early-bird matinee only fifteen minutes away, he couldn't spend time gloating. He strode to the ticket booth, which stood under the marquee, a small compartment unto itself that was outfitted with velvet curtains and a parlor lamp. Chester Benton himself was just as dapper in his pinstriped suit, polished brogans, and blue-tinted spectacles that hid his clouded eyes. Brain fever had rendered him stone-blind when he was eight.

Approaching the booth, his leg wacked against the hard metal mouth of a waste basket.

"I've told you a million times that can belongs in the booth with you." Chester's voice was strident as he squeezed into the compartment alongside Maxine, his thirteen-year-old ticket-seller, who was perched on a stool inside. "Now I'll have a God-awful bruise on my shin."

"But Mr. Benton, there's not room for it in here. I can barely cross my legs."

Chester shoved the can beside her stool. Maxine sighed.

"And is that Juicy Fruit I smell?" he asked. "You know the rules. Spit it out."

"Yes, Mr. Benton. Sorry."

"You're not wearing lipstick, are you?"

"No," Maxine said, quickly swiping her Red Glo–coated lips with
the back of her hand.

"I can't afford to lose patrons because of a slovenly, gum-chewing,
lipstick-wearing ticket seller."

"Yes sir."

"Do you have enough change?"

There was a rattle of coins in the cash drawer.

"Twenty-four quarters, five dimes, thirty pennies."

Satisfied, Chester eased back outside. Behind him came the click of
a lipstick tube and the rustle of magazine pages, but he chose to ignore
Maxine's transgressions for the moment. Stepping out from under the
canopy, he tilted his head. The sun beat down. Blue skies meant folks
would be up and about and feeling snappy. In thirteen minutes the curtain
would rise, and if he sold twenty tickets, there would be enough to make
the rent. He grinned, allowing himself this nip of optimism, knocking it
back same as a shot of Four Roses. Making rent had not been an issue until
two years ago. It was then that the nickels that once jingled plentifully
in men's pockets and ladies' cookie jars became scarce. Everyone started
thinking twice before spending money on anything that didn't put food
on the table or keep the roofs over their heads. The Depression and the
drought had walloped Oklahoma with a one-two punch.

In the good years, the twenties, Chester had made a decent living.
Bought a radio and an overstuffed chair for his apartment upstairs. Invested
in a fine wool suit. Squired Lottie Klein, the head clerk and buyer at her
father's clothing store, to dinners at the Crystal Hotel and treated her to
biannual train trips where they sipped Four Roses in the club car.

He was a sharp-looking man, according to Lottie, who had regularly
remarked on his pencil-thin Clark Gable mustache. The mustache was
gone now. He'd had to give up the weekly expense of a barber's trim.
But Lottie said that his naked upper lip was not a deal breaker and that
hard times called for economizing. She was a shrewd businesswoman and
spoke her mind—qualities Chester admired. He figured she was in her
late thirties or early forties. Her standard reply when anyone asked her
age was, "None of your beeswax."

At precisely 11:35, Chester took up his position at the ticket bin
inside the lobby. The first patron to step up to the pulpit was Mrs. Reed,
as regular as clockwork. The woman wore too much perfume but her
voice was pleasant enough.

"And thank you very much," he said, as she dropped the ticket into his upturned palm. He ripped it tidily in half and handed her the stub. "To your right, please."

Depositing the pasteboard in her coin purse with a loud click, Mrs. Reed said, "Tell me frankly, is this one as good as Fred and Ginger's first?"

"Beyond a shadow of a doubt."

"But *Screenland* said . . ." Mrs. Reed began before Chester overrode her.

"So there you have it. Next?"

Mrs. Reed moved along with hesitant steps, as if a pupil returning to her desk after a scolding. Two more moviegoers approached Chester. "Left, please," he said.

Soon there was a gratifying crush of patrons, whose voices he knew by heart. Plus, there were at least five or six strangers, most who seemed to be CCC boys—their clothes sweetened with a scent of resin.

An audience of twenty-three, according to his count. He'd brought in enough to make rent. Enough to avoid the indignity of Dish Nights that so many other theater owners had been forced to succumb to. The idea of passing out free cereal bowls or coffee cups to entice patrons inside, as if he were a waiter or, worse, a volunteer at a soup kitchen, turned his stomach.

Relieved, Chester counted off fourteen paces to the stairs. Trailing his hand along the cool plaster of the stairwell, he mounted the steps to the projection room. Earlier he'd clamped the news and feature reels onto the two projectors. He'd had to let the kid who ran the projectors go. At first, Chester had been afraid he wouldn't be able to operate the equipment by himself. But then he'd gotten the idea of slipping a nickel into the sprocket, right near the hub, so he'd know when a reel was nearing its end. When the coin clattered onto the hardwood floor, Chester got ready to start the second projector. Now he flipped a switch and frenzied violin strokes heralded the first frames of the newsreel.

Back downstairs, he marched across the lobby. Maxine might need change for the two p.m. show. As soon as he pulled open the outside door he heard a faint thrumming of wind that resembled the plucking of thick guitar strings. Chester paused. There it was again, the opening chords of a storm. A duster coming and him with two dozen patrons inside. He'd never had a dust storm collide with a picture show. Damn it. Damn it to hell. He listened once more. The chords seemed fainter. Maybe he'd been wrong. He stepped toward the ticket booth and smacked into Maxine.

"A duster!" she shouted, her words rattling.

"How far out?"

Maxine was wailing: "Tall as a mountain! Oh my God! I've never seen one this big!"

Chester's mouth pressed into a rigid line. "I need you to tell me how much time before it hits."

"I don't know!" She was so nerved up that the air around Chester pulsed.

"Step out onto the sidewalk and tell me what you see."

She balked. He felt it, in the manner that a mule driver feels his animal stiffen along the telegraph lines of reins.

A second later she was back. "Just beyond the tracks." The flesh of his arms broke into goose pimples. The temperature had dropped at least thirty degrees. The dust storm would slam into town in five minutes, at most.

"Let's keep our heads. I'll turn on the house lights and let everyone know what's coming. Meanwhile, you shut off the projector."

Chester pivoted, yanked down his cuffs, and strode inside. Maxine followed him into the lobby. Behind her, the doors rattled and banged. Fingers of wind and dust wriggled under the sills and across the carpet. The fronds of the potted palms flanking the candy counter shivered. Maxine eyed the snug telephone booth in the corner and thought of squatting inside. An image of Mr. Benton's stern lips, however, sent her up the steps to the projection room two at a time. Peering through the booth's narrow window she watched the theater owner make his way down the aisle, then flick on the house lights. The audience moaned. Taking her cue, Maxine cut the projector. On the screen, the newsreel decelerated, then froze altogether.

"Hey!" shouted a young man.

Downstairs Chester held up his palms. "Ladies and gentlemen, I'm sorry to interrupt the show but it seems we have a duster bearing down on us and—"

Several people quickly rose as if to leave.

"You all need to stay seated. It'll be on us any second and this one is particularly big."

The theater abruptly went black.

"Electric's out," came a voice from the left.

"Oh, yes," Chester flushed, then called up to the projection booth. "Maxine, bring the lanterns."

Mrs. Laycomb, the judge's wife who had brought her elderly mother-in-law to the movie house, could be heard shouting into the old lady's ear: "See if he doesn't try to gyp us out of a refund." Then Mrs. Laycomb's sturdy oxfords clomped up the aisle. "I'm going to see what's going on out there for myself," she announced.

Springs squeaked as everyone else dropped back in their seats, having gotten used to hunkering down wherever a dirt cyclone found them—in church, at a neighbor's, in their own porous house outside of town. Within seconds Mrs. Laycomb returned, reporting it was as black as night beyond the lobby doors.

"Up here too," Maxine muttered aloud, slowly feeling her way down the stairs from the booth. Why did *she* have to get the lamps? Mr. Benton was used to the dark. The utility closet smelled of kerosene and floor wax. She bundled three old lamps with oily, blackened chimneys against her chest, undoubtedly smearing her best blouse, and stumbled back through the lobby and into the theater. Sand and topsoil hurtled down on the roof as she traipsed along the aisle. Maxine cringed. *What if the roof gives way?* Suddenly a load of dirt and a blast of cold air shot in from the left. The exit door must have blown open. She was showered with a spray of sand. Several patrons commenced hacking.

"Shut the door!" a woman yelled. Maxine crouched in the aisle, making herself as small as possible. After a second or two, the heavy metal door to the alley slammed shut. She rose slowly, still clutching the lamps, and found her way to the foot of the stage. Mr. Benton's voice rose suddenly in her ear.

"You've got the lanterns?"

As Maxine lit the wicks, weak applause broke out. Above the ornate plaster ceiling, the rafters creaked and shifted.

Chester spoke: "Everyone stay calm."

There was a general shuffling as the patrons changed seats, moving closer to the light and warmth. Chester was suddenly overwhelmed with fatigue. The unexpectedness of it all had tangled up the careful web of routine that kept his world intact. And then there was the rent money. He was cradling his head in his hands when the sound of Maxine's shoes on the carpet intruded.

"Mrs. Laycomb is raising a fuss, saying her mother-in-law is hungry. Should I bring something from the candy counter?"

Her God-awful lipstick smelled like clotted candle wax. "Why not? Bring enough for everyone," he replied, irritation clipping each syllable.

"What should I get?"

Chester made a brushing motion with his hand. "I don't care. Why should I care? The bank will have it all soon enough."

After a pause, Maxine's voice came out low, as if she'd dropped her head: "I'll need the keys to the counter."

"I know that," he snapped, although he'd forgotten that detail. He removed a key ring from his jacket pocket. "It's the one with the bit of adhesive tape on the top."

Returning with yellow candy boxes clasped in her arms, Maxine noted, despite the dim light, that the patrons were settling in. Mrs. Laycomb's mother-in-law pulled out needles and a ball of worsted from a lumpy knitting bag. Miss Boyle and Miss McDonald, English teachers at Vermillion High, whispered together, their identically crimped heads touching. The loose-limbed CCC boys sat cross-legged on the carpet in front of the stage playing cards. Maxine passed out the Raisinets and found she had two extras. She shrugged, took a seat a couple of rows behind the CCC boys, and opened a box for herself. Three of the boys were sort of cute. She removed her glasses and tucked them in her pocket.

An hour later, the wind still bellowed. Everyone in the county had lived through at least a dozen dust storms and knew what to expect. But Chester was alert to every howl and this storm was the loudest. It seemed as if wagonloads of sand and soil were being flung at the Jewel, scouring its brick walls and hammering the roof with the unceasing cacophony of ball-peen hammers. Layered upon that was the crackle of plaster as the walls heaved under the assault. Behind Chester, the velvet stage curtain released a musty scent.

Just when he thought he could not stand a second more, the air washing around the doorjambs subsided, the wind's screams dropped a few decibels, and the size of the clods slamming into the Jewel grew finer—turning to silt, then powder. Chester rose stiffly.

"The lights are back on," Miss Boyle called out helpfully.

"Thank you. It sounds as if . . ." Chester began, but then had to stop and clear his throat of grit. "It sounds as if the storm has moved on. If you CCC boys would clear the front doorways, that would be a help. The rest of you, please be patient for just a couple of more minutes and then we'll have you on your way."

"Are we going to get our money back?" Mrs. Laycomb's voice rang out.

Chester hesitated, then drew himself up. "Certainly."

Chester and the boys scooped dirt from the front doors and dug a path to the sidewalk. Mrs. Laycomb was the first out, dropping the refunded nickels into her purse and commenting to her mother-in-law that they'd at least gotten to see the newsreel. And for free. When the last of the moviegoers had left, Maxine asked if she should stay for the afternoon show. Chester shook his head.

"I'll have to cancel. Everyone will be digging out. But the seven o'clock is still a go, so be back by six thirty."

As her footfalls receded, Chester slumped against the lobby doors, sliding down until his rear bumped against the floor. He sat for quite a while, gathering himself. Then he made his way upstairs. In his bedroom, he removed his suit jacket, tie, shirt, and trousers, hanging each in its assigned place in the closet. The Oklahoma School for the Blind had taught him and the other boys the importance of consistency and organization. And as a result had turned out a gaggle of fussy housewives, he thought grimly. *A place for everything and everything in its place.* But the system largely worked. His biggest terror, until ticket sales began drying up, had been mismatched socks.

He pulled on an old mechanics jumpsuit and got to work in the auditorium, pushing the carpet sweeper up and down the aisles and wiping the armrests with a wet rag.

He moved on to clear the fire exit, shoving on the push bar, but the door wouldn't budge. Odd. He kicked the toe plate until he managed to squeeze through, stepping into at least six inches of dirt that buried his shoes and poured into his socks. From across the way came the sound of Ernie, the owner of the Maid-Rite Dinerette, scraping down the grill. Chester's stomach rumbled. He hadn't eaten since breakfast and here it was—he flipped open the crystal on his wristwatch and fingered the braille numerals—2:45. But he'd have to shovel out the fire exits before getting a bite. The last thing he needed was a citation from the fire marshal.

Chester bent over the wheat scoop. It didn't take long to scrape the asphalt near the door. He dug toward the Maid-Rite, the smell of fried eggs and bacon real enough to chew. Suddenly the scoop rammed into a drift. Chester groaned. His muscles already ached. He arched backward to flex his spine. How high was this pile? He raised the scoop, then plunged it in into the drift as a measuring stick. Instead of thudding against the pavement, the shovel's edge bounced against something slightly springy, several inches down. He drove the scoop into a different spot. Same thing. Maybe the storm had torn off an awning. Chester kneeled. He wormed his fingers into the mound and felt cloth. Not an awning; the material was too thin. And underneath there was something supple. He inched his fingers forward. The fabric gave way to a smooth narrow band. Leather. He yanked his hand away. Lord! A belt. It was a belt. Someone was buried in the drift. He shoved both hands in, digging frantically. The silt poured back down almost as quick as he scooped it. But he managed to unearth the back of a leg. A man's calf. The poor fellow was facedown. Was he breathing? Chester couldn't tell. "Ernie! Help! I need some help out here!"

He clawed at the mound. His fingers lit on an ear. *Get to the mouth. The mouth, damn it.* The dirt fought back, reburying what he cleared. Ernie didn't answer. A tooth scraped Chester's thumb. *There!* He wiggled two fingers past the teeth, scissoring the jaw open. Inside was more dirt. The mouth was packed solid. *Damn!* But maybe he could clear it. He shoved his index finger in as far as it would go. Nothing but more dirt. Probably all the way into the lungs. He pulled his fingers out; sat back on his heels. Poor sap. Probably some bum sleeping one off when the duster powered into town. What a way to go. Chester stood and brushed off his trousers. He trudged inside to telephone Sheriff Jennings. Jennings would need to pinpoint the cause of death and identify the deceased. All that would take time. Both evening shows might have to be cancelled. Chester's hope of making rent evaporated.

C HAPTER THREE

EARLIER THAT SAME DAY, as Chester was greeting the dawn with worries about rent, Sheriff Temple Jennings was steeling himself for the sorrowful task of foreclosing on the Fullers' farm. The acreage, livestock, and household goods, all part of the bitsy holding scratched out by Jess and Hazel Fuller, was going on the block. Darnell, the banker, would take in the cash while Temple stood alongside, rifle in hand, guarding the bank at the expense of those down on their luck. A couple of years back, Temple had tried to wriggle out of safeguarding the auctions, but Darnell had contacted a state judge who sent a sharp letter stating that foreclosure work fell under a sheriff's legal duties. And because Temple was a man who stood by the law, even when it left a bad taste in his mouth, he obeyed. He and Etha exchanged words about this sort of thing all the time.

This morning was no different. He was mopping up yolk with a piece of toast at the kitchen table when she brought it up.

"For pity's sake," she said, her back resting against the sink, coffee cup in hand, "why should you carry water for the bank? Don't go out to the Fullers' today and then see if Mr. Darnell has the constitution to turn a hardworking family out of their home."

"It's my job. The bank loaned the money in good faith and it wasn't paid back and now it's a legal matter." The last bit of egg was refusing to be corralled by the toast.

"You done?" Etha asked, whisking away his plate before he could answer. She plunked the dish into the sink with clattering efficiency. "But there's nothing that says you can't send your deputy. Besides that, you think the banks play fair?"

Temple sighed. "Probably not."

"'Course not! I bet there's a healthy number of businessmen in town who are behind on their payments, but Darnell isn't going after *them*."

Temple pushed away from the table. "Best get going."

Drying her hands on a towel, Etha turned to him. Her face softened. "Now your tie's all crooked," she said, adjusting the knot. On tiptoes, she pecked his cheek.

Although it was an hour before he was needed at the Fullers' place, Temple bypassed his office, perpetually awash in paperwork, climbed into the county sedan, and motored into the countryside in search of fresh air. Unnerved by Etha's comments, his stomach was rebelling. He pulled onto the shoulder at the crossroads twelve miles outside of town. Clambering out of the stuffy car, he shook his legs, loosened his shoulders. For the first time in months, the sky was high-vaulted and seamless. A cloudless expanse of blue that bleached white at the horizon. Temple leaned back against the sedan, elbows resting on the hood, long legs crossed at the ankles. He shut his eyes against the clear sunlight and inhaled. It could have been the air of fifteen years ago, when he and Etha had first moved out from Illinois. When the winds blew strong like a tonic. When, across the flat expanse, a man could tell where a stream flowed by its hem of leafy cottonwoods.

He opened his eyes and the illusion evaporated. Nowadays, Oklahoma was nothing but a battlefield of shifting sand dunes and emaciated stalks.

And not for a minute did he think that the rainmaker hired by the Commerce Club was going to change anything. Last night Temple had been hunting down a whiskey still hidden in a stand of sumac when the TNT blasts reached his ears and his spirits sank. Earlier in the day he'd heard about the huckster rolling into town, heard that the merchant class had been fool enough to consider the man's pitch. The detonations rocking the prairie had confirmed the sheriff's fears—they'd taken the bait. Temple never trusted anyone who showed up with only a business card and a handshake.

Now, dazed by the blighted view on this brilliant morning, he stuck his head through the open window and plucked a bottle of stomach tablets from the glove box. Foreclosures sickened him. How long could he keep swallowing the skunk oil while pretending it was soda pop?

Thinking back on his exchange with Etha, Temple beat his dusty Stetson against his thigh. *A rock and a hard place, that's what this job was. Shoot.* All he wanted was to get today's foreclosure done and over. That's what he wanted with all of them but this one was particularly tough. The Fullers had a boy, about the same age as he and Etha once had. And Temple knew that kiddie with his string bean legs would be watching the whole sorry occasion. He checked his watch. The hands had hardly budged.

Various signs leaned every which way, clustered around the crossroads, crying out to drivers. Temple strolled over. *Vermillion Up Ahead! Population 7,261,* was the biggest, erected by the Commercial Club a couple of years back. That number would need to be changed, he thought, with all the farmers packing up and moving west. His eyes fell on a newly planted marker: *Civilian Conservation Corps Camp Briscoe—5 miles.* Since the camp opened a year ago, Roosevelt's boys had done a lot of good. Planting windbreaks and grading roads. But there'd also been some scrapes between the fellows in the camp, and Temple had been called out twice to handle knife fights.

His eye fell on a poster stapled to a telephone pole: *Vince Doll for Sheriff—#1 Protecting Citizenry.* How many had Doll printed up? Every time you turned around, there was his stern mug plastered on a pole or propped up in a storefront window. Despite Temple's assurances to Etha that the Democratic primary, a little over two weeks away, was a sure thing, he was far from certain. This was the first time Temple had butted up against an opponent since coming to town and successfully winning the position of sheriff, pretty much because no one else wanted it. A couple of months back, Vince Doll, who owned the county's grain elevator, had gotten it into his head that the sheriff's office would be better served by a businessman who had also helped found the town back in '93. And, surprise, surprise, Doll himself fulfilled both qualifications. Another reason his gut was doing cartwheels. Being that there was no one running for sheriff in the Republican primary, largely because there were no Republicans in Jackson County, the winner of the Jennings-Doll contest was a shoo-in come November. Now, all of a sudden, Temple's chances seemed rocky. He checked his watch. Forty-five minutes to kill. Temple snorted and climbed into the driver's seat. He turned over the engine and twisted the radio dial until he landed on a peppy tune.

He drove without direction, past skeletal stalks of wheat and alfalfa and derelict barns. Most of the farmhouses, once whitewashed, had been scalped of paint by the blowing sand. And there were still a fair number of soddies, erected during pioneer times, which were nothing more than bricks of turf stacked on top of one another.

After a time, Temple grew drowsy. He pulled off by a row of fence posts, some crowned with crows baking in the sun. The posts, the crows, seemed to be sending a message. The dots of the birds. The dashes of the fence posts. Dot, dash. Dot, dash. Feeling his lids begin to lower, he leaned back. That whiskey still, once he'd found it last night, had taken hours to break up. The clock had read 2:36 when he'd finally slid under the sheets beside Etha.

Now settled in his car, he tipped his hat over his eyes and drifted off beneath the warm felt, sliding into a dream about fishing. He was squatting on the banks of a muddy creek, spearing a worm onto his son Jack's hook. The little boy squeezed his eyes and mouth into a tight kernel of disgust. Jack was wearing the sweater he refused to take off, the one with moth holes and unraveled cuffs. Seeing the delicate knobs of his son's wrists, Temple's heart swelled. *Why, he's not dead. He's as alive as can be. Why did I think he was dead?* Relief, cooling as summer rain, pattered at the edge of Temple's consciousness. But then, suddenly chilled, he woke with a start. He was huddled tight as a pill bug against the car door. He jerked upright. The air had changed. The clear sky had thickened and dulled to pewter. And, on the horizon, a four-thousand-foot-tall mountain of dirt was boiling. A dust storm. The biggest he'd ever seen and it was coming fast. Temple watched it churn toward him, his mouth slack with wonder and fear. A shrieking flock of crows unscrewed into the sky. Jarred into action, he scrambled out of the car, hauled an oily length of chain from the trunk, and hooked it to the bumper. The dry air of dust storms generated enough static electricity to short out a car engine. Everyone kept a chain in their vehicle to channel the electricity into the ground. Back behind the wheel, his heart thrumming, Temple tried to think. Carrying tons of swirling topsoil, the deadly blizzards of dust could turn day into night, suffocate cattle, and bury a car within minutes. Four weeks ago the Clapsaddle boy had gotten caught in one walking from the barn to his house. They'd found his body a day later, swallowed in a dune not a hundred yards from his mother's kitchen door.

The sheriff itched to turn the wheel, smash his boot against the accelerator, and drive to town as fast as possible. Through the sedan's windscreen he saw the vast billows piling on top of one another, gaining height and speed. His roiling gut told him there was no way he could outrun the thing and get to town in time. He had to shelter now. Where was the closest farm? He knew the answer even before it coalesced in his mind: the Fullers'. The last family he wanted to beg a favor from. The family, for God's sake, that he was turning out of house and home. But Temple didn't have a choice. He gunned it west, gravel flying beneath his tires.

Within minutes, the car was engulfed in a howling thunderhead of topsoil from Colorado, Kansas, the Panhandle—hell, from China, for all Temple knew. The bright afternoon plunged into brown twilight. Spectral glimpses of telephone poles kept him on the road. *What if I drive right on past the Fullers' and don't even know it?* He gripped the wheel as if it were a dousing rod, as if he were dying of thirst and it was leading him to a deep pool of clear water. Etha's heart-shaped face rose before him. He clutched the wheel harder and drove on.

Suddenly, the gay red paint that Hazel Fuller had chosen for the farm's mailbox materialized. "Praise the Lord!" Temple shouted into the howling gale. He turned right, missing the drive and plowing into a culvert. The car stalled out at a cockeyed slant. He wasn't sure where the farmhouse stood; his sense of direction was completely off-kilter. Unknotting the bandanna from around his neck, he counted to three and leaped from the car. Flinging up the hood, he fumbled for the radiator in the dim brown light. After a minute, his fingers found the cap. He unscrewed it and stuffed the bandanna into the water. Pulling it back out, he pressed the wet rag over his nose and mouth and ran, head down, toward a hazy rectangle of light. Beneath his boots, drifts shifted and pulled as if quicksand. He stumbled onto the porch and pounded at the door. No answer. He pounded louder. The storm was full upon him now, its roaring load of dirt and sand blocking every sound.

After an eternity, Jess Fuller's voice cried out, "Someone there?"

"Let me in!" Temple shouted through the clotted bandanna.

The door opened a crack. Temple stumbled over the threshold and into a damp shroud. Every housewife in Jackson County hung wet sheets over doors and windows to keep out the dust. But it made no matter. It found its way inside, passing through walls as flour through a sieve. Jess stood on the other side, his eyes dark in the weak flicker of a kerosene lantern. "Well, look who it is."

Temple lowered the bandanna, now stiff with a muddy mix of soil and saliva. As his eyes adjusted to the light he took in Hazel, sitting stoically at the kitchen table, her arms around the huddled boy.

"Ma'am," the sheriff nodded.

Jess stood with legs dug in, arms across his chest. "You must be disappointed that the auction is a bust. Leastwise for today."

"Not so."

Jess snorted. Pressure rose in Temple's chest.

A particularly strong blast walloped the frame house, setting the door and windows jittering. The boy whimpered. Hazel shushed him.

Temple saw fear flicker in the child's eyes. "You know, we can holler ourselves hoarse at each other or we can sit ourselves down and reassure your young'un that everything will be all right."

Jess didn't answer, but yanked out a chair, plucked the kid from his mother's side, and settled him in his lap. The boy curled into his daddy's chest with a snivel. Temple perched at the opposite end of the table. He studied Jess's boyish face, now screwed into a scowl. No mystery in that. But when he turned to Hazel, Temple detected something unexpected—a gleam of triumph, as if she'd been in a protracted battle and had, at last, emerged victorious.

She rose. An enamel coffee pot sat on the stove. She lifted it, nodding at Temple. "Want some? Cold but strong."

"Don't you give that man a drop!" Jess barked. "Don't you dare. I mean it. If it weren't for this duster, we'd be watching that pot and everything else we scraped for being sold off. And you know what this man," here he paused and jerked a thumb toward Temple, "you know what he'd be a-doing, right? Standing to the side, rifle at the ready, making sure you and me don't put up a fuss."

He slammed his fist on the table, the noise setting his little boy to wailing. "And Mr. Sheriff, when you and that banker pull it off, that's the kiss of death on your reelection. You can forget about it. Over at the grange hall? That's all they're talking about. Who's the friend of the farmer? And it sure as heck ain't shaping up to be you. My place is auctioned? You can count on losing at least thirty votes right off the bat." He snapped his fingers. "Like that."

Temple stiffened. He knew that he was on thin ice with the folks in town, who seemed to be backing Doll, but the farmers too? He'd believed that the rural folks appreciated his fairness and plain talk. That they understood the foreclosure auctions were not his doing. That they recognized Temple would do his best by them, including stalling off auctions until they had a chance to pack up. But now Jess was telling him different.

Hazel hadn't moved. The coffee pot was still aloft. She slowly lowered it. "It ain't the sheriff's fault. He's doing his job. And besides that, I'm not going to make any sort of fuss when the auction comes off. I'll be smiling and clapping because there is nothing for us here. Nothing. And the sooner we are shut of this place, the better."

A load of grit slammed against the farmhouse. The lamp wick wavered but held. Hazel pulled a cup from a basket that had been packed for travel, blew into it, and filled it with coffee.

She offered it to Temple. As he reached out, it crossed his mind that Jess might rise up and strike it from his hand. And Temple couldn't really blame him. He'd do the same, if he was in Jess's position. But then Temple's gaze fell on the child's pinched and dirty face and he knew Hazel was right. This was no place to raise a family. Not anymore. Not since the drought bore in and the dusters started. Temple took the cup and raised it to his lips. At that moment, the storm hit full force. Gravel pelted the window, breaking one of the panes. Sand and grit swooped in, choking off the air and dousing the lantern. The cup in Temple's hand vanished as did his fingers; that's how dark it was. Impenetrable and thick as the bottom of a barrel of crude oil. He squeezed his eyes and mouth shut, tugging the bandanna up over his face and fighting to get air in through his nose. The tempest of dirt and sand roared as if a freight train was pounding over them, squeezing them between the rails as the colossal engine thundered inches above their heads, throwing off heat and pouring soot into their mouths while they screamed.

C HAPTER FOUR

As the duster raged, Temple sat stiffly at the Fullers' table with Jess glaring, the boy sniveling, and Hazel pouring coffee, her chin cocked. A loose shutter banged without mercy. After a while, however, its clatter slowed, then stuttered. Temple timed the intervals between gusts. As soon as the pause reached five minutes, he snatched his hat, thanked Hazel for her hospitality, and strode into the choking brown landscape. As he excavated the car, he worried about how Etha had fared back in town even though the courthouse was sturdy and she was unflappable.

After twenty minutes, he got on the road. Dunes rippled across the highway as if the denuded land were trying to draw a blanket over its naked limbs. Every half mile or so, the road was completely clogged. Temple jerked on the brake, hauled himself, and dug. Even on these back roads, Doll posters had been stapled onto pretty near every telephone pole. Bending over the shovel, Temple ruminated. If he lost the primary, he and Etha would have to move. He'd have to find work in a country that was already awash with bread lines. And he'd have to live with the fact that he'd drug her all the way out here, away from her hometown, away from their boy's grave. Overrode her objections and drug her out for this job that might now disappear.

The drive back to Vermillion took two hours instead of the usual forty minutes, and so it was midafternoon when the Jackson County Courthouse came into view, its brick walls rising above the flat prairie town. It had been built in 1903, ten years after Vermillion was founded. Ten years after thousands of white settlers raced to claim plots in Indian Territory. The cannon on the courthouse lawn was a replica of the one that had announced the government-authorized land grab in 1893 with a tremendous boom.

Temple pulled around back. All the county offices, including the sheriff's, were on the first floor, their pebbled-glass doors surrounding a large three-story foyer. Temple strode inside and found Deputy Ed McCance on the telephone. Ed was a former CCC boy from Chicago who had been finishing his stint at the Vermillion camp six months earlier when Temple got the go-ahead from county council to hire an assistant. Ed had filled out an application within the hour. Temple still hadn't figured out how the boy had heard about the job so quick. But that kind of instinct would make an effective deputy, he'd reckoned.

Spotting Temple, Ed said into the horn, "The sheriff just walked in. Here he is," and stiff-armed the receiver in the sheriff's direction.

Temple raised his brows. Before taking the call, he started to say to Ed, "Any sightings of my—" when the deputy interrupted him.

"Etha's fine. Poked her head in here after the storm passed to check on me." Then he added, "It's Chester from over at the Jewel. Got a dead man in his alley."

Temple pushed a flop of hair off his forehead. "Jeez." Into the receiver, he said, "What's going on?"

He listened. Chester's voice rattled faster than a telegraph key.

"We'll be right over. Don't touch anything in the meanwhile." He turned to Ed. "Grab your camera. I'll join you after I wash off some of this dust."

"Yes sir," Ed said, hurriedly unrolling his shirtsleeves.

"Anything else going on?" Temple asked. "Reports of storm damage?"

"Yeah, lots of calls but nothing that can't wait."

"All right by me. We can't handle anything more right now."

Settling the camera straps around his neck, Ed said, "Oh yeah, Mr. Hodge called again. Said that Peeping Tom he's been hollering about for the past two weeks was back last night."

Temple sighed. "We've checked that out twice already. What more does he want us to do? Camp in his backyard?"

Ed laughed. "Sort of. He said if we don't catch the creep within twenty-four hours, he's calling his friend the governor to complain."

Temple rolled his eyes. "I'll try to get over there later today."

As Ed hustled out, Temple crossed the foyer, mounted the marble stairs, passed the second-floor courtroom, and continued up a wooden staircase. At the top was a small vestibule. Straight ahead, behind a steel door, was the four-cell jail, and to the right, the sheriff's residence.

His fingers grasping the apartment's doorknob, Temple was startled when it was yanked from his hand. Etha stood in the entrance, her brows furrowed. "I thought I heard you. I've been worried sick. Had visions of you blown into a ditch." She wrapped her arms around his waist.

He kissed the part in her salt-and-pepper hair. "Made it safe and sound."

The door led directly into the kitchen. The smell of soap flakes told Temple that Etha was already laundering the curtains despite the haze of soil that lingered. Temple filled her in on Chester's phone call.

"He was clearing the fire exit. Found the remains in a drift. Sounds as if maybe someone got caught in the duster and suffocated."

Etha brought her hand to her mouth. "Oh dear God. Man or woman?"

"Man. Probably a drunk or a drifter from down by the tracks."

Etha clicked her tongue.

"You make out okay? Worst roller I've ever seen," Temple continued.

"Lucy was cutting down an old dress and needed help. We were having coffee and cookies when it hit."

"Ah, Lucille's cookies," Temple said. "The week-old cracker variety?"

Etha sighed. "Bless her heart. We holed up in the cellar. You?"

Temple snorted. "You won't believe where I ended up. Had to shelter with the Fullers. It was the closest place."

"Warm welcome?"

The sheriff shrugged. "Could have been worse. Jess was mad as heck."

"And Hazel?"

"Sort of smug. I'm feeling she can't get away from that farm fast enough."

"Still and all, being run out of your house is not the way it should happen." Etha turned and took a wet rag to the top of the icebox. "You best go wash up and get moving."

"'Spect so."

Bent over the bathroom sink, Temple sent up a prayer that Chester's discovery was going to be easily explained. A simple accident needing a thorough but quick investigation, a hat-in-hand notification to the next-of-kin, a final report. Over and done. Anything more than that, manslaughter or worse, would explode smack in the middle of the primary. And that would be bad news. Those kinds of cases never moved fast enough for the voters or county officials, who seemed, as the drought stretched onward, to have become more prickly and impatient. As if the cooperative salve of the frontier had evaporated along with the rain.

Five minutes later, Temple planted a goodbye peck on Etha's cheek.

"I'm thinking you won't be home for supper," she said.

"Doubt it."

"You walking over to the Jewel?"

"Guess I could. It's only a couple of blocks. You need the sedan?"

"I could bring a hot meal over to you and Ed later if you leave it here, is all."

"Appreciate that."

Temple descended the stairs and stepped out onto the street. Cleanup was underway. Shop owners were shoveling off their sidewalks and unfurling canvas awnings. A broken gutter lay across the curb and someone's laundry line, with housedresses and coveralls still pegged to the rope, was wrapped around a telephone pole. Temple cut through the neighborhood behind the main drag. Mrs. Keller, handkerchief tied around her mouth, was walloping a throw rug against the porch railings. She returned his wave.

The sheriff trotted the final block toward the Jewel. There were a few more folks out, all trying to make the best of a market day hogtied by the storm. A farm family emerged from their jalopy. When the farmer turned his pocket inside out a plume of dust bloomed.

"Caught out on the slab?" Temple called.

"Stuck for two hours. Would've gone home but we were already halfway, so . . ." The man shrugged.

An old guy who Temple didn't recognize ambled over to the family. Temple heard him ask for a ride out of town. His car had stalled out. Day-old growth peppered his narrow chin, his lower lip folded inward—a mostly empty wallet with only a few coins. The old-timer's wind-burned cheeks were the color of dried tobacco leaves.

Entering the alley, Temple spotted Ed kneeling beside a partially excavated drift. Four or five kids leaned out of the Maid-Rite's back door and another cluster of spectators huddled at the far end of the alley. When Temple shouted, "Folks, please go about your business, we need some privacy here!" most of the lookie-loos melted away.

With a small grunt, Temple crouched beside his deputy. The dead man lay on his stomach. Someone, likely Chester, had cleared the face of its shroud of dust, but most of the fellow was buried.

"Took twelve snaps so far," Ed said.

"Take a couple more, then we'll dig out the rest of him."

When Ed rose, Temple noticed that the deputy's trousers were rolled up. Before joining the CCC, Ed had been nothing but a street tough from Chicago's infamous First Ward. Rough around the edges. But now he was laboring mightily to file those down. For one thing, he'd taken to favoring an old man's wardrobe of pleated pants, tan suspenders, and soft white shirts. Temple's granddaddy would have been at home in the high lace-up shoes on the deputy's feet.

While Ed snapped away, Temple asked, "Where's Chester?"

"Inside. I told him to stay put until you're ready to talk to him. And you can guess what he said."

"*And just where would I be going?*" Temple smiled. "Snappish and high-strung as usual. Most stone-blind are."

The sheriff inspected the body, his face grave. "Don't recognize him."

After a dozen or more flashbulbs flared and died, Temple said, "Let's dig him out."

Ed settled the bulky camera on top of a nearby ash can and grabbed the shovel that Chester had parked by the Jewel's side door. He scraped away at the edges of the drift while Temple used his hands to scoop gently around the limbs and torso. The dead man lay with the toe of one shoe planted downward and the other splayed to the right. His store-bought suit was of a modern cut. Temple was surprised to see he was wearing a jacket since the last few days had been scorchers. Local men had an unspoken understanding that on the hottest days, shirtsleeves were acceptable. Even Darnell the banker walked to lunch at the Crystal Hotel with his jacket slung over one shoulder. The dead fellow's collar had flipped up and a tie with bold geometric shapes that Etha would have pronounced *gaudy* was visible.

Temple pushed on his thigh and levered himself up. The dead man's head was turned sideways as if the fellow was doing the crawl stroke, with his mouth and nose positioned to pull in air. Dried blood, crusted with dirt, ran from one nostril and the exposed ear. The deceased looked to be in his thirties with a strong jaw and a nose with a cleft at the tip. He'd been a handsome man.

"Accident?" Ed asked.

Temple made a clucking noise with his tongue. "Can't tell just yet. Could be, I guess. Hoping so. Seems to be a fair amount of dirt underneath him. Could have stumbled out here in the middle of the storm and cracked his head against something." He lightly touched the blood around the nose. "Tacky. Didn't happen too long ago." Working his fingers around the back of the skull, Temple said, "Uh-oh. Here we go." He brought up his hand. Blackened blood and dirt smeared his fingers. "A goodsized gash."

Ed snatched up the camera and squatted beside the sheriff.

Temple gently rotated the head so that they could get a better look. The concave, saucer-sized wound was a stew of blood, matted hair, and dirt.

Ed whistled, then snapped off a few shots. "That seems deliberate. Stove in with a bat or something."

"Could be." Temple scoured his face with a palm. "Shoot." What a way to go, he thought. Without knowing what hit him. Without knowing that the end was upon him. Mouth stuffed with dirt.

Unbidden, the image of his first grade teacher materialized. Her bloated body facedown in the silt of the Little Conemaugh, whose waters had famously flooded Johnstown, back in Pennsylvania. He pushed it away, then rose and wiped his fingers with his white handkerchief, aware too late that Etha would have a fit. "Get some more photos. I'll call Hinchie."

Inside the Jewel it was cool and shadowy. Temple tugged at his shirt where circles of sweat bloomed under his arms. He found Chester in his office, cranking an adding machine.

"Come to interrogate me?" the blind man asked.

"Not yet," Temple said. "I need to get ahold of the doc before we move the body. Can I use your phone?"

"Sure, sure." Chester rose from the desk.

"Appreciate that." Temple settled into the office chair and pulled the telephone toward him.

"The seven o'clock show is still a go, right? No reason not to. I mean, you'll have everything taken care of by then?" Chester's hands had a life of their own. Right now, they were alternately clutching one another like passengers on a sinking ship.

Temple paused, his finger in the rotary. "Do what I can."

Chester headed down the stairs, muttering.

Hinchie's wife answered on the third ring.

"I'll send him over as soon as he beats the parlor rug. I asked him to do it forty minutes ago and he's still fussing with his tomato plants. As if they're going to pull through."

Minnie was a tough nut. "I'm hoping you'll tell me that rug can wait. I've got a dead man outside the Jewel. I need Hinchie. Quick."

A short intake of breath came through the line. "Dead? Who?"

"Don't know."

"A stranger? Goodness! I'll send him right over."

Temple was hanging up when Chester entered with a sweating bottle of pop. "This might cool you off."

"Thank you kindly," the sheriff said, downing a healthy gulp.

"Now do me the favor of hurrying this whole thing along so I don't lose my evening box office," Chester said. "And make sure the telephone is in the exact spot you found it in. I have a system, you know."

Temple rolled his eyes. "As soon as Hinchie finishes, I'll be back to talk with you."

Ten minutes later Hinchie was trotting down the alley, despite his weak ankles. A cigarette wagged from the corner of his mouth. Dr. Wilburn Hinchie was not only the town's general practitioner but the medical examiner as well. When a medical opinion on cause of death was needed, Hinchie got five dollars a day for his services that included testifying at the inquest. Everyone in town, including Minnie, knew he used the extra money to buy hooch and cigarettes behind her back. He was of the impression that she was unawares.

"Get to that rug?" Temple asked.

"No . . ." Hinchie was breathing heavily. "I did not. But it will be waiting when I return." He gazed skyward, inhaled a lungful, and returned Temple's gaze with a smile. "All righty. What do we have?"

Temple filled him in as the doctor bent over the body. The sheriff stopped when he saw disappointment cross the man's face.

"What?"

"It's the rainmaker," Hinchie said, straightening.

Temple's brows shot up. "From last night? You sure?"

"Indeed." He took off his jacket and handed it to the deputy. Squatting beside the body, he probed the head wound. "Nasty. Pushed bone a couple of inches into the brain," he said, wiping his fingers on a piece of gauze from his doctor bag.

"You think this could happen from, say, staggering into a wall or maybe an ash can?"

Hinchie gave this due consideration. How many times had a patient told him that an accidental fall caused the gaping cut on the head, the broken arm, the deeply bruised ribs? 'Course that happened plenty. But also plenty of times it was due to drink or fisticuffs or an epileptic fit that no one wanted to admit to. Just last week he'd treated the wife of a prominent citizen for a nasty bruise on her jaw. Slipped on a rug had been her story. He'd heard it all from her over the years and it sickened him. He was sick with rage at her husband for beating her and sick with loathing at himself for not having the guts to speak out about it.

Now Temple was clearing his throat, and Hinchie answered, "Not in a million years. If I had to guess, I'd say he got slammed in the back of the head by a board or a pipe. That sort of thing. Undoubtedly went down like a sack of feed."

"Shoot," Temple said, turning to Ed. "This is going to be complicated."

Hinchie said, "Almost certainly you've got an intentional act here by an unknown party or parties, as they say."

The doctor unbuttoned the dead man's jacket, slid his hand inside, and drew out a brown wallet with rounded edges. He handed it to Temple. With Ed observing, the sheriff pulled out a healthy stack of small bills, a shriveled four-leaf clover folded inside a scrap of paper, and a receipt for *r. beef + mashed* from a restaurant in Alva, Oklahoma. There were also a bunch of business cards imprinted with:

Roland R. Coombs
Rainmaker and sewing machine repair
Work guaranteed
Francis and Fourth
St. Joseph, Mo.

"You were right, Hinchie," Temple said.

"I'm surprised you boys didn't recognize him."

"I missed the fireworks," Temple said. "There was a still out near Boiling Springs that needed smashing."

"And I'm not one for that kind of voodoo," Ed said.

The three men studied the body. Hinchie snorted. "Sewing machine repair? If I'da known that, I wouldn't have put up a nickel."

Temple laughed. "You were in on it with the Commercial Club? A man of science?"

"Listen. If Vermillion goes the way of rest of the towns around here, just how do you think I'm going to earn a living? I thought it was worth a shot." Hinchie did not add that he'd ponied up the last bit of his old-age savings to help hire Coombs. Seventy-two and still a fool, he derided himself. The possibility of putting his black bag away for good seemed more remote than ever.

Excavations of the deceased's pockets yielded half a stick of chewing gum, a pack of cigarettes, and a key from Mayo's Rooming House.

Temple counted the cash. "Two hundred plus or minus. Was that what the Commercial Club put up?" At Hinchie's affirmation he added, "Not a robbery."

While Ed snapped more photos, Temple quickly canvassed the alley for a weapon. But the drifts were too deep. He'd get Ed back on the shovel in a bit.

Temple clapped his hands. "All right, gents. We'll get Mr. Coombs here over to the undertaker so you can give him a good going over, Hinchie. Say in about an hour?"

The doctor nodded.

"And Ed, watch the body until Musgrove gets here with the hearse. In the meantime, dig into the bigger dunes. Keep sharp for anything that might be connected to Coombs or the killer. And a possible weapon. That duster is going to complicate things. I'll interview Chester and then be back to help."

As Temple was entering the Jewel he spotted Etha hurrying up the sidewalk with two tin dinner pails. He was surprised to see her wearing an old wrap dress and a shapeless felt cloche; Etha was a stickler for correct street attire. And rightly proud of her trim figure.

"I was afraid I'd miss you," she said, slightly breathless.

He pecked her cheek. "Almost did."

She held up the pails. "Brought you both a bite."

Temple lifted one of the lids. Fried chicken and mashed potatoes. "Much appreciated. Could be late when I get home."

"Who was it? Anyone we know?"

"No. That rainmaker fellow. Name of Coombs."

The tight corners of Etha's lips relaxed. "At least it's not a local. But that poor man. A stranger and all." Then her gloved hand flew to her mouth. "Oh no. How will you let his family know?"

Temple shook his head. "Have to track them down. His business card has a St. Joe address." He watched in sorrow as Etha's eyes welled. She quickly pulled out a hankie, dabbing the edge along her lower lids. With any death, the first thing she worried about was the family getting word. She'd been that way ever since their son Jack had wandered off and it was eighteen agonizing hours before a Peoria patrolman had come to their door, hat in hand.

She blew her nose. "But it was an accident?"

Temple raised his angular shoulders. "Not sure."

Mrs. Albright and her daughter strolled by with polite smiles. Everyone exchanged greetings. After they passed, Etha sniffed and wiped her nose again. "Now one of these pails is for Ed."

"'Course." He bent down to kiss her. "Sorry, sweetie, I've got to get along and—"

"I know, I know. I was just wondering if I could keep the car. Only for an hour. I've got some errands."

He pushed his hat to the back of his head in the way that reminded her of his hero, Will Rogers. Temple had that same hank of hair always falling onto his forehead. "Now?" he asked. "The roads will be a mess. Can't it wait?"

"I promised the McDonalds a couple of care packages. They're not far out," Etha said, running her words together. "I heard they were trying to swap Mary's great-grandma's best china platter for a bag of sorghum."

"You're a big-hearted woman. Be careful out there."

She watched him stride into the Jewel with the loping gait that had caught her eye on his first visit to her music studio. Such a sweet man. She hated deceiving him.

CHAPTER FIVE

NOT FAR FROM TOWN, Etha turned off the highway onto a dirt road. Before her, railroad tracks zippered toward the setting sun. To her left, tucked along the rails sprung the clump of cottonwoods she'd been scouting for. As the sedan bumped closer she spotted a glimmer under the darkening trees that swiftly swelled into a campfire ringed by dozens of ruddy faces. A spore of fear swelled in her gut. Real men and boys squatted under the trees. The kind who slept rough. Who reeked of woodsmoke and sweat. Who slunk through town pleading for handouts.

What was she thinking, driving out here with her boxes of fried chicken, a pound bag of sugar, and the sack of coffee? When it had come to her last Tuesday, the idea had seemed sound, jolting loose some long-buried enthusiasm that Reverend Coxey's sermons on charity had not. She had stopped by the Maid-Rite for a cup of coffee. It was late afternoon and the wooden stools around the U-shaped counter were empty. Only Ernie, the owner and cook, was there.

"Take a seat, young lady. There's nothing deader than a café between lunch and dinner," he had called from the steam table. He was arranging and rearranging a heap of loose meat with broad strokes of a spatula. Spread across his belly was the usual apron marbled with grease stains. As Etha sipped her coffee, half listening to Ernie's circular chatter, a skinny figure appeared at the back door. It was a kid, not more than twelve. He knocked timidly. Ernie kept on talking.

"Someone's out back," Etha said.

Ernie didn't turn. "I know. If I gave handouts to every kid riding the rails I'd be out of business. I do my share but there's a limit to my good nature."

Etha had known, of course, that most Vermillion shops and houses got regular visits from tramps squatting in the hobo jungle by the tracks.

They offered to do odd jobs in exchange for a sandwich, a slice of bread. No one stopped at her house. Being it was three floors up in the courthouse and next to the jail, the vagabonds kept their distance.

The kid rapped a couple more times before slinking away. Her thoughts leaped to her son Jack, as they did whenever she spotted a vulnerable boy.

Now here she was, out on the prairie with night approaching and on what Temple would have called a *cockamamie* good-works mission, if he'd known about it. All because of some nameless kid who'd made her think of their son Jack, dead for fifteen years. A nameless kid to rescue because her own lost boy was beyond reach.

She braked and shakily exhaled, her hands pattering on the wheel. Shadows quivered thickly behind humped backs circling the fire. The heavy air absorbed the metallic tang of unwashed bodies, of urine-sour loins. I can't do this, she thought. I'm too scared. She abruptly clutched the gear stick, shoved it into reverse. Then her headlights caught two young men ambling toward the car. She pressed her elbow into the lock button inside the door.

"Ma'am, you lost?" asked the taller of the two.

"I just thought . . ." Etha heard her voice shaking just a little. "I thought that you all might be wanting some homemade fried chicken."

"Sure enough we would!" He broke into a face-splitting grin. "I'm Gil and this here is Carmine."

With that smile, Etha's fears dwindled. "Pleased to meet you. Now, you best help me unload." She climbed out and retrieved a box, passing it to Gil, who sniffed mightily and exclaimed, "Wee doggies!"

Turning to slip a crate into the arms of Carmine, Etha caught her breath. The young man, who was wearing a denim shirt, bore a resemblance to Jack. There were the same dark waves of hair and eyes set close to the nose. She struggled to gather herself.

"Guess I picked the right time to pay a call," Carmine said with laugh, revealing an overbite.

When she saw that, his similarity to Jack faded slightly. Her gut unkinked. He's not Jack, but I know boys like him, she thought. I know him.

They hefted the boxes to their shoulders and loped toward the clearing. Etha followed. The short path led to a fire ring near three patched tents and a couple of lean-tos made of boards and flattened tin cans. A pocket mirror was nailed to the trunk of a cottonwood. From the tree's branches swung an empty pot and a couple of straight razors.

Carmine called out, "Hey, fellows, dinner's on!"

At least two dozen men and boys turned Etha's way. Dungarees and overalls hung from their boney hips. Some were shirtless. Most wore cracked-soled shoes.

With all those eyes on her, Etha's pumps wobbled on the path. One of the older men, a fellow named Murph, rose from a stump and swaggered over. "Put them boxes down," he told the boys, then turned to Etha. "Excuse me, ma'am, but what are you doing out here? This ain't no place for a lady." The fellow was short but beefy, his cheeks gravelled with gray and black stubble.

Etha flushed. "I just figured you all could use a good meal. I had extra so . . ."

"More than extra, I'd say." The man peered into the boxes. "Seems as if you did this on purpose. I ain't saying we don't appreciate it, but I've been on the bum for four years and know that there's a string attached to every little thing. Everybody's working an angle. Even if it's a nice-looking lady. You with the church?"

Etha wasn't prepared to explain herself. "No. I mean, I go to church of course, but this has nothing to do with that. Well, it does in a way. As far as following the Golden Rule, but this is all my own doing."

The tramp considered her words, tipping his head from side to side. "Maybe not, maybe so. Anyways, you're here now and we're hungry now." He turned to the men, most of whom were standing, ears alert, a pack of dogs. "Divvy it up," he said, waving a hand at the boxes. He turned back to Etha. "Okay. You done your good deed. We'll sleep with full bellies tonight thanks to you. I don't mean to sound ungrateful, but no one from town ever comes out here except to shoo us away."

"Guess I'm an exception."

"Could be."

Etha watched as the jungle's older residents sauntered over to claim drumsticks before returning to the deepening shade of the cottonwoods. They leaned against the trunks, chewing hungrily. The younger ones squatted on their haunches, ripping into the meat. Cicadas filled the hot air with their cyclical thrum. The cords of the immense night sky loosened, expanding the shadowy spaces beyond the cottonwoods.

"As I said, thank you kindly for the food," Murph said.

Etha, lost in her thoughts, jerked her head up. "Mind if I stay awhile?"

Murph raised his brows. "Night's coming."

She scanned the sky. A log collapsed with a brittle *shush* in the fire ring. They're out here in the middle of nowhere and far from home, she thought. Like me. "I won't stay long."

Murph shrugged. "Do as you want. That's the motto here."

He ambled back to the log and applied himself to a tin plate with chicken and a heap of boiled potatoes and cabbage from the stewpot.

Etha hesitated. The cicadas pulsated. Gil approached. "You want to sit a spell, that's fine by us," he said, pointing to the cluster of young men on the far side of the fire. Most appeared to be in their late teens—faces still open despite the old-timer stoops draped across their narrow shoulders. They made room for her on the beaten ground. She sat gingerly beside Carmine, pulling her dress over her tucked-in legs, aware of Murph's wary glance from the other side of the fire. In the light of the logs she noticed that Carmine's shirt bore a CCC patch on the pocket.

"You from the camp?" she asked.

He nodded. "Passing through here on my way back to the bunkhouse."

For a while there was only the sound of night insects and chewing. Then a boy on her right said, "You make chicken just as good as my ma's." He wore a soft-collared shirt and trousers with suspenders. His nose had grown faster than the rest of his face.

"Where you from?" Etha asked.

"Kentucky."

Etha frowned. "That's mighty far."

"Trains will take you anywheres. And I needed to get out. There were too many of us. That's what Pappy said. Too many mouths, so I had to leave. Told me so right in the middle of breakfast. I didn't take another bite. Put the fork down, stood up, and walked out with nothing but what I'm wearing. Been traveling ever since."

Etha had read about young men cast out, set loose because there were no jobs, no food.

Kentucky added, "It ain't so bad. I'm not any hungrier than I was at home and have gotten to see a lot of sites."

Another kid, who introduced himself as Abe, boasted he'd been in eight states in the past three months.

"And where are you from?" Etha asked.

"Illinois."

"Me too!" Etha said, and the kid's face lit up.

"Where abouts, if you don't mind."

"Peoria. You?"

"Macomb."

Etha stretched out her hand. "Howdy, neighbor."

"Howdy-do to you too."

After that, the fellows sitting around Etha loosened up. They commenced swapping stories about encounters with railroad bulls, about sleeping rough, about homesickness and how they came to ride the rails. Some had taken to the road for adventure. Most, though, had been forced from home by parents who couldn't water down the stew anymore or who hoped the young men could earn enough to send something home. As they talked, she studied Carmine. He had the wiry body of early manhood while her Jack was forever the fleshy schoolboy. She most always thought of her son in this way. Or as a baby with those little legs pumping when Temple clucked over the crib. But now she considered how puberty might have molded Jack's features.

Abe pulled a bottle out of his bundle. "Mind, ma'am?" he asked and, after she shook her head, swallowed vigorously before passing it to his neighbor. Across the crack and leap of flames, someone was singing an old-timey hymn. Dusk flowed from the shadows, saturating the sky's blues with rose, orange, lilac.

When Etha turned back to her boys, for that was how she was beginning to think of them, they had shifted from stories to jokes. The bottle went around a few more times and the jokes edged toward the off-color. Etha blushed but the boys seemed to have forgotten she was there. Some stretched out full-length on the ground, elbows bent and heads resting in their palms.

"I know you've heard this one, but it's worth hearing again!" Abe shouted as the laughter grew. "See here, it's about this muff who agrees to take a salesman behind the barn."

"You mean behind *her* barn?" someone said, jumping up and thrusting his hips forward and back. There was more loud laughter.

Etha's blush deepened. As far back as her teenage years, she had been dimly aware of stag films and roadhouses. Of dirty jokes and crude language. Rough places where men, even good men, gathered occasionally. But first her father and brothers, and later Temple, had shielded her from that sort of thing. Still, it was out there; a trickle of dirty water in a drainage ditch. When she had business at Phillip's Sunoco, Etha diverted her eyes from the wall behind the counter where a girlie calendar hung.

Now Carmine had gotten into the act. "I've got a good one, fellows." He licked his lips. Etha scooted away from the fire, into the shadows, and plugged her ears. She squeezed her eyes shut. But in the darkness behind her lids, Jack's form blossomed. It was a teenage Jack, wearing a sly expression. Her eyelids flew open. She never saw him that way; not with his schoolboy innocence shed like a snake's skin, part of the hidden world of men.

Another boy jumped up to speak; his silhouette magnified in front of the leaping flames. He swayed a bit from the drink. I've got to get out of here, Etha thought. All was darkness beyond the blaze. Where was the car? As her eyes darted around the clearing, Murph, the hobo leader, emerged from the gloom.

"Willing to share a pull?" he asked, gesturing to the bottle that was still making the rounds. Abe handed it over and Murph took a long swig, then delicately licked his lips. "Mighty fine. Not the usual." He held the bottle up to the firelight, tipping it this way and that. "Where's this from?"

"Town. Some lady gave me a sack of potatoes yesterday when I knocked," Abe said. "Found the bottle at the bottom."

"Really? Did you mark the house?"

"Sure 'nuff. Put a big old circle with an X right on the back gatepost."

Etha had seen tramp signs chalked on fences and barns. She'd never known what they meant.

Murph said, "If you fellows plan on draining this bottle, don't you forget we have a lady present. She asked to sit awhile, but I don't think she signed up for this. She expected us to be gentlemen. With tea and cookies and maybe singing duets. Ain't that right?"

Etha bristled. A moment ago, she'd wanted nothing more than to leave. Now, hearing a challenge thrown, she felt differently. With six brothers, she had learned to stand her ground. "I thought no such thing." The bottle had made its way to Murph. She grabbed it from his hand and took a long pull. The whiskey pricked the inside of her throat, like seedpods clinging to a sock.

"Careful, ma'am. It's strong," Abe said.

Etha cleared her throat. "I'd say you're right." She surveyed her audience. Most were grinning. She took another gulp and decided she'd stay longer.

Murph squatted and poked the fire. Carmine pulled a harmonica from his pocket. After a couple of tentative puffs, he blew out a song or two. The tramps gradually stopped talking when he hit the notes of "Brother, Can You Spare a Dime?" Some bent their heads. Others stared into the flames.

The tune ended. No one spoke.

Abe jumped up. "What is this? A funeral? Dump the dirges. We need something with some pep. How about 'Keep on the Sunnyside'? Know that?"

"Lemme see." Carmine studied the sky then put the mouth harp to his lips. After a tentative start, he built up the pace and volume until the tune emerged full blown. Swaying from side to side, he shook one foot out, then the other, until he rolled into a solo version of the Lindy Hop. Alternating sides, he lifted a leg, knee bent, and gave it a shake. All so fast he was moving in a blur. Bouncing from one leg to the other. Soon there were five or six dancers jumping and jiving.

The bottle came around again and Etha, who had been clapping along, paused for another swallow. When Carmine switched to a rag and Abe held out his hand, she took it, bounced to her feet, and twirled beneath his rotating wrist. Although Etha never taught her piano students anything but classical music, when she was alone on the third floor she sometimes let loose with a boogie or two. Now she felt the juice in her limbs as Abe spun her, cinched her close, and cast her out in a breakaway. As she whirled dizzily, she glimpsed Murph's face once or twice. Was that a grimace or a smile?

Carmine ended with a long high blast.

Etha stumbled back, a bit off-balance. Breathing hard, she said, "My." And then, "I haven't danced for ages."

Abe bowed low. "Thank you, ma'am. Hope your husband wouldn't take offense."

"Oh no! He won't dance. But he doesn't mind when I do."

"Won't dance?"

Etha waved Abe off. "Temple thinks it'll compromise his dignity." Her head felt light.

"I a-told you she was a church lady. A church lady married to a preacher." Murph wagged a finger. "Nobody more worried about his dignity than a preacher."

Etha laughed. "No. Temple hasn't been to church in months. He's not a preacher. Fact is, he's the sheriff."

As soon as the words jumped out of her mouth, Etha regretted them.

Murph snorted. "Guess that explains everything. Sent you here to spy? I'd say that's pretty low."

"No!" Etha said. "He doesn't even know I'm here. I did this on my own." She glanced around at her boys. Most studied the dirt. A few met her gaze with sour expressions. "Truly, this was all my . . ." Her voice fizzled out.

Someone tossed a stick into the fire. The dry wood snapped loudly, releasing a shower of sparks.

Carmine stepped to her side. "Let me walk you to your car. I need to hoof it back to camp anyways."

Etha let the boy take her gently by the elbow. He opened the car door for her. Down the line a train whistle blew. Carmine turned to listen. She caught his profile and was struck again by the echo of Jack. His face shimmered. She blew her nose.

"Don't cry," Carmine said. "Some of the men have had some rough brush-ups with the law, that's all. I'm sure you didn't mean any harm."

At that, Etha broke down completely. She finally stopped when she noticed Carmine's panicked expression.

"Please, ma'am," he said.

"I'm all right." She sniffled. "Did you get kicked out of home too? Like some of those other boys? I can't believe your ma would do that."

"Probably not. But she died way back."

Etha covered her mouth. "I'm so sorry."

Carmine shrugged carelessly, but sorrow thickened his eyes. "Anyway, I had my reasons for leaving Kansas City. Pa's still there with my younger brothers. The CCC sends him most of my earnings. That's why I joined."

Etha dabbed a corner of the hankie under her eyes. "Good for you." Then she frowned. "Why aren't you at the camp?"

"Had a beef in town last night. That's all. I'm going back to the bunk now. Pa needs the scratch. And if I went home, I'd only be a burden."

Etha reached outside the car and grabbed his arm. "Don't ever think that. No parent ever sees a child as a burden."

A slight grin crossed Carmine's face. "Maybe. But I'm not a child anymore. I got to make my own way. You okay to drive back to town?"

Etha nodded. After blowing her nose again she turned over the engine. "Do you want a ride?"

"Naw. My legs need to shake off that hooch. But I'll watch until I see you've made it to the turnoff."

Etha maneuvered the sedan up the dirt road. Right before bumping up onto the asphalt highway, she glanced back. Carmine still seemed to be standing there, nothing but a smudge against the parched vista. Maybe it wasn't even him at all but another boy or a fence post. You really couldn't tell. But even that uncertain glimpse pierced her heart.

C HAPTER SIX

CHESTER CROSSED HIS LEGS ONE WAY, then the other, then back. He ran a finger over the braille numbers on his watch. Forty-five minutes before the seven o'clock show and here he sat in the theater's back row, twiddling his thumbs.

When the side door finally clicked, Chester bolted to his feet.

"Mighty hot out there," Temple said.

Chester's words spilled out in a rush: "What about the seven o'clock?"

Temple paused. "I'm sorry, but it's a suspicious death."

Chester collapsed in his seat. "You're sure? How about the nine o'clock?"

"Nope. Ed and I need to give the alley a good going over and it'll take awhile to get it all dug out. I know this is tough."

Chester snorted. "You've no idea. Who was it anyway? Someone from town?"

"That rainmaker."

"The con artist who killed off my Friday-night receipts?"

Chester's famously snappish tone brought out Temple's grin. "I need to take a statement. Your office?"

"I've got nothing better to do. You've seen to that," Chester said, flinging up a hand.

Upstairs, the theater owner settled into his desk chair and smoothly pulled a pack of cigarettes from a drawer. He lit one with a match and took a long drag. Temple drew a notebook-and-pencil setup, jerry-rigged together with a string, out of his coat pocket. The string had been Etha's idea.

"Let's start with how you discovered the body."

Chester forcefully discharged twin columns of smoke from his nostrils. "Per directives from the fire marshal, I was shoveling out the fire exit. If only I'd ignored that regulation—as so many of the other merchants do, I might add—that fellow would still be sleeping peacefully under the dust, my screenings would be running, and no one would be the wiser."

"But that wasn't what happened."

"No," Chester sighed. "What happened was my shovel connected with something under the drift. I thought maybe it was a hank of awning ripped off in the storm. I dug around and pretty quick I knew it wasn't an awning."

"Then what?"

"Then I started clawing the dirt away, feeling for the mouth, thinking the fellow was alive but passed out. I hollered for Ernie across the alley but he didn't answer. When I got to the face . . . well, you know what I found."

Temple resettled himself, propping his right ankle on his left knee. "And when were you last in the alley before that?"

"I'd say around eleven. I always check the fire exits before the first show." Chester efficiently discharged the ash from his cigarette into a large pink cake plate on his desk. While the blind girls had been in crochet class, Chester and the other boys taught each other to smoke behind the manual arts building. "And there was no body there then."

"You sure?"

Chester shrugged. "As far as I could tell. I checked the entire space around the exit. Paced it off. You should ask Ernie. I think he'd have noticed if a dead man was stretched out not far from his back door. By the way, you going to close the Maid-Rite too? I mean, just because I found Mr. Coombs doesn't mean this had anything to do with the Jewel."

"I'm aware. Might have to do that, but—"

A door slammed downstairs and Ed McCance called out, "Sheriff?"

"Upstairs."

The deputy hurried up. "Sorry to interrupt," he said, "but just before the funeral director pulled up, I decided to go through Coombs's pockets one more time. I found this stuck in the seam." He handed a pasteboard ticket to Temple.

"What is it?" Chester asked.

"A stub from the Jewel. Seems our man was a patron of the arts," Temple said.

Chester ground his cigarette butt into the plate. Temple tucked the stub into an evidence envelope and folded it into his shirt pocket. "Okay, Ed. Keep shoveling out the alley and I'll be down as soon as I'm finished here. Then you and I are off to Mayo's to check out Mr. Coombs's accommodations."

After Ed clattered downstairs, Temple said, "Mind if I ask why you're using that cake plate as an ashtray? Etha would have my hide if I did that."

"It's a sample from a salesman. Trying to talk me into holding Dish Nights. I take great satisfaction in defacing this cheaply made knickknack."

Temple laughed. Chester allowed a thin smile.

"Moving on, it seems that Mr. Coombs attended your feature."

"Could be. I didn't even get to the main attraction. The storm hit in the middle of the newsreel."

Temple made a note. "How many in the audience?"

"I took twenty-three tickets. I'd guess, of those, at least five or six were strangers, including a few CCC boys."

"Plus the regulars?"

"Of course. Mrs. Reed. Mrs. Laycomb dragging along her mother-in-law," Chester said. He stood and began to pace. "And that girl who goes steady with the Avery kid. What's her name?" He snapped his fingers in rapid succession. "Cora? Carrie? Clara. Clara and Leroy."

As Chester kept talking, Temple jotted down all the names he mentioned. He and Ed would need to interview the entire list. That would take time, and time was something he didn't have. Not with the primary coming up fast and Doll hovering like a long-legged mosquito hungry for blood. In all, the theater owner unequivocally identified fifteen locals in the audience.

"And you think there might have been three or four CCC boys? Let's say four. That adds up to twenty. Still missing three. Is there someone you forgot?"

Chester fingered his upper lip while Temple glanced around the small office. A low shelf to the right of the desk held a stack of trade magazines. Battered film boxes, scabbed with labels from movie houses across the West, were piled under the window. The desk was bare except for a typewriter, the cake plate, and a small fan that pushed out hot air smelling of dust and oil. No framed photograph of Lottie, of course. Chester had never seen her face. Temple couldn't imagine not being able to watch Etha's fingers running up and down the keyboard or admiring her slim figure when she rose on her toes to slide clean dishes into the kitchen cupboard.

Chester's words intruded: "No. I'm positive that's everyone I recognized. You'll have to talk to my ticket seller Maxine about the CCC boys. How many there were and all that."

Temple uncrossed his long legs. "Guess that'll do it for now. Unless you can think of anything else?"

Chester shook his head.

Temple tucked the notepad in his pocket alongside the evidence envelope and stood. "I'll let you know when you can open up."

As he let himself out, Temple heard the click of the lighter. Another cigarette that would be smoked to the butt and then smashed into the pink cake plate.

C HAPTER SEVEN

AN ORGAN'S THICK CHORDS BLARED FROM THE PARLOR of Mayo's Rooming House as Temple and Ed mounted the porch steps.

"Myra's program," Temple said, checking his watch. "Eight o'clock on the nose."

The two lawmen had spent the past hour scouring the dirt where Coombs had lain and the remainder of the alley, coming up empty-handed. Not a weapon, not a button yanked from the killer's coat, not a clue of any sort. They'd gulped down Etha's dinner and hustled over to the boarding house. Temple was feeling the pressure to hurry, to scrape together the facts of the case, squeeze them into a narrative. The breath of Vince Doll burned his neck.

Two men occupied kitchen chairs on Mayo's porch. Their legs were crossed in the languid posture of men who have no place to be at that hour of the day or any other. They seemed oblivious to the radio program washing through the windows behind them.

"How do? Mrs. Mayo in?" Temple asked.

A fellow wearing the striped billed cap of a farmer nodded. The other lit a cigarette and tossed the spent match into the dusty weeds skirting the porch.

Itinerant peddlers and bachelor shop clerks traditionally made up Mayo's clientele, but recently lone farmhands on their way to California and tramps who had saved up enough scratch to treat themselves to a bed for a night had joined their ranks. The town's well-heeled visitors lodged at the Crystal Hotel which boasted carpets, felted cotton mattresses, and telephones on every floor.

Mayo's didn't aspire to those lofty heights. Two days after opening in 1900, Edward Mayo keeled over from a massive stroke. It was speculated that the effort of getting the place built to Mrs. Mayo's liking had contributed to his death. The widow immediately took on the job of running the place, despite her persistent gallbladder, spleen, and bunion problems. In recent years, she had handed off most of the menial tasks to her spinster daughter Beatrice. Still, Mrs. Mayo ruled the place with an iron hand. She kept the books, enforced the rules ("No spitting," "No cussing"), and performed daily room inspections. Despite her efforts, Mayo's had grown tatty. The yellowed shades continuously flapped against the windows, inhaling and exhaling stale air; the wallpaper was blistered at its seams and the baseboards bore permanent scars from a procession of sturdy boots. The screens bowed outward like the bellies of middle-aged men.

Temple tapped on the door and called into the dark hallway, "Miss Beatrice?" No one stirred.

After two more attempts, Ed said, "I don't see how she could hear you over the radio. It's turned up awful loud."

"She hears us. Just taking her time. It's her way of getting back at her mother."

After a bit, a fleshy woman of forty in a matronly housedress emerged from the shadows of the hallway. Her warm brown eyes and finger perm were not unattractive but she had an unfortunate receding chin that melted into an elongated neck.

"Just finishing up the dishes. Come on in," she said.

"Thank you. Appreciate it." Temple removed his hat. "Full house?"

Beatrice shook her head. "Only eight. Who you tracking down?"

It was not unusual for Temple to seek out Mayo's guests, who were often good sources of information on the location of stills around the county and the comings and goings of itinerants.

"Your ma."

"Oh. Well, she's in her room. You know the way." Beatrice retreated to the back of the house.

Temple wasn't sure how cooperative Myra would be. After all, Vince Doll was married to her sister, and if he won the election, she'd have a lawman who took her side when neighbors complained about roomers whooping it up, passing out on the porch, or spitting tobacco juice on the sidewalk. Halfway down the hall a door stood open. Temple tapped on the frame.

Myra Mayo lay stretched out on the bed, fully clothed, including her shoes, which rested on a newspaper protecting the white chenille spread.

Her eyes were shut. Myra, at age sixty-two, was half her daughter's weight. But she made up for that with a pair of heavy lace-up pumps that, at the end of her thin legs, resembled anvils.

She held up a hand and announced, without opening her eyes, "Just a minute."

"*Stop it. Stop it, I tell you. I had no reason to kill him!*" Helen Trent, the radio drama's heroine, exclaimed from the parlor. There was a pause, followed by the purr of the announcer's voice: "*Join us tomorrow for the next chapter in* The Romance of Helen Trent, *the story of a woman who is out to prove that romance need not be over at age thirty-five and beyond.*"

Only when the final notes of the theme song faded did Myra's eyes snap open. "My doctor says I'm to lie down after I've et. Since they took that fibroid out I've had terrible spells with my gallbladder. Big as a grapefruit, they said. Never seen one bigger." She swung her legs off the bed, her weighty shoes thudding against the floorboards. The bedside table was cluttered with medicine bottles, wadded hankies, eyedroppers, and a frame displaying three images of Myra's younger self. "What can I do for you? Must be important to come at this hour."

Temple said, "We have some questions about Roland Coombs. He's rooming here?"

"Yes, but he's not in. He went to the Maid-Rite this morning and I've not seen him since." Myra turned to a blue parakeet hopping energetically in its pagoda-shaped cage. Tilting its head, it observed her with a silken black eye. "Does Sweetsie want a snack before beddie-bye?"

Temple caught Ed rolling his eyes and shook his head. The sheriff cleared this throat. "We know he's not in. His body was found in the alley next to Chester's this afternoon."

Myra paused with a pinch of birdseed between her fingers, but didn't flinch. Temple hadn't expected her to. You don't operate a rooming house for thirty-odd years without running smack into the seamy side of things. Drunks, gamblers, fast women, and the occasional body.

After a tick, Sweetsie got his treat and Myra played patty cake over a tin wastepaper basket, spattering the remaining seeds clinging to her fingers. "All I can say is at least he was paid up."

Temple said, "We need to know when he got here. What he did. That sort of thing. Can we go someplace to talk?"

"The kitchen. But you know I don't pry into my roomers' business dealings."

"Of course not," Temple said smoothly.

The hallway was dim, but lights blazed in the kitchen where Beatrice was folding towels on an ironing board. Myra, Temple, and Ed sat at the table.

"Go turn the radio down," Myra said to Beatrice. "And give us some privacy." She shook a finger at her daughter. "You're a Nosy Nora if I ever saw one."

Beatrice clamped the stack of towels against her bosom and silently marched out.

Myra finger-combed her hair. "I must look a sight. Anyway, Mr. Coombs showed up with two suitcases about noon yesterday. I figured he was a salesman. I can spot them a mile away. Grins too wide. Hand out for a shake, even from a lady. He wanted a room for three weeks. One in the back, he said. I guess he thought he was at the Maid-Rite ordering roast beef and mashed. I showed him one at the front and he took it. He stayed up there until suppertime and then didn't get back here until the Idle Hour closed. Two in the morning. I heard his footsteps on the stairs."

Ed broke in: "How did you know he'd been at the Idle Hour? Did he say that's where he was going?"

"No. But where else would a fellow be until that hour and come back soaked in beer? I smelled him." Myra stood and set a kettle to boil on the range. "I'm to have a cup of hot water an hour before bed. Doctor's orders for my spells." She took a china cup and saucer from a cupboard. "Naturally, Mr. Coombs didn't get up until late this morning. Beatrice was complaining to me that she couldn't get in there to clean the room but he must have eventually got on his hind legs since she stopped yammering about it." She poured out the steaming water and sipped.

"Did Mr. Coombs tell you why he was in town?" Temple rearranged his long legs under the table in search of a comfortable position.

"Said he'd been hired by the Commercial Club to make it rain. I said, *Good luck to you.*"

"Did he say where he was from?"

Myra studied the far wall. "Might have. Let me think. He said he'd come in by way of Kansas. Coldwater, I believe. I didn't get the impression he was from there, though."

"Any mention of a truck?"

Myra leaned against the counter. "Parked over by the freight yard, he said. Seeing it was loaded with TNT, that seemed a sound idea."

Temple turned to Ed. "Make a note. We'll have to secure those explosives." Swiveling back to Myra, he asked, "Mind if we check out his room?" He employed his Sunday manners. He didn't want Doll trying to make the case that his sister-in-law had been manhandled. "Then we'll get out of your hair. I know it's late. We'd surely appreciate it."

Myra's brows, which had been plucked within an inch of their life, rose. "No skin off my back. I'll get the keys."

Coombs's room was of the austere rooming house variety, with a steel bed frame, straight-backed chair, and washbasin on a stand. A cheap dresser occupied one wall with a brush, comb, and shaving kit arranged on top. A suitcase was lying open on the floor. In years past rooms such as these harbored the dreams of young men pushing west, excitedly hoping to make their own stake on the land. The rooms had smelled of raw lumber and new paint. The dreamers themselves were green, with the vigor of growing wheat. But since the drought began and the Depression set in, the air in the rooms had taken on the stale scent of a closed-off attic. The men who collapsed onto the cotton ticking were worn and brittle.

Temple pointed at the bureau. "You start there, Ed. I'll tackle the suitcase."

Myra leaned against the doorway, cupping the china just below her chin. "My mister never was one for shaving lotions and all that. He always said, *Leave that stuff to the ladies.*"

The two men worked in silence. After a bit, Ed said, "These are empty." He scraped the drawers shut. "He must not have had time to unpack."

"Or maybe he wasn't sure how long he was staying," Temple said. He kneeled beside the suitcase, slowly pulling out clothing and examining each piece. "He said three weeks, Myra?"

"Yes. And paid for one, which is standard. I don't have to give that money back, do I? After all, it's going to be tricky renting out the room of a dead man."

Temple laughed. "Yeah, your clientele is awful persnickety."

Myra sniffed. "Some are."

Ed sorted through the toiletries on top of the dresser. "Our man was worried about losing his hair." He held up a bottle of tonic. "Just socks, shirts. The usual. Nothing personal." From his jacket pocket, he removed a notepad and jotted a few lines.

Myra stabbed a finger at the bureau. "Check under the drawer liners. Sometimes they tuck stuff underneath."

Temple smiled slightly. "Thought you didn't pry."

"I don't." With that, she turned away. "Let me know when you're finished," she called over her shoulder.

"Got her back up," Ed said with a grin after she'd left.

Temple sighed. "Hard not to."

There was nothing but bare wood under the liners.

Voices floated up from the front porch along with the sweetish scent of cigars. There was a phlegmy sound as someone gathered saliva and spit. Temple studied the ceiling abstractly. What kind of fellow pulled into town and within twenty-four hours or so managed to rile up someone bad enough that he got his brains bashed in?

"Well, well. Looky here," Ed said slowly. He drew out a small photo from a barely visible fold in the leather shaving kit. It was of an older man and woman posing stiffly in their best cloths. Across the bottom of the image was stamped, *Olsen Photography, St. Joseph.* "Probably his folks." Ed handed it to Temple.

"Good find," Temple said, slapping Ed on the shoulders. "St. Joe again; same as on his business card. Maybe a place to fill in the missing pieces about Mr. Coombs."

Ed nodded. "No wedding ring."

Temple cocked a finger at Ed. "Speaking of which, I better call Etha before we leave and let her know we have one more stop to make."

"Yeah?"

"The Idle Hour. I trust Myra's nose. Sure as shooting, Roland was there last night just around this time. So the iron is hot for striking, as they say. I think we checked everything . . ." Temple gazed around the room. "Except here." He sat on the bed. Its springs creaked in rebuke. There was a single drawer in the rickety bedside table. Inside, a tattered dime novel and a couple of loose cigarettes kept company with a tiny megaphone, no longer than an inch.

Before Temple could examine it, Ed snatched it up and, seeing the puzzled frown on the sheriff's face, said, "Know what this is? Check it out." He put the small end of the megaphone up to his eye and blew out a slow wolf whistle. "Roland here preferred ladies on the buxom side." He handed the viewer to Temple.

"I would say so," the sheriff said, taking his turn. A dim photograph of a young woman as nature made her smiled back at him. As he rose from the bed the springs repeated their chorus of sighs. "And make a note for me too, before I forget, about talking to the boys at the CCC camp. Chester said he was sure some CCCers were at the movies today. Maybe they noticed something."

"The CCC? Uh, sure. But I'd be glad to save you a trip. I know the place inside and out, after all."

"I know, but this is something we need to do together. I don't want to be accused by anyone, primarily Doll, of conflict of interest. Just make a note of it in that pad of yours." Temple's eyes swept across the room. "I think we're done here for now. Bring the shaving kit with the snapshot and let's hit the Idle Hour."

Temple and Ed were descending the stairs when Beatrice stepped into the hallway. A stack of linens was still pressed against her bosom, though the pile was considerably smaller.

"You're working late," Ed said.

Beatrice shrugged. "Sometimes it takes all day to clean the rooms and wash the linens. You finished in there?"

"We are. But we're going to need to keep it locked for another couple of days."

Tipping her head toward the room she'd just left, Beatrice whispered, "We need to talk."

"All right," Temple said slowly.

Inside, she dropped onto a straight-backed chair, still hugging the towels to her chest. "Close the door."

Ed swung it shut.

"This morning when I went in to clean Mr. Coombs's room, his handkerchief had blood on it."

"A lot?" Temple's voice rose in surprise.

"Yes. It's not unusual to have a couple of spots from shaving nicks, but this was a gusher. Probably got punched in the nose. I didn't think much of it. Only that it was going take a lot of work getting the blood out. I soaked the hankie in bleach, then tossed it in the tub with the rest of the stuff. It still had some rust spots, so I put it aside to soak again."

"Where is it now?" Ed asked.

"In the laundry room."

Temple mused that there were some daughters, grown women even, who were eternally outshone by their mothers. Seemed to be a combination of a daughter who was by nature reserved, and a mother who clung with ferocity to the glory of her own youth. The sort whose bedroom was ornamented with framed photos of her younger self. He wanted Beatrice to understand she had his full attention. "We appreciate you letting us know."

A slight smile crossed her lips as she leaned forward and dropped her voice: "That's not all. When Uncle Vince was here earlier, I told him about the blood and he said not to mention it."

"Really?" Temple said.

"He told me, *The sheriff doesn't need to know about this. He'll just be sniffing around Mayo's all the more and you all don't need that kind of attention.* Ma was here with us and backed him up. But I didn't think it was right."

Temple gazed abstractly out the window. The sky was quiet. Clearly Doll had gotten wind of the murder. He might be trying to slow down the investigation—tarnish Temple's record. Maybe Doll was even mixed up in the killing somehow.

"You've done right. Thank you, Beatrice."

"You won't say anything about Uncle Vince, will you?"

Temple shook his head.

As the two men descended the stairs, Temple stopped abruptly and asked Ed, "Where were the matches?"

"What?"

"Matches or a lighter. Roland was a smoker, right? Cigarettes in his jacket, in his room. But nothing to light them with."

"Think that's something?"

Temple shrugged. "Could be. Write it down just in case."

He poked his head into Myra's room, where she was back in bed resting her gallbladder; he thanked her and met Ed outside. The porch was empty. The boarders were either already in their rooms or had sauntered over to the Idle Hour for a beer.

"What do you think about Coombs's bloodied handkerchief?" Ed asked.

"Could be nothing. Could be something."

The night air was still, holding the day's heat as a mother cradles a fevered child. Temple speculated on who might have told Doll about the dead body. And once again felt Doll's hot breath on his neck.

CHAPTER EIGHT

ED DREW OUT HIS NOTEPAD AS TEMPLE TRAMPED into the Idle Hour. Months ago, just minutes after Temple's call letting Ed know he'd been hired, the young man had hustled to Model Apparel for a smart silk necktie. As he handed a five-spot to Mr. Klein, a display of narrow pocket-sized notebooks alongside the cash register caught his eye. A well-dressed businessman with a coat casually thrown over his elbow and a suitcase beside his well-shod feet was rendered in blue ink on the covers. *Beach's "Common Sense" Travelers' Note Book*, it said. That's for me, Ed had thought. Professional. Serious-minded. Not a bum or CCC pity case.

Now he was using it to take notes on his first murder investigation.

The Idle Hour's bar ran down the left side with booths on the right. Three loners, sitting two or three barstools apart, hunched over beer glasses. The remaining clients filled one of the wooden booths and more—overflowing so that several had pulled up chairs and another was leaning against the booth's coat rack. Ed immediately recognized Vince Doll and his cronies, including the lawyer John Hodge, who had been griping about the Peeping Tom. Temple's back stiffened. Ed and Temple had not talked much about the primary, but the deputy knew that his boss, underneath his composure, was worried. And Ed walked his own tightrope. If Temple lost, God forbid, he'd be depending on Doll for the deputy job.

"Let's go say howdy to the boys," Temple said.

Doll was holding court, leaning back on a chair with his legs crossed. A cigar was pinched in one hand and he gripped a cane with the other. There was something prideful about his paunch, festooned with a double watch chain.

"Look who it is!" Doll exclaimed as Temple and Ed approached.

Everyone exchanged small nods. Doll was joined by Hodge, Darnell the banker, a couple of shop owners, the Methodist minister, and three county clerks. There had been several rounds of drinks, judging from the number of shot glasses and steins on the table. The entire scene reminded Ed of the Christmas basket packed with oranges, nuts, a dressed turkey, and candy that the Democratic precinct captain used to bring to his family's apartment. He'd strut into their kitchen, install the basket crinkling with red cellophane on Mom's kitchen table, pump Dad's hand, and sweep out into the hall where a group of sycophants stood at the ready with more baskets. Growing up in Chicago, Ed knew all about the political machine's barter system. Christmas baskets, loads of coal, city permits, and rounds of drinks for the house—all greasing the gears to ensure election. And the currency of highest denomination was patronage—choice jobs in city hall or public utilities. Ed eyed the county clerks.

Doll gestured with his cane. "Get our sheriff and his deputy chairs so they can sit a spell and have a beer with us. You do have time, I'm hoping. Nothing pressing?"

Ed assumed Temple would brush this aside and get down to business so he was surprised when the sheriff said, "Kind of you. We could use a drink." While Temple eased himself into the offered chair, Ed stood behind—legs planted in a wide stance.

"I've got a beef with you," Hodge said, pushing a finger toward Temple. "Someone been lurking around—"

"Cool down, John. Ed told me you called and I promise we will look into it as soon as we get past the storm cleanup."

"What's this about?" Doll asked, looking at the lawyer.

"Sheriff's business," Temple said, putting a period at the end of the sentence.

Once the beers arrived, Doll began speaking: "That was some duster. Never seen one so big. I was at my desk ordering seed when the whole place went black. Black as pitch at noon. Never would have believed it. Couldn't see my hand in front of my face. And choking. I swallowed enough dirt to plant wheat in my belly."

"It was nasty," Temple agreed.

Doll pointed his cigar at the sheriff. "Heard you had to take shelter outside of town."

"Heard right. The Fullers took me in."

"You mean the family you and Walter here were supposed to

foreclose on today? That must have been a might uncomfortable."

Several members of the entourage laughed. Ed saw Temple's jaw muscles tense.

"They're good people and were nice enough, considering the circumstances. That's one part of my job that I find distasteful."

Doll narrowed his eyes. "Now that's where you and me differ. I'm all for pruning away the withered vines. Those not strong enough to survive a couple of bad crop years. I expect our lawmen to flush out the weak sisters. Vermillion would never have been on the map if it hadn't been for men and women with strong backs and stronger stomachs. I've said this many a time but it's worth saying again: I was all of seventeen when I took the train up here from Texas. When I stepped off, there was nothing but the station platform. And you all know what I mean by *nothing*. Prairie grass, blue skies, and sun white enough to blind a man. Not a building, not a windmill, not a tree. Staring out at the flatness, our eyes were just begging for a mooring, a speck of something to build on. But there was nothing out there. Just a big old armful of air. It all had to come from in here." Doll thumped his chest. "Not out there. But we made it something. Built from the ground up. I've seen worse times than these. Way worse." Webs of spit glistened at the edges of his mouth.

"Yes indeed," the banker murmured.

Temple settled his elbows on his knees and clasped his hands loosely. His voice dropped to a confidential tone: "I tip my hat to any man or woman who came out here in the early days. I can't begin to imagine what it took to build this county from the dirt up. And I know that there are some who came later and maybe took all that'd been done for granted. Who grabbed a piece of land when those cannons went off in '93 and didn't know two hoots about farming. But the Fullers aren't those people. They tried to make a go of it but the weather was stacked against them. I'm not saying the bank isn't owed its money. I'm not saying I won't uphold the law. I'm just saying I don't believe it's all as clear cut as some think and it gives me moral indigestion."

Doll started in: "But let me tell you that—"

"I'm sorry we can't hash this out right now and I promise we will," Temple cut in, "but tonight I need to talk business. Ed and I are trying to cull out the comings and goings of that rainmaker and Myra tells me he was in here last night. Did any of you see Mr. Coombs?"

For a moment, the only sound was the irregular whir of a fan with a bent blade. Ed drew out the notebook and positioned his pencil.

Doll knocked cigar ash onto the floor with a firm tap. "Not me. I spoke to him a few minutes after the detonations but that was all. Went straight home afterward. Why? Is he missing? I hope to God he didn't take off with our money."

Temple ignored Doll and examined the other faces. The banker and minister shook their heads. One of the county clerks, a young man with a fringe of silky hair on his upper lip, said, "We was here. The three of us. Coombs come in about ten. He was belly to the bar drinking a beer when we left twenty minutes later. We didn't speak to him or nothing."

"Was he alone?" Temple asked.

The second clerk, sporting a snappy bow tie, jumped in: "There were three boys from the CCC with him. They were all hooting and hollering. I heard him say he'd buy the first round."

The pencil froze between Ed's fingers. CCC fellows? He'd only been out of the corps a couple of months and knew everyone in the camp. It sickened him to think that a CCCer was somehow mixed up in this. The corps had been his salvation. Sure, it had taken the townsfolk and farmers months to warm up to the fellows sleeping in the bunkhouses, clearing brush, and planting trees. To trust they weren't a bunch of young hellions. But eventually they'd see its true merit. If a CCCer was involved in Coombs's death, it would bust up all that goodwill.

Temple was still talking. Ed turned back to the notebook, reminding himself that even if Coombs was drinking with some of the boys the night before, he'd been murdered that afternoon.

"Now I have a question for you, sheriff," Doll said, holding up his empty glass which one of the clerks promptly carried to the bar for a refill. "If you remember, I notified you last week of a big old still set up beyond the Copes' abandoned soddie. As far as I can tell, nothing's been done about that as yet. When do you think you might get around to it?"

The sheriff took his time answering. His right foot, propped on his left knee, jiggled double time. Ed recognized how deeply exasperated Temple was, although his face was as still as a low-water creek.

"Ed and I will take care of it first chance we get. Now let me ask you this: why did you try to hide the fact that Myra found a bloody handkerchief in Mr. Coombs's room? As a citizen, she has an obligation to report anything that might have a bearing on—"

"An investigation?" Doll broke in. "Is that what this is?"

"I could charge you with interference."

"I didn't think it was important and would be bad for her business, that's all."

Temple stood. "And yes, to answer your question. It is an investigation. Mr. Coombs was found dead in the alley outside the Jewel this afternoon. If you come across any other information that might help us with this, I'd appreciate your cooperation."

"Jeez," one of the clerks said, lowering his glass with a bang on the table. A few of the others pulled their heads back in surprise.

Doll said, "Dead? That's a shame. Seemed like a nice enough fellow. But if you find any money tucked somewhere, remember that's the Commercial Club's. And of course I'll cooperate." He waved his cane dismissively.

"Promise to do that," Temple said gravely.

The chink of toasting glasses accompanied Temple and Ed to two stools at the far end of the bar. The sheriff pulled out a pack of cigarettes and offered one to the deputy.

"What can I get you gentlemen?" the barkeep, Ike Gradert, called from his station at the taps.

Temple snapped a dime, in the manner of a tiddlywink, onto the bar's polished wood. "Two beers."

Ike, a man of middle age with a face that sagged like overalls on a wash line, filled the glasses and shuffled over, slopping liquid on the floor.

Temple raised the dripping glass and, as was his custom, said, "To you, Ike."

Across the room, chairs scraped. Doll and his pals prepared to depart. As they filed out, Doll spoke for the group: "'Night, gents. And good luck, sheriff." The screen door bumped behind them.

Ignoring the interruption, Temple said, "We need to talk about a customer you had last night."

The barkeep glanced at the wall clock. "Could you give me five? Got stew going in the back."

"Sure thing."

Ike traipsed into the kitchen and Ed took a swallow of beer. It went down smooth. "So, did you buy Doll's story about the handkerchief?"

Temple snorted. "I think he's hankering to gum up our case, hoping to improve his chances."

"Agreed."

The two men fell silent. Ed chewed over which CCC boys had been in the Idle Hour with the rainmaker. He contemplated the bar's uneven tin ceiling and the squat coal heater with its stovepipe exiting through a poorly plastered wound in the wall. This place was a pity case if he ever saw one.

Tapping the bar with an index finger, Temple said, "And he's trying to pile on the work so that we can't keep up. That's why he brought up the still. I'd bet my last dollar." The sheriff sighed and stubbed out the half-smoked cigarette. "Why don't you question Ike? I'm wore out."

"Well, ah, sure," Ed said, trying to tamp down the excitement in his voice.

The swinging door to the kitchen flapped open and Ike reappeared with two small bowls. He plunked them down in front of the lawmen, and wiped his hands on his apron. "Tell me what you think."

Temple put a spoonful of stew in his mouth. "Right fine."

Ed nodded his assent. He slid the bowl to one side and, after wiping the counter with his handkerchief, opened his notebook and began questioning the barman. The Idle Hour had been deserted while the TNT show was on, Ike said. After the explosions, the regulars trickled in and the place steadily filled up. Ike agreed with the clerks' description of the rainmaker's arrival.

"Came in sort of cocky, with three of those kids from the camp. And . . ." Ike paused. "Say, aren't you a CCCer? I remember you coming in here in the uniform awhile back."

Ed stiffened. "Yeah, I was. Now I'm the deputy."

Ike leaned against the counter with folded arms. "You appear on the up-and-up, but some in the corps are nothing but young toughs. Last night one of your CCCers sucker-punched Coombs. And that was after the man had bought him and his buddies a couple of rounds of beers."

Ed's stomach dropped. The fan's thwacking drone seemed louder.

"Ah, jeez," Temple said.

"Yep. It was coming on closing time. I was washing up," Ike pointed to bar sink, "when I heard shouting up front. It was a CCCer and Coombs ripping into each other. I couldn't tell what about. Coombs shoved the kid's shoulder and then *wham*, the kid socks him in the nose. Must have broke because it was a gusher. Coombs was dripping all over but got in a healthy punch before heading out."

"Did you recognize the kid?" Temple asked, then turned to his deputy. "Oh, sorry. Go ahead."

Ed said, "Did you?"

"He'd never been in before but I'd know him now. Short. Dark hair. Close-set eyes. Wore his hat brim snapped back."

Ed ran through the faces in the chow hall, the bunkhouses. He couldn't come up with a match, but new fellows arrived all the time. "Did you hear what they were arguing about?"

"Nope."

Ed asked a few more questions but didn't get any more useful information. He closed his notebook and tucked it in his pocket.

Temple finished his beer. "Okay for now, Ike. Thanks for the help."

Outside, the air was slightly cooler. The two men walked toward Main Street—Temple on his way home and Ed to the room he rented from the Murphys.

"Do you know who the CCC fellow might be?" Temple asked.

Ed shook his head. "Maybe a new guy. Could be Ike got the details wrong." Either way, Ed thought, I've got to check this out quick. If it was true, if someone in the corps fought with Coombs, he wanted to be the first to know. He had a better chance of making it clear that the kid was just a bad egg. And if the fellow had nothing to do with the murder, that was something else Ed needed to find out too. Right away.

Temple was saying, "Okay, we'll drive out to the camp tomorrow. Together."

At the courthouse steps, the sheriff put his hand on Ed's shoulder. "We're just starting so don't jump ahead of yourself. Get some sleep. Tomorrow will be another long day. Meet me at nine sharp at the Maid-Rite. We need to know if Ernie heard anything during the storm. Then we'll follow up on the CCC lead and make time to secure that truck."

Ed nodded and watched Temple stride toward the back entrance. He waited until the light in the top floor's hallway snapped out. If he walked at a good clip he'd get to the camp in an hour.

From the hallway window, Temple watched Ed turn away from the direction of the Murphys and trot out toward the highway leading to the CCC camp. He'd figured as much. Would have done the same when he was Ed's age. Temple sighed. I've got no energy to chase him down tonight, he thought.

Closing the apartment door quietly behind him, Temple pulled off his boots and padded to the bathroom. He splashed water on his face and brushed his teeth. In the bedroom he removed his trousers and shirt and slid into bed beside Etha. She fumbled for his hand and squeezed it. Her voice was groggy. "You home?"

"Yep."

"Everything okay?"

"Pretty much. You have some sweet dreams." He kissed her on the cheek.

Etha mumbled and rolled onto her side. As she did, Temple caught the faint scent of woodsmoke. His brain started to puzzle on that but sleep overtook him.

Dust swirled around Ed's legs as he hiked west. Solitude no longer made him jumpy, as it had in those first lonesome days when he'd arrived here, fresh from Chicago's raucous streets. Now it was a balm. The same as all those saplings he and the crew planted for windbreaks were a balm to the stripped earth. We are both trying for a cure, Ed thought, this barren ground and me. His mind turned to the fistfight between Coombs and one of the boys. The corps' reputation could be destroyed in a blink of the eye by rumors spread by some of Doll's pals. That the killer might be a CCCer wasn't even to be considered. Ed had to get this cleared up before Temple turned his gaze to the corps.

It was past midnight when the dark shapes of the camp buildings appeared up ahead. Skirting the gravel entrance road, Ed trotted along a beaten shortcut. It circled around the wood-framed mess hall and latrine, their tar-paper roofs one with the night sky. Four barracks, lined up side by side, faced the flagpole. Ed kept to their backs, his trouser cuffs brushing the dried grass. His old bunkhouse was third from the right. He still had a couple of buddies there. Johnny and Al would know who'd been with Coombs at the bar. Ed stopped at a window, its shutter, hinged at the top, propped open with a long pole. The uneven exhalations of forty fellows sprawled in camp beds met his ears. The revelry grounds were submerged in shadows—no one stirred. The door on the bunkhouse creaked if opened too fast, but Ed knew how to finesse it. Inside it smelled of pine boards and the canine stink of young men in an enclosed space. Johnny's bunk was third on the left. He was sleeping on his back, mouth wide open and legs splayed, as if he'd collapsed from exhaustion in midsentence. Ed crouched beside his ear.

"Johnny," he whispered. When he got no response, he shook his friend's shoulder. "Johnny."

Johnny's left eye cracked open, then shut.

"Hey, it's Ed."

Both lids rose slightly. Johnny wiped spit from the corner of his mouth. "What you want?" His voice was thick with sleep.

"It's Ed. I need to ask you something."

The words penetrated. Johnny pulled back. "What are you doing here?"

"Working a case."

Johnny pushed himself up. "A case? For real?"

"Quiet down, fellow. This is on the hush-hush for now."

"Okay, okay. Gotcha."

"I need to ask you something. Saturday night, one of the CCCers got in a fistfight at the Idle Hour. Do you know who it was?"

"One of our guys?"

"You haven't heard anything?" Ed asked, his voice sinking.

"I was on KP. Stuck in the kitchen washing dishes. Sorry. Say, what's this about? I heard a body was found in an alley. Is it true? Hot damn! You're tracking a cold-blooded killer, aren't you?"

"I can't say." Ed cocked a finger at Johnny. "But *you'll* be the first to know."

"Yeah, right."

"Is Al still bunking at the end?"

Johnny nodded.

"Get some sleep. And keep this quiet," Ed said, rising.

As wide awake as Johnny now appeared, he flopped back onto the mattress without protest. Ed could swear he was snoring before he himself was halfway down the aisle.

Al would be different. While Johnny was an eager farm boy who followed directions, Al was a smart aleck from St. Louie. Ed would have to impress on him the importance of secrecy. If Temple got wind that Ed was pursuing the case on his own, he'd likely be fired on the spot. Ed found Al on his back in his bunk, arms crossed behind his head, staring at the open rafters. He was wearing a sleeveless undershirt, displaying bushy hair in his armpits.

"I heard you talking to Johnny," Al said without a glance Ed's way.

"Guess I wasn't being as quiet as I thought."

"Guess not."

"I need the lowdown on something."

Al turned on his side toward Ed, who crouched beside the bunk. Al's curly hair, greased back with pomade, released its sweetness. "What can I do for you?"

"Any idea who got in a scrap last night at the Idle Hour?"

Al drew a toothpick from above his ear and chewed on it reflectively. "Not directly. I was involved in a serious poker game. Went all night," he said slowly. "But my bet would be on Carmine. A hotheaded kid. Someone said he and his buddies went to town last night to see the fireworks. Haven't seen him around here since."

"Where's he bunk?"

"Over in Four. So you got yourself a real job, huh? Has the sheriff got you doing his dirty work—still smashing and bum running?" Al's brown eyes flicked over Ed's uniform.

"There's some of that. But other stuff too."

"You always was a hustler. That's good. But I myself can't see staying out here in this hick town for any longer than I have to. I need to get back to St. Louie." Al yawned. "Anyways, good to see you."

"Thanks for the tip."

Ed stepped into the night. Number Four was dark and quiet, same as the others. Problem was, Ed had no idea what Carmine looked like or which bunk was his. And what will I do when I find him? he thought. Maybe the kid would raise a stink and wake up the whole camp. Then Ed would be out of a job for sure. But saving the CCC from a black eye was worth the risk. And Ed felt deep in his gut that a CCCer wouldn't kill a man. Not when life was looking so much better for him.

All this cogitation was wasted, however, because Ed didn't get two steps inside before a heavy hand clamped on his shoulder and a low voice muttered in his ear, "No unauthorized persons permitted in the barracks, McCance."

Ed turned. Senior Leader Don Davies loomed above him, his face as pale as cheese. Ed and Davies had never gotten along and the deputy knew there was no use arguing. Davies, twenty-eight, had worked in logging camps and freight yards before the hard times set in. He was the oldest CCCer in camp. Ed decided it was best to leave with speed and silence. Raising his hands in a *you win* gesture, the deputy turned and strode out. Davies stood in the doorway until Ed reached the road. The deputy had come a long way with nothing to show for it.

The hike back to town was misery. It felt as if he was toting a knapsack—one of those hand-me-down canvas packs from the soldiers in the Great War. And its leather straps were rotten. And it stank of sweat. And it was packed with rocks.

CHAPTER NINE

RIGHT ABOVE THE TOILET, AT EYE LEVEL, was a nail hole from Sheriff Wright's days. Temple often speculated as to what had hung there. Wright's razor strop? His wife's shower cap? Recently, as late middle age exerted its pull, Temple had more time to speculate as he waited for his bladder, or whatever was causing the slowdown, to release. On this morning, the process was particularly protracted and Temple contemplated asking Etha to hang a picture there. His mind moved on to consider his body's small treacheries as it inched toward sixty. When he slept too long on one side his hip ached the next morning. Taking a wrench to a stubborn bolt left his hand trembling for an hour or so afterward. And when had he fallen into the habit of grunting whenever he rose from a chair? His inner workings awoke at last and Temple finished his morning ablutions.

Etha, her church dress covered with a clean apron, was in the kitchen scrambling eggs. Normally Sundays found her humming a favorite hymn as she whisked, but this morning she was quiet.

Temple parked himself at the kitchen table. "I'll be sorry to miss the service, but Ed and I need to stay on top of this murder."

Etha slid a plate of eggs and buttered toast in front of him. "I'll explain to Reverend Coxey. He'll understand." She sat down opposite him with only a cup of coffee.

"No breakfast? You seem sort of down-at-the-mouth," Temple said, his own mouth full of egg and toast. "Feeling poorly?"

Etha waved a hand. "Nothing to worry about. No zip, I guess."

"Yeah, we're not getting any younger. I was thinking on that just now."

"Home for supper?"

"Doubt it."

He finished the eggs and put the plate and coffee cup in the sink.

"You still my old sweetie pie?" he asked, bending down to kiss her powered cheek.

"'Spect so," she said, smiling.

Ten minutes later, as the courthouse clock struck nine, Temple walked through the Maid-Rite's door. Ed was seated at the counter in wrinkled trousers and with a crease across his cheek. Slept in his clothes and just got up, Temple thought.

Ernie shoved a brimming coffee cup across the counter. "'Morning. Etha feed you?"

"Yes indeed. That woman can cook almost as good as you," Temple said.

The two older men laughed. Ed stared into his cup.

"Up late?" Temple asked, turning to his deputy.

"Sort of."

"Finish your coffee, that'll help. And get your notepad out."

"The boy ain't eaten yet," Ernie said, his back to them as he worked the grill. He made up a plate of ham and eggs. Then, drawing up a corner of his grease-mottled apron to grip the dish, he plunked it down in front of Ed. As an afterthought, the cook swiped his thumb around the plate's rim, removing some errant yolk and licking it off.

Ed glanced at Temple, who nodded. Five minutes later Ed pushed the empty plate aside, belched, excused himself, and opened the notebook. This was another reason Temple had hired Ed straight from the CCC, besides the fact that the kid had gotten his application in so quick. At the interview, Ed had displayed both deference to Temple's authority and an undercurrent of eagerness.

Temple began: "All right, Ernie, I think we're all set. Regarding that body found—"

"Rainmaker, right?" Ernie interrupted.

"It'll be in tomorrow's paper, so, yes, Mr. Coombs met with foul play. Tell us about the last couple of days here. Beginning Friday night. Who came in, what your routine was. All of it."

Ernie rested his arms across the bib of his apron and studied a twist of fly paper and its deceased cargo hanging from the ceiling. "Friday night. Let's see. Had a good supper crowd. The special was roast beef hash. I ran out by five thirty. Didn't see Coombs, if that's what you're getting at. Undoubtedly ate with the Commercial Club fellows over at the Crystal. Things trickled off by closing time. I cleaned up and was home by eight."

Home for Ernie was a three-room apartment over Model Apparel. His proximity to fancy duds, however, had no effect on him. Underneath the tent-size apron, he wore a once-white shirt, brown trousers, and black brogans whose sticky soles emitted ripping noises as he plodded from grill to counter and back.

Temple sipped his coffee. "Did you get to Coombs's fireworks?"

"Nope. And I didn't put any money up, neither. Rattling every window in town ain't going to make it rain. Told that to Doll too. He'd come around late Friday afternoon passing the hat."

"What time did you open Saturday?"

"Opened at the usual—six. But got here at five to prep." A fat fly dived toward the grill. "'Scuse me," Ernie said, snatching a swatter tucked beside the register and taking aim. The fly dropped to the counter, legs up. The cook pinged it into oblivion with thumb and forefinger.

"When you opened," Temple continued, "did you see anyone lurking out back?"

"Nope. No one later either, besides Chester checking the fire exit."

"You sure?"

Ernie nodded. "My garbage cans are out in the alley. I'm in and out of there at least half a dozen times before lunch. That's how . . ." He paused and snatched the swatter. "That's how . . ." *Thwack!* "Got you," Ernie bragged to the smashed fly. "That's how I get so many durn insects in here."

Temple laughed. "Point made. Good breakfast crowd?"

"The regulars. And Coombs showed at maybe . . ." Ernie pursed his lips, twisting them to one side, "maybe ten? Around then. He sat two stools down from where your deputy is planted. Ordered eggs and bacon. Started right in gabbing with the Johnson boys."

The Johnsons were brothers who farmed off Route 16. Bachelors in their forties, with morose expressions and sun-bleached blue eyes, they ate breakfast at the Maid-Rite seven days a week. No one knew their first names.

"Of course, they didn't say much, but that didn't faze him. Then Darnell came in and Coombs dropped the Johnsons like they were a sack of alfalfa overrun with weevils. He sweet-talked the money man and then, when Darnell left, he asked if there was an early matinee and I said—"

Ed broke in, "Did anyone hear him ask about the movie?" Then he caught himself. "Sorry, sheriff. Got excited." He lowered his head over his notepad.

Temple grinned. "That's okay. You're on track." He turned to Ernie. "Who might have overheard Coombs? We need to know everyone who was in here then."

Ernie scratched his chin. "The Johnson boys for sure. Two teacher ladies from the high school were sitting at the end of the counter. Bill Owens and his kid. A CCCer. I think he was still here then. It's hard to remember. I know I had two or three farmers come in sometime that morning. No one I knew by name. A couple of them might have been here the same time as Coombs. And, oh yeah, John Hodge and Reverend Coxey. They took up two stools for at least an hour arguing scripture. I normally tell lingerers to move on. But, you know, can't do that with a lawyer and a clergyman!" Ernie laughed raucously.

Temple smiled. "Anyone else? Think hard. It's important."

Ernie pressed his lips together and, after a couple of seconds, shook his head. "Can't think of a one."

Temple turned to Ed. "Did you get all those folks?"

"Yep."

"So what did you tell Coombs?"

"That there was an early-bird matinee every Saturday at quarter to noon. Then I peeped at the clock and said, *You've got ten minutes.*"

"Then what?"

"Then he tossed two bits on the counter and left. That was it."

"Anyone else leave at the same time?"

"Don't think so. I remember putting the money in the register. Clearing away the dirty dishes. Scraping down the griddle for lunch. Then the duster hit. Came out of nowhere. The plates rattled on the shelves and—*boom*—it was on us. Everyone cleared out straightaway. Throwing change at me on their way out the door. I hustled to fasten the shutters. By the time I got to the last one it was pitch black. I hunkered down behind the counter, just praying the roof would hold. Only tarpaper up there. You know, this was nothing but a lunch wagon when I bought it. Took the wheels off, set it on a foundation, and plumbed it up. Not all that sturdy. When the blowing was over I shook off the dust and checked for damage. Everything held except some porch lattice covering the crawl space. It pulled off on the alley side, but I tacked it up, no problem . . ."

As Ernie talked, Temple leaned over and rolled a toothpick from the metal dispenser. Picking your teeth was vulgar in Etha's household. Temple indulged when he was out and about. He pointed the pick at Ernie. "So, I need you to think. Did you take notice of anything out of the ordinary during the storm?"

The cook snorted. "Hell no! With all that sand and wind? I thought a freight train was busting through town. Clanking, howling, and dark as pitch. There was no way to hear or see anything. Why, if Eleanor Roosevelt herself had blown through the door I'd never had knowed it."

Temple smiled again. "All righty. I think that's all for now." But something Ernie said jabbed at the back of his mind. An image floated up. His grandmother's porch. Rocking chairs, ferns—and a skirt of crisscrossing lattice. The crawl space under the porch floor concealed by lattice had made an irresistible hidey-hole for little boys. He asked, "Mind if I take a gander at that lattice you tacked up?"

"Fine by me. But I'm a cook, not a carpenter. Just so's you know."

The three tramped out the back. Ernie pointed to where the skirting had pulled away. Temple saw some cracks in the wood. He kneeled. "Mind?" he asked Ernie, pulling out a jackknife.

"Be my guest. Just put it back when you're done, otherwise there'll be rabbits nesting there for sure."

The three nails eased out and Temple drew back the framework. He stretched out on his belly, knowing Etha would pitch a fit about the dirt on his clothes, and peered into the crawl space. It was surprisingly clean. A low pile of bricks and a couple of stray tin cans were all Temple saw. Then, farther back, he caught a glimpse of something else.

"Ed, I need your eyes," Temple said, and the deputy promptly dropped down beside him. "See that there?"

"What, those bricks?" Ed replied.

"No. To the side of them."

"Yeah. I see something. Can't tell what."

Temple called over his shoulder to Ernie, "We need a broom."

After a couple minutes of unsuccessful fishing with the broom, Ed shoved it aside and wriggled halfway into the cramped underbelly of the Maid-Rite. When he squirmed back out, he was dragging a long wooden handle.

"Familiar?" Temple asked. And Ernie, wiping his own brow after observing so much exertion, said, "Nope."

"We'll let you get back to your customers, then."

"Suits me." Ernie disappeared inside.

The lawmen examined the find.

"Might be the murder weapon. It's pretty clean. Not been under there long," Temple said. "Definitely a tool handle. Oak, I'd say."

There was a square metal grip at one end. The other was snapped off by a fresh break, with a rust-colored stain on the splintered edges.

"Could be blood," Temple said, squinting at the tip.

Ed's stomach dropped. He'd clutched many a handle like it in the corps. It was an army entrenching tool, another Great War castoff that the CCC inherited. He recognized it right off, despite the missing shovel blade.

"From a pick or a hoe, maybe," Temple was saying. "What do you think?"

Ed shrugged, not trusting his voice and dodging an outright lie.

Temple used Ed's handkerchief to lift it by the steel grip, dark with age. He knew a few things about tools. His grandfather had owned a hardware store in Johnstown, at the base of Pennsylvania's share of the Allegheny Mountains. As a kid, he spent Saturdays roaming its cluttered aisles, learning the trade. Each week, he'd been drilled by Grandpa Jennings on its sprawling inventory. The first lesson had been memorizing the types and sizes of shovels—the narrow post-hole spades, the general-use shovels with their broad blades, and the short-handled scoops for grain. By the time he was eleven, Temple had worked his way up to the saws. And then came the great flood, the roiling wave of water, silt, uprooted trees, and drowned cattle that crashed down the mountain and into the valley. As the first alarms had sounded, Temple, his ma, and his little sister Nan had scrambled up the attic stairs of their house on Green Hill, above the city proper. He'd crept to the gable window and caught glimpses of the Little Conemaugh River bucking and roaring out beyond the railroad tracks. A torrent of muddy water inundated the shops, churches, and his school. Grandpa's store, with its red tin roof, began to list. The flood swept away Johnstown's houses, schools, and churches. And Grandpa's store. And Grandpa himself.

Now, balancing the broken stick, Temple said, "Let me correct myself. Not a hoe. A shovel handle. Bet the house on that." He stretched, relieving the stiffness in his spine. Ed, he thought, looked puny. "Buck up, boy, we've got a heap of work. You can take a snapshot of this at the office and then I'll drop it off at Hinchie's. See if he can tell us if that's blood at the break. If you ask me, the killer used this to bash Coombs's head in and then tossed it into the crawl space with a *good riddance*."

Seeing that handle left Ed gut-punched. They needed to solve this case fast, before the primary. No way, Ed thought, is Doll going to hire me if he steps into office. But Ed couldn't stomach having to choose between keeping his job and sullying the CCC's reputation. And it seemed to be going that way.

Usually Etha looked forward to Sunday afternoons, when she and Lottie Klein, the head clerk and buyer at her father's clothing store, sat at the upright piano in the Kleins' house for Lottie's weekly piano lesson. Etha critiqued Lottie's technique, Lottie raced through the scales, and both of them gossiped and laughed.

Lottie favored blue or red frocks designed for much younger women. Her berets, always cocked to one side, and ornamented with a pheasant feather or rosette of ribbon, were the bright spots in Etha's dusty landscape. How Etha missed the varied hues of Illinois! The jade of tender corn husks, the violet shadows of distant trees, the furry scarlet spears of sumac.

In Oklahoma, the palette was nothing but brown. Brown bridal trains of dust billowed behind tractors. Curtains turned from white to strong coffee. Folks spit river mud after a duster. Washes of beige, cinnamon, and umber bled into the blue sky, depending on which direction the wind blew. The people, the land, the buildings absorbed the dust. All other colors leached away, while brown and its infinite variations remained.

On this Sunday, Etha raised her hand to knock on the Kleins' door without her usual verve. Last night's trip to the hobo jungle weighed on her. She had lied to Temple. She had sought out an isolated camp full of strange men. She had drunk whiskey. And, most troubling, somehow young Jack's image had been supplanted with an older, unrecognizable version of the child she'd lost. When she had awakened and his visage appeared as it did every morning, unbidden and often too painful to bear, it had been of a young man. His features had meshed with Carmine's adolescent form. It was all wrong but she couldn't shake it.

Mrs. Klein's was voice booming from the kitchen when Etha knocked. "*Gib zikh a shuk!*" This being a frequent command in the Klein household, Etha knew it meant, *Give yourself a shake,* and understood it was directed at Mr. Klein. The family's lapdog yapped in support of his mistress.

Abruptly Mr. Klein, with his kind round face, appeared in the doorway. He held the screen door open for Etha. "Come in, young lady. You're a breath of fresh air."

"You know from nothing! Isn't that what I was just saying?" His wife waddled over busily from the kitchen, the dog wriggling and yipping from his podium on her jutting bosom. Etha smiled. Part of the weekly drama in the Klein household was Mrs. Klein's insistence on a Sunday drive and her beleaguered husband's lack of enthusiasm.

Lottie, already seated at the piano, turned and waved Etha over. She wore a red striped seersucker playsuit and her hair was up in curlers—a getup too youthful for someone pushing forty, but she got away with it.

"Ignore them and come sit." She patted the chair beside the piano bench. Etha settled herself and dropped her handbag on the floor. On cue, the screen door slapped and then a car engine rumbled to life just beyond the window. As usual, Mr. Klein's determination had wilted under the onslaught. Mrs. Klein, radiating victory, asked Etha if she wouldn't appreciate a cup of tea and rushed to fetch it before Etha could answer.

Lottie shrugged. "Nothing changes around here. That was the duster of all dusters, wasn't it? Where were you?"

As Etha relayed her experience in Lucille's cellar, Mrs. Klein reappeared with a cup and saucer—a cookie and two sugar cubes snugged alongside the cup. Mrs. Klein, too, was vain about her appearance, but that was to be expected. The Kleins operated Vermillion's only clothing shop, Model Apparel. In addition to her fashionable attire, Mrs. Klein wore rouge and lipstick and her hair was meticulously dressed. Etha suspected that it was also dyed. If Etha had encountered Mrs. Klein as a stranger on the street, she might have guessed her to be fifty. Ah, but her hands, Etha thought, as she thanked her hostess and took the cup. The hands always gave away one's age and Mrs. Klein's hands said she was approaching seventy. As a piano teacher, Etha was intimate with the anatomy of knuckles, veins, tendons, palms, and wrinkles that, similar to rings on a tree, revealed a person's true years no matter how much care was taken with face and figure. And it worked the other way around too. More than once she'd bought eggs from a farm wife whose weathered face and faded hair belonged on a sixty-year-old. But as the woman nestled the eggs in a straw-filled box, Etha would be shocked to see the firm hands of a young person.

Etha dropped in a sugar cube, crushing it with a spoon. Mrs. Klein snatched up the dog again and swooped out to the waiting car. The two women at the piano grinned.

"That's a relief," Lottie said.

Etha sipped. "Was the store full when it came through?"

Lottie's shoulders slumped. "Never is, these days. Just Mrs. Hodge. She was there for a fitting but her husband was late. A very smart print with side tiers starting at the . . . well, never mind. Anyway, she tried it on and it fit like a dream. Spectacular, even with that God-awful scarf around her neck that she refused to take off. But Mrs. Hodge won't make a decision without the mister so we were waiting maybe ten minutes when the sky went black. I've never seen one come up so fast. Papa herded us into the back office where we huddled on the floor as if we were a bunch of sheep. If those weren't the longest two hours I've ever spent. Mama and Papa bickering, Nudnik howling, and Mrs. Hodge quivering."

Etha put the teacup down. "Wait a minute. Her husband was coming to the fitting? Temple wouldn't do that in a million years. And doesn't John keep Saturday hours at the law office?"

Lottie yanked out and rerolled a rubber curler that had come loose. "Go figure. Yesterday was the first time she'd ever set foot in the store without him. I think she's poorly. Even our smallest size has to be taken in. He's playing nursemaid, I'd say."

"I never knew. Maybe I'll stop by this week," Etha said. Then she drew a page of sheet music from a stack on top of the piano. "Ready for some scales?"

For the next twenty minutes, Lottie labored through the drills and then plowed into a Haydn sonata. Half of Etha's mind was tuned to Lottie's efforts—correcting clumsy finger work and uneven pacing—but the other half dwelled on her trip to the jungle. What had she been thinking?

After plunking out the final fortissimo chords in the rondo, Lottie announced, "I need a cigarette."

They retired to the back steps. Lottie lit a Lucky for herself and one for Etha and passed it over. They smoked in silence, the only sound being the tutting of chickens from a coop two yards over.

"I have a confession," Etha said, as she stubbed out the cigarette under the ball of her shoe. "I drove out to the shacks by the rails yesterday. I got it in my head to take the tramps some food and, well, it was a mistake."

Lottie jumped in quickly: "Did something happen? Did they try to take liberties?"

"No, no. But I didn't tell Temple anything about it and . . . it got sort of out of hand." She told Lottie about the hooch, the off-color stories, the dancing.

Lottie gave a low whistle. "Close call. Here, you need another." She handed Etha a cigarette and puffed. "What about Temple?"

"I don't think I'm going to tell him for a while. Not with the primary and the murder investigation. It's the last thing he needs." Etha lit the cigarette, watching the smoke dissolve in the dun-colored air. "But I will tell him at the right time. I've never kept anything from him and I'm sick about it."

"He's a good man," Lottie said. They both stared abstractly across the scorched yard. Then Lottie slapped her thighs. "So, what about that Coombs? Chester is beside himself. He's afraid the murder will affect business, which is already at rock bottom. I think he's all wrong. I told him last night that he'll sell *more* tickets. It's a Charlie Chan movie come to life!"

Lottie and Chester had been dating for ten years, "with no end in sight," as Lottie said. The theater owner was very stuck in his ways. It came from the blindness, Etha thought, and needing to have everything, including his clothes and desk, arranged in the same way.

Etha and Lottie had been friends since Etha and Temple moved to town. Lottie had knocked on their apartment door and said she'd heard Etha taught piano. Their first lesson, that very day, hadn't gone well. Lottie could hardly sit still, which irritated Etha. Finally she'd said, "Miss Klein, what seems to be the problem? You're too old to be squirming."

"That jail cell is giving me the willies," Lottie confessed.

Etha had twisted to glance through the hallway into the kitchen. One corner was enclosed with iron bars—a small cell rarely used. Although this setup was not unusual in the homes of rural sheriffs, Etha, too, had been unsettled when they'd first moved in.

Temple had said, "Doubt I'll ever need it. These things are only used for overflow or if we get a lady prisoner." It was, Etha found, handy for storing potatoes and canned goods.

Since that day, the two women had gradually become friends despite their age difference. Now Etha's throat swelled; thinking of all the times they had shared some laughs, some petty complaints about their men, some gossip. And how she had unburdened herself to Lottie, especially in those early days when Jack's death was still fresh. Temple had uprooted

Etha, moving her to Vermillion, barely two months after their little boy wandered off and drowned in the Illinois River. He had thought it best to make a fresh start in a place not weighted down with memories. But it had pained Etha to leave behind the house that Jack knew as home. And just as crushing was the thought that she would not be there to pull the weeds around his headstone or to lay the traditional Christmas blanket of evergreen boughs on his grave. The move away from the cemetery, from Peoria, had punctured Etha's heart and she was grateful that Lottie listened patiently whenever the wound reopened. In all their years in Oklahoma, a day had never passed that Etha didn't want to move back to Peoria to be by her son's side.

Lottie suddenly clapped her hands to illustrate a point and abruptly brought Etha back to the Kleins' back steps. Her friend was recounting the plot of the latest Charlie Chan movie.

"... and *bang*, just like that," Lottie said, smacking her palms together again, "the case was solved."

Etha took the long way home from Lottie's. Temple wouldn't be back for hours. She paused at the plate-glass window of Quality Grocery. Recently she'd speculated on what might happen if Temple lost the primary. Would he give in and take her home? Beside a pyramid of canned peas was propped a *Vince Doll For Sheriff* poster. The candidate stared out confidently.

Etha leaned toward the window, her breath fogging the glass. "I hope you win," she whispered.

C HAPTER TEN

AFTER INTERVIEWING ERNIE AT THE MAID-RITE, Ed hurried back to the office to set up the camera equipment. Temple stayed behind for a second cup of coffee, and then followed him to the courthouse.

The sheriff's office was austere. It was furnished with two desks, three straight-backed chairs, and a poster-sized calendar advertising insurance. Temple had dodged Etha's suggestions of a rug and bookcase, but had finally given in to a potted rubber plant, now a denuded stalk, on the windowsill.

When Temple walked in, Ed was shooting stills of the handle they had discovered under the diner. The click of the shutter, followed by the crackling concussion of the flashbulb and the rattle of the spent bulb hitting the floor, beat out a syncopated rhythm. Temple dropped into his desk chair. The message spindle was filled with notes from Viviane, the courthouse secretary. He thumbed through the slips of paper, each recorded in the young woman's fluid script. T.S. Dibbert's push mower had been swiped. Musgrove, the undertaker, expected a particularly rowdy funeral on Wednesday and requested that the deputy be on hand when the drinking started. Two reports of whiskey stills. A missing cow. A report about tramps bedding down in the cemetery. John Hodge with another Peeping Tom complaint.

Ed finished up and all was quiet. Being it was Sunday, the rest of the courthouse slumbered. There were no jangling file drawers, brisk footfalls, or the snap of suspenders underlining a point from down the hall. A good day for thinking. Temple tipped back and stretched his legs across the desktop. He admired his boots. They held their rich mahogany shine darn near all day. Well-polished boots, he believed, let folks know he took his job seriously.

"Pull up a chair. I want to talk out what we've got so far."

Ed scooched his desk chair over and pulled out his notebook. "Shoot."

"This Roland Coombs shows up Friday. He tells Myra that he's driven down from Coldwater. We'll need to check on that. We can call the sheriff up there. Somehow Coombs makes contact with our Commercial Club. Make a note about finding out who he spoke with. The club agrees to hire him and pays the initial fee. According to Ernie, some in the club then treat Coombs to dinner at the Crystal. That evening, a crowd gathers outside town and Coombs sets off the first round of explosives. After the show he's drinking at the Idle Hour in the company of three CCC boys. A couple of beers later, he and one of them get into a scrap. I need to know who those three were, especially the one who popped him." Temple paused. "You were up to the camp last night, right?"

Ed, who had been scribbling industriously, stopped abruptly. A flush washed up his cheeks. "Uh . . . I thought . . ."

Temple waved him off. "I understand. I'm assuming you were going to tell me."

Ed studied his lap. "I absolutely apologize. That was out of line."

"Did you find out anything?"

"Just that a fellow named Carmine cracked Coombs in the nose. I don't know the guy. Didn't get a last name. I was sneaking in to talk to him but got chased away by the senior leader before I got two steps inside the bunkhouse."

Temple pointed at Ed. "We all make mistakes. You get one pass and now you've used it. Understood?"

Ed nodded.

"Okay. So Coombs and this kid get in a scrap. Coombs goes back to Mayo's where he cleans up his bloody nose, maybe spends a few minutes with Miss Peep Show and then falls asleep, we presume. We'll need to find out where the kid slunk off to after the brush-up. I'm assuming it was back to the camp."

The phone rang. "Sheriff's office," Temple said into the receiver. He listened, issued a few affirmative grunts, and ended with, "I certainly will."

Ed raised his brows.

"Hodge again. Anyway, late the next morning Coombs turns up at the Maid-Rite where he talks to the Johnson boys, the banker, and asks about the movie times. For now, we'll assume he went to the matinee because you found the ticket stub in his pants. We'll need to confirm that with Maxine. We have a lot of questions for her, in fact. Given what we know so far, I have a gut feeling that Coombs steamed up a fellow enough—either at the fireworks, the Idle Hour, or even Mayo's—to want to hurt him bad, if not kill him. The murderer maybe was in the movie theater with Coombs and followed him out or came on him by chance in the alley right as the duster rolled through. Either way, he took the opportunity to whack Coombs but good. Then tossed the handle in the crawl space. Remember that Ernie said the lattice started flapping around that time."

Ed had stopped writing and was staring abstractly out the window. "That duster seems mighty convenient."

Temple lit a cigarette. "Agreed. Maybe the killer was willing to wait it out for the right moment to come along. Somebody with time on his hands. And when the storm rolled in, he jumped on the chance."

Ed snorted. "That doesn't narrow things down a bunch."

Temple grinned. "True." He dropped his legs to the floor and slapped his thighs. "That sums it up for now, I'd say."

"Now what?"

"We need to interview Maxine. Was Coombs at the matinee? Who else bought tickets? Did she notice if anyone left right before the storm? Or even during it? You know what to ask."

"Me?"

"I'm thinking a good-looking guy might make more headway than this old dog."

Ed flushed and Temple was reminded of the day he'd offered the young man his job. The kid was humble. When you were hoping to teach someone the tricks of the trade, as Temple intended to do, that was a good trait.

"Meanwhile," the sheriff said, "I'll call on the CCC boys. Track down this Carmine."

"Don't you think it'd—a—it'd be a good idea for me to go with you? After all . . ."

"I do not. Not at this time. Maybe later, after you're squarely in my camp. Right now you're like a snake shedding its skin. Not wholly one or the other. Go interview Maxine. It's important." Temple stubbed out the cigarette. "I'm going to drop the handle off with Hinchie. We'll catch up here later."

* * *

A boy in overalls answered the door at Maxine's house. "Whatever you're selling, we don't want any." The kid casually plunged his fist into a ratty baseball mitt bound with black electrical tape.

Ed's brows shot up. If he'd spoken that way to a grown-up, his father would have socked him. "Your parents home?"

"Nope. Just *Maxine*," he scoffed.

"Can I speak with her?"

"Who's asking?"

The brass deputy sheriff's badge he pulled out of his pocket was not as ornate or heavy as Temple's, but it did the trick. The boy stepped back with wide eyes. "Yes sir. Come on in."

Ed slapped the badge back into his pocket and stepped into the living room. It was bigger than the kitchen, dining room, and parlor combined of his family's Chicago apartment. Against the far wall, a resplendent cabinet radio, its wooden grille shined to a high gloss, held court. A large fern sat on top, its fronds unfurling into green tendrils.

"She's in here," the boy said, leading Ed through a rounded archway. The deputy skirted a scatter of metal jacks on the rug and followed him into the dining room.

"Who was at the . . ." an older girl wearing round spectacles and a frown was saying as Ed walked in. She had risen from her chair behind the dining table, but upon seeing Ed, she abruptly sat down. "Oh! My folks aren't here."

Across the table, pieces of a jigsaw puzzle were meticulously spread. The upper right corner of the puzzle was taking shape: leaves against a blue sky.

"I'm Ed McCance, the deputy sheriff, and if you are Miss Saunders I am hoping we could talk." Ed produced his badge a second time. "We're investigating the murder of Mr. Coombs and think he may have attended the matinee yesterday. There's a good chance the killer followed Coombs from the Jewel into the alley."

Maxine sucked in her breath. "He was *murdered?* And the killer was in the Jewel? I sold a ticket to a killer?" she yelped. Behind the spectacles, her eyes went wide.

"We're not sure. That's why I'm here."

After a long exhale, Maxine said, "Cliff, get lost. But stay in the yard."

Ed pulled out a chair across from her.

The kid said, "Nuts to you. I ain't going nowhere."

"Don't say *ain't* and I'm in charge. Mommy said so. Out."

Cliff darted to the table, scrambled Maxine's assembled pieces into a jumbled pile, and scooted out, the screen door banging in his wake.

"You brat!" Maxine yelled. To Ed she added, "So juvenile."

Ed smiled. "I have three little brothers myself."

"You do?"

"Back in Chicago. That's where I'm from." He plucked the notepad from his pocket.

"How'd you get out here?" Maxine already knew the answer. Harriet, her best friend, had told her all about the good-looking deputy with the Dick Powell eyes. Harriet would turn green when she found out that Mr. McCance had come asking for Maxine.

"CCC. Best thing that ever happened to me." Ed cleared his throat. "Could I trouble you for glass of water?"

Maxine jumped up. "Sure thing. Back in a dash."

She filled a tumbler at the kitchen faucet. From the pocket of her housedress she fished out her lipstick. Harriet had been right. What a dreamboat! Her baggy ankle socks had to go. She snatched them off and stuffed them in the first place she could think of, which happened to be the bread drawer. Dipping her fingers in the glass of water, Maxine tweaked the curves of her bob.

When she reentered the dining room, Ed was bent over the puzzle. "Trying to patch up the mess your brother made. I haven't done one of these in ages."

"They pass the time when I'm minding the holy terror," Maxine said, handing him the water.

"Thanks." He drained the glass and picked up his pencil. "All right. Let's start with the particulars. Your name, age, and how long you've worked at the Jewel."

Maxine was considering if his full name was Edward or Edwin. She preferred Edward, like the prince of Wales. Edwin sounded rather prudish. "Maxine Ruth Saunders. Thirteen and eight months. I've been working for Mr. Benton for almost two years. I started out stocking the candy counter and now I sell tickets too."

"Good. Now, tell me about yesterday. What time you got to work, who bought tickets. The works."

As Maxine described her routine she fiddled with the puzzle pieces, turning them this way and that. When she found a match, she tapped the interlocking pieces so Ed would notice. "I got to the theater at eleven and first thing I always check the counter. It's funny how some days almost all the Boston Baked Beans are gone. Other days it's Raisinets. You never know. Then I emptied the torn stubs from the ticket bin. Mr. Benton hits the roof if that overflows. It was getting close to opening, so I started setting things up in the booth. Mr. Benton brought out the change drawer. He came back again, fussing about something. I don't remember what. Then I just waited for customers."

The puzzle's upper border of trees and sky were taking shape again. Maxine began concentrating on the lower right corner. "Oh look!" She held up a piece with most of a woman's face. "Do you think she's pretty?"

"Umm. Sure," Ed said. He cleared his throat again. "I want you to think carefully. Who bought tickets? Mr. Benton says he collected twenty-three. Some customers he knew by voice. But some he didn't. If you can remember all of them, all twenty-three, that would be great."

"Jeez. Is this a quiz? I'm not too good at those." Maxine screwed her lips to one side. "Mrs. Reed bought the first ticket. She's a regular. Then Clara and Leroy, they're going steady. That's only three. This is going to be hard."

After five minutes she had remembered a total of twenty. The list included two high school teachers; the two Mrs. Laycombs, the judge's wife and mother; three nurses from the hospital, still in uniform; Mr. Hodge the lawyer; Viviane Gilbert from the courthouse; three county clerks spiffed up on their day off in suits and ties; a guy and a girl, not together, who she figured, by their clothes, were from nearby Woodward; and three CCCers. Ed's stomach lurched.

Maxine tapped the table with all ten digits. "And Mr. Coombs."

Ed's brows rose. "How did you know it was him?"

"He told me. When it was his turn at the booth he slid a business card into the slot. He said, *I'm the fellow you're hearing about that's going to make it rain. How about a free ride?* Then he flashed a big grin. As if I was some kind of ninny."

"What'd you do?"

Maxine huffed. "I said no, of course. Pushed out my chin to show I meant business."

"And?"

"And he winked to let me know it was all a joke, paid his nickel, and strolled inside." Maxine flopped back in her chair. "How many is that? Must be twenty-three."

"Nope. Three more."

"Jeez. I can't think of anyone else." She leaned over the table. "Did you ever notice how when you're doing a puzzle and the radio's on, the story sort of mixes with the pieces? See this section I'm working on here? Somehow the people we're talking about are part of it."

Ed nodded. "I think I know what you mean." He picked up a piece. "This goes here." He tamped it down alongside the woman's face. What is this a picture of, anyway?"

"It's called 'In the Garden of Dreams.' I've put it together bunches of times. There are these two women in togas and some swans. Sometimes I pretend I'm one of the ladies." After blurting this out, Maxine blushed. *Pretending? He must think I'm a little kid.* But when she peered at Ed, he was examining a piece.

"Is this water or sky, do you think?" he asked.

After a few minutes of quiet assembly, the deputy picked up the pencil again. "So, we'll come back to the rest of the ticket buyers. Tell me what happened when the storm started up."

"It was the worst I've seen. I'm not a scaredy cat, but I was shaking in my boots. I told Mr. Benton. He sent me up to shut off the projector while he calmed the customers. They all wanted to leave, of course, but it was too late. They would have been blown to Kansas. It took some convincing to make them stay. Mrs. Laycomb stomped out as if she was fixin' to go, but flew back in when she saw for herself how bad it was. We were stuck at least three hours with the wind howling and so much sand and dirt thrown you couldn't hear yourself think. Luckily, the kerosene lamps fired right up."

"So you could see?"

"Sort of."

Ed looked away in thought. "I want you to close your eyes."

It crossed her mind that he was going to kiss her. Maybe she should take off her glasses, but her hands were shaking too much. She lowered her lids in fear and excitement. But it was just more pretending and she knew it.

The deputy was giving directions: "Think back to that scene. Is Mrs. Reed there? Do you see her?"

Maxine screwed her eyes tight. "Yes. I remember! She wears those silver bracelets and I heard them jangle when it was blowing so hard."

"Okay, good." Ed consulted the list of names she'd given him. "How about Clara and Leroy?"

Smacking noises rose from Maxine's puckered lips.

In the end, she remembered seeing most of the ticket buyers seated in the theater but wasn't sure about five or six. For some reason, she could only conjure up two of the three nurses. Had the lawyer stuck it out? She wasn't sure of that, either. And the same with the CCCers. Two had stayed—but all three? Maxine shrugged.

Ed sighed. "All right. Mr. Coombs?"

Maxine opened her eyes, snapped her fingers. "You know, I didn't see him. I know that for sure because I checked. I was going to tell Mr. Benton about the trick he tried to pull and I looked around but he wasn't there."

"Yeah, we figured he might have slipped out. But this confirms it. Good work." Now Ed put down the pencil. "Maybe more patrons than Coombs scooted out?"

"Could have happened while I was up at the projection booth."

Ed nodded. "Makes sense."

"And," Maxine said in a rush, "and I think someone might have left while I was bringing in the lamps. It was pitch black, the duster was right on top of us, and the side door, the one on the alley, blew open. At least I thought it did, but maybe someone was, you know, ducking out."

"The door slammed open?"

"Yeah. A load of dust and sand blew in. Someone yelled to shut it."

"How long was it open, do you think?"

"A couple of seconds."

"Long enough for two people to leave?"

Maxine pulled back. "I see what you're getting at. I think so." She shivered. "This is giving me the creeps." She couldn't remember any more details.

The screen door to the house slapped and Cliff clattered in. "The guys got a ball game going behind the school. Can I head over?"

Maxine's eyes narrowed. "All of a sudden you're asking instead of just running off? What have you been up to that you don't want me to know about?"

Her brother frowned. "Me? Nothing. I've been staying in the yard just like you said."

"I've got to move along too, Miss Saunders. You've been a great help." Ed stood and tucked the notepad in his pocket.

"Happy to oblige." Maxine's Red Glo lips glistened.

"If you remember any more ticket buyers or anything else, call the sheriff's office right away."

"I will."

As he adjusted his hat, she imagined him sweeping her up into his arms and promptly felt sick at the thought. She watched from behind the front curtains as he headed down the sidewalk. When he was out of sight, she slumped onto the sofa. Dejected but also relieved. Pretend boyfriends were safer.

In the solemnity of the blistering Sunday afternoon, Ed walked the quiet streets back toward the courthouse. Chicago's clamor was thousands of miles away. He grinned. Got a lot accomplished, he thought. Might have nailed down the victim's movements just before he was killed. Got a bunch of possible suspects. A number of sturdy young men, capable of killing someone with a strong hit to the head, had been at the Jewel that day. Of course, that was assuming the murderer was at the theater at all. But how else would he know Coombs was in the alley at just that time? So, the county clerks were possibilities. That lawyer, Hodge, might be another. Ed considered the clerks and wondered if they had been among the entourage fawning over Doll at the bar the night before. Could there be some connection between the killing and the campaign? If this was Chicago, the answer would be yes. But here? Ed doubted it. He wished Maxine had eliminated all the CCCers. He thought of Temple up at the camp right at that moment. Ed trusted his boss to be fair, to do the right thing. He just hoped the right thing wasn't arresting Carmine.

C HAPTER ELEVEN

AFTER ED LEFT TO QUESTION MAXINE, Temple wrapped the shovel handle in a sheet of the *Gazetteer* and drove over to the doctor's house. Minnie received the bundle and Temple's request with a sniff, explaining that she had other plans for Hinchie, which involved burning the week's rubbish.

"You're a hard-driving woman," Temple said with a laugh.

He climbed behind the wheel thinking of the set of Etha's mouth when she had something she wanted to accomplish. "They are the backbone," he said aloud, turning the sedan westward toward the CCC camp.

After the previous day's storm, the horizon was still choked in a thick yellow haze. With so many fence posts buried up to their necks, unsettled crows flew in circles, searching for places to roost. Temple strode up the path to the CCC commander's office, tapped on the door, and walked in. Army Captain Leroy Baker oversaw the site from behind a dented metal desk that appeared, like all the CCC's gear, to be an army castoff. But Baker himself was first rate, in Temple's estimation. The army reservist's posture was straight, his gestures efficient, and word was that he ran a well-oiled operation and didn't play favorites. With his black tie tucked between the second and third buttons, and high lace boots, Baker looked the part.

"Long time no see," Baker said. "Where you been a-keeping yourself?"

"Here and there. We've been meaning to have you to supper. Really, Etha has been poking at me to invite you. Think you could get one of your subordinates to babysit the corps one night?"

"That'd be swell." Baker had a ruddy face that lit up like a lantern when he smiled. "Haven't had a home-cooked meal in I don't know how long."

Temple's eyes fell on a cluster of topographical maps, covered with pushpins, papering the walls. "What are these here?"

"Trees planted. Windbreaks to hold the soil in place. Each pin is a hundred trees."

Temple gave a slow whistle. "That's a lot of holes dug. You've got the boys on their toes."

"Sure enough."

"Good bunch?"

"Best so far. Hard workers even though they get here mighty scrawny. It takes two weeks of three squares and calisthenics to get them even halfway conditioned."

Temple shook his head. "A shame what's happening to this country." He meandered to the opposite wall where supplies were neatly stacked on wooden shelves. Along the top were small hand tools—hammers, screwdrivers, and such. Boxes of bolts and nails, each labeled as to size and length, were one shelf down alongside hand drills, pliers, planes, and files. On the bottom were saws, picks, and at least half a dozen shovels with square metal handles.

"You got a whole hardware store here."

"Trying to teach these boys something about forestry and carpentry. The army supplies us."

"My grandfather had a hardware store. I recognize most all of these. I can tell you the difference between a ball-peen, ripping, riveting, and bell-face hammer," Temple said with a grin. "But I don't recognize this here." He picked up a handled shovel, balancing it between his two hands, judging its weight.

"And you wouldn't, unless you served in the war. That's an army entrenching shovel. Specially designed for digging trenches. Every soldier who fought was issued one, along with a mess kit, wire cutters, and a gas mask. After coming home from France, I'd hoped never to set eyes on one again but crates of them keep turning up here like bad pennies."

Temple made a clicking noise with his tongue out of the side of his mouth. "Learn something new every day." He laid the shovel back in the pile. "Each of these accounted for?"

"Not really. Those on the shelves are extras. Most are stored in the supply room. Why?"

Temple pulled the visitor's chair away from the desk to make room for his legs and settled himself. Ed must have handled one of those shovels every day when he was in the CCC, but hadn't said a word when he'd pulled one from under the Maid-Rite.

"I'm investigating a murder and one of these shovel handles may or may not come into play. Don't know yet. What I do know is that a CCC boy got in a fistfight with the victim Friday night."

Baker, who had been absently tapping a pencil on the desk, halted it in midair. "You're sure?"

"A couple of witnesses have told us so, but that's why I'm here. To talk to the fellow. You didn't hear anything about this?"

Baker rubbed his face. "No, I did not. And there will be hell to pay because no one reported it. Everyone here knows they have to toe the line. That's the first thing we drill on."

"You get a couple hundred young men thrown together, it's bound to happen," Temple said.

Baker rested his forehead in his palm, eyes closed. "Who got killed?"

"Traveling rainmaker by the name of Roland Coombs."

"Do you have the CCCer's name?"

"Just the first. Carmine."

Baker pulled out a file drawer and flipped through the tabs while he talked. "Carmine DiNapoli. He's one of the new intakes. Arrived July 15. Think he's from . . ." He tugged out a manila folder and flipped it open. "Kansas City. Age nineteen. Before joining the CCC he'd been delivering groceries. Says here he completed his sophomore year then quit school to help support his family." Baker glanced up. "At least every other one of our boys have dropped out to work. The other half got told to leave home by their ma or pa—some nicely, some not—because the family couldn't afford to feed them."

Temple pulled his pad out and started taking notes.

Baker went back to the file. "Five feet eight inches and a hundred thirty-three pounds in July. He's gained a few by now, I'd bet. Assigned to Bunkhouse Four. That's about it."

"I need to talk to him."

Baker put the file back and rose. "'Course. Sundays the corps has the day off. We organize activities. Today are the boxing finals and a baseball game. I'll walk you over to the rec fields."

Temple stood. "I'm sorry for this. And my deputy, well, you can guess how down-at-the-mouth he is. He credits the CCC with turning his life around. Sometimes I think he's more a CCCer than a deputy."

Baker laughed. "Ed's got a fidelity streak a mile long."

He led Temple between the two rows of barracks. A couple of young men were crouched in doorways, bent over writing tablets. The thick thrum of a guitar came from the shadowed interior of another. Otherwise the bunkhouses appeared empty.

At the far end was a dining hall. Competing aromas of roast chicken and dish soap wafted from the windows.

"We try to give the boys something special for Sunday supper, although it is questionable if that is necessary since they inhale whatever is put in front of them," Baker said over his shoulder. Up ahead, hoots and whistles could be heard. At least two hundred young men were spread across two large playing fields. A baseball game was underway on one. The batter, a lanky kid with a heavy hank of hair falling in his eyes, swung and missed to a chorus of jeers from the outfield. Opposite, a thick crowd surrounded a crude boxing ring made up of a planked floor enclosed by thick rope tied to iron piping. Inside the ring, two boys circled one another.

"Come on, Jimmy, sock him a good one!" someone shouted, and one of the boxers sprang toward his opponent, attempting an upper jab that failed to connect. The other kid, shorter and wiry, pranced backward out of range, a pair of too-large gloves shielding his concave chest. Someone struck a cooking pot with a metal spoon to end the round. The two fighters retreated to their corners where they wiped the snot from their noses and got an earful of advice from supporters.

Jimmy was outfitted like the real McCoy in a pair of sateen basketball shorts and a sleeveless undershirt. He was bent over, sucking in air. His opponent, in sagging trousers and bare chested, seemed scarcely winded as he shifted back and forth on the balls of his feet. He poured a ladle of water over his head from the corner bucket and shook it off like a nerved-up terrier.

An eager spectator leaned forward. "You show 'em, Carmine. Show 'em for us new guys."

DiNapoli nodded as if to say, *Will do*, and turned back to the ring.

The pot was struck and the two boxers moved warily toward one another. Jimmy was still breathing heavily and DiNapoli seemed to sense this. With a series of jabs, he backed the boy into the ropes and landed a solid hit to the abdomen. Jimmy doubled over, the ref split them up, and DiNapoli glanced out at the crowd with the start of a grin. It abruptly vanished when his eyes fell on Temple's uniform. Jimmy got back on his feet and the ref gestured for them to continue the fight. DiNapoli grabbed the closest corner post and vaulted over the ropes.

"Hey, what the heck!" someone shouted as the boxer dashed away from the ring.

"Ah, jeez," Temple said. "Let's go." He and Baker set off at a trot.

DiNapoli was sprinting, despite the heavy boxing gloves. Temple shifted to a walking pace, knowing there was no sanctuary for the kid out there. No alleys, no apartment house doorway—just wide-open prairie.

"Let him run it out," Temple said to Baker.

Eventually DiNapoli slowed to an open-mouthed jog. Then a walk. The kid's knees buckled and he slumped to the ground. Temple and Baker caught up a minute later.

"Let's go," Temple said.

Panting, DiNapoli pushed up onto all fours, wobbled, and stood. Temple untied the knots on the gloves. Wordlessly, the three walked back to camp.

"Go in and clean up," Temple said to DiNapoli as they approached the washhouse. "I'll wait."

The barracks were deserted. Everyone, including the letter-writers and the guitar player, had been herded to the baseball field by the camp staff. The kid emerged from the washhouse with face and bare chest dripping. Lean but with some muscle on him, Temple noted. DiNapoli's chest, neck, and arms were tawny. Funny. Coming from the city, you'd think he'd be paler. Had he been in camp here long enough to brown up?

DiNapoli had one of those streetwise faces. Opaque. Closed in. And he had an older purple bruise along his jawline as if he'd gotten punched a day or so ago. Say, Friday night.

Baker offered Temple the use of his office before moving off toward the ball field.

"Follow me," Temple said. DiNapoli nodded.

Once inside Baker's office, the sheriff pulled the two chairs across from one another and indicated that DiNapoli was to sit in one. He took the other, pushing it back a bit so he could cross his legs comfortably. DiNapoli sat with thighs wide, forearms resting on each, head bowed.

"Son, why did you run?"

DiNapoli shrugged. "Don't know."

"What?"

DiNapoli raised his head. His eyes narrowed. "Said I don't know."

"You've got to have some idea. You took off like a jackrabbit right in the middle of the round. One you seemed to be winning, by the way. Caught a glimpse of me and off you scooted."

DiNapoli shrugged again.

A fly whizzed past Temple's head, banged against the window glass. Searching for an escape route. It looped around to another window and finally commenced a twanging barrage against the screen door. It was the only sound for a full minute.

Eventually Temple uncrossed his legs. "Okay. We'll go into that later. I'll tell you why I'm here. I have reports from several witnesses that you got into a fistfight with a Mr. Roland Coombs on Friday night. That so?"

DiNapoli raised his eyes to the sheriff's. The gaze was unreadable. "Yeah."

"And you've heard that Mr. Coombs's body was found outside the theater yesterday?"

DiNapoli jumped in, his voice raised: "I heard. But I didn't have nothing to do with that."

"All right." Temple's tone was measured. "But could you tell me about the fight? How it came about? How you met up with Coombs?"

DiNapoli tilted his head back, shut his eyes, and sighed. "It being Friday night, me and a couple of guys went to town to, you know, have a couple of beers, play some pool."

"Did you walk in?"

"Started walking but a farmer gave us ride in the back of his truck. He said a rainmaker was set to shoot off explosives at the edge of Vermillion and he was going. Sounded fun. We asked if we could come along."

Temple tipped his chair back and laced his fingers behind his head. "Good show?"

"The aces." DiNapoli sat up. "Bam. Boom. Louder than fireworks. I thought for sure it'd start pouring right then. Afterward we talked to Coombs. Found out about his setup. How he rigged the explosives and all. Then he said he'd give us a ride back to town and buy us beers if we'd help him load his truck."

"When did you get to the Idle Hour?" Temple asked.

DiNapoli thought for a moment. "Somewhere around ten."

"Big crowd?"

"Guess so. For around here. Not the same as in Kansas City where you've got to squeeze inside it's so packed. And that's on a weeknight."

Temple turned his eyes away for a minute. "St. Joe's close to Kansas City, right?"

"Guess so. I've never been."

"Did you know Coombs was from St. Joe?"

DiNapoli shook his head. "Never said where he was from."

"All right. You're at the Idle Hour . . ."

"Coombs bought us the suds. Then we all bought each other rounds."

"Get drunk?"

"I was pretty pickled. Coombs talked with us for a bit, then drifted away. An hour or so later, he was back."

"And that's when the fight happened?"

"I was out of matches and asked him for a light. Coombs tosses me his lighter. A spiffy sterling-silver job. I must have forgotten to give it back and he forgot to ask. But then he did ask, so I checked my pockets and couldn't find it. He accused me of filching. We were both blotto by then. He wouldn't let it go. Shoved me. I shoved back. He shoved me again. Then I let him have it. He got one across my jaw. I knew I'd overstayed my welcome. When I got outside, the fellows had ditched me."

The sheriff shifted in his seat. So far, the kid seemed to be honest. After so many years questioning moonshiners, he could tell when a man was telling the truth and when he was lying. Couldn't explain it. Something in the eyes and hands.

"Go on."

"I thought about walking back to camp but I was too drunk. I needed to sleep it off. I'd missed bed check but nothing I could do about that. I stumbled down a couple of alleys and found an unlocked shed. Nothing inside but a bunch of garden tools and a sack of ground cobs that made an okay mattress."

Temple grunted. "Passed out cold?"

"Yeah—no, wait. I was soused but woke up at some point. Heard the back porch steps creaking, like someone didn't want nobody to hear. I rolled over and looked out through a crack in the wood. There was a dark shape, but that was all I could make out."

"Man or woman?"

DiNapoli paused. "Man. Not a big man, but bigger than a woman. He was stooped. Maybe an old guy? I didn't come to again until morning. I peeked out. There was a woman cranking clothes through a washer on the back porch. She'd have seen me if I tried to leave. I lay back on the cobs and must have drifted off."

The shouts and hoots of young men rose in the distance. Someone on the diamond had likely scored, Temple thought. "And then what?" he asked.

"And then the shed door was rattling. It was the wind. Howling and spraying dirt through every opening. There was a window but it didn't do no good since I couldn't see a thing. That was one hell of a dust storm. I was pinned down for a couple of more hours, knowing that whole time I'd be in big trouble at camp, but there was nothing I could do about it."

"How long were you in the shed?"

"However long the storm lasted. When it stopped, I started hoofing it to camp. I thought I'd get a ride along the way but no go. My stomach was yapping something fierce. I hadn't eaten anything since dinner the night before except a couple of Saltines at the bar. So when I spotted a campfire by the tracks I made a beeline. There was a whole crowd of fellows there. Had some chicken that some . . . that some fellow cooked up. Finally crawled back to camp around midnight. Got caught by the senior leader and put on KP for a month."

Temple stood, stretched his legs. He wandered over to examine the wall map. "So you're telling me you were nowhere near the Jewel on Saturday?"

"The movie theater? No sir, I wasn't."

"Anyone see you around the shed or when you headed back to camp?"

DiNapoli shook his head.

"Where was the house? What street?"

"I don't know. A couple of blocks from the bar."

"Would you know it if you saw it again?'

"Maybe. But I was pretty blotto."

"So you got drunk, got in a fistfight with Coombs, staggered into someone's toolshed to sleep it off, and then, after the storm the next day, walked back to camp after taking a detour at the jungle beside the tracks. And you never saw Coombs after he left the bar on Friday night?"

"That's right."

"So why did you run when you saw me?"

DiNapoli shook his head. "Instinct, I guess."

"Have you had run-ins with the law before?"

"No sir."

Outside, the wind picked up. A metal chain on the flagpole took to clanking.

Temple said, "Let's go over to your barracks. I'm going to need to see the clothes you were wearing Friday."

DiNapoli paled. "Sure."

In Bunkhouse Four, DiNapoli led Temple to his bed, which was made up army style with a wool blanket stretched tight. A row of hooks had been nailed above the beds and from DiNapoli's hung a white duffel bag.

"Dirty laundry's in there," he said. "Clean stuff's in the footlocker."

Temple took down the bag, tugged the drawstring, and dumped the contents on DiNapoli's bed. A wrinkled green uniform, socks, and underwear tumbled out.

"What were you wearing Friday night?"

Pulling his hands from under his armpits, the boy poked through the pile. "These trousers, I think. And this." He picked up a CCC shirt.

Right away, the sheriff saw what might be dried blood on the pocket and on one of the cuffs. "Your blood?"

DiNapoli dropped his head. "Coombs's. At the bar. I got him between the nose and the lip. It was a real bleeder."

"Not the next day? Not in the alley?"

DiNapoli's eyes widened. "No! Jeez, you don't really think I killed him, do ya? 'Cause I didn't. I swear on my mother's life."

Temple put the shirt aside. As he picked up the trousers, something fell out of a pocket and onto the floor. "This the lighter?"

DiNapoli scratched his neck and gazed away. "Yeah."

"So you didn't forget to give it to him?"

"No. I boosted it. I boosted it and I smashed him in the face at the bar, but I didn't kill him."

Temple shook his head. "This isn't looking good right now. You know that?"

"Yeah." The kid sniffled, wiped his nose.

Temple gathered up the trousers and shirt, put the lighter in an envelope, and tucked it in his shirt pocket. "I'm going to need to talk to you again tomorrow. See if we can't locate that shed. In the meantime, don't even think about running. I'm going to let Commander Baker know and ask that his entire staff keep their eyes trained on you. If you take off, it'll only be harder on you. Understand?"

DiNapoli nodded.

"Okay. Let's go talk to the commander."

The wind battered the sedan's snub nose mercilessly as Temple drove home. With dusk coming on, the dust swirling darkly across the asphalt blurred the boundaries of road and field. He tried to sort out his thoughts. Was a barroom fistfight enough of a motive for DiNapoli to hang around town overnight, track down Coombs's whereabouts the next day, and wait for the odd chance to knock him off? Might be enough for a hotheaded kid. DiNapoli certainly had access to the type of weapon used, and his shirt was bloodied. Temple could be easily persuaded that DiNapoli was the killer. And a liar too. He'd lied about stealing the lighter. And, Temple thought, maybe about his life before the CCC. DiNapoli had known how to hunt down a place to sleep it off. Probably he'd spent some time bumming around, maybe riding the rails—acquiring that tan, learning the rules of the road, using people to his advantage. Another thing was the St. Joe connection. That needed more fleshing out but something could be there. Maybe Coombs and DiNapoli had butted heads before Friday.

Temple absently scratched his chin. But then there was DiNapoli back at the camp and signing up for a boxing match. If he had killed Coombs and was expecting the sheriff to come after him, why hadn't he just jumped the first freight out of town from the hobo jungle? Why make the hike back to camp at all? Maybe, Temple reasoned, he didn't think he'd get caught. But surely with that fight in the bar witnessed by so many, DiNapoli knew he'd be a suspect. So how come he'd waited until today to run? And another thing: when the kid heard *why* Temple was questioning him, wasn't there a spark of surprise in his eyes? They wouldn't be closing the case today, that was for sure. But there was a healthy chance of an arrest before the primary.

Temple pulled behind the courthouse and parked. On the third floor, the open kitchen window glowed. He sniffed, then grinned. Sunday pot roast. As he stepped out of the car, his legs, protesting against the cramp of the footwell, moved like rusty jackknives. Being long-shanked was a scourge.

The courthouse clock struck six, its toll displacing the sparrows atop the gabled roof and rattling Etha's cut-glass tumblers in the china cabinet for a solid minute.

After returning from Lottie's, Etha had tied on her apron and scrubbed the vegetables for dinner. The carrots were knobby with cracked skins and the turnips bore black spots. She'd decided that telling Temple about her trip to the jungle would do no good. It would just worry him for no reason. And hadn't it all worked out? As she knifed potatoes into

quarters, Etha's brain kept murmuring, *But then again . . . But then again
. . .* But then again, she'd never withheld anything from Temple. Not in
thirty-two years of marriage. Was that true? She had withheld some of
her innermost thoughts . . . about Jack, about her desire for another child
after his death. But she'd never failed to tell him what she'd been doing
or where she'd been or purposely mislead him as she had this time. Green
shoots sprouted from the onions. She clipped them off and was pulling
out the roasting pan from the oven when the bell struck six. She watched
Temple walk toward the back entrance down below; he took off his hat
and waved it at her. As gallant as a rodeo rider. Her stomach dipped. *I
can't lie to this man. I've got to tell him.*

"Smells mighty fine," he said, settling in at the kitchen table.

"The same roast I make every Sunday. Some of the vegetables are
long in the tooth, I'm afraid."

Temple laughed. "Same as me. I tell you, Etha, I'm feeling my age
today." He pulled off his boots, then his socks, and massaged his feet.
"How are things with the Kleins? Same old Sturm und Drang?"

"That setup isn't going to change. Bertha badgering Meyer about a
Sunday drive. The dog barking its head off. Lottie rolling her eyes. Go
on and wash up, change your shirt. I'll set the table." She plucked two
knives, forks, and spoons from the drawer.

Temple headed down the hall. He peeled off the uniform shirt and
trousers, stuffing them in the bedroom hamper. In the bathroom he bent
over the sink, splashing tap water on his face and the back of his neck. He
swabbed his underarms. Coffee-colored water swirled down the drain.
He shuffled back to the bedroom and pulled on the frayed blue shirt and
soft trousers with holes in the knees that he wore around the house. The
bed, with its tufted chenille spread, called. Temple flopped down, trying
to empty his mind, but something bristled up through his thoughts.
Something about the expression on that kid's face was not lining up but
he couldn't put his finger on it. Temple lay back to rest his eyes for a
couple of minutes.

"Dinner," Etha called. At the same moment, the phone in the hallway
rang. Years of late-night calls about strangers in someone's barn or a
fight at the Idle Hour had trained Temple to go from a dead sleep to fully
awake in an instant. He jerked upright on the bed and moved to answer
the trill. Etha, trained by the constant interruptions, slid the roast back
in the oven.

Temple had the receiver in his hand and Walter Darnell's voice in his ear. The banker was the only man in town with the wide desk, leather chairs, and hooded lamps of a city-style office, yet he did business everywhere but. Darnell was known to discuss loans, mortgages, and new accounts in Trinity Episcopal's parlor during fellowship hour, in the bleachers at Vermillion High's varsity game, and astraddle a stool at the Maid-Rite. Now Temple envisioned the banker stretched out on Mrs. Darnell's floral davenport, his stockinged feet propped on the armrest.

After an exchange of niceties Walter said, "The auction at the Fuller farm is on for tomorrow at noon. Can you or Ed be there?"

Temple groaned. He'd been hoping that after Saturday's postponement, he'd have at least a week to focus on the Coombs case. But First National rolled on, no different than the flooded Little Conemaugh River rampaging through Johnstown, heedless of mankind's tragedies and sorrows. And keeping the law was his job, in matters big and small.

"I'll be there."

A rustle of paper told Temple the banker was already on to his next task. "Much obliged. I find these foreclosures as distasteful as you do, but the big picture is we've got to protect the bank's assets and this is just one of those necessary evils to make sure First National stays afloat."

Walter gave out this little speech whenever a foreclosure came up. And it was, Temple thought, getting as drained of meaning as an ancient vaudeville gag. "All right, then. See you at noon." He let the receiver fall into the cradle with a thunk. "Sorry, Etha, but that—"

The telephone rang again. This time it was Ed.

"Hey, sheriff, I need to fill you in on questioning Maxine."

"All right. Hold on a minute." Temple laid the receiver on the small table and walked into the kitchen.

Etha was at the table, flipping the pages of a magazine. She seemed nerved up about something; probably fretting about the roast turning to shoe leather.

"It's Ed and this will take a bit. Sorry to make you hold dinner."

She gave a half smile. "Not your fault. Although I don't know why people don't think about folks trying to eat Sunday dinner before they ring."

He walked over and kissed her on the check, inhaling the sweet scent of her face powder. "Thanks."

Back on the telephone, Temple leaned against the wall, propping his forehead between thumb and index finger to listen. Ed described the interview and ended with reading off Maxine's list of who bought movie tickets on Saturday morning.

"We were right, then, about Coombs ducking out in the middle of the storm," Temple said.

"Yeah, and maybe there was someone else right behind him. Maxine's a pretty observant kid. Despite the spectacles."

"Good to know because we're going to need her for an identification."

There was silence at the other end of the line. After a moment Ed said, "What'd you find out up at the camp?"

"The news isn't good. I had to chase him down, but I did talk to Carmine DiNapoli and . . ." Temple was saying when Etha's scissors clattered to the kitchen floor. He watched her hesitate before stooping to pick them up. Temple continued, "He admitted to the fight but says he didn't kill Coombs. Says he was sleeping one off in someone's toolshed during the storm and then hiked back to camp on Saturday night. Trouble is I found blood on his shirt and Coombs's lighter hidden in his dirty laundry. DiNapoli admitted pinching it. And then there are those entrenching shovels all around camp, as I'm sure you know. Same as what was used to bash Coombs's head in."

Ed's voice trickled weakly across the wires: "So, you're thinking it's this kid?"

"Right now, if I was a betting man, I'd lay some money down. But there's still a couple of strings dangling. We need to see if Maxine recognizes DiNapoli as one of the CCCers at the Jewel on Saturday."

"How we going manage that?" Ed asked.

Temple scratched his chin. "I don't want to do a police-style lineup."

"Yeah, I'm not sure how Maxine would take to that. She's just a kid."

Temple made a sucking noise with his teeth. "How about you drive her out to camp tomorrow? Maybe park in front of the office and we could ask Commander Baker to meet with a few of the corps about something, I don't know what, and include DiNapoli as one—"

"And have her eyeball him from the passenger seat?" Ed broke in.

"Exactly."

"Guess that would work."

"Good. I'll call Baker tomorrow and then you and I can set it up," Temple said. "Did you get those photos of the body developed yet?"

"On my way over to the *Gazetteer* right now."

The sheriff's office had an agreement with Hank Stowe, the *Gazetteer*'s publisher, to use the newspaper's dark room when Ed needed to print crime scene photos.

"Then see you in the office first thing." Temple tugged on his lower lip in thought. He wanted to trust Ed's professionalism in dealings with the CCC. He thought it doubtful that Ed would purposely try to confuse Maxine somehow and stack the deck in favor of DiNapoli. His deputy wasn't that kind.

It was after seven o'clock when Temple and Etha sat down to eat. The roast was dry, the potatoes shriveled, but Temple's empty stomach didn't care. He filled Etha in on his trip to the camp and talk with Baker.

"I invited him over to dinner some night soon. I hope that's all right."

"Of course," Etha replied. "So, you've got a suspect, then?"

"Think so. Not hungry?" Temple asked, and Etha opened her mouth to answer when the phone rang again. "Ah, jeez." Shoving a forkful of carrots in his mouth, he made another trip to the telephone.

Hinchie was already launched into midsentence: ". . . had me so busy I only got around to studying the handle you dropped off earlier."

Ignoring the gap, Temple said smoothly, "What'd you find?"

The doctor sipped something, almost certainly a whiskey, and cleared his throat. "First, that is definitely blood on the wood. Human blood. Type A. Same type as the victim's. Of course, there are lots of folks who are type A. Then I compared the handle with the indentations on Coombs's skull. As far as I can tell, it matches up perfect. Also, there is a hair stuck in the splintered end. I don't have the equipment to analyze it, but the boys at the state lab do. For what it's worth, Dr. Hinchie's naked eye test says it's a match."

"I'd back that test any day. Much obliged that you got to this on a Sunday."

"No problem. With the election coming, I'm not all that fired up to give Doll any kind of advantage. He's always struck me as a self-promoter. Of course, that's not for general circulation. I wouldn't want to get on his bad side if, well . . ."

"If he wins," Temple finished the sentence. "Don't worry. I know we're all walking on a tightrope around here. No crops, no money, no rain will do that. I'd give a lot to know who tipped Doll off on the murder, though."

"My money's on Musgrove."

Temple reared back. "The undertaker? The man doesn't speak!"

"He's not much of talker; that is true. But Doll's sister-in-law over in Woodward is poorly. She's a rich woman and maybe Musgrove is smoothing the way, hoping he'll get the business of doing up her funeral. Get on Doll's good side."

"Jesus. Well, that answers that." Temple shook his head. "One last thing. Can you tell if the handle was broken off recently? I mean within the past week?"

"I'm not an expert, of course, but the break strikes me as old. The edges are dried and dark. Not the light color of newly snapped wood."

Etha was cutting off a generous slice of apple pie when Temple stepped back into the kitchen.

"Let me guess," she said, wedging the triangular pie server under the crust and efficiently transferring it to a plate. "Hinchie."

Temple laughed. "Yes ma'am. You get a gold star for that correct answer." He swatted her lightly on the bottom. "Old Hinchie came through. I'm feeling much better about this case than I did when I walked in tonight."

After Temple had a second piece of pie, the couple retired to the living room. He snapped on the radio. Seven thirty on the dot. *The Gulf Headliners with Will Rogers* was his favorite program. Temple and Etha had staked out their preferred spots, as long-married couples often do: he in the upholstered armchair with small tufts of stuffing sprouting from its worn arms and she in the narrow straight-backed chair with a pillow tucked in the curve of her spine and a bridge lamp behind. The workbasket at her feet was a muddle of stockings with holes and shirts without buttons. She pulled out one of Temple's brown socks, located the scarred darning egg and set to work.

A protracted musical number opened the program. As always, the pianist irritated Etha. Much too showy with fancy glissades and trills that affected her stomach the same as a birthday cake with too much icing. She eyed Temple, who was chuckling over the *Gazetteer*'s funnies. Still a boy, she thought. My boy. A smile started to crease her lips but then her deception about driving to the jungle welled. Disappointing him, seeing the hurt darken his eyes, would break her heart. But concealing her dishonesty was worse. It was tainting every mundane exchange, every routine act that they had built up over the years; those little things which comforted them, that bound them, through which their devotion was made manifest. And now, besides her dishonesty, there was the added worry about Carmine. The sock with the darning egg inside dropped to the floor.

Etha opened her mouth to speak when the program's soprano launched into a solo. Temple crumpled the newspaper into his lap.

"I can't abide that woman," Temple said. "Why don't they put on Will? If I'd wanted to listen to opera, I'd have tuned into another program." He glanced at his watch. "This will go on for another couple of minutes at least." He turned the volume down. "Sorry. I'm out of sorts. Something's making me burn."

Beneath her face powder, Etha blanched. "I've been meaning to talk to you—"

"It's that DiNapoli kid," Temple cut in. "You know, he lied right to my face. Right to my face. I asked if he'd boosted Coombs's lighter and he said no. Knowing that it was back in the bunkhouse. Did he think I wasn't going to search his things? I can tell the fellow's not stupid. Far from it. So why? Why lie? I can't understand it. Can you?"

Etha's tongue was a husk. She couldn't speak. Just then Will Rogers's voice, as familiar as your next-door neighbor's, broke in. Familiar but tart. Spoke his mind about the need for a trickle-up economy. Suddenly the anger melted from Temple's face. He raised the volume, put his feet up, his head back, and closed his eyes.

As Rogers launched into a story about deer hunting that was, sure as shooting, going to end up as a political barb, Etha willed her hands to stop shaking. This wasn't the time to confess her deceit. She studied her husband's face, glowing in the lamp light, his half smile gradually relaxing as he drifted off to Rogers's prattle. She knew that there would be another chance. She hoped she would rise to the occasion.

CHAPTER TWELVE

SMASHING A CENTIPEDE with Granny's flat iron, Viviane Gilbert, the courthouse secretary, silently raged at life in a house built of sod. Despite the carpet tacked over the dirt floor and sheets of newspaper covering the walls, the centipedes squirmed in, dropping from the ceiling with squishy plops onto Pa, Ma, her four brothers, and Granny. It being a weekday morning, she set the coffee to boil, pumped a bucket of washing-up water, and rousted her little brothers. She washed and dressed behind a sheet that hung in the corner.

On this particular Monday, she pulled on the print frock, wet-combed her hair, and stepped outside to wait. After milking, Pa would drop her off at the courthouse before continuing on to the train yards where he unloaded freight.

As they jolted away from the farm in Pa's truck, Viviane's mood lifted. The shame of eating and sleeping in the cramped soddie with dirt and bugs constantly sifting onto her dinner plate faded. They rode silently. Pa was a man of few words. And Viviane was lost in her favorite daydream where she was a secretary in Oklahoma City. By the time she tapped up the courthouse steps, she had shaken off the sod house completely and entered the world of plaster walls and paperwork. First thing after she settled at her desk in the county office, two clerks strolled in, jawing about the Cubs' shellacking of the Reds the day before.

"Morning, doll," the lanky one with big ears said. The other winked. Viviane shot them a cool glance. Shrugging, as if she couldn't take a joke, they loudly resumed their discussion of the previous night's game.

Annoyed, Viviane was sorting the day's filing when Deputy McCance strode in. The clerks abruptly stopped their chatter. Lordy, Deputy McCance surely put them in their place, she thought. Viviane's irritation, which had been crawling up her neck like one of those nasty bugs, vanished.

Hiding a smile and calling up her most polished secretarial tone, she asked, "How can I help you, Deputy?"

Since the sheriff's office had no secretary of its own, she often typed warrants, mailed reminders for overdue fines, and processed invoices—all swell, in her mind. The chores carried with them a whiff of cops and robbers—broke the monotony of routine.

So today, when Deputy McCance politely handed over the rainmaker's business card and asked for her help contacting next-of-kin, Viviane responded in her best secretarial voice, "I'll see to it right away." She picked up the telephone receiver. "I need to send a telegram to St. Joseph, Missouri, please." Her tone was crisp.

Ed smiled inwardly. Viviane was way more businesslike, even just out of high school, than the two shirkers snickering across the room. "Let me know if you run into a brick wall on this. And thanks," he said.

Returning to the sheriff's office, he bent over the photos of Coombs's body spread across the worktable. They stunk slightly of developing fluid.

Temple gave his dinged-up letter opener a rest, laying it beside the considerable stack of mail. "How'd you make out with Viviane?"

"Fine and dandy. She'll get back to us."

Temple perused the front page of the *Gazetteer*. "That bugger of a storm we had Saturday? Well, it hit five states. Carried soil all the way to New York. They're calling it the worst duster in history. Some folks thought it was the end of the world."

"I believe it."

Temple folded the paper and spun his chair around to face his deputy. "Let's talk."

"Sure thing." Ed put aside a close-up of the glistening black mass that was Coombs's head wound, and drew the notepad from his shirt pocket.

"First, give that Coldwater sheriff a call to confirm that it was indeed Coombs's last stop before here. Find out if the rainmaker got involved in any brush-ups out that way. Then contact Darnell at the bank. I'd like to know which member of the Commercial Club Coombs first made contact with when he rolled into town. Then I want you to call Mrs. Saunders. Get permission to take Maxine out for a gander at a group of CCC boys. See if DiNapoli wasn't one of those at the matinee."

Ed's shoulders slumped slightly at the last edict, but he gripped the pencil and noted Temple's orders.

The sheriff continued, "I phoned Commander Baker. He'll be ordering a dozen of the boys to stop by his office, individually, beginning at noon. You okay with driving Maxine up there?"

Ed nodded.

"I mean, will you be able to handle it if she recognizes DiNapoli? I'm not questioning your integrity. Just need to know if you can handle it."

Ed's ears reddened. "Yes sir, I can. I've thought it through and if there are bad apples among the corps, they need to go."

"Glad to hear it. Also, the foreclosure auction at the Fullers' is a go for this afternoon. I'll be holding the reins on that. I should have time to secure Coombs's truck on my way there."

Within five minutes Ed had completed his first two assignments. The Coldwater sheriff confirmed that Coombs had spent about five days in town, peppering the skies with TNT, and when not a drop of rain appeared, he'd been politely escorted to the city limits. Darnell the banker had himself been the first to hear Coombs's pitch and thought it worth a listen by the Commercial Club.

Getting through to Maxine's mother took longer. The telephone operator informed Ed that Monday was laundry day at the Saunders house and calling before ten thirty a.m. would be futile. There was no way in heaven that Mrs. Saunders would answer the phone when she was operating the crank washer. So it was not until late morning that Maxine's trip to Camp Briscoe for a possible identification was arranged.

Meanwhile, Temple rang the state crime lab, telling them to expect the bloodied shirt and possible weapon. Then Walter Darnell called.

"Some paperwork has come up regarding the Fullers' foreclosure. Got to postpone the auction until Thursday."

Temple frowned. "You know I've got a murder investigation going on. I set aside time for this. Time I don't have."

"Nothing I can do about it. See you Thursday," Darnell said, and clicked off.

Something didn't smell right. There had been word from other counties of protests at farm auctions. Farm folks banding together against the banks. Maybe Darnell had heard rumblings of something similar in Jackson County. Or maybe this was an irritant purposely planted by Doll to trip Temple up. Either way, it added up to a headache. The only bright spot was there would be plenty of time to give the rainmaker's truck a good going over and secure the TNT.

* * *

Chester's schedule, too, had been disrupted. At noontime, Lottie came up the stairs to his office and announced she was treating him to lunch at the Crystal even though it was a weekday. His protests, citing the inappropriateness of a lady paying, the state of his bank account, and the change in their usual routine, did not penetrate.

At the Crystal, they were escorted to the small window table they preferred and Chester busied himself straightening the silver and china while Bessie, the waitress, informed Lottie of the day's specials. Chester always ordered the same meal at the Crystal; he had no need to listen and so he didn't.

After Bessie thumped toward the swinging kitchen doors, Chester adjusted the place setting one last time, then propped his elbows on the table and folded his hands. "And now I need to know the nature of this favor. For certainly that is what this is all about."

Lottie spoke bluntly: "All right. From what I hear around town, Temple's not going to survive the primary. Doll is pushing hard and a lot of the money people are backing him."

"Really?"

"If Temple loses, Doll is going to collude with Darnell to go after even more foreclosures. You know Temple has talked Darnell out of foreclosing on farmers who are only a couple of months behind. That whole policy of granting a grace period will end. And then who do you think will be around to buy movie tickets or new hats or anything? Nobody, that's who."

Chester grimaced. "I am more than aware that there aren't the patrons there used to be. But I'm not all that convinced that Temple can do much about that either way. The drought and the Depression are crushing us."

Lottie bore down: "But he can help a few farmers hold on for another six months or a year, and by that time the drought could very well be over. And another thing—Doll is letting it be known that he'll bring in a deputy who is paid on commission. Same as they've got in Dewey County. I've heard stories about those men."

Bessie arrived with heavy china plates of roast beef and chicken hash. Lottie leaned forward to whisper, "Meat at six o'clock, mashed at nine."

Chester took up his knife and fork. "Go on."

"I've heard those deputies are nothing more than grave robbers. They lurk around funerals, knowing there will be a lot of drinking, and hoping for fistfights so they can make arrests. That's how they get paid: number of arrests. They do the same at revival meetings—expecting somebody to get riled up about what's true religion and what's false. And farm foreclosures where things might get ugly."

Chester chewed thoughtfully. "As if things aren't bad enough. That's not going to encourage law-abiding straight-and-narrows to stick around."

"Exactly. And those folks make up most of our business." Lottie nibbled at a small forkful of hash, and then reached for the salt and pepper.

"I see your point, but why am I being plied with this overcooked beef?"

"You run daily ads in the *Gazetteer*. You and Hank Stowe pal around—"

"I don't *pal around* with anyone. The publisher and I are associates who enjoy one another's company over an occasional glass of beer."

Lottie rolled her eyes, which she was sure Chester detected, and continued, "Anyway, I think you should ask him to publicly back Temple for sheriff. Endorse him on the editorial page."

From the kitchen came the sounds of breaking glass and then a metal bowl hitting the floor. Chester winced.

"So, will you do it? Ask him?" Lottie pressed.

"I'll have to think about it. You know I loathe politics."

"Yes, but—"

Chester held up his hand. "Please don't push. I promise to give it due consideration."

Lottie opened her compact and began applying a fresh coat of lipstick. "Please don't take too long," she said between strokes, "the primary is in just over a week."

Ed pulled up at the Saunders's bungalow where Maxine and another girl were perched on the porch swing with hands lightly folded and ankles crossed, looking suspiciously posed.

"Afternoon, Maxine." Something was different about her; Ed couldn't put his finger on it. Could be a new hairdo. Girls her age were always fiddling with their hair. They giggled. *This* was who the sheriff's office was relying on to identify a killer? She hadn't seemed so giddy yesterday. "I need to talk to your mother before we drive out to camp."

"Around back hanging laundry."

More tittering followed as he turned the corner of the house. Mrs. Saunders was shoving a clothespin over the far end of a tablecloth flopped over a line. She was a flabby woman with large wheels of perspiration around the armholes of her housedress. The laundry cord sagged with sheets and pillowcases hanging in the hot air.

Ed showed his badge. "I called earlier about Maxine helping with the investigation?"

Mrs. Saunders stooped to retrieve another soggy piece of linen from the basket at her feet, straightened, and sniffed. "I'm not sure how much help she'll be. She's at that silly stage."

"We just need her to identify someone who might have been at the movies on Saturday. I've got younger brothers so I know how they can be. But this is as straightforward as it comes." After a pause, he added, "Ma'am."

"Get her home by four o'clock."

"Yes . . . ma'am." The hairs on the back of his neck bristled. For God's sake, she's treating me as if I'm a teenager picking up Maxine on a date.

"And Cliff's going along."

"What?"

Mrs. Saunders lifted her chin from its pillow of fat. "He's chaperoning or she's not going."

Ed paused to gather himself. "I understand your concern but I can assure you—"

"No go."

Minutes later Ed was in the driver's seat and Maxine in the passenger's while Cliff bounced on the leather upholstery in back, emitting the oscillating whistle of a police siren. Maxine's friend Harriet stood on the porch to see them off.

As Ed shoved the car into first gear, Maxine turned on Cliff and muttered, "If you don't sit still and shut up I'm going to paste you one. And you know I will."

The kid paled and pinched his mouth shut.

"Sorry," she said to Ed.

As they pulled away from the curb, Harriet waved frantically from the porch. Maxine waved back with a wide grin.

CHAPTER THIRTEEN

BRICK DAVIS LEAPED ONTO THE SEDAN'S running board, tommy gun pressed tightly against his ribs. The car, packed with fellow G-men, veered away from the curb in pursuit of the getaway car. For a minute it seemed as if the notorious McKay gang had made a clean break. Then, up ahead, Brick spotted the crooks' taillights. The sedan rocketed down the street as Brick rammed the gun's stock into his shoulder, aimed, and drew back the trigger, shattering the mobsters' rear window with a burst of fire. "Pow! Ka-powpowpow!" The gunmen returned fire. Brick aimed for the tires. "Pow! Ka—"

"Didn't I tell you to keep your trap buttoned?" Maxine shouted, leaning over the backseat and shaking a fist in Cliff's face.

"Keep your mitts to yourself." He slapped her hand away.

Maxine's eyes narrowed. "When we get home I'm telling Mom you interfered with the sheriff's business," she said, facing forward.

"Tattletale."

Deputy McCance rolled his eyes as he turned onto the highway.

Maxine smoothed her skirt. Under Harriet's tutelage, she had practiced some feminine gestures designed to draw Ed's attention. Smoothing her skirt was one. Idly zippering her locket back and forth on its chain was another.

Harriet had said, *It'll highlight your neck.* To which Maxine had replied, *Why would I want to do that?*

Now she toyed with her necklace. Her stomach flip-flopped between attraction and fear. The deputy's eyes remained on the road. She zippered louder. Cliff mumbled threats from the backseat.

"Enough. Both of you. This is serious. Got it?" Deputy McCance said. "We're almost there and I need quiet and cooperation."

Cliff twisted his mouth to one side. Twice he'd seen Jimmy Cagney play Brick Davis in *G-Men* at the Jewel and he knew all about being a government man. This guy thinks he's a big shot but he ain't. Not like Brick.

The deputy turned onto the camp drive. Ahead was a cluster of small buildings. They looked like the motor court where Danny Leggett, Public Enemy No. 1, was holed up. Cliff silently tucked Brick's machine gun into his shoulder.

The deputy pulled into the gravel space to one side of a small building labeled *Office*. He yanked hard on the hand brake. "You two wait here," he said. "I'll be back in a couple of minutes."

Inside the car, Maxine cranked the window down to inspect a shabby chicken pecking around the front tires.

"Rat-a-tat-tat! You're dead." Cliff aimed at her head.

"Stop that or I'm—"

"No you're not, because if you tell on me, I'm telling the deputy that you aren't wearing your glasses."

Maxine's cheeks darkened. "So?"

"You can't see a thing without them."

"I can too and don't you dare say a word."

"I'm going to tell him that you didn't want anything to get in the way of making goo-goo eyes at him. So, bang, you're dead."

Deputy McCance emerged from the office and slid behind the wheel.

"All set." He glanced at his watch. "The commander asked eight guys to stop by the office to update their records. He'll be talking to them one at a time. All I need you to do is let me know if any of these fellows bought a ticket from you on Saturday. Just focus on their faces. Simple as that."

From the backseat came a snorting laugh.

"And you, zip it," McCance said to the boy. Cliff paled. "All right?" the deputy now asked Maxine. "Nothing to be scared of."

"Sure." Her voice was uneven. "But what if I don't recognize any of them?"

McCance shrugged. "Then you don't. That helps too."

He drew out his notepad. Maxine fidgeted, picked a scab off her ankle. Within minutes a group of young men were milling around the office door. One or two glanced disinterestedly at the county car. Maxine counted. They were all dressed alike in the CCC uniform of denim trousers and shirts. She squinted at the blurred patterns of eyes, noses, and mouths. A tall man with a clipboard appeared in the doorway and read off names.

"Concentrate on each one as he goes in and again as he comes out. That way you're sure to get a good look. One at a time," McCance said. "If one is familiar, give me a nod."

Right away Maxine knew that she'd never seen the first three. They all had some quirk that she was sure she would have noticed and remembered: bushy hair, an enormous Adam's apple, and a big old honker that even her nearsighted eyes picked up. The middle three she wasn't so sure about. As they marched into the office and then out, there was nothing in their blurry faces that caught her attention. She tucked her lips under her front teeth.

"Nothing so far?" Deputy McCance asked.

"I'm not sure. Not the first three, but . . ." she shrugged, "the next ones. They all look sort of the same."

"Take your time. I can ask the commander to call them back in again if you need a second look." He tapped his pencil on the notepad, same as Miss Jenkins did when she was waiting for an answer from one of the slow boys in the back row. Cliff was steadily kicking the back of her seat.

"No. I don't need a do-over. Let me just think." Maxine pulled on her lower lip, then remembered how Harriet had lectured her on that habit. *It gives you a fish mouth*, her friend had said. Maxine quickly pulled her hand away. "I'm certain now. None of those middle ones were there on Saturday."

Two were left. The last fellow in line was the shortest. She made out dark hair parted on the side. When it was his turn he shambled forward, same as Leon Smith, the slowest of the slow boys, when he was called to the chalkboard.

Tap tap tap went the pencil. Was it clicking faster? Yes, she thought it was. Like a telegraph key. "That's him," she said. "The last in line."

The pencil stopped. McCance straightened. "You sure?"

She nodded. "Positive."

"It's okay if it's not any of them."

"I know. But it's him."

"All right. I'll let the commander know we're all set and then I'll get you two home."

Maxine wasn't sure at all that the boy she'd identified had been at the Jewel. Ever. But it was too late now. Deputy McCance hopped back behind the wheel after a minute's conversation with the commander and they were off. She decided she'd tell the deputy that she was just a teensy bit unsure. But then she'd have to explain why, and the whole scheme of leaving off her glasses would have to be explained. She'd rather die.

But no, she couldn't stand thinking about that poor fellow getting arrested because of her. She'd tell Deputy McCance when they passed the courthouse. But when the big sandstone building came into view, her voice stuck in her throat as if she'd swallowed a wad of gum. So then she decided she'd speak up when they crossed the tracks. That would be the landmark. But the tracks came and went and she still couldn't get her tongue unstuck. The longer she waited, the harder it got. When they pulled up to her house she sat frozen while Cliff bounded out with a "See ya" and a wave. She thought maybe once her brother was out of the car she'd find her voice. But she didn't.

Finally, after the deputy had thanked her twice more, she tugged up the handle and got out. Cliff raced past her screaming, "Bang bang, you're dead," as she stood on the sidewalk in the bright heavy air. She hung her head. There was blood on her best anklets where she had picked off the scab. Mother would be furious.

While Ed was up at the CCC camp with Maxine, Temple made the rounds chatting with folks who had taken in Coombs's pyrotechnic display. While he was banking on Maxine identifying DiNapoli, he also wanted to make sure other possible suspects weren't overlooked. From what he'd gleaned about Coombs, it was not improbable that the glib rainmaker had riled up someone else in town.

Temple found Pastor Coxey in the church basement, boxing up extra hymnals no longer needed for his shrinking congregation. The green cloth covers gave off a musty odor. Yes, Coxey had been at the demonstration, had even offered up a prayer before the blasts. No, he hadn't seen any confrontations; he had seen nothing on the gathered faces but grim determination.

Temple ambled over to Quality Grocery where Toot Morris, wearing a stained grocer's apron, was doodling on a scrap of butcher's paper. The pleasant aroma of sawdust and refrigerated meat hung in the air. Why of course Toot had been at the big blast. Wouldn't have missed it. Most excitement the town had seen since the Fourth of July parade. Everybody was pleased as punch. What? No! No feathers ruffled. Coombs was the man of the hour. Everyone agreed on that.

At the edge of town, Lou Harriman occupied a kitchen chair outside his service station, a pile of whittlings accumulating between his ankles. He hadn't taken note of anyone who seemed to have a grievance with the rainmaker. But Lou himself was angry as hell. He'd chucked in what he could toward Coombs's fee and not a drop of rain to show for it. And did Temple know when the Commercial Club would get back the cash it had handed over to the fellow? It was all around town that $217 in small bills had been found in the deceased's pocket. Lou said that he sure hoped that money would be distributed right quick. With the primary coming up and all. And did Temple know that Doll was spreading rumors that the sheriff office's gasoline usage was out of line? "I sure would hate to have to vote for that no-count," Lou added as Temple climbed back into his car.

After three casts and no nibbles, Temple decided it would be a waste of time to pursue further inquiries—at least until learning how things went with Maxine. He swung by Coombs's truck and later, back at the courthouse, checked in with Viviane who was still awaiting a response from the telegram to St. Joe.

Five minutes later Ed appeared.

"Well?" Temple asked.

Ed leaned against the doorframe.

"It's him," he said, his voice flat.

"She's positive?"

"Yep."

"You told her that it might not be any of the men she was looking at?"

Ed nodded. "I was very clear about that. She is 100 percent. Now what?"

"Now I get a warrant from Judge Laycomb and make the arrest."

"Think we have enough?"

Temple studied the dusty street beyond the window. "I do." He tapped his fingers one by one. "Opportunity, access to weapon, blood on his clothes, motive."

Ed rapped a knuckle hard on the doorframe. "I got to be there."

"I don't think that's a good idea."

"I'm asking as a favor."

Temple said, "Last one."

On the drive out, Temple filled Ed in on Coombs's truck. Inspecting it, he said, took all of five minutes since the cab had nothing in it but a

couple of maps and a few greasy rags. Temple had arranged with the
foreman at Public Oil to haul it away and secure the TNT for the time
being. It was after five p.m. when Temple and Ed pulled up the drive at
Camp Briscoe.

Ed checked his watch. "Everyone will be at the flag-lowering
ceremony."

"And?"

"Can we wait until it's over and the guys head to dinner? I mean, it'll
really take the starch out of the fellows if they have to watch a CCCer
led away in handcuffs."

Temple pulled beside the office and set the brake. Twisting to look
Ed in the eye, he said, "I know this is tough. But you've got to remember
which side your bread is buttered on now."

Ed nodded.

The two men sat silently in the sedan until the corps began streaming
toward the mess hall. Commander Baker spotted the lawmen and trotted
over.

Temple climbed out of the car and extended his hand. "Sorry to be
here with bad news, but we've got a warrant for DiNapoli."

"I figured, soon as I saw you pull up. I'll have him brought up from
the mess hall. He's on KP. Why don't you fellows wait inside my office?
I'll send someone for him."

"Appreciate it."

Temple stood looking at one of the maps while Ed paced. Baker
settled behind his desk. No one spoke. Five minutes later, Senior Leader
Davies knocked on the door.

"Reporting with DiNapoli as requested, sir," Davies said.

"We'll talk to him privately," Baker responded. "Go get some chow."

"Thank you, sir." Davies spun on his heel and marched out.

Baker turned to Carmine. "The sheriff here asked to see you."

Carmine sagged but kept his eyes on Temple's face.

The sheriff began: "I'm here to arrest you for murder in the first
degree of Roland Coombs on August . . ." As he pulled a paper out of his
pocket and read out the warrant, Carmine shook his head.

"This ain't right. This ain't right." The young man's voice was low
and steady.

When Temple was finished, Carmine turned his back so Ed could
clamp on the cuffs.

As they pulled out onto the main road, striations of pink and orange flowed from the setting sun. At the courthouse, Temple led the way through the back door and up to the third-floor cellblock. He glanced at the door to the apartment. Mondays Etha oversaw the church auxiliary meeting and, in the absence of cooking smells, he figured she was running late. He inserted the spike key into the steel door of the jail. The air was stuffy. There had not been a prisoner since earlier in the month.

"Get him settled," Temple said to Ed. "I'll be downstairs filling out the paperwork."

Ed led Carmine into the first cell and removed the cuffs. A narrow metal bed with a thin mattress covered in blue-striped ticking stood beside a porcelain sink and a toilet bolted to the wall. The odor of urine and bleach was strong. Carmine dropped onto the mattress with his elbows on thighs, his head in his hands. From a cupboard by the cellblock door, Ed drew a blanket and towel and handed them over. Then he pulled the cell door shut with a firm click.

"We'll bring some dinner," Ed said. "Anything else you need?"

Carmine shook his head.

"The sheriff is fair. He'll make sure you get treated fair."

"Didn't do it," Carmine said, staring at the floor.

Ed felt as low as he had in a long time. He headed out into the hallway. Every fellow in the corps was a down-and-outer by definition. But still, he couldn't figure how anyone could throw away three squares and a chance to earn some dough. How come Carmine let a two-bit fight with a fast-talker get the better of him?

Down in the sheriff's office, Temple was hunched over a half-completed report. Ed lit a cigarette and began typing up his notes. Neither man, caught up in his own task, heard Etha come in the back door and mount the steps, although she was making no particular effort to be quiet. Up in the apartment, she shucked off her street clothes and pulled on a housedress. Temple would have to be satisfied with creamed beef on toast. She found a note taped to the icebox: *Prisoner in cell #1. Needs dinner.* Oh God, she thought. Her stomach wobbled.

Snatching the cellblock keys off the ring by the door, she dashed into the hall. Her fingers jittered as she struggled to fit the key into the lock. Inside, the last bit of daylight fell on Carmine, who lay on a cot, stiffly staring at the ceiling, the boyish charm drained from his face.

Her voice was thick: "No!"

He jumped up. "What? What are you doing here?"

"Our apartment is next door." She cocked her thumb toward the hall, then approached the cell. "What happened?"

Carmine's eyes pooled. "It's a mistake. I didn't do what they said. I didn't."

Etha pulled a chair over to the cell and settled herself. "What *did* happen?" she asked in a quiet voice.

He scoured his running nose and eyes with a shirtsleeve. After a moment he gathered himself. "You see, we was joking around at the bar. I'd had a couple of beers. We all did. It was the first time I'd gotten a town pass since coming into camp. I was dying of thirst. Then the explosives guy pulls out this silver lighter. My grandpa had the same one. With fancy swirls and whatnot. Nonno used to sit me on his lap and let me thumb the wheel. You know, strike it up. So when I saw that same lighter, I wanted it." He squeezed his eyes shut.

"Go on," Etha said.

"You're going to think less of me, but I used to boost stuff all the time. But I haven't swiped anything since I've been at camp. I swear."

Etha studied her hands. "I believe you."

"But the lighter was different. So after I lit my smoke, it slipped into my pocket nice and snug. At first, the fellow didn't take note. But then he did. I guess I could have laughed it off, like I did it without thinking. You know, *Oh, sorry.* But I couldn't. It was as if it were Nonno's—the only thing I was ever going to have of his. The fellow pushed me. Started yelling. People stared. Something inside me exploded. Bang! I shoved back. He darted for my pocket to grab the lighter and I popped him in the nose. Got him good. A real gusher. My buddies hightailed it." He fell silent.

"And then what?" Etha asked.

"Usually when I paste someone, they go down," Carmine continued, gesturing with both palms up, "but that Coombs was no slouch. He came back and caught me in the jaw so hard I swore it was broke. I'm ashamed, ma'am. Yes I am. But I didn't hunt that man down and kill him. I holed up in town, in someone's backyard shed. Then the next day, after the storm, I started hoofing it back to camp. Stopped at the jungle for a bite, where you saw me, and then on to camp. Never laid eyes on the fellow after Friday night. I'm not a killer. I'm not."

Carmine pressed his forehead against the iron. Etha's gaze slid away to a steamy afternoon not long before Jack died. He and his gang were sprinting through the neighborhood's open yards in a game of tag. Etha, who was pinning towels to the clothesline, noticed the feebleminded boy from one block over flitting along the sidelines. As Jack raced past the boy, she heard her son yell, "Hey, dummy . . ." The rest was lost amidst the shouts of the other boys. Her eyes had widened in anger. She snatched him by the shirt as he flew by, yanked down his trousers, and spanked him with a hard hand.

"Don't ever let me hear you use that word again," she had hissed as he struggled to tug his pants up over skinny hips, his face slick with tears and snot and humiliation.

"What word? What?"

Jack, she knew, was entirely capable of fibbing and evading, especially when scolded. Yet as she had studied his face that day, she saw nothing but confusion.

"What did you shout at Davey just now?'

"Asked him, *Hey, do you wanna play?* Like that."

Etha grabbed his arm. "Is that the truth?"

"Yes ma'am."

"You didn't call him a dummy?"

"No!"

She pressed her hand against her mouth. "I'm sorry. I thought I heard something else."

There was a tick of silence. Then he mumbled, "Can I go now?" When she reached out to ruffle his hair, he'd ducked and trotted off. For the remainder of the day he had dodged her touch. The next week he was swimming with his gang in the Illinois River and never surfaced.

Etha thought of all of this as she studied Carmine's face.

"I'm not a killer," he said.

She bit her lower lip. "I believe you."

"You do?"

Etha nodded, gingerly passing her hand through the gap between the bars to touch his dark waves.

Back in the kitchen, as she whisked milk and flour and tossed in chips of dried beef, Etha began laying out an argument for Carmine's innocence.

His kindness had been evident from the moment they'd met in the hobo jungle on Saturday evening. It was, in fact, only a few hours *after*

Coombs's death at midday. Only a few hours and yet it had been Carmine who had showed compassion when she had foolishly driven out to the edge of the tracks. He had been one of the first to greet her. And it had been Carmine who walked her to her car after she had blurted out that her husband was the sheriff. Thinking back on that moment, she tried to recall how Carmine had reacted when the words flew from her lips. Murph, the old hobo, had immediately condemned her and there had been fear and shock in the eyes of the others. But what about Carmine? As Murph denounced her, Carmine had gently taken her arm. There was no fear in his eyes. No terror. Which would surely have been the case if he had killed a man earlier that day. Indeed, he had escorted her to the sedan as if they were concluding a social engagement. He promised to make sure she got back on the main highway safely. He had remained in her rearview mirror as she bumped down the dirt road and finally reach the asphalt. He was a young man who kept his word.

While the sauce thickened, Etha pulled a metal tray from the cupboard and wiped it clean. She toasted two slices of bread, laid them in a shallow soup bowl, and ladled the chipped beef on top. There was room on the tray for the bowl along with a slice of yesterday's pie and a glass of milk. Everyone knew that growing boys needed milk. Etha picked up the loaded tray and moved slowly, so as not to spill, into the outer corridor and on into the jail. Carmine stood at the cell door, his fingers wrapped around the bars.

"Smells mighty good," he said.

"I have been known to scorch the cream."

She passed the tray through the open slot in the cell door.

Carmine sat on the cot, carefully balancing his dinner across his knees.

"Did you wash up?" she asked.

"Yes ma'am."

Etha took her seat.

"Can't remember the last time I've had home cooking," Carmine said, his voice thick with pie. "Guess it was that chicken you brought out to the jungle. But that's been it for a while."

"Do they feed you well at camp?"

"Oh, yeah. You can fill yourself up. But it's nothing like this."

"And before you joined the CCC? When you were on the road? Did you have enough then?"

Carmine scooped the remainder of the pie into his mouth, flicking his tongue around a glob of filling sticking to the corner of his lips. After swallowing, he said, "It was hit and miss out there. Most days I lived on stale bread. Canned beans or sardines pretty regular too." He wet his finger, scraped it across the residue of sugar and cooked apples stuck to the plate, then licked it clean. "'Course, I got many a handout . . . bologna sandwiches, a glass of milk, whatever the housewife had in her icebox. A lot of them didn't have nothing much on hand and some didn't even have an icebox. You always remember those folks that have nothing and still give you some."

Etha's icebox had never been empty. She pressed her fingers to her mouth. "Oh Lordy."

Carmine shrugged. "Take what you can get. Sometimes, when I hopped off in a town, I'd stroll into a restaurant and tell the waitress I was waiting for someone. She'd show me a table and bring a glass of water. Most places had bottles of ketchup and crackers set out. I'd pour the ketchup in the water and stir in the crackers. Helped kill the hunger pangs."

Etha rose. "I'm going to bring you another piece of pie right this minute."

"Wouldn't turn it down."

"Hand me the tray."

As she hurried through the outer hallway, Temple was climbing the stairs. "Got the prisoner fed?"

"Yes. Just need to bring him a slice of pie."

Temple lifted his brows. "Getting fancy with the jailhouse menu?"

In the kitchen, Etha hastily shoved the dirty pie plate under the soup bowl. "We have plenty."

Temple shook his head. "Don't forget he's been charged with killing a man. Bashing in his skull. Don't let DiNapoli hoodwink you. I mean it." He strode down the hall. Water splashed in the bathroom sink.

Etha slid the second slice of pie onto a dish and hustled back to the cellblock. "Here."

Carmine took the plate and held it up, admiring its contents. Etha walked toward the hallway.

"Can't you stay?" he asked.

"No. I've got to get the sheriff's dinner." When she turned at the door, he was sitting on the bunk, the pie untouched, and looking so forlorn her heart ached.

Over dinner, Temple didn't want to talk about the arrest. Instead he went on about Doll's claim that when he was elected sheriff, the county would save on gasoline.

"He's saying he can cover this county on less than fifty gallons a month. That's of bunch of hooey. Pardon me," Temple said, gliding his fork over his empty dessert plate. "Any more of this pie by chance?"

Etha flushed. "Sold out. Coffee?" As she set the cup and saucer on the table, she said, "That Doll surely has an inflated opinion of his merits. Do you think people are buying it?"

Temple studied his coffee cup. "Hard to say since no one is going to tell me straight to my face that they aren't voting for me. But I've got a bad feeling in my gut. Too many foreclosures, too many stills busted up, too little rain. Folks are angry and they're looking for someone to blame. I don't want to scare you, but I'm worried."

The living room was the coolest spot in the apartment; its north-facing windows captured whatever breeze happened by. After switching on the radio, Temple took up the newspaper and dropped into his chair. Rudy Vallee sang "I'm in a Dancing Mood." Etha started to work her knitting needles on what was to be a cap for the Bonwells' new baby, but a book on the shelf had fallen sideways and she got up to straighten it. She sat down again. Then she noticed the geranium needed water. All the while she fretted about Carmine.

Temple shook the newspaper. "Will you listen to this! Rogers says in his column here that he's flying to Alaska this week. He and Wiley Post are off on a sightseeing trip."

"Umm . . ."

"You all right, sweetheart? You don't seem yourself."

"I don't know. Guess I'm a bit all-overish tonight." She took up the needles again.

Later, as Temple climbed into bed beside her, she tried to lose herself in a novel recommended by Vermillion's librarian.

Temple stretched out on his back and bent his arms behind his head. "You know, I just can't figure why that kid did it."

Etha tensed. She tented the book on her stomach. "Oh?" she said, trying to keep her tone even. "How so?"

"It would make a lot more sense if DiNapoli went for Coombs right after their fistfight. Followed him out of the bar and whacked him on the head. A crime of passion. But for DiNapoli to plan it out. To wait until the next day and then trail the fellow to the pictures. All because Coombs accused him of nicking a lighter?"

Etha chose her words with care: "It does sound improbable, now that you say it."

"Except that I've got him with access to what I think is the weapon— I'm waiting for Hinchie to take a closer look at it—and what is almost certainly the victim's blood on his shirt, *and* a witness who saw him at the movies on Saturday."

He leaned over and kissed her. "I'm too tired to think on it anymore. Sleep well."

But Etha couldn't sleep. Not a wink. After mindlessly turning the pages of the book for a few more minutes, she clicked off the bedside lamp. Temple snored lightly. She thought over the bits of Carmine's story that she knew, worrying about him alone in the cellblock.

At 2:13 a.m., Temple snorted mightily and woke himself up. After tossing and turning for hours, Etha was still staring at the ceiling.

"What's wrong?" he asked.

"Fretting about Carmine."

"That's what's troubling you?"

"Yes. All by his lonesome. He's just a kid, you know. I think you should move him into the kitchen lockup. That way he'd have some company."

Temple exhaled heavily. "Didn't I warn you not to let yourself be scammed by that kid? He knows all the angles—grew up streetwise, then bummed around the country. He's staying in the cellblock." With that, he rolled over on his side and slid effortlessly into sleep.

But Etha's vigil continued until dawn leached through the curtains, when, surrendering, she rose, found her slippers, and shuffled into the kitchen.

CHAPTER FOURTEEN

TWO DAYS LATER, ON WEDNESDAY, the state of affairs was unchanged. Temple remained confident he'd arrested the right man, but Etha's thoughts were evolving. Very early that morning she had concluded it was not enough to believe Carmine innocent. She needed to prove it. Living with a sheriff had taught her there was always the possibility of stones unturned. And after a lifetime in small towns, she knew how to navigate the gossip, rumors, and webs of family relationships that muffled and hid realities; thick layers of paint that had to be chipped away to get down to the bare wood of truth.

After washing up Temple's breakfast dishes, Etha added a ladle of hot water to the pot of coagulated oatmeal and sugared it up good. Putting on a falsely cheerful face, she carried the tray with the oatmeal and two cups of coffee next door. Carmine was at the sink, head bowed, hands gripping the sides of the porcelain as if steadying himself in a fiercely pitching rowboat. When he turned to face her, pink rimmed his eyes.

"I imagine you're hungry," she said.

A half smile hung on his face then dropped away. "Not really, ma'am."

She kept one of the cups for herself and passed the food through. "Have some coffee with me, at least."

Carmine lowered the tray to the bed. "The sheriff was just here. Said my lawyer would be coming by again. My arraignment is this afternoon and . . ." Carmine rubbed his mouth with a palm, his eyes glazed with dread. "Do you really think they'll charge me with murder?"

Etha swallowed her mouthful of coffee. Leaning forward, she fixed her eyes on Carmine. "Listen. Mr. Jennings is a fair man. You are not guilty and when evidence is assembled that proves that, the charges will be dropped. He will make sure of it."

"But he must think he's got all the evidence he needs."

"He might think so now, but I'm going to do some digging on my own. If I can find some facts to the contrary, he will listen."

Carmine shrugged without expression.

She continued: "But you'll have to tell me exactly where you were, from the time you left the Idle Hour on Friday to when I met you out by the tracks on Saturday night. That's the crucial time. And no hooey or whitewashing. If you vomited in someone's bushes, if you took a joy ride in the minister's Ford, I need to know."

"I told you all that already."

"Tell me again."

Carmine walked her through the details of Friday night and Saturday. Etha listened; asked a few questions. As he finished she studied the grounds at the bottom of her cup.

"The first order of business is to find that shed you slept in. Ask the owners if they saw you sneaking out after the storm. That would establish your alibi." Etha stood up. "Now, get some rest. I don't expect you slept much last night."

Back in the apartment, she changed into her street shoes, gathered her pocketbook and hat. On the first floor, she was heading for the front doors when she heard Temple's voice coming from his office. She froze. If he spotted her would he question where she was going? Don't be silly, she scolded herself. She ran errands all the time and he didn't think a thing of it. Still, she wheeled around and crept out the back.

Outside another broiler of a day gathered steam. Etha decided to start at the Idle Hour and retrace Carmine's steps as best she could. Peering into the bar, she envied the men seated on the stools in the cool darkness. Rivulets ran down the glasses of beer in front of them. And there she stood in her felt hat with the sun beating down.

She closed her eyes and tried to imagine herself as Carmine, stumbling out in the night with a bruise blooming on his jaw. Which way would he turn? Not right, she decided. Down that way was a padlocked warehouse and not much else. It would be dark when he lurched out of the bar. Left then, toward the lights of Main Street. Two blocks down, she paused in the shade of the Quality Foods awning. Now where? Carmine had remembered the shed as being behind a house on a quiet street. She had a choice to make. Down a block and to the right squatted the clusters of simple porchless homes ubiquitous in the town's early years. Farther down and to the left were the newer, grander homes. Lottie and her parents lived there, alongside other well-to-do citizens. A toss-up. Etha went with her gut. It told her that a drunk tends to wander. Has trouble leaving the bar, but once in motion will stagger around for a good long time. That was the complaint of her sister in Arkansas, anyway. She often grumbled about tracking down her drunken husband a mile or two outside of town and finding him propped against a fence post.

Keeping to the shadier side of the street, Etha made her way toward Lottie's neighborhood. Carmine had mentioned spotting the shack from an alleyway. In this section of town, grassy byways where families stowed garbage cans and kids played leap frog hemmed the small backyards. As she turned down the first alley, Etha suddenly became aware of her street shoes and purse. They were out of place in these private domestic spaces. She dreaded being accused of snooping. But midmorning on a scorcher, folks generally sheltered inside home, barn, or office. She took a chance. The first alley yielded nothing. Not a single outbuilding in sight. Two streets down she sauntered by three backyard sheds. Too big and no windows. Carmine had mentioned watching the storm through rattling panes.

So far, Etha had not bumped into a soul. This changed with her next move. Halfway down the third alley, she spotted a housewife kneeling outside a backyard fence, industriously pulled weeds. How to explain herself? Maybe Etha didn't have to. Maybe she could just exchange the customary greeting about the heat and forge ahead. But that was not the small-town way. Etha would need to explain the nature of her errand. She cast about for a reason but couldn't think of one. The housewife, as Etha got closer, turned out to be Mrs. Lawson, the mother of Vermillion's switchboard operator and a sponge for tidbits of any kind. The standard niceties were exchanged.

"With this drought and all, thistles are the only things that grow and they're tough as nails to get out," Mrs. Lawson said companionably, waving a wilted stalk. "What brings you out in this heat?"

Etha bit her lower lip. Her mind was blank. And what with the heat and not sleeping the night before, she suddenly felt dizzy. She swayed and grabbed the fence post.

"Are you all right?" Mrs. Lawson asked in alarm. "Let me get you some water. You're pale as milk."

"No, no. I just need to stop and rest a bit."

"I insist." Mrs. Lawson brushed off her housedress and hastened toward her house.

Etha watched until the housewife was inside. Then she straightened. The dizziness had passed. She hurried farther down the alley. A shed, small and with a window, caught her eye on the left. She darted into the yard, again with no plan to explain herself if the homeowner emerged. The lawn baked silently in the heat. Etha approached the outbuilding and peered in. The glare of the sun and the interior darkness blinded her, but in a couple of moments she could make out long-handled tools hung neatly against one wall. She glanced over her shoulder. A door slammed down the way. She waited tensely but there were no other sounds and she turned back to the window. Besides the tools, there was a push mower and, yes, in the far corner, a large burlap bag. Etha pressed her face hard against the glass. The sack was at an odd angle. She squinted. Corncobs. It said *corncobs!* Could this be where Carmine hid until the storm passed? Maybe. But his movements would need to be confirmed by someone seeing him entering or leaving the outbuilding. And the likeliest witnesses would be the homeowners. Etha scooted past the bungalow's tidy back porch, alongside a wall of shrubbery, across a shallow front lawn, and to the sidewalk. She paused to pat her hat and straighten her dress. All was quiet. She turned to face the house. Why, it was the Hodges! Although Etha and Temple didn't know them well, the lawyer and his wife went to the same church as the Jennings. This was all working out just fine. Mrs. Hodge would welcome her in and hopefully offer a cool glass of lemonade. Then Etha could casually bring up the storm. But wait, Lottie had said Mrs. Hodge was trying on a dress when the sky blackened and that Mrs. Hodge and the Kleins had ridden out the storm together. But what about Mr. Hodge? He was supposed to be at the fitting but he'd never come. Maybe he had been at home. Both the screen and front doors were shut, despite the heat. Etha pressed the bell. When no one answered, she tried again. The street was quiet. As she turned to leave, she noticed the sheer curtains sway slightly in the parlor window. Mrs. Hodge's strained face swam briefly from behind the organdy before receding. All right then, Etha thought, you are home. She spun around and knocked hard. There was a sound of footsteps and then Mrs. Hodge opened the door.

"Yes?"

"Good morning, Mrs. Hodge. I'm sorry to trouble you but . . ."

"Oh, Mrs. Jennings. What brings you out in this heat?" The woman produced a watery smile.

Yes, the heat, Etha thought. "I was running some errands just down the block and started to feel dizzy. I remembered you lived here and wondered if I could rest inside for a moment."

"Here?"

"Well . . . yes."

Mrs. Hodge touched her throat. "I don't know. Mr. Hodge will be home for lunch soon . . ." Her voice dribbled away.

Removing her hat, Etha fanned herself. "Just for a few minutes."

"All right, I guess."

The inside of the house was dreadfully close. Etha wondered if she could even continue the charade of coming in to cool off. She dropped onto a stiff cane-back chair. "I'll just sit here in the hall and catch my breath, if you don't mind."

Mrs. Hodge pushed up a sleeve to check her wristwatch. A violet bruise was imprinted on her forearm. "Could I bring you something to drink?" she said at last.

"That would be very kind."

Mrs. Hodge practically sprinted to the back of the house and returned almost immediately with a glass of lukewarm water. "I'm sorry I don't have ice cubes to spare. Mr. Hodge expects a full glass of iced lemonade for lunch and I don't want to run short."

Etha sipped and smiled. "This is just right. Refreshing." Sensing that the skittish Mrs. Hodge would be pushing her out the door any minute, Etha said, "Say, how about that storm? Lottie Klein said you got caught in the shop."

"Goodness. It was a nightmare. And the house filled up with dust. I don't know how it gets in. I'm still wiping down baseboards. The mister demands a clean house."

"Yes, men can be particular. By the way, did your husband get caught out in the duster?"

"No. He was at the office."

"Oh? I imagine something came up at the last minute, then. Lottie said he was expected at the fitting."

"Something did. Yes. Something came up."

On a low console table at Etha's elbow was the morning's copy of the *Gazetteer*, still tightly rolled. Etha gestured toward the newspaper. "My husband also has a lot on his plate these days, as you can imagine. What with the murder investigation."

Mrs. Hodge frowned. "In Vermillion?"

"Yes. It's been in the paper."

"Oh, I don't read it. Mr. Hodge makes sure to keep me up to date on matters that concern me. Someone in town was killed?"

"That rainmaker who came in on Friday. Chester Benton found his body in the alley outside the Jewel after the storm." Rising, Etha started to hand the empty water glass back to Mrs. Hodge but saw that the little bit of color in the woman's cheeks was now entirely washed away. "Are you all right?"

Mrs. Hodge planted two fingers on the console to steady herself. She inhaled sharply. "Fine."

"Are you sure?"

"I just don't like to think there are people in our town capable of that sort of violence. That's all. I'm fine." But there was no reassuring smile punctuating her stilted words.

"You know, let's call one another by our first names. Mine's Etha. And yours?"

The woman spoke to the floor: "Florence."

"Florence? Is that what you said?"

"Yes."

"My, what a pretty name."

When there was no response, Etha added, "Thank you again. I'll see you on Sunday at church."

Back outside, which now seemed cool after the airless heat of the shut-up house, Etha considered Florence. Such a sad woman. Why hadn't she noticed that before? Why had she only now learned the woman's first name? It was as if Florence Hodge was as unremarkable as her parlor curtains. Passing down the sidewalk, Etha's thoughts turned to Carmine. It seemed possible that no one had witnessed him slipping out of that shed, or it might not be the right shed anyway. Still, as her father had remarked when her eight-year-old self was banging away on the family's upright, practicing the same sonata over and over, Etha was dogged. Since she had a bit of time before her first piano student of the day, she decided to get a look at the murder weapon, if it was still at Wilburn Hinchie's office. That was another thread that appeared to connect Carmine to the killing.

While Etha made her way to the Hinchies', Viviane concluded a long-distance call. "Yes sir, I will certainly convey your message to the sheriff."

A burst of static emptied into her ear.

"You'll have to speak up," she said loudly.

Another volley of unintelligible sound was launched.

"I'm sorry, we have a bad connection!" Viviane shouted. "I'm going to hang up but I'm sure the sheriff will be in touch!"

Without taking the time to transcribe her notes, Viviane hurried across to the sheriff's office and strode in without even bothering to smooth her skirt.

"I just got off the phone with St. Joe," she said in a rush. "I think I've got something."

Temple and Ed looked up from their desks.

"Great," Temple said. "Ed, get this young lady a chair."

Perched on the edge of the rail-back, Viviane became conscious of her flushed cheeks. *Mind before mouth* had been the motto of her clerical teacher at Vermillion High. Now Viviane wished she had taken the time to collect her thoughts.

She cleared her throat. "The owner of Blodgett's Boarding House in St. Joe telephoned. He received the telegram that I sent at your request. It seems Mr. Coombs was a resident of Blodgett's for five years but has been away on business for the last, ah . . ." she consulted her notepad, "two weeks. He asked me why Jackson County was wanting to contact Mr. Coombs's next-of-kin. Of course, I declined to answer."

"Good," Temple broke in.

Viviane smiled. "Then he said, and I'll quote." She glanced down at the notepad in her lap. "He said, *If that no-count is dead, I want it on record that he owes me eighty dollars for storage of his trunk at ten dollars a month.* I asked him if he knew of any of Mr. Coombs's kin and he said there was an uncle by the name of Bert Coombs in town. Then Mr. Blodgett asked if Fenton was in Oklahoma and I informed him it was not. He said someone from Fenton's merchant association had come nosing around for Mr. Coombs a month ago with," here she read from the notepad again, "*with blood in his eye.* The man claimed Mr. Coombs had fleeced his town out of five hundred dollars by swearing he could make it rain. Then the connection broke up. Mr. Blodgett insisted he wanted the eighty dollars he was owed if Mr. Coombs had any money on him and I assured him you would be getting back to him, Sheriff." She looked up. "I hope that was all right?"

Temple smiled. "Sounds as if our man was none too popular. Did the landlord have a number for this uncle so I can notify him of his nephew's death?"

Viviane slapped her hand across her mouth. "I forgot to ask."

"Don't fret. We can get that, I'm sure. I appreciate your help."

She smiled broadly. "Anytime."

"And by the by, your father telephoned from the depot. I guess you were on the other line and Shirley put him through to me. They need him to work the night shift. I told him we'd make sure you got home, no problem. Ed's going to drop you off."

Viviane blanched. "But. Oh, that's not necessary. I'm sure . . ."

Holding up his hand, Temple said, "Won't take no for an answer. You come by here when it's quitting time and Ed will run you out in the county car."

Hugging the notepad to her chest, Viviane trudged out into the foyer. Everything had been going swell. Now Ed, the fine-looking deputy, would see that she lived in what amounted to a heap of packed earth, busting at the seams with children and grown-ups and alive with bugs. It would be as bad as someone seeing her saggy homemade underwear with the stretched-out elastic. Sniffling, she blew her nose twice before entering the main office. She knew the eyes of the two county clerks would be on her as soon as she stepped inside. They watched her every move as if they'd never seen a woman before.

Peering through the Hinchies' screen door, Etha observed Minnie, the doctor's wife, on her hands and knees in the entrance hall, her broad fanny raised in the air. At Etha's knock, Minnie waved her in while straightening her stout body in segments like an articulated measuring stick. Scattered at her feet were scraps of cardboard, a ruler, scissors, a single shoe, and a number of hairpins.

Before Etha could even say howdy-do, Minnie announced, "And to think I've come to this." She gestured at the littered carpet. "Father warned me about marrying a doctor. He said, *Minerva, Wilburn is a good fellow but he is not the provider you need.* I should have listened to him."

Along with Lottie, Minnie was one of Etha's closest friends. Like Etha, she was from east of the Mississippi—in her case, Cincinnati. Minnie fashioned herself as a woman who had come down in the world, a woman who had been destined to continue along the path of engraved silver pickle forks until Wilburn Hinchie had strolled into her sickroom one afternoon, palpated her swollen adenoids, and stolen her heart.

Now that romantic impulse was long past. Minnie's eyes snapped in her long face that conjured the image of an outraged horse, Etha mused, before brushing the unkind thought from her mind.

"What's got your feathers ruffled?" Etha asked

In answer, Minnie stomped over to the stairway landing where a magazine lay open. Snatching it up, she waved it in Etha's startled face. "*Simple instructions on repairing one's shoe with cardboard.* Hah! First, it is not simple at all." She kicked the bits of cardboard. "I've done four tries and haven't gotten close to making it work. Then there is the bigger outrage of having to patch a worn shoe. When I was a girl, my foot never *knew* a resoled shoe. And now, not only am I reduced to that, but using cardboard! Oh my God. I'm nothing better than a tramp in one of those shantytowns. What are they called?"

"Hoovervilles," Etha murmured, stooping to pick up the rejected shoe. She wiggled her finger through the hole. "I might be able to make this work."

Minnie flapped her hand. "Forget all that for now. I'm sick over the whole thing. Let's have an iced tea."

The two women sat at the kitchen table. There was a sharp smell of rubbing alcohol from Dr. Hinchie's office, which was attached to the house. Voile curtains as ruffled as a young girl's party dress hung at the windows. While walking over from the Hodges', Etha had decided to speak plainly to Minnie about Carmine's case and her desire to inspect the murder weapon.

"We both have husbands whose work intrudes directly into our home lives. Work that often demands discretion. So I know you will understand when I tell you privately that there is a young man jailed for murder in the cellblock next to my apartment as we speak."

Minnie sometimes assisted her husband with autopsies and so Etha gambled there would be no ladylike gasps. There weren't.

"But I know he didn't do it. Yes, the—"

"How do you know?" Minnie interrupted.

Etha paused. "This sounds naive, but he told me he is innocent and I believe him."

Minnie's brows rose toward the marcelled waves that began at her part and continued down the side of her head like a corrugated metal roof. "Really?"

"Yes. I am telling you this confidentially, but I had already met the boy on Saturday when I took some food out to the hobo camp near the tracks."

"On your own? You went to the jungle by yourself?"

"Yes. It was fine. That's not the point. I know he's not capable of murder."

"Far be it for me to criticize anyone for naïveté when I eloped with a man who promised me that after five years doctoring here we'd be able to buy a ranch and live in style. Twenty years later, here we sit. Still, I don't know how you can be so sure."

Etha couldn't explain it. "I'd bet my life on it. But I need to prove it. Temple says the evidence is solid. I understand what might be the murder weapon is here for Hinchie to examine. Some tool that the CCC camp stocks?"

"And you want to see it?"

"Yes!"

Minnie shrugged. "Fine by me."

She led Etha into the hallway where a door connected directly with the examining room. When she and Minnie got together for coffee, more often than not the door was open and Hinchie had his ear to the chest of some weathered farmer. Today, however, the doctor was making house calls, Minnie explained, and the office was empty.

"Wilburn mentioned something about it, but I didn't see it myself," Minnie said, flinging open the doors on a white-enameled cabinet full of various medical instruments. "What are we hunting for?"

"Temple didn't say exactly."

The two women searched the exam room, careful to return everything as they had found it, although Minnie dryly observed, "He wouldn't notice if we tipped the exam table on its head. Not a very observant man except where his patients are concerned. Then he doesn't miss a pinprick."

Beyond the exam room was a cramped waiting area and off that, an even smaller consultation office. Hinchie's desk was awash with piles of papers that spilled over onto two chairs and from there onto the floor. Minnie pounced on a brown parcel atop one.

"This might be it," she said.

The two women huddled over the desk as Minnie slowly unrolled the wrapping paper. Inside was a wooden shank with a square metal handle attached at one end and a ragged break, where the wood had been snapped off, at the other. The wood was pale yellow except on the jagged tip which was stippled dark brown. Both women recognized the stains. Dried blood. They observed the same whenever their monthlies came around.

"Is this from a hoe?" Minnie asked.

"I'm not sure. I'm going to make a sketch," Etha said, removing a clean sheet of paper from Hinchie's typewriter roll.

Through the open window came the sound of an auto drawing up to the curb. Both women froze.

"It's Hinchie," Minnie said.

The car door slammed.

Etha quickly drew a rough outline of the handle and stuffed the paper in her pocket. Minnie was rewrapping the parcel as footsteps crossed the porch. Her hands shook. But then Hinchie paused and a moment later the scent of pipe tobacco eddied through the window. Soundlessly, the conspirators hightailed it back through the exam room and into the house. Minnie closed the connecting door with a soft click. They leaned against the wall of the narrow hallway, catching their breath.

Etha said, "Close."

"But what a thrill!" Minnie whispered.

Ten minutes later Etha started for home. Her face as innocent as a lamb's, she waved to Hinchie, who was holding the office door open for an elderly patient.

Nearing the courthouse, Etha checked her watch and saw she had ten minutes before she needed to be home. Out front of Mitchem's Hardware a rack of brooms, a line of galvanized watering cans, and two rolls of asphalt shingles were making a feeble appeal to attract nonexistent passersby in the noonday heat. Etha found Cy Mitchem at the back of the store, scooping nails into paper packets. Cy, at age thirty-one, was a man born into the wrong profession. He had inherited the business from his father, and while eager enough, Cy had no head for numbers. And his ineptitude with tools was common knowledge. The joke around town was that the chicken house he'd hammered together for his wife was so poorly constructed and lopsided that the eggs rolled around like ball bearings. Still, he was invariably cheerful, his favorite saying being, *It don't help none to squawk.*

As Etha approached the counter, Cy rapidly shoved the nails aside as if he couldn't get shut of them fast enough. "Hot one," he called out, a grin breaking out below his closely cropped mustache, skinned by a razor at one end.

"Sure enough." Etha pulled off her hat and fanned herself.

Cy came around the counter. "Election's almost on us."

"That's so." Etha suddenly realized that in her preoccupation with Carmine, she'd forgotten all about the election. What if Doll won the primary before she had time to prove Carmine innocent? That would be a disaster. No longer was she ambivalent. Temple *had* to win.

Cy was saying, "You don't have to worry none. Everybody's voting for Temple. But you know that. So, I got a sale on today. Garden lime five cents a pound, if you're interested."

"I certainly would be. That truly sounds like a bargain but we live up on that third floor and don't have a garden so . . ."

Cy bumped the heel of his palm against his forehead. "What was I thinking? Jeez. So, what'll it be then?"

From her handbag, Etha pulled out the sketch she'd drawn at Hinchie's. "I was wondering if you have anything that has a handle similar to this. Maybe a hoe or rake?"

Cy studied the drawing. "Could be," he said finally. "Sort of seems familiar. Let's go have a look-see."

Etha followed him to the back of the store where a line of long-handled tools hung on a pegboard. Glancing at the sketch every couple of seconds, Cy slowly perused his stock.

"Just not seeing anything that . . ." he started to say, shaking his head.

Etha stooped to a lower shelf. "What about this?" she asked, pulling out a shovel.

Cy reared back. "Didn't know I had those."

"Sell a lot of them?" Etha asked.

"To be honest, I'm not sure what that particular scoop is for."

Applying the voice she used to steer a lazy piano student into choosing the most difficult practice piece, Etha said, "Maybe Ruthie-Jo would know?"

Ruthie-Jo was Cy's wife. She kept the books and tracked the inventory and everyone knew that if you needed help with getting the right-sized nail, she would be the one to ask. But the asking had to be done over the telephone and conveyed through Cy since Ruthie-Jo never left their house.

Cy snapped his fingers. "Yep. I bet she does. I'll give her a ring."

"And see if any have been sold recently," Etha called out as Cy hurried to make the call. "Please," she added, afraid she had been barking orders.

While she waited, Etha examined the square-handled shovels. There were three and all were dusty. She doubted that they were top sellers. But if even one had been sold, it would indicate that the murderer didn't necessarily have to be a CCCer. Didn't have to be Carmine.

After a few minutes Cy returned. "Ruthie-Jo says it's an entrenching shovel. We got a few in as army surplus."

"Did she remember how many came in?"

"Yep. No one keeps a ledger as particular as my Ruthie-Jo. Got . . . let's see," Cy said, squinting at his notes on a scrap of wrapping paper. "Got five in a year ago. Sold one right off the bat and then not another until this past Friday."

Etha's heart lurched. Friday, the day before the murder! It could very well have been bought by the killer. A killer who had access to an army shovel that came from someplace other than Camp Briscoe.

"Who bought it?"

Cy frowned. "Ruthie-Jo didn't made a note of that. 'Course, she doesn't work the counter. I must have sold it but I can't remember . . . No, wait. I wasn't here Friday afternoon. It must have been then. Had a nasty toothache so I got the Clanton boy, you know the Clantons? Got him to watch the store."

Shoot, Etha thought. No time left today to track Jimmy Clanton down. She had four piano pupils in a row starting, she glanced at her watch, in three minutes. Then she became aware of Cy's eager eyes.

"So, did you want to buy one?"

"What? Oh, no," she said. But then, touched with guilt, she added, "But I could use a couple dozen laundry pegs."

"Sure do got those!"

Hurrying to the courthouse with her superfluous purchase, Etha knew she didn't have enough evidence to present to Temple yet. But it was a start. The rest of the day whizzed by and she didn't have a chance to update Carmine on her progress with anything more than a whispered, "I'm working on it," as she passed him a dinner of navy bean soup, cornbread, milk, and two slices of pie.

That night, after washing up the dishes, she and Temple settled into the living room. During the *New York Symphony Hour*, Etha planned her next moves. Talk to the Clanton kid for sure. Maybe call on Mr. Hodge to see if, by chance, he was home and not at the office during the storm. Then her mind turned to Carmine, who was surely feeling blue, what with being on his lonesome over in the cellblock.

Abruptly, Etha said, "I think I'll bring Carmine that book I got from the library. It might take his mind off things." She shoved the yarn back into her work basket.

Temple uncrossed his legs. "Hold your horses. That's not a good idea. These young fellows riding the boxcars, joining up in the CCC, idling around city street corners—some have come up rough."

"But Carmine's not like—"

"Let me finish," Temple said. "They're unemployed and hungry. They learn to sweet talk to get what they want. Don't you remember that rash of scams over in Enid with that slick salesman peddling monthly sheet-music subscriptions door to door?"

"I'm not stupid, you know."

Temple held up his hands. "Didn't say that. But all those women got for their dime was a single piece of music as ancient as the hills. I'm just making sure you don't get suckered in by this kid who, I will remind you again, killed a man." Putting the newspaper aside, he clicked off the radio.

"I disagree," Etha said. Her chin rose.

"I know. But the price might be high if you're wrong on this one."

Temple passed down the hall and into the bathroom from where, in short order, came the brisk burr of his toothbrush. Etha wanted to tell him how certain she was Carmine didn't kill anyone, but that would mean revealing she'd met the boy at the hobo camp. So, instead, she clicked off the living room lamps. A wave of fatigue spread across her shoulders. In bed, she sank gratefully into the mattress. But despite exhaustion, sleep wouldn't come. Beside her, Temple seemed restless too.

She said, "It would be a help if you could move him into the kitchen cell."

His response was a grunt.

"My arms are sore from carrying those trays."

A deep sigh. "Then I'll have Ed carry them. I'm not moving the prisoner. Now get some sleep."

He kissed her gently on the cheek, then rolled onto his side and within minutes was snoring gently—his breath rising and falling in small chuffs. If only it would rain, Etha thought. She longed for the comforting splatter against the bedroom windows, the steady thrum on the gabled roof. In the streets beyond, the dust lay silent, but Etha, her ears as wide as funnels, listened and prayed.

CHAPTER FIFTEEN

"GRAZING ON DIRT," McGreevy the auctioneer announced, clucking his tongue as he pried open the mouth of Jess Fuller's best heifer. The animal tossed her head in protest, but McGreevy managed to prize her mouth open enough to reveal teeth ground down to the gums. "Bet her stomach's full of it too." He pressed his hands against the heifer's slack hide.

"What'd you expect?" asked Jess, who was holding the guide rope. "Every cow left standing in the county is just as pitiful. Where have you been, man?"

The foreclosure auction on the Fullers' farm, cancelled once because of the Brown Blizzard, as it was now being called in newspapers across the country, and again because of some bungled paperwork, had been rescheduled for this day, Thursday, at noon. And Jess was prickly as hell.

McGreevy shrugged. "Maybe get twenty dollars for her."

Jess wouldn't be seeing any of the profit. Why did he care what the heifer sold for? Still, he was deeply insulted. He'd birthed this heifer and five others. When they'd gotten scrapes from barbed wire, he'd rubbed ointment on the cuts. He'd trimmed and scrubbed their hooves. And since the dusters started blowing in, he'd applied wet rags to their lashes when dust and tears glued their eyes shut. A low bid would be a slap in the face. It was the same as saying, *You don't know your stuff,* when none of this had anything to do with animal husbandry and everything to do with the drought. With the rainmaker's death, Jess's last hope had been killed off too. Only anger was left.

For another hour, he led McGreevy around the homestead as the auctioneer made notes on a clipboard. In the machine shed, Jess confessed that the patch he'd applied to the wagon hitch hadn't held so good. And after he mended the tractor's crankcase it still leaked some. Might as well bend over and show everyone the hole in the crotch of my overalls, he thought.

Finally, Darnell the banker pulled up the drive in his Ford and McGreevy trotted off to report on the auction's sorry forecast. Jess hunkered down on the splitting block, casting his eyes over the barn and house with their cluster of outbuildings. Above him, the windmill's blades turned sluggishly.

His brooding was broken by a rise of dust delineating the road. A stretch of trucks came into view. Farmers from the surrounding homesteads, some who Jess knew, were arriving to pick over the Fullers' meager belongings. A few would hang their heads, embarrassed, as he had done himself not so long ago. But others would be as bold as brass, as if they, too, weren't a step away—a failed well or another dry month—from the same. Jess stood, stretched his legs, and walked toward the gathering crowd.

Behind him, a screen door slapped. Two women from First Methodist, with pitchers, bedding, and bookends clutched to their bosoms, advanced across the lawn with Hazel. They kneeled under the cottonwood, adding their burdens to the household goods already spread on display. Earlier, Hazel had painfully culled the can-do-withouts from the necessities. The essentials—mattresses, cookpots, and Gram's hope chest—were already strapped to the swayback truck. After the auction, they'd squeeze in and drive east to her folks.

"Now Hazel, you gotta keep your washboard," Mrs. Rayburn said.

"Mother's got a wringer washer. Electric."

"Well then."

Hazel smiled inwardly. Oh, happy day to be shut of this place. She'd been counting down the hours since last week. No more sweat poured into cleaning the house, feeding the hogs, tilling the fields, all to have it blow back in her face. She surveyed the hodgepodge of bedsheets, horsehair chairs, and young Fred's iron bedstead, laid out in the open air.

Mrs. Rayburn pulled a hankie from her sleeve and handed it to Hazel. "But surely not your oak sideboard! You saved up egg money for a year to buy it. It's your pride and joy."

"It's hard to part with, I'll admit, but it will bring a good price and we get to keep the money from the household goods. It's the first thing people notice when they visit. Everyone comments on it. I figure maybe eighty dollars."

The farmyard was filling up with bidders and lookie-loos—farmers in mended overalls and wives in sagging sweaters. A stranger stopped to scrutinize the dishes. The ones with the daisy pattern. Hazel had fed her family three times a day on that china, had memorized every petal on every flower as she washed, dried, and stacked. And now they were nothing more than secondhand plates to some stranger, wiped clean of meaning.

Hazel's eyes welled again and she pushed past the church women. Leaning against the back porch railing, she had a good cry. After a while she gathered herself and blew her nose into Mrs. Rayburn's hankie. There was the muffled crunch of boots on gravel. The sheriff strode toward her from the direction of the barn. Hazel's spirits lifted. She trusted Temple, no matter what Jess said. She knew it wasn't his fault they were losing the farm. He was a fair man caught up, as they all were, in the swirling haboob that was the Depression and the drought.

Temple pulled off his hat. "Afternoon."

Smiling, Hazel dabbed at her nose. "It's a warm one. Can I get you some water? I think I've packed all the glasses, but I'm sure I could scare up a canning jar."

Temple chuckled. "Naw, but thanks. Sorry about this." He glanced over his shoulder at twenty or so farmers who had convened around one of their number, listening intently as the man spoke.

Hazel shrugged. "You know how I feel, but it's still upsetting. All we worked for . . ." A pained expression crossed Temple's face. Hazel saw she was making him uncomfortable. "But I can't tell you how much I need to set my feet on the homeplace back east."

"Etha feels the same."

"Not you?"

Temple grinned. "In my way of thinking, moving on means moving west. I started in Pennsylvania and never have looked back. If you don't move on, move forward, you get mired down. But Etha and I have never seen eye to eye on that." After a pause, he settled his hat back on his head. "Guess I best get going before Mr. Darnell comes a-looking for me."

Hazel said, "You don't want to cross that man. You want a banker on your side. Believe me. I've learned that lesson."

As Temple ambled around the side of the house, Bob Ellis, a farmer from down the road, waved him over. The two men shook hands.

"What can I do for you, Bob?"

Bob's wind-burned face seemed to deepen a shade. "I don't know how to . . . Well, I believe in letting a man know how I stand. So as while I think you are a good person, I won't be voting for you this time around. It's nothing personal. Just, Doll might do more for the farmer. Wanted you to hear it from me."

"Appreciate that," Temple said slowly, the pleasant expression frozen on his face. "I'm not thinking we're in agreement on this!"

"Har har!" the other man barked.

"What exactly do you believe Doll can do that I can't?"

Bob turned aside politely and discharged a jet of tobacco juice. "I just think he will have more pull in the statehouse and such. He's one of the town founders. Been here his whole life. Jackson County is hurting and we need to use every connection we got. Sorry, but that's a fact."

Temple inhaled heavily. "I appreciate your honesty though I hope you might rethink this. But anyways, give Cora my regards," he said, turning away.

Temple passed into the front yard, his spirits low. How many other farmers thought as Bob did but didn't have the courage to say so? The raked dirt that passed for a lawn was alive with women pecking through the detritus of Hazel Fuller's cupboards. The scene was oddly jarring, like the house had its innards busted open. He'd seen this kind of thing before. Not just at auctions either, but back in Johnstown when he was a boy; the day after the big flood. He thought about that morning, when he'd slogged alongside his father, down from the safety of the hill where his family had sheltered during the night, and into the valley. Where businesses, shops, the courthouse, and his grandfather's hardware store had once stood. On that morning it was nothing more than a grotesque welter of chairs, roofing, chamber pots, baby carriages, and sodden bedding. There was hardly a landmark that remained standing except the sturdy brick offices of Cambria Iron and a couple of houses washed off their foundations and leaning at crazy angles. Temple's legs shook as he and his father picked their way through a foul stew of smashed and torn debris. They had turned left toward the river and come upon a pile of shattered window frames and bricks. A single bloody leg with shreds of skin and arteries dangling sat atop the heap, a bit of stocking clinging to the naked skin. The bile had risen in Temple's throat and then the vomit gushed out, spattering his shoes.

"Come on, son," his father had said. "Hands are needed down at the bridge."

The massive stone railroad bridge, with burning debris jammed against its pylons, loomed in Temple's inner eye. From deep within the mass, voices had screamed out for relief, their agonized wails pouring into his ears. In the distance, someone hollered his name. At first, Temple imagined the cry rose from the pyre. But as he pulled himself away from the nightmare, he recognized the banker's voice.

"Temple? Where you been at?" Darnell asked.

"Sorry. Lost in thought," Temple mumbled.

In a cleared area beside the barn, the auctioneer had set up shop on Hazel's kitchen table. He was instructing two teenage boys: "Bring the household goods up first. Then we'll move on to the machinery."

McGreevy smacked his gavel and waved the crowd of a hundred or more forward. Temple eyed the side of the barn, which was shady and a prime spot to rest your back against. But standing prominently next to the banker was his job. It telegraphed the message that these were legal proceedings. He straightened the brass star on his shirt pocket.

"We're about ready to start," McGreevy called out. "But first Vince Doll has an announcement."

Temple frowned. There was movement in the sea of hats before Doll emerged. Licking his lips in the way of a trumpet player preparing for his solo, the candidate took the gavel in hand and pounded twice.

"Ladies and gentlemen, I just want to take a moment of your time. As you all know, I've been a proud resident of Jackson County since it was incorporated. Here from the beginning. A pioneer settler, as they say. And I've been hearing about other towns in these parts boasting how they're prepared to tough out these hard times. That their spirits are higher than any. Well, I'm here to show them they're wrong! None are as hard-nosed as us! Hard-nosed, ornery, stubborn, and just mean old cusses! We can outlast any drought, any . . ."

Why, the man was hijacking the auction and whipping up the crowd with a campaign speech! Temple wondered if he should try to put a stop to this or would that make him seem as if he was afraid of some competition? Coming down on the side of the law, Temple stepped toward Doll as he switched gears.

". . . and to show our neighbors we are fighting back as hard as they are. Harder! We all know that the jackrabbit population is out of control. This season's small-crop production is being made even smaller by these menaces. And next season, when the rains come back, the jackrabbits

will too, unless we do something about it. That's why I'm sponsoring
Jackson County's first jackrabbit drive next Wednesday. Bring your bats,
your shovels, and your thirst. We will rid our land of these hordes and be
prepared for a good strong crop next year."

At this, a burst of whooping and hollering commenced.

"My boys and I will corral a three-acre pen of rabbits for you to
smash and bring something to wet your whistle afterward. Spread the
word. Ten a.m. at the Campbell farm. See you there!"

Doll waved his hat at the throng, who answered with more cheering.
As he passed Temple, he said in a low voice, "You don't need to be there.
My boys will make sure things are under control."

Temple put on a tight smile. "Appreciate that, but it's my duty to keep
the peace."

As Doll strutted away, Temple removed his hat and pushed back his
sweat-damp hair. McGreevy had returned to the table, clipboard in hand.
"Let's get this rolling. Boys, bring in lot number one."

The auctioneer's two assistants trotted up with several filled crates.

"Lot one is miscellaneous household goods. Everything your little
lady would want or need to set up a house or replenish her cupboards.
Don't miss out on this one." McGreevy now launched into his chant: "I'll
take a quarter for the lot, a quarter for the lot. I see I have a quarter, how
about fifty? Will someone give me fifty? Fifty cents, now seventy-five.
Will someone give me seventy-five? Seventy-five? Once, twice, gone for
fifty cents."

And so it went, with the dregs of the Fullers' life on the plains sold
off. The sun boiled thickly through a copper haze. Hazel sat on the porch
step alongside Mrs. Rayburn, waving a palmetto fan. Hazel had sent
her boy off to the Jewel with two precious nickels and told him and a
neighbor kid not to come back before suppertime. No reason he had to
see this.

Finally her oak sideboard was carried up front.

"Here you go," Mrs. Rayburn said, nudging Hazel's ribs.

The auctioneer started in: "Purdy is as purdy does. What husband
wouldn't want to make his wife a gift of this sideboard? Practical as it is
refined. She can put all her best tableware inside and display knickknacks
on top. Take note of the inset mirror. That's a nice touch, don't you think?"

He paused, then sprang into his chant: "I'll take nothing less than a
hundred dollars for this fine piece. Hundred for it. You know it's worth

twice as much. Hundred now, looking for a hundred. Now who'll give me a hundred? All right. Who'll give me ninety-five? Ninety-five? Do I hear ninety? Who'll give ninety?"

And so the numbers slid until Hazel was pressing the hem of her dress to her eyes and Mrs. Rayburn put an arm around her shoulders.

With a crack of the gavel, McGreevy finally announced, "Sold for $4.25. You got a good buy, sir. Now, let's move on to the farm equipment."

Shame rolled over Hazel, as if she had done something foolish and been caught out. Foolish to think that her best piece wasn't anything better than cheap pine covered in veneer and tarted up with a mirror. "My stomach's turned," she said, then stood and walked away from the house, out back to the truck, tilting under its burden of trunks, chairs, rolled mattresses, the galvanized washtub. She sat on the running board, eyes shut, fingers tight in her ears to block the noise of the auction.

From his vantage point beside the banker, Temple noticed Hazel slinking away, same as a wounded cat. Beside him, Darnell hummed something jaunty under his breath, his hands deep in his trouser pockets. Sure this is legal, Temple thought, but is it right? Until recently, he had assumed the two went hand in hand. But now he thought differently. He moved away from Darnell out to the shady place he'd spotted earlier. Close enough, he decided. He joined a man in frayed overalls and a greasy hunting cap.

"How do," the man said as a formality, not a question.

Temple nodded. It was a relief to lean against the barn's rough planks. After a bit he turned to the man. "Don't believe we've met."

"Not lived here long. They call me Trot," he said.

Jess was driving a hog to the auction table, the first of the livestock to be sold off.

"Took a gander at her. Sound," Trot said.

"That so?"

"Yep." A week's worth of stubble overlaid a gaunt face. The farther Temple traveled west and away from Johnstown, the more monosyllabic the natives became. He found that refreshing. Not true of everyone, of course. Doll and his kind, the townsfolk, talked a blue streak while holding back their cards. Farmers were different. Temple inhaled the air, which smelled a tad clearer.

"Seems as if more folks are moving out of here than coming in," Temple said.

"Yep."

In a voice like a megaphone, McGreevy rattled off the hog's attributes and then slid into his pitch. "Starting at forty dollars. Who will give me forty for this fine sow? Looking for forty." He kept at it for a while. A phalanx of local farmers was at the front of the crowd. McGreevy pointed to members of this group. "How about you, sir? Give me forty dollars? Will you give me forty dollars?"

The young farmer, a man by the name of Hartsell, shook his head.

McGreevy cocked a finger at the next man. "You there, I'll take thirty-five. Take thirty-five. Will you give me thirty-five for this fine specimen?"

Instead of bidding, the fellow studied his boots.

Jess, who up until this point had been taking no interest in the auction, only in the hog that was wallowing in the dust at his feet, glanced up with a confused expression.

For the next five minutes, McGreevy kept the patter going, giving ground inch by inch until, with a worried glance at Darnell, he called, "Rock-bottom price. Ten dollars. Rock-bottom."

Far back among the throng, an arm came up but it quickly retracted, as if its owner had been encouraged to rethink his position.

Jess turned to McGreevy and, after a pause, raised his hand. "Two dollars."

McGreevy balked; then continued as if Jess hadn't spoken: "Ten, who will give me ten?"

Nothing but silence until a stern voice called out, "Take it. Take the bid."

In an instant, the starch went out of the auctioneer. His mouth, the tool of his trade, hung open. Finally, he pronounced, "Sold." The formality of the gavel was forgotten.

Darnell swore under his breath, then waved McGreevy and Temple over. "What the hell is going on?" The banker looked from McGreevy to Temple and back. "Is this legal?"

McGreevy, apparently stupefied, was mute. Temple answered, "As far as I know, there's no law that says a man can't bid at his own auction."

Darnell, his cheeks scarlet, whipped around to McGreevy. "You agree?"

"I, ah . . ." His tongue stalled, then caught hold: "Never seen anything like it. But I've heard rumors from Iowa and thereabouts of farmers colluding to, you know, help out a neighbor."

"But is it legal?"

"Not sure," McGreevy said, flinching, as if anticipating a blow.

Darnell glanced away, his jaws clenching and unclenching. "All right. I'm not calling this off. That will give these troublemakers more to yammer about. But as soon as Doll is elected, and he will be, Temple, he will get the law set right. He'll put a stop to this tomfoolery."

Temple bristled. "I'm still sheriff and intend to stay so. And you know as well as I do that sheriffs don't make the laws. We enforce them."

The auction resumed. Temple retired to the shade.

"Mutiny?" Trot asked.

Temple laughed grimly and lit a cigarette. He needed to parse this thing out. There was the fact that the bank had loaned Jess money that he hadn't paid back. When you can't make your mortgage, the bank has a right to foreclose. That was clear-cut. But what if hundreds of folks couldn't pay back what they owed? And all due to the same hard times that were pulling everyone down? No one could argue that every single one of those belly-up homesteads was the fault of poor farming. And what good did it serve to push people off the land? If they stayed on, at least most of them were still able to feed their families. Listen to me, he thought. I'm sounding like a socialist. Will Rogers was right. Nothing makes a man broad-minded more than adversity. Or watching your fellow man lose everything. Temple flicked the cigarette butt.

And so the remainder of the afternoon churned on, a rowboat in rough seas. Five heads of cattle went to Jess for one dollar each. The plow, tractor, and baler were sold back to their owner for $6.25. Machinery, hand tools, sacks of feed corn, a half-consumed salt lick, lengths of irrigation hose, two rusty pitchforks, and the disk seeder were all paraded out of the barn, greeted with silence until Jess spoke up in a bewildered voice, and then returned to their places.

By late afternoon it was all over. Darnell stomped off to his flivver. The tight group of farmers that Temple had noticed as he talked with Hazel before the auction, mostly locals, surrounded Jess, slapping him on the back with their big rough hands and handing him wrinkled bills to cover his bids for the equipment and the land. Jess himself had the slack-jawed expression of a man taken by surprise.

Temple found Hazel sitting on the running board.

"All over but the shouting?" she asked, her face grim.

"As a matter of fact, the farm's still yours. Seems that your neighbors had a plan. No one bid except Jess. You should have seen Darnell's face, it was . . ." Temple's voice trailed off as Hazel jumped to her feet, throwing her hat on the ground.

"I'm not staying. You know that, don't you? I don't care if someone hands this place to Jess on a silver platter. There is nothing here for us but heartache, and if he don't see that, then he is just fooling himself. Stay out here long enough and you get delirious."

Temple hung his head. "I'm sorry, Hazel," he said softly.

Ten minutes later, as he swung the sedan around to head out, Temple observed Jess and Hazel beside the loaded truck. Jess leaned toward her, flinging his hands to make a point, his face knotted in anger while Hazel's fingers struggled to untie a bundle from the roof. It was a single bedroll. She tossed it at her husband's feet. Temple wanted to leap out of the car and shake Jess's shoulders hard, to tell him to listen to his level-headed wife. He wanted to shout, *Wake up, man!* But instead, he stepped on the gas pedal. Not ready to face the office, he drove west, away from town; shadows of telephone poles zippered across the roof of the car.

Not a quarter of a mile down the road, he spotted Trot walking back toward the Fullers'. Temple pulled over.

"Forget something?"

Trot leaned into the open passenger window. "Nope. Car troubles."

"Need a lift?"

"Appreciate it. If you could just get me home, I'll go back later and fix the rattletrap."

"Sure thing." Temple pulled the gear knob and off they went.

"See there?" Trot said as they passed a Model T parked cockeyed at the edge of the road. The man exuded the sour odor of sweaty clothes and unwashed hair that Temple associated with lifelong bachelors. There was no chatter on the ride, which was fine by him. Trot directed Temple by pointing this way and that until they ended up at a soddie at the tail end of a lane. Temple recalled a couple with a large brood of kiddies farming here not long before.

Trot raised the door handle. "Thank you kindly."

"You're welcome. Can you could spare a glass of water before I head back?"

Temple followed Trot. Inside, his hat brushed against yellowed newspapers covering the low ceiling. The essentials—a chair, table, a rag rug, and narrow bed—were worn but clean.

Trot removed a glass from a cupboard in the kitchen area. There was the inhale-exhale of a rusted pump handle. Temple examined a photo propped on a rough shelf. It showed a young man wearing the tunic, cinched belt, and puttees of a soldier in the Great War—the spitting image of Trot. So he has a son, Temple thought. Wrong about the bachelor part.

Trot handed the filled glass to Temple.

The sheriff gulped it down. "That hit the spot."

"Can't believe that boneshaker broke down again. Thought I had her all fixed up. She did the same after the fireworks. Had to walk all the way back to town that night."

"You mean the rainmaker's demonstration? You were there?"

Trot shrugged. "Something to do."

"I'm working on a case. He was killed the next day."

"Heard that."

"Did you notice any harsh words exchanged?"

"Not that I can say." Trot's lips worked in and out over his mostly bare gums. "Nope. Purdy sure not."

Temple shrugged. "Well, we already made an arrest. Just wanted to make sure I didn't miss anything."

"An arrest?"

"A CCC boy. So what'd you think of the explosives?"

Trot coughed and spit a wad of phlegm onto the floor. "Noisy as all get-out. Stirred up a fair amount of dust. Sort of akin to a stockyard that way. Surprised you arrested someone already."

"Yeah, well. Come up from Texas, did you?"

"Naw."

Trot didn't volunteer anything else. Temple figured the man was squatting and didn't want to be caught out by the law.

Driving back to Vermillion, he thought about the photo of the young soldier. Would his own Jack have grown up to take after him? The boy had the makings of it. Same eye and hair color as Temple. But hard to say. Etha's siblings all had widow's peaks that had been passed along to Jack. And he had the Hart family's oval face. The kid was sort of a mutt, Temple thought, which for some reason made him smile.

Earlier in the day, the movie house owner had also been reflecting on the past. Midmorning on a Thursday and Vermillion, in years gone by, would have been thrumming with voices and vehicles. But nowadays there was only the muffled emptiness of hard times. It amplified the sound of Chester's shoes as he returned to the Jewel, bearing a handful of overdue bills from the post office. It conveyed the town's hollowness up through his soles. The doorway of the vacant drugstore next to the theater stank of stale urine.

Five days before, Chester had wrestled with the adding machine an entire afternoon, and no matter which way he punched the keys, it came out the same. The Jewel was sinking fast, with profits no longer even treading water. It was hard medicine to swallow. He required a long night of drinking and the patient ear of Hank Stowe, the *Gazetteer*'s publisher, before he could even contemplate bringing that particular spoon to his lips. On Monday, Chester had telephoned the Salem China outfit. The eager commercial traveler on the other end of the line said he could be in Vermillion the next day to get the Jewel started on a dish promotion, but Chester put him off. "I've other appointments," he'd said stiffly, knowing that his daily calendar was as empty as half of the town's storefronts. "Thursday at eleven thirty will suit."

Chester had asked Lottie to join him for the huckster's pitch. Pleasant but firm in dealing with salesmen that called at her father's store, she would make certain that the dish patterns and posters were as tasteful as possible in what was, Chester believed, an abomination on the silver screen's high culture.

Now Lottie's voice rushed to meet him from behind the candy counter: "There you are! I thought you'd jumped ship, leaving me standing alone on the deck in one of those unbecoming life vests."

"Please, no melodrama," Chester said, striding the twenty paces between the lobby doors and the refreshment stand. "Get me a pop, will you? My stomach is unsettled."

As Chester lifted the bottle to his lips, the salesman breezed into the lobby, trailing a cloud of aftershave and peppy lingo. Unsnapping his case, the commercial traveler by the name of Russ drew out a large variety of dishes. As Russ talked up the attributes of the various place settings, Lottie described them to Chester.

After twenty minutes Chester interrupted: "I get the picture. Please take yourself outside for a smoke so the lady and I can discuss this in private." Five minutes later, Chester settled on Lottie's recommendation—the Monticello pattern. The three retired to Chester's office to sign the contract.

Russ dropped into a chair and busily made check marks in the margins of a black notebook while Lottie read the agreement aloud. When she finished, Chester nodded grimly, slid his wooden writing board under the paperwork, and used its horizontal notches to execute a signature straight enough to center the bubble in a spirit level.

"You won't regret this. You have my word on it," Russ said, tucking the papers and money in his breast pocket. "Thank you for the . . ." he glanced at his watch. "Whoa doggies! I'm late. I'll bring the crate into the lobby and be on my way."

"Where you headed?" Lottie asked.

"Elk City. Just hoping the lodgings have been deloused. I got a nasty case of bedbugs in St. Joe's not long back. The bane of the traveling salesman. I was talking to a fellow roomer there and he said the bedbugs hereabouts have nothing on the grasshoppers. Grasshoppers as big as prairie dogs is what he said. Come to think of it, I believe he was coming down this way too."

"Vermillion is overrun with salesmen," Lottie laughed. "Drummers hawking jabots, cancer cures, encyclopedias, udder balm. You name it, they've been here."

"I'm not sure what he was peddling. Something that required a truck. And know-how he'd picked up as a doughboy. He was bragging on that. As if getting conscripted as cannon fodder makes you top dog. One of the other boarders took offense at all his boasting. Told the fellow to shut his trap. Drew out a pistol. But nothing came of it." Russ appeared downcast.

As Chester put the writing board back in the drawer and reordered his desk, Russ mentioned an article he'd read in *True Detective* about a particularly gruesome killing of a schoolteacher. Lottie had heard about the case too, and began quizzing Russ about the details. The conversation then turned to gangland shoot-outs and other murders of the day. Chester shot his cuffs. He cleared his throat. The talk continued around him. I might as well be invisible, he thought. Their voices whirred on. The cruel irony of the sightless is that we are mostly unseen by the rest of the world. But not here. His status as a businessman, a person of import, and a stylish dresser with an eye-catching lady friend had rendered him highly visible in town. Now, however, the Depression and the dust were taking all that away, snatching it from his fingers. And Lottie and Russ were prattling on as if nothing had changed. Rage rose in this throat. He stood abruptly and leaned toward them with whitened knuckles planted on the desktop.

"Get out! Both of you!" he screamed. "Who cares about a husband who is a cuckold? The death of a two-bit gunman? A woman strangled by her stockings in Chattanooga? Who cares? You are nattering about things that don't matter while I lose everything! Everything I've worked for. Do you have any idea how hard it is for a blind man to stand upon his own two feet? To be independent? And now I'm being carved away in bits and pieces until I am nothing but raw flesh. Until I'm helpless as a child and there is nothing I can do about it. Nothing I can do to stop it. Get out. Both of you."

Neither moved. Then all was motion.

Russ jumped up and clattered down the steps. Lottie reached for Chester's arm but he yanked it away.

She cried out, "I'm sorry, I had no—"

"Leave." Chester's teeth were clenched, his jaw rigid.

"Oh God." Sobbing, Lottie stumbled back, knocking over a chair. She ran down the stairs and through the lobby, her footsteps fading.

When all was silent, Chester grabbed the pink cake stand, laden with ash and crushed cigarette butts, and hurled it across the room where it crashed down the stairwell, spinning out broken shards as it fell.

CHAPTER SIXTEEN

IT WAS NOT UNTIL THE NEXT DAY, Friday, that Etha had time to fill Carmine in on her findings. The young man's jaw was now a mottled shade of chartreuse and his unwashed hair stuck up in greasy peaks. She told him about her visit to the Hodges' house and described the setup.

"Does that sound like the place?" she asked.

Carmine swished a mouthful of coffee from one side of his mouth to the other. "Could be. Yeah."

Pushing her back into the chair, Etha grinned. "Good. So I'm going to be paying Mr. Hodge a call today. We know his wife wasn't there to witness your departure, but maybe he was. What do you think?"

Carmine stared past her shoulder, his eyes fixed in thought. Finally he said, "I'm grateful for all you're doing. Really and truly. But I don't deserve it. I mean, I didn't kill that man, but you know, I've done other things, and maybe this is just settling the score."

Etha stiffened.

"Things I'm not proud of."

"What things?"

He exhaled. "I don't want to say."

"I need to know if I'm going to help you."

Carmine wiped his nose on his hand. "Are you sure? It's not pretty."

Etha nodded.

"We was living in some crummy apartment on the South Side. This was after my mom died. Someone showed my dad how to rig a meter box and skim off the electric. He had a bad knee and so sent me up the pole outside our building. I was twelve. Something like that. I got a jumper line hooked up and it worked. Pretty soon everyone on our street was asking me to do the same for them. I rigged at least twenty over the next couple of years. And they were all good. I swear it! I was careful. But then there was this place across the street with maybe twenty apartments. Someone from over there, someone with a lot of kids, asked for my help. I must have cut a main without knowing it. The whole place burned to the ground."

"Oh Lord." A hollow opened in Etha's breastbone. "Surely no one would blame you for—"

"Six dead, three of them kids." Carmine pressed his knuckles to his lips. "I knew right away I'd done it. Dad said I'd better beat it west before the cops came sniffing around and asking who jigged the wires. He gave me ten bucks and hustled me over to the freight yard. Haven't been back since." He paused. "Anyway, that's why I ran when I saw Commander Baker pointing me out to the sheriff. My legs took off."

"Do you know for sure the wiring caused the fire?"

Carmine shrugged. "Dad said so. But things were bad then. Sometimes I think maybe he just wanted one less kid at the dinner table."

"You'll need to tell Mr. Jennings about why you ran."

"You still willing to help me?"

"Yes, of course. You were just a child," she said. "And I know you didn't kill Mr. Coombs."

They sat in silence. Then Etha raised a finger. "Be right back." She returned with the library book. "See if this doesn't take your mind off things for a while."

Later that afternoon, Etha shut the courthouse door firmly behind her and set off to talk to Jimmy Clanton, who had filled in for Cy at the hardware store and possibly sold the entrenching shovel. The Clantons occupied rooms above a now-shuttered millinery shop. When Etha pressed the buzzer at the bottom of the stairs, there was a quick flurry of heels crossing above her head and then Georgina Clanton's tightly bobby-pinned head poked from the apartment's doorway.

"Yes?"

"It's Etha Jennings."

Georgina squinted. "Come on up."

Etha adjusted her handbag. "I'd like to, but I've got a list of chores a mile long." This was a common complaint among the women of Jackson County. For housewives, the hard times had brought more work as the necessities of "make-do" expanded to include repairing upholstery, taking in boarders, and sewing every stitch of the family's clothes from underwear to coats. For Jackson County menfolk, especially farmers, it was the opposite: they spent most of their days in town, squatting on their lean haunches, their empty hands limp between their knees.

Etha said, "I'm wanting to talk with your Jimmy."

"At the ball field. Or that was where he was headed an hour ago. What's he done?"

"Nothing."

"You know he's never going to submit to piano lessons, if that's what you're after."

Etha laughed. "It's not that. Has to do with a customer at the hardware store."

"Try the ball field."

At a rough baseball diamond with sawdust-filled gunny sacks for bases, two youths tossed a ball back and forth. Etha tromped toward them, sandy soil spilling into her shoes. Jimmy was wearing a cap slung sideways with its brim flipped up. He stopped pitching when he caught sight of her.

"Forgot your mitt?" he asked, a one-sided grin breaking across his face. That grin sold many a cookpot and laundry starch on the two afternoons a week he clerked at the store.

"Want to loan me yours?" Etha shot back.

She recognized but didn't know the name of Jimmy's buddy, whose cheeks and chin were riddled with pimples. Etha recalled her first boyfriend. Each time he'd called at her parents' house, she'd struggled to keep from staring at the angry eruptions. But after a few minutes the pimples seemed to recede, until she forgot them altogether. Funny how we manage to trick our eyes.

"I'm hoping you can help me," she said.

"Sure."

"My gardening shovel is busted. I have my eye on a replacement, but it's a little pricey. Mr. Mitchem said you sold one last week."

"You came all the way out here to ask me that?"

Although Etha detested lying and wasn't good at it, she stuck it out. "Yes," she said, knowing Jimmy wouldn't question an adult beyond a certain point.

And he didn't. "Since I only sold one shovel this whole month, I know which one you mean. Trench digger?"

She nodded.

"I was sort of surprised he wanted one. He doesn't seem the gardening type."

"Who bought it?"

"Mr. Hodge," Jimmy said.

"Really?" More than once she and Temple had sat in the pew behind the Hodges and she couldn't envision his fleshy form, always clothed in business suits, nor his smooth-skinned hands with their carefully pared nails, turning over soil in the garden.

Jimmy raised his palms. "Surprise, ain't it?"

Walking back across the lot, Etha mulled over Jimmy's information. Beyond the incongruity of the stolid lawyer planting seeds was a more worrying issue—where had he stored the shovel? If he'd hung it in the outbuilding, which was probable, that would add to the weight of evidence against Carmine. On paper, it now seemed that the boy had two chances to steal the type of shovel used to kill Coombs. Her spirits flagged.

Back on the sidewalk she emptied her shoes, brushed off her dirty soles as best she could, and headed toward the law office of John Hodge, Esquire. The only blemish on her conscience would be the new lie she was now concocting. She couldn't just march into the lawyer's office and demand to know if he'd seen a young man sneaking out of his yard on Saturday. Another lie, but a small one, was required.

Hodge's offices were a block from the courthouse, above the telephone exchange. The attorney's secretary was Alice Ames, who had briefly taken lessons from Etha before defecting to Vermillion's other piano teacher. The one who pasted gold stars on the sheet music of even the worst students.

"Afternoon, Mrs. Jennings. Can I help you?" Alice asked, her face a polite mask.

Figuring that a false compliment might win her ten minutes with Hodge, Etha replied, "My, isn't that blue blouse becoming on you."

Blushing, Alice took the bait: "Why thank you. I wasn't sure . . ."

"Oh, it absolutely works. I was hoping Mr. Hodge might have just a few minutes for me. It's a church matter of sorts."

Alice glanced at the closed door to her right with Hodge's name stenciled in gilt. "He usually doesn't want to be disturbed. But since it is church business, let me check."

And in this way, Etha was ushered into the lawyer's inner sanctum.

He had pen to paper and, holding up one finger, signed the document laid
out before him with a flourish. After setting the paper aside, he raised his
immense head. Hodge was beefy all over but his head was huge, with a
jowly moon-shaped face and fleshy ears. All this was set off by a stiff shirt
collar that Etha knew, by the sweetish smell, Florence had achieved with
heavy doses of starch.

"And to what do I owe this honor?" he asked.

"I'm sorry to intrude. I hope this isn't a bad time."

He laced his fingers over the mound of his belly and tipped back.
The springs of his chair squealed. "There is always work to be done. But
I certainly have time when a lady from my church calls about some little
matter. That's my duty as an elder."

She smiled tightly. He was the last person she would seek advice
from, spiritual or otherwise, but she'd do this for Carmine. Removing a
hankie from her sleeve, she patted her forehead. "This will sound foolish,
but I am here about one of our shut-ins. Mrs. Hargrove?" She noticed
that the lawyer's fingers were squeezing impatiently. Strong piano hands,
she thought.

"I believe the church women have arranged to bring her meals?"

Etha nodded. "My day is Sunday. When I got to her house this
week—she lives a block down from yours as a matter of fact—she was
in a dither. Her cat had slipped out during the storm the day before and
hadn't come back. As of today he still hasn't turned up. I've been asking
neighbors if they might have seen the cat on Saturday taking shelter right
before the duster. I thought perhaps he got shut in a . . . an um . . . a
garage or shed. You have a shed out back, don't you?"

"I didn't see any cat. However, I will ask Florence."

"Oh, but Florence wasn't home during the storm. She said so herself
when I stopped by yesterday."

"You were at the house? Florence didn't tell me." Hodge's face
contracted.

Etha hastily added, "I was only there for a minute. She probably
forgot. I was running errands and felt faint. With the heat and all. Your
wife very kindly gave me a glass of water." Why did Etha suddenly feel
as if she had to protect the woman? "We chatted about the storm. It
occurred to me that maybe you caught a glimpse of Mr. Jinx."

"Who?"

"The cat. Mr. Jinx. It's a silly name, but you know how people—"

"I didn't."

Etha pushed on: "I thought maybe if you noticed something right before or even during the storm, you might have seen the cat . . . or something."

"Actually, I was at the pictures on Saturday. So, it seems I can be of no help on this little matter." He rose.

This didn't sit right. First, the idea of the lawyer attending a Saturday matinee by himself was almost as ludicrous as the image of him planting tomatoes. There was also a discrepancy between his account and Florence's. For a man who usually insisted on accompanying his wife to a fitting, as Lottie had said, why had he skipped out to the movies and then told his wife he was at the office?

There was no way to ask. She saw he was clearly expecting her to politely thank him and leave. Pronto. The room was sweltering. Trying to maintain the demeanor of the well-meaning church woman, Etha thanked him for his time and hurried out the door.

Later, when Etha delivered dinner to the cellblock, Carmine was sitting on the bunk, head bowed so low that his eyes were hidden. All she could see was the greasy crescent of hair flopped across his forehead.

"You must be starving," she said lightly. He mumbled and Etha had to ask him to repeat his words.

"Thanks, but not hungry."

"Goodness." She paused and set the tray down. "What's wrong?"

"My lawyer stopped by. Told me it doesn't look good—that the case against me is strong."

Etha stiffened.

Carmine shrugged. "So what's the use of eating? In a couple of months I'll be strapped into the chair and that'll be it."

"Don't even think that. I'm making progress on—"

"I'm sorry, ma'am, but I don't feel like talking."

And no matter how many times she tried to coax a word or two out, he refused until she finally slid the tray through the slot "for when you're hungry later," and slipped out the door feeling gut-punched.

Two floors below, Ed was gathering himself to ask Viviane to join him at the Maid-Rite later that evening. He waited until the two clerks were out to slip down the hall. He didn't want an audience if she turned him down. When he strolled in, she lifted her face from her typewriter. He took in the cool milk of her cheeks, the wash of freckles across her nose, the heavy brown hair.

"What can I do for you?" she asked.

Ed broke out in a sweat. "I'd like to treat you to a hamburger after work today. If that's okay with you, that is. I can drive you home afterward."

Viviane's lips, Ed noticed, were a particular shade of pink. She was saying something. The words eventually reached his ears: "Why yes. I'd like that."

And so, shortly after the courthouse clock struck five, Ed escorted Viviane out through the foyer. There wasn't much said during their walk to the Maid-Rite. Ed thought he might have mentioned the drought. Viviane may have answered. But something busted loose between them after they settled on two stools at the end of the counter and ordered. Ed suddenly found himself telling Viviane about his year in the CCC. The joy of toeing a shovel into the soil during a morning of honest work. It was like throwing open a window on the first warm day in May, he said. Welcome fresh air after a cramped winter. He told her about growing up in Chicago and the grimness that fell on the city after the economy soured.

When Ernie slid two hamburgers, buns glistening with grease, their way, Ed continued to talk and Viviane to listen. After a bit, Ernie came back, pointing out, fussily, that their supper was getting cold. Ed and Viviane grinned and dug in. Then Ed ordered a piece of pie to share. Viviane talked about the degradation of the soddie. How humiliated she had been when he drove her home that first time. How when she climbed out of bed each morning, an imprint of her head, outlined in dust, remained. She said her dream was to leave Jackson County. And that she was going to move to Oklahoma City or maybe even Chicago as soon as she could.

As they ate and talked, the life of the diner surged around them. An overalled man sat down on the stool next to Ed and nursed a cup of coffee for a long while. The Johnson boys, the quiet bachelor brothers, came in for their nightly supper of corned beef hash. Two teachers in print dresses spent twenty minutes gabbing about the upcoming school year as they fastidiously crushed Saltines into Ernie's chili.

It was going on seven o'clock when Viviane, glancing at her watch, exclaimed, "Goodness! I've got to get home. Let me run and powder my nose."

Ed paid up and watched as she made her way down the narrow hall to the ladies' room.

"That one's a keeper, I'd say," commented Trot, who was the latest occupant of the stool beside the deputy.

Ed, unaware of the comings and goings beside him, turned with a start. Trot produced a sunken grin. The smell of whiskey was strong. "Yes, well . . ."

"You know, when I was young I had a girl just as pretty. But I had to go away for a while and when I got back she was gone. Don't let that happen." Trot shook a finger at Ed. "Biggest mistake . . ." His voice dribbled off.

"Sorry to hear that," Ed said politely and turned away, but Trot had not yet run out of gas.

"Another thing. I see your badge there." He flapped a hand in an exaggerated fashion toward Ed's shield. "Got a ride from one of your kind after my machine broke down at that there auction. Much appreciated."

"Oh, yeah. The sheriff, I guess," Ed said, with his head still turned away and watching for Viviane's reappearance.

"'Twas him," Trot said, too loudly. "Told me about the arrest. CCC boy? Hard to believe. Just a kid."

"They grow up fast."

"I just hope you're sure of what you're doing. Hate to see an innocent kid take the heat."

Ed frowned. "If you're saying we're railroading the suspect through the system, you'd be wrong."

"Not saying that."

Viviane returned and Ed ushered her away from the old coot and out the door. As they drove to the soddie, Viviane complained about the county clerks, and Ed, half listening, plotted his next move—which was to invite her to the movies.

When he pulled down her lane, her parents and grandma were seated outside in the twilight while her brothers chased each other around the pump. They invited Ed to sit on one of the straight-backed chairs brought from the house. There was not much talk, just a silent appreciation of the cool air. The scrub turned from silver to purple and, far off, a single cottonwood stood sentry on the flat prairie. How beautiful, Ed thought, as desire and contentment rose in his chest.

C HAPTER SEVENTEEN

THE NEXT MORNING IT WAS BARELY EIGHT A.M. and yet, if hung outside, tobacco would cure in an hour—the air was that hot and dry. Another tick mark on a desiccated year. The fan in the sheriff's office blew hot air on the lawmen's necks. Temple was taking a phone call. Ed typed.

"I'll be snookered," Temple said at last, dropping the receiver into the cradle.

Ed glanced up. "What?"

The sheriff stepped to the bulletin board, thickly feathered with an array of foreclosure announcements and county regs, with the only visual relief being a couple of *Wanted* posters in garish fonts. With his thumb and middle finger, Temple thumped the mug shot of a spectacled man. "Alvin here and his pal Harry have been arrested."

Ed jumped up. "No kidding."

Both men were well-known criminals. Alvin Karpis, in and out of prison since he was sixteen, was wanted for kidnapping a banker and murdering a Missouri sheriff. Harry Flanagan was his getaway driver.

"Yep. The Texas boys tracked them down. Both are being escorted to Missouri under armed guard for extradition."

Ed emitted a low whistle.

"And guess what lockup the rangers are asking to use for an overnight stop?" Temple pivoted. "As if we don't have enough work with the Coombs case and the usual bunkum."

The telephone buzzed again. The caller's voice commandeered the receiver even before Temple could identify himself.

After a couple of minutes, the sheriff managed to wedge his toe into the flood of words. "Just the one," he said loudly. "Got a separate women's lockup but I don't see—" Another monologue overran Temple's voice. He rolled his eyes at Ed, then sighed, said, "Yes, I do. I'll take care of it. Will do."

"Now what?" Ed asked.

"Now they're wanting us to clear out the cellblock and move our prisoner to the kitchen lockup. Seems Alvin and Harry are at high risk for escape and the rangers don't want any back-and-forth between them and other inmates."

Someone tapped on the office door. Ed startled as if the two public enemies were busting in then and there. But it was only Viviane with a stack of papers that needed signatures.

"Put them with the other stuff I'm not going to get to," Temple said.

Viviane began tidying up the sheriff's desk, aligning the edges of the papers, brushing off eraser crumbs. She glanced shyly at Ed who smiled tightly in return.

Temple moved toward the door. "I'll let Etha know. Then we'll move DiNapoli."

Stepping into the apartment, Temple heard little Sally Clark lurching through a Mozart sonata as if she were a mule staggering under a load of bricks.

Temple leaned through the dining room doorway. "When you're finished," he said to Etha.

Ten minutes later, Sally was galloping out the kitchen door as if the place were on fire.

Etha trailed behind. Temple poured a cup of coffee.

"Problem?" she asked.

He raised the cup as if in toast. "You'll be happy to know we're moving DiNapoli into the cell here."

Etha pressed her palm against her chest. "Thank you."

"Don't thank me. Thank the Texas Rangers." He filled her in on the transport of the two criminals.

"Do you think it's safe? Having them next door?"

"Four rangers on duty around the clock. Steel doors. Wrist and ankle shackles. It's safe."

Etha exhaled. "I've been wanting to tell you that Carmine hasn't eaten since yesterday's breakfast. Just sits on his bunk studying his hands. He thinks he's going to the chair."

Temple rolled his lips between his teeth for a couple of beats, then said gently, "Honey, that is a possibility. If he is found guilty he—"

"But he's not!"

"That's for the jury to decide. I don't have time to nursemaid DiNapoli. We've got hardened killers on their way. Get this cell ready so we can move him over. Please."

Making sure a boy is fed and housed isn't coddling in my book, Etha thought with a sniff. She hauled two bags of turnips and a crate of canning jars from the cell and into the hallway. Then smoothed the wool blanket on the cot and brought in an extra pillow.

Twenty minutes later, low voices trickled from the cellblock. Then came the clank of shackles. She rushed to the bedroom, unable to bear the sight of Carmine in chains. After Temple's and Ed's footfalls receded to the lower floors, she emerged. Carmine was curled like a snail on the cot, his back to her. She studied the line of his shoulders, his skinny haunches.

"Hungry?"

He shook his head.

"I was going to bake up a big old pie."

Nothing.

The flour and lard were warm in her hands. After shaping the dough, she wrapped the ball and set it to chill in the icebox. Carmine's feet hung limply over the end of the cot. How to settle his mind? She drifted into the dining room to tidy up the sheet music scattered across the top of the upright. Music could take you away from your worries, sure enough. Carmine had been blowing on a harmonica the night she met him. She absentmindedly collected the loose song sheets. *Wonder if his harmonica is up at the CCC? Wouldn't hurt to take a drive over there and find out.*

Past the edge of town, Etha cranked down the car window to inhale the sun-baked grasses and dilute the reek of gasoline. The sedan lumbered along comfortably and her hopes lifted for some unknown reason.

She pulled into camp. The clusters of bunkhouses and open spaces were deserted. She stepped out of the car and adjusted her hat. Through the screen door of the office she spotted the commander. She tapped lightly.

"Can I interrupt?" she asked.

Raising his head from paperwork, Baker smiled and rose. "Sure enough. I don't get many visitors." He pushed open the door and gestured toward a chair. Etha settled in with her pocketbook on her lap.

"What brings you here?"

Etha had met Commander Baker only once, and her first thought had been of how well-ironed his shirt and pants were despite the fact that he was unmarried. It was the same today. The creases looked as sharp as knife blades. Above the pressed collar, his face was unreadable.

"It's about Carmine. He's in an awful spot and is just as nerved up as can be. He hasn't swallowed a morsel since yesterday noon."

"Sorry to hear that."

"And so I was thinking that maybe having his harmonica would help ease his mind."

The commander cocked his head. "Didn't know he played."

"He's quite good. I heard . . . I heard someone say so. And I was wondering, if his harmonica was here, if you'd let me take it to him."

Baker studied his laced fingers. "Don't see any harm. His things are here for safekeeping. I was getting ready to ask Temple what to do with them, as a matter of fact."

Etha smiled. "I truly think it will do him a world of good."

The commander crossed over to a large wooden storage cupboard. "Our first group of CCCers built this for me. Did a pretty good job, I'd say." He yanked on the door, which stuck a bit, and pulled out three canvas duffel bags. "We've had a couple of the corps run off in the middle of the night. Couldn't take the discipline, I guess. Not sure which bag is Carmine's."

He peered inside the first two and tossed them back into the cupboard. The third he plopped on his desk chair, yanked its drawstring, and reached in. Out came a crumpled work shirt with *DiNapoli* stenciled inside the collar. A thin towel, four pairs of rolled socks, two *Popular Science* magazines, and a battered edition of *The Maltese Falcon* emerged.

"He might want that," Etha said, reaching for the book. "If you don't mind."

Baker waved. "Sure. Not locating a harmonica as yet." He dug deeper.

Etha absently flipped through the *Falcon*'s pages. A snapshot that had been tucked between the leaves fell to the floor. Before an ivy-covered wall, a woman in a limp dress posed with a baby. Both stared directly into the lens. Her heavy-lidded eyes were dark, as were the child's.

"Carmine and his mother! Don't you think?" Etha exclaimed.

Baker squinted at the photo. "Could be."

"It is! Spitting image." Etha patted her mouth. "Such a shame to lose his mama. Does she look poorly to you?"

Baker leaned forward. "Maybe." His fingers deep in the bag, the commander's face lit up. "Got it."

The dime-store harmonica had been played hard. Its frilly engraved lettering was mucked with sweat and saliva.

"Seen many a mile," Baker said, handing it to Etha, who wrapped it in a clean hankie and tucked it into her purse along with the book and the snapshot.

"I can't thank you enough," she said, rising and smoothing her dress.

Back home, Carmine was stretched out on the cot, motionless as a rabbit gone to ground.

"I brought you a few things from camp." No response. Etha decided to carry on as if they were having a conversation. "Your harmonica and the detective book."

Nothing.

She kneeled and slid them under the bars.

"Now I'm going to bake up that pie. I'm betting you're a pecan man, right?" Etha drew the apron over her head, removed the dough from the icebox, and lit the oven. She hummed "Let Me Call You Sweetheart," a song from her girlhood. As she smoothed the dough, she kept her eyes on the rolling pin, thinking Carmine was more likely to thaw if unobserved.

When the pie was assembled and ushered into the warm oven, she finally turned. Carmine was sitting up, more or less, with his chin sunk to his sternum and arms limp. But he was upright. *The Maltese Falcon* was not in sight.

Etha drew up a chair. "Any chance you know 'By the Light of the Silvery Moon'?"

Carmine raised his head sluggishly, his eyes dull with misery. "No ma'am."

Hearing the heaviness in his words, Etha wanted to cry but pushed her voice into the upper range of false cheer. "Yes, I guess that's before your time. How about . . . well, what do you like to play?"

He shrugged.

"Oh, come on."

He picked up the harmonica off the floor. Rubbed it against his thigh. The bang of a door slamming two floors below echoed up the stairwell.

"Guess this one, sort of." Carmine pursed his lips and, warming up, blew out a couple of scales. The opening notes of "California, Here I Come" issued from his lips, warbling through the reed.

Etha smiled. "Give it some snap."

Carmine picked up the pace; the notes straightened their spines.

"Hey, I've got sheet music for that. Hold on."

Carmine smacked the mouth organ into his palm, clearing it of spit.

Etha rushed into the dining room. "Got it," she called out. She settled herself at the keyboard, fingers rounded. "Come in on three."

Etha counted off loudly, then they both jumped in. They ran through the song twice.

Back in the kitchen Etha said, "We're getting there. You need to slow down on the chorus. And come to a full stop on the fourth bar."

"Bar?"

Etha knuckled her hips. "You can't read music, can you?"

He shrugged.

"I'm going to teach you." She snatched the key to the lockup from off the nail beside the door and opened the cell. "Come on. I'll show you what I'm talking about."

Carmine hesitated. "I don't think I'm supposed—"

"Don't be silly. The piano's this way." Etha marched toward the dining room. Carmine hesitated again, then followed, the harmonica pressed to his breastbone.

Patting the bench, Etha said, "Sit beside me. Now, see this big fat note all alone? That's the *come* as in, *California, here I come.* You're not sitting on it long enough. Listen."

Etha hit the keys firmly, depressing the A down good and long. "Hold it for four beats. See?"

"Maybe."

"Let's run through it again. Watch my fingers and try to match my rhythm."

By the time they zipped through the sixth run-through, Carmine was swaying side to side and, Etha noticed, his eyes were clearer.

"Again!" Etha shouted, and Carmine stomped his foot three times to get them started. They were generating speed and bringing it home—

"What in the hell is going on?" Temple thundered, striding across the room and grabbing Carmine by the arm. "Are you crazy, Etha? He's been arrested for murder. Bashed a man's brains in. He could have done the same to you just now."

"He wouldn't!" The words burst from Etha's mouth.

Temple pushed Carmine back toward the kitchen.

Etha wailed, "I'm sorry! I'm sorry!"

Temple turned, his lips pressed into a tight line. "This kid is accused of murder. I don't know why you can't get that through your head."

She opened her mouth to reply but no words came out. He gave DiNapoli another shove and the boy stumbled forward into the cell. After locking it, Temple moved to hang the key on its hook, but paused, then pocketed it instead. Slamming the apartment's outer door, he stomped down the front steps flushed with rage.

Out on the broad granite steps of the courthouse, he lit a cigarette. His hand shook. Usually in late afternoon, the air softened so that the ever-present dust on the cars and awnings took on a velvety nap. But today the sun reflected harshly off cars and sidewalks. Temple ground out the butt until it was nothing but a mush of tobacco and shredded paper. He lit another. Letting DiNapoli out of the lockup to roam freely in their house. Playing a hootenanny with him, for God's sake. What was Etha thinking? Temple snorted. He knew exactly what she was thinking. She'd mixed up DiNapoli with Jack somehow. I'll be damned if I see it, he thought. She's talking herself into something that isn't there. DiNapoli's nothing more than a city tough. And hotheaded to boot.

Temple's anger was still at full boil when two black sedans, heavy as tanks, rolled up the street from Route 34. The rangers and their captives had arrived. Temple shouted for Ed to open the cellblock, then hurried to wave the sedans into the courthouse lot. The first car was driven by a lanky ranger in a frayed dress shirt and trousers. There was another lawman in the front passenger seat and, in the back, two more sandwiching a slumped and shackled prisoner. Temple's first thought was that the convict, who he didn't recognize, must be sweltering, packed like a steer in a crowding pen—the final stage before the chute and slaughter floor. The second car had an identical set of passengers. Except Temple knew the criminal right off. Alvin "Old Creepy" Karpis was well known to most lawmen. Once the hand brakes were yanked on the sedans, the cars emptied, with the drivers and passengers flexing themselves.

"Long drive?" Temple asked the lawman who was approaching, hand extended, with a gold Texas Ranger badge glinting on his shirt pocket.

"You can say that again. I went to spit and it turned to steam before hitting the asphalt. I'm Captain Yarbrough."

Temple grinned. "Sheriff Temple Jennings. Welcome to Oklahoma."

"Not much different than Texas. So, you all set to show our lodgers to their rooms?"

The lawmen closed ranks around their prisoners and followed Temple into the courthouse. The drivers stayed in the shade of a cottonwood as the sedans' radiators cracked and cooled.

It took awhile to get to the top floor as Yarbrough refused to unshackle the prisoners' ankles. "Those two," he said, jabbing a finger toward Old Creepy and Flanagan, "can't be trusted. If given half a chance, they'll leg it for sure. Those irons stay put until we turn them over to the feds. Then this pair is *their* problem."

Ed, his face tense, led the prisoners to the two cells at either end of the block. When Creepy was secured, Ed's eyes darted to Temple, who gave a slight nod of reassurance. Flanagan, just a kid with barely enough whiskers to grow a downy mustache, crumpled in a heap on the bunk, awkwardly drawing his knees up to his chest. Creepy toured his cell as if he was deciding whether to move in or not. He fingered the woolen blanket, flushed the john, and twisted the tap this way and that. Then, with a disturbing grin, from whence his nickname came, he said, "Got a complaint here about the blanket. I'm allergic to wool."

Yarbrough, ignoring the remark, directed the four rangers to take the first watch—two inside the jail and two standing in the hallway. As Creepy continued to make a case about the blanket, Yarbrough turned to Temple and Ed, gesturing them toward the outer door.

"Got a good setup here. I appreciate your cooperation."

Temple nodded. "I'll ask my wife to make some sandwiches for your men. And I've arranged for two rooms at the boarding house a couple of blocks from here so you all can rest up between shifts."

Yarbrough extended his hand. "Thank you kindly." He began to turn away when Temple grabbed his arm.

"One other thing. My wife and I live right here." He pointed to the apartment door. "I'd appreciate it if you would advise your men of that. It makes me nervous, I'll admit, to have those two only a wall away from my Etha."

Yarbrough grinned. "Don't you worry. My fellows are as sharp as they come. Handpicked for this detail. You can sleep sound tonight. You've got my word on it." The captain then said to Ed, "Tell the drivers I'm on my way."

As Ed hustled down the stairs, Temple chuckled. "This is his first encounter with professional killers. I'm betting he's happy as a clam that he won't be sleeping here tonight."

Earlier, after Temple had roughly deposited Carmine back in the lockup and stomped out, Etha had first retreated to the bathroom. When she finally emerged, blanched and drawn, Carmine was on the bunk facing the wall. Seeing the curls budding at his neckline where his haircut was growing out made her weepy. Oh for goodness sake, she admonished herself. She had come down to the empty courtroom below the apartment to pull herself together. After a good long cry she blew her nose and felt better. It was then she heard Temple talking on the landing outside the courtroom. She opened the door a crack.

". . . and I'm sure he'll get right on it," Temple was saying to a uniformed man who nodded and jogged down the steps.

Etha opened the door wider. "We need to talk."

Startled, Temple pivoted. "What? What are you doing there?"

"Needed a quiet place to think. We need to—"

"This is not a good time. I'm right in the middle of something, and besides that, I'm still mad as hell. I don't want to say something I'll regret." His cheeks reddened.

"It's important. You know I wouldn't ask if it wasn't."

"Give me five minutes. The Texas Rangers brought in their prisoners and I need to make sure everything's nailed down."

Etha covered her lips with her hand. "I forgot all about that."

"So now you can understand why I'm pressed." He descended the steps, his footfalls echoing heavily down the stairwell.

It was not five but a full thirty minutes before Temple reappeared. He slid a chair out and sat at the table across from his wife. "Okay. Shoot."

"First off, I want to apologize again for letting Carmine out of the cell. That was foolish and—"

"I don't give a damn about the foolish part. I care about the danger. You don't seem to be able to get it through your head that DiNapoli is accused of crushing another man's skull in, and who's to say he wouldn't have done the same to you and then run off?"

"I know he wouldn't do that. He's not a killer."

Temple squeezed his eyes shut. "It's bad enough you put yourself in danger, but when I can't trust that you will obey the workings of my office, when it is clear you have taken to deciding on your own who is innocent and who is guilty, then I am pushed way past my limit. It is for the judge and jury to decide DiNapoli's fate. It is my job, not yours, to gather the evidence and make the case."

Etha felt as if she were young child receiving a scolding. "That may be true. But this time, you got it wrong. I've been doing some checking and the story you have built up about Carmine has holes in it."

Neither spoke. The regulator clock mounted behind the judge's bench ticked loudly. Etha slapped her hands on the desk. "So," she began, dropping into a softer tone, "Saturday, when I borrowed the car, I didn't go where I said. I had got it into my head to take dinner to the tramps out by the tracks. Foolish. I know. But seeing a youngster begging at the back door of Ernie's got me going. I pulled into the camp with boxes of fried chicken, sugar, and coffee. I almost turned around, I was that scared. But when Carmine and another boy trotted over, eager and hungry, the heebie-jeebies vanished. There must have been twenty tramps, at least half of them just teenagers or even younger, hunkered around a fire. You should have seen them dig into my chicken! I stayed awhile. Carmine tooted on the harmonica and someone else brought out a bottle and I took a sip or two. It felt good to let loose."

Temple tilted back in his chair. "Go on."

"Anyway, at the end of the night I let slip that my husband was sheriff, and you can guess how that went over. But Carmine didn't flinch, he walked me to the car and made sure I got on my way without a problem. If he'd been guilty, he would have been shaking in his boots when he found out who I was. But he was as steady as they come. You know how it is when you meet someone for the first time and you see right off they're good through and through? That's how it was with Carmine. Knew it in my heart. So when you told me that he'd gotten into a fight with Coombs, that Coombs had turned up dead the next day and that you suspected Carmine, I knew he couldn't have done it. No matter how bad it seemed. So I set out to prove he didn't."

Temple's chair slammed onto the floor. "What?"

Etha focused on his eyes. "Just hear me out. Then you can holler all you want." She explained how she had found what might have been the shed with the sack of corncobs where Carmine had bedded down after the fight at the Idle Hour. How it was in the Hodges' backyard and the place fit Carmine's description to a T. Then she fessed up to sneaking into Hinchie's office with Minnie to inspect the murder weapon. She described how she'd learned that the hardware store sold the same army shovels that the CCC boys used and discovered Hodge had purchased one last week.

"So," she wrapped up, "Carmine was telling the truth about the shed. And he was not the only person with access to those kinds of shovels. In fact, at least a dozen locals plus other CCCers could lay their hands on one without batting an eye." She folded her hands on the table. "That's what I've found." She waited.

Temple ran his tongue over his bottom teeth. "I think that you proved the murder weapon was widely available. But that's all. DiNapoli still has the strongest motive, access to the victim, blood on his clothing, the man's lighter stashed in his duffel, and he's a hothead. So, I heard you out but my mind is unchanged." He rose, tucking the chair under the table with exaggerated precision. "I'm going back downstairs to finish the paperwork. It's been a long day."

CHAPTER EIGHTEEN

IT MIGHT HAVE BEEN FIVE MINUTES OR AN HOUR. Etha lost track of time as she paced the empty courtroom, jerking wayward chairs into place, yanking the long blinds up and down. Temple hadn't listened to a single thing. Her findings about the shovel had been as tidy as a trimmed seam. Surely they had enough substance to merit at least *considering* other suspects. And hadn't she practically groveled? About something as minor as tiptoeing behind his back for the trip to the tracks? She was on a mission of good works, for God's sake, not committing a federal crime.

Back in the kitchen, Carmine was softly blowing on the harmonica. He quickly put it down and stood as she walked in.

"Did the sheriff blow a gasket?" he asked.

"Yes, but he's angry with me, not you. And I'm angry with him, so we're even."

Carmine sat on the bunk with a thump.

Etha slipped her apron over her head. She dipped into the icebox and pulled out a pound of sliced bologna. "It'll be slim pickings for the lawmen's lunch. But I think I have enough to make a couple of sandwiches for you too. Tide you over until dinner."

In the dining room that evening, Temple and Etha ate in silence. Afterward, Temple excused himself. "Going over to make sure the rangers are settled in."

"Of course," Etha said.

As she washed up, she noticed that Carmine was lost in the final pages of *The Maltese Falcon.* She had read it and, with a cold feeling in her gut, remembered those last few lines where Sam Spade says, *If they hang you I'll always remember you.* She scooped a generous spoonful of cobbler into a bowl and passed it through the bars.

"Late-night snack."

Carmine glanced up with a wisp of a smile, and again, in the tilt of his head, for a quick second, she saw Jack. "Thanks, ma'am. If I wasn't in so much trouble with the law, I would say being here with you has been the closest I've been to home since . . . well, for a long time."

Etha hurried into the living room and turned on the radio. It wasn't going to help Carmine to see her bawling.

She jerked awake near midnight. She was slumped sideways in the armchair with the radio humming. She walked stiffly into the bedroom to change and saw, with surprise, that Temple wasn't there. Maybe, she thought, he'd gotten an emergency call, but it was more likely he was still fuming. She'd never seen him so angry. But then again, she'd never been this angry at him. She changed into her night clothes, turned on the bedroom's electric fan, and shuffled into the bathroom where she brushed her teeth and twisted her hair into pin curls. Sliding between the sheets she thought to stay awake until Temple came in, but her eyelids drifted downward and she gave up.

The stalemate between Etha and Temple continued through Sunday. As dawn broke on Monday, she was sunk in a dream. Shouting, pushing her way through a crowd toward Carmine's body collapsed in a chair, his arms strapped down with thick black leather belts. Her thumping heart woke her, panicked and disoriented. Then the familiar wooden dresser came into view as did the curtains and the buzzing fan. She turned to see if she had awakened Temple but he must have come and gone. The sheets on his side had been slept in but were now empty.

All right, mister, she thought, if you're going to dig your heels in, so will I. She bathed, dressed, and made breakfast while Carmine slept heavily. After slipping a plate of biscuits into the lockup, and delivering trays to a ranger for the cellblock inmates, she marched downstairs. Ed was in the office. Temple, he said, was out answering a call about a stolen heifer. The rangers were due to get on the road with their prisoners in about an hour, he added.

"If he comes back and asks for me, please let him know I fed the prisoners and I'm out running errands," she said in a businesslike tone. Temple couldn't accuse her of forgetting her duties as jailhouse cook.

In the middle of the night it had occurred to Etha that Roland Coombs might not have been able to bring rain—that it wasn't really possible.

Not a thing he or any other man could call down. Maybe someone from another town, who had paid Coombs good money for nothing, had come after him. A bit of research at the library was in order.

The first time she had stepped into Vermillion's library, Etha was crestfallen. The entire one-story wooden structure could fit easily into the vestibule of Peoria's grand two-story brick-and-granite institution. And the shelves were woefully skimpy, with many of the books hand-me-downs from local families. More than once Etha had eagerly plunged into a novel only to find crucial pages missing. But over the years she had made peace with the place.

Miss Fisher sat behind the circulation desk, sorting check-out cards into tidy piles. The librarian had an extensive collection of matching earring-and-brooch sets. Today, tiny enameled blue flowers graced her ears and bosom. After exchanging greetings, Etha entered the reading room on the right. Dictionaries and almanacs dominated the small reference section tucked in one corner. The *Encyclopedia Britannica* was missing volumes 5 and 19, but was otherwise complete. Not whole but serviceable, like an old man's teeth, Etha thought. The rainmaking listing referred Etha to the entry on magic. The subsection of *pluviculture* yielded a lengthy description of a certain Dieri tribe in Central Australia. The Dieris summoned rain by slashing the arms of young men and dripping their blood onto two elders. The blood represented rain. Other men tossed feathers into the air, signifying clouds.

"My," Etha said loudly, before remembering where she was. She glanced around guiltily. Miss Fisher remained bent over the typewriter. The reading room opposite had a single occupant. All Etha could see of the woman were her substantial legs, sturdy enough to support a piano, the remainder being concealed behind the generous sheets of the *Oklahoma City Times*. Both the librarian and reader seemed oblivious to Etha's outburst. She returned to her research, but it was soon clear that the encyclopedia wasn't going to bear fruit. There were a few other mentions of rainmaking ceremonies performed by ancient tribes before the entry ended. Even though she had not been at Coombs's public event, Etha certainly would have heard if he'd been smearing onlookers with blood or tossing feathers. Disappointed, Etha slid the volumes back onto the shelf.

Returning to the circulation desk, she asked Miss Fisher about scientific periodicals that might report on modern-day rainmaking methods. The librarian cast her gaze upward. "Of course, my first thought on that is *Popular Science*, but we don't subscribe. Too expensive. I may have . . . Just a minute." She jumped from her seat and raced into the stacks. A few minutes later, she returned empty-handed. "I thought that maybe a chemistry textbook might have something on that, but no go."

Etha sighed. She'd have to look elsewhere to find out whether Coombs's methods were scientific or pure bunkum. However, Miss Fisher beamed when Etha asked about a Hammett mystery.

"I've got everything he's published," she said proudly. "Short stories and novels. Have you read *The Red Harvest*?"

When Etha shook her head, Miss Fisher chirped, "You must! It's his best. Better than the *Falcon*, in my opinion."

As Etha turned to leave, with the novel in hand, the woman in the reading room lowered the newspaper to turn the page.

It was Minnie Hinchie. Etha had not seen her friend since they had crept into Dr. Hinchie's office for a peek at the murder weapon. Minnie spotted her at the same instant.

"What brings you here?" Minnie asked, indicating the armchair beside hers. "More detective work?" she added in lower tones.

"Sort of, but no luck. You?"

"I'm hiding. Mrs. Fitzgerald is due at the office," she glanced at her watch, "right about now with three kids, all under the age of four. Seems they are coughing their heads off. I took the phone call and could hear them in the background, hacking like coal miners. As soon as I gave Hinchie the message, I fled."

Etha laughed. "And I see you had success with your shoes."

Minnie stretched out one leg and twirled her ankle. "Of a sort. The cardboard slips some but if I walk very slowly it works." She put the newspaper aside. "Actually, I've been wanting to talk to you. I'm worried about Temple's chances in the election."

Etha frowned. "What?"

"A lot of Hinchie's patients *and* the ladies in my sewing guild told me they aren't voting for him."

Etha straightened, her voice strident: "Why not?"

"It seems that while everyone likes Temple, there is a strong feeling that he isn't forceful. That he has a soft spot for the down-and-outers. A lot say he's too easy on the moonshiners."

"That's not true!" Etha shot back.

"I know, but that is what they're saying. There's also talk that he should have stopped those low-ball bids at the Fullers' farm auction. I'm guessing that Vince Doll is spreading rumors and some folks are swallowing them."

"I don't understand. Why would anyone turn against Temple for looking the other way when a man is trying to feed his family? Goodness, everyone in the whole county is a down-and-outer."

Minnie leaned forward. "But they don't see themselves that way. Most of these folks are from town. They forget that they're stuffing cardboard in their shoes just like everyone else."

Etha studied the map of the Oklahoma Territory hanging on the opposite wall. "Even if this is so, even if most of Vermillion's swells are supporting Doll, that still leaves all the farm folk. Surely they're on Temple's side. And they are in the majority."

Minnie shook her head. "Not anymore. At least half have decamped for California. Hinchie says he's lost at least fifteen patients in the past six months."

Etha thought of her own shrinking cadre of piano students. Thunderclouds massed in her stomach, moved north into her ribs and throat. "But if Temple loses, what will happen to us? Where will we go?"

Patting her friend's hand, Minnie said, "The primary isn't lost yet. But Temple needs to glad-hand. Make his case known."

"But he's already overextended, what with the murder case plus the usual—"

"I know, but it's the hard truth. He needs to do some old-fashioned campaigning. When I hear this kind of talk about Temple not being the man for the office, I give folks a piece of my mind, but they want to hear it from him." Minnie sat back. "I don't like to be the bearer of bad tidings, but . . ."

Etha smiled weakly. "No, I appreciate it. I'm just not sure if he'll listen to me on this." Or anything right now, she thought.

"I can prod Hinchie into talking to Temple, if you think that would help."

"Thanks. Yes." Etha stood. "I've got to scoot. Piano lessons."

On the way home, Etha felt as if every little bit of joy had been squeezed out of her. She wasn't any closer to proving Carmine innocent, Temple was so furious he couldn't even stand to be around her, and now this.

She was passing the alley beside the Jewel where Coombs was killed when Minnie's warning about the election really sank in. Etha had understood all along that Temple's job was on the line and that meant their apartment was too. Vermillion had never truly been home, and just last week hadn't she thought that a primary loss might be the best way to get Temple back to Illinois? But now everything was different. It wasn't the job or the apartment, it was Carmine. If they moved away she would be separated from him. The young man who had brought back a bit of Jack. The young man who needed her. Even if he ended up in prison, she could travel to the state penitentiary for visits. But she was going to make sure that didn't happen. And somehow make sure that Temple was reelected.

Etha quickened her pace. The election was just over a week away and time was suddenly speeding up.

At the courthouse, the sheriff's office was empty. She hustled upstairs. Opening the apartment door, the first thing she saw was that the bedding in the lockup was missing. Carmine's pitifully small pile of belongings was gone, as was the young man himself. Her heart thudded. Had Temple transferred Carmine to the federal prison because of Etha's foolishness? She pressed her fingers against her lips and the tears came.

When Temple strode in she was slumped with her back against the sink, her face wet and blotched. His eyes were not unkind, but exasperation lingered around his mouth. After thirty years of marriage, she could read the smallest twinges in his face. Stubborn man.

He handed her his clean handkerchief. "Your boy's all right, if that's what you're going on about. I moved him back to the cellblock."

"I . . . Can I see him? I brought him a book from the library." She blew her nose vigorously.

"Give it to me. Ed'll take care of it." Temple drew his hand heavily across his jaw. "You still don't get it, do you? DiNapoli is up for *murder!*"

"You're still angry with me."

"What do you think?"

She pulled up her chin. "I think you're a bull-headed fool. And Minnie says the primary is on the line."

Temple chuckled grimly. "You sure do know how to make a fellow feel good."

"I just wanted to lend him this to pass the time."

Temple raised his arms. "Uncle! Go on and do your good deed. I've got work to do." He strode out abruptly.

He might have been soaring over Alaska with Will Rogers, he seemed that far away. In the mirror above the bathroom sink, where Etha was shakily patting cold water on her face, she saw the stiffness around her mouth. She hated it when she and Temple fought. But this time she knew she was right, and although it shook her, she was not bending. Etha retrieved *The Red Harvest* from the kitchen counter and was almost out the door when she noticed a scrap of white under the lockup's cot. It was the snapshot that had been tucked in *The Maltese Falcon*. It must have fallen out when Carmine was moved back to the cellblock. Etha picked it up, taking a moment to gaze again at the hollowed-out woman clutching the baby in frilly clothes, and then tucked it in her pocket.

Carmine was slapping the harmonica in his palm when she entered. Seeing her, his face brightened. "Back to square one," he joked sourly.

"Not for long, I hope. In the meantime, I got you another Hammett."

She passed the book through the bars and Carmine immediately flipped through it. "Swell!"

"And," she said, drawing out the photograph, "this got left behind."

Carmine flushed and hurriedly slotted it into the book.

"Your ma?" Etha asked quietly. "And you?"

He nodded.

"You are her spitting image. You know that?"

After a moment of silence, Carmine's words came out low and throaty: "She was a waitress."

"What about your pa?"

"He had a bunch of jobs. None stuck for long."

"And then?"

"And then Ma got an ulcer in her, ah . . ." He pointed to his chest.

Etha covered her mouth. "I'm sorry."

"Yeah, well."

"How old were you?"

"Eight."

Etha groaned.

"I remember getting back to the apartment after the funeral and thinking she would be there. What a dumbo."

"No! Not at all. I lost a son. He was the same age as you when your ma died. I thought the same thing. Still do, sometimes." Etha gestured at the bars. "And don't you worry, I'm going to make this right."

* * *

When the afternoon's piano lessons were over, Etha took a paring knife to the membrane of that evening's liver. As she slipped the blade under the transparent tissue, she thought of her next move. The idea that Coombs's killer was a previous client of the rainmaker, one who had discovered a flimflam, was still worth pursuing. If only she could find out if Coombs's effects included a client list. Temple isn't going to tell me, that's for sure, she thought. But Ed . . . now that was a possibility. First thing in the morning she'd make a point to talk to the deputy. She'd have to get him alone for a minute, but that could be handled by asking for his help with the kitchen faucet or something. If Coombs did have a list of clients, she could be on the phone and maybe have a suspect or two by the end of the day. Something to give Temple pause. Think that maybe he needed to look beyond Carmine.

The liver was overdone by the time Temple made it home. Their meal was another silent affair, both resentfully chewing on the tough meat. After plunking down the pie and a cup of coffee, Etha retreated to the living room. The radio buzzed, there was a swirl of static, and then a strident dance tune surfaced. Still seated at the table, Temple pressed a finger above his right eye where the throb of a headache bloomed. His anger at Etha and his worries about the election pressed in from all sides. He jerked his chair back, called out, "Going for a drive," and was out the door.

The night was oppressive. The sedan's steering wheel was hot to the touch. Temple drove aimlessly for an hour. Many of the farms were deserted, with shreds of lace at the windows and voiceless dinner bells standing sentinel on poles. He drove by open stretches that, in the twilight, might pass for a field of sweet potatoes, but in reality were sowed with nothing but fine silt. Not a living thing was about except for the occasional jackrabbit whipping past. Temple's mind emptied and then gradually filled.

The primary. That was a big knot. Was it really on the line, as Etha had said? It seemed that most folks, except maybe Jess Fuller and other farmers he'd had to evict, were satisfied enough. Temple prided himself on fairness. Getting the job done but bending a bit when someone couldn't pay their fines right away. He was known to issue warnings instead of warrants to first-time offenders. But he had to admit that he hadn't done much campaigning. Wasn't keeping the peace enough to get the vote? He drove by the Fuller house. Dark. Temple had heard that Jess was still living there even though Hazel and the kids had moved out. Jess was likely at the Idle Hour, he thought. That's where I would be if Etha picked up and left. And Etha. Why in the hell was she championing that no-count kid? Snooping around town to dig up proof that didn't exist. And letting him out of the lockup. DiNapoli could have run off, and how the hell would that have looked to voters? Or worse, he could have taken liberties with Etha.

Canopies of dust draped the night sky. Temple traveled randomly, following whichever patch of asphalt presented itself in the headlamps' brilliance. After a time, he pulled over and stepped out of the sedan, its motor clicking as it cooled. From not far off came the stink of burning cow chips. He glanced around and saw that he was at the same intersection he'd stopped at on the day of the Brown Blizzard. The wooden CCC sign and Doll's election placards stood as they had a week ago. But now everything had changed.

Temple scooped a handful of stones from the sandy soil and began pitching them, one by one, Dizzy Dean style. *Phumpf.* The rock hit hardpan. Etha had lied to him. Had there been other lies that he didn't know about? The dry earth absorbed the stoning. The cartilage in his shoulder ground and still he threw fast and hard. She could not let the boy go. Refused to let their boy Jack go. It came down to that.

CHAPTER NINETEEN

ETHA AWOKE TO AN EMPTY BED the third morning in a row. Temple had slipped in and out without a word. She was a light sleeper. He must have taken extraordinary measures not to rouse me and fall into another quarrel, she thought glumly. She was, however, still determined to find Coombs's real killer, even if it meant a week of the silent treatment. Wheedling information out of Ed was at the top of her list.

After breakfast, she hovered at the kitchen window, eyeing the county car that Temple drove on midmorning patrols. Within ten minutes she spotted him walking across the parking lot, then heard the engine sputtering. She hustled downstairs.

Ed stood at the overstuffed filing cabinet trying to jimmy a folder into a drawer. A wry smile crossed his face. "Either we need another file cabinet or less paperwork."

"Could be." She crossed over, took the file from his hand, and neatly finessed it inside.

Ed laughed. "Guess it's my technique. Temple's on morning rounds."

"Actually, I wanted to talk to you about . . ." Etha began, when Maxine hurried in.

"Sorry I'm late," she said to Ed. "I had to babysit the brat again."

"Understood," Ed said. "Mrs. Jennings, is this something that could wait? I have some paperwork for Maxine to sign."

Maxine, Etha observed, was wearing a floral-print dress that suspiciously resembled her Sunday best, and white anklets with low-heeled sandals that might have belonged to her mother.

Suddenly, as if she'd just noticed Etha, Maxine said, "Gosh. Am I interrupting?"

Etha smiled. "Nothing that can't wait for a bit. Ed, just give me a buzz when you're through here?" Moving toward the door, she turned and saw Ed gesturing to the chair beside his desk. Maxine sat, coyly arranging her skirt.

"I need you to sign here and here," he said, tapping a paper with his index finger.

Etha noticed that Maxine was leaning eagerly toward the deputy. Was she wearing lipstick? She had certainly made an effort with the dress and shoes and a couple of bobby pins. Something else was different too, but Etha couldn't puzzle out what it was. As she trudged up the three flights, her brain picked at the knot. It was not until her hand fell on the knob of the apartment door that it came to her. Glasses. Maxine wasn't wearing her glasses. She froze for a moment, then clattered downstairs. When she reached the vestibule, Maxine was already walking through the courthouse's tall oak doors.

Etha called out her name, and when Maxine turned, her face was as naked as the day she was born. Inside her rib cage, Etha's heart beat wildly. "Tell you mother I said hello," she called, her voice choked with excitement.

Back in the sheriff's office, the deputy plucked at the typewriter keys.

"I need to ask you something," Etha said hurriedly.

Ed laughed. "I was going to call you, honest. Just need to finish up."

He pounded out a couple more lines. Etha skittishly sat on Temple's chair as if it were made of glass. At last Ed was pulling the paper from the carriage.

"Okay. Shoot."

Etha inhaled. "I want you to think carefully before you answer. Promise?"

"Do my best."

"When you drove Maxine out to the CCC camp the other day for the identification, was she wearing glasses?"

"What? Sure! I mean I think—" He broke off.

A shade slapped in a sudden gust of wind. Ed turned toward the window, gazing out abstractly. Shadows pooled under the awnings of the storefronts across the way. They appeared cool and inviting, but not everything was as it seemed. Ed pushed his thoughts back to the first time he had interviewed Maxine. He'd helped her with that jigsaw puzzle. She was nothing but a kid. And she had been wearing specs. Definitely. He remembered her pushing them up on her nose as she bent over the pieces. But what about when he'd driven her to the lineup? He tried to conjure her face, but couldn't remember. Walk yourself through, he thought. Pulled up at the house. Maxine was on the porch, whispering with a girlfriend. She'd seemed different, older somehow. Her mom was around back hanging laundry. He remembered the unsavory thought that this was being treated like a date. Then off they went, with Cliff bouncing in the backseat, squealing like a siren and Maxine shushing him. The CCC boys milled outside the commander's cabin. Ed remembered cautioning her to take her time, to look carefully. And then her profile emerged in his mind's eye. The sharp chin, the barrette angled above the ear, her eyes narrowed into a squint. But no glasses. *No glasses!*

He turned to Etha with a stricken face. "She wasn't wearing them. How could I have been so stupid?" He dropped his head into his hands.

"Don't be hard on yourself," Etha said softly.

Ed jerked up. "I've got to tell Temple right away. Maxine's identification made the case. He'll be mad as hell. Pardon me. I've made us look like fools!"

"He'll get past it," Etha said. "No matter what, Temple wouldn't want to have a hand in the conviction of an innocent young man. At least it didn't go to trial . . ." Her voice petered out.

"Yeah," Ed said morosely.

Etha stood and squeezed Ed's shoulder. "It'll be all right."

"Maybe."

The phone rang and they both jumped.

Ed took up his pad and pencil and lifted the receiver. In a flat tone he said, "Sheriff's office."

Etha retreated, closing the office door carefully behind her. She couldn't believe it. Could Carmine be freed as easily as that? The tight space beneath her breastbone expanded. She took a deep breath for the first time in days.

As she passed the cellblock she hesitated. The urge to rush in and tell Carmine was strong but she thought better of it. It was not her place and might be premature at that. But she was bursting to talk. The second she walked in the door, she went straight to the phone. Minnie answered on the first ring.

"I've got good news!" Etha exclaimed giddily.

Minnie sighed. "I could use some. Mrs. Fitzgerald and her brood are back. Seems the children don't have colds but dust pneumonia, poor things."

"That's awful!"

"Hinchie is trying to talk her into taking the kids . . ." A barking cough in the background drowned out Minnie's voice for a moment. ". . . to the hospital in Enid. Get them away from the dust. In the meantime, I'm smearing their nostrils with Vaseline. Seems to give some relief. What's your news?"

Etha launched into her story of noticing the missing glasses and the possibility that Carmine was wrongly identified. "So it seems likely that he'll be released. I mean, without the identification, the case is pretty weak. Temple said so himself. I can't tell you what a relief that would be."

"Certainly that's good news for the boy. And for you. You seem fond of him."

"He's a good kid with no mother to stick up for him."

"But you do know that arresting the wrong man will not help Temple's stance with the voters. Not one iota. So, while you celebrate with the boy, you better be also thinking about ways to get Temple reelected."

Etha grew still. "I hadn't thought of that."

"And I hate to pile on more gloom, but on my way home from the library I stopped by the *Gazetteer* offices to have a frank talk with Hank about the election. He's not hearing good things about Temple's chances either."

"No!"

"If he says there's a problem, I believe him. Hank knows the county like the back of his hand. Apparently Jess Fuller, the farmer from last week's auction, is still fuming even though it turned out he's hung on to his property for now. He's spreading venom about the bank, the auctioneer, the sheriff's office—anyone and everyone involved."

Etha dropped down into the chair beside the telephone table. There was silence on the line and finally Minnie said, "I've gotta go. Hinchie needs a hand."

"Of course! I'm sorry to keep you."

Etha slowly lowered the receiver into the cradle. Temple might very well lose, she thought. She gazed around the living room. At the walls she'd papered with the large gray-and-mauve fern pattern. At the matching bridge lamps, the walnut knickknack shelf, the desert painting above the radio. This was home. It had been for a long time, even without her knowing it. Her eyes fell on Temple's chair. These days it was not uncommon for men, good men, who lost their jobs, couldn't put food on the table or shoes on their kids' feet, to drift away. Women woke to permanent hollows on the other sides of their beds. Children sat at the table while suppers cooled, waiting for Pappy, who had "stepped down the street for a pack of cigarettes" and never came home.

All the joy that had bubbled up at the prospect of freeing Carmine fizzled out.

Ed was at his desk, hammering the typewriter keys as if they were nails, when Temple strode in from morning patrol. The deputy abruptly stopped typing and stood.

"Sir, we need to talk."

Temple caught the urgency in the deputy's voice. He removed his hat, hung it on the rack, and dusted off his cuffs, then lowered himself into his chair. "Let's hear it."

Haltingly, Ed described how Etha took notice that Maxine was not wearing glasses and how he, after careful thought, was sure she didn't have them on for the identification up at the camp.

Temple exhaled heavily.

"I'm so sorry, sir. There is no excuse and you will have my resignation—"

"Whoa. First, did you confirm any of this with Maxine?"

When Ed shook his head, Temple told him to get over to Maxine's pronto and confirm what was at this point only speculation. "Then we'll see where we are."

Ed hustled out the door, his boyish face stiff with remorse. Temple attempted to gather his thoughts. It was noontime and the metal desk fan, whirring on top of the file cabinet, was no match for the stagnant air. He pushed his face into its tepid breeze and studied the framed portrait of George Washington hanging on the wall. The first president appeared to be ascending from a cloud. The same print had been suspended above the chalkboard in his third grade classroom and it wasn't until many years later that Temple had learned that, in fact, Washington wasn't emerging from a heavenly cumulus but that the portrait was simply unfinished. Temple, too, felt submerged in thick fog—the murkiness of the case, the uncertain outcome of the primary, the discord with Etha.

Ed returned within twenty minutes with the unhappy news that Maxine had confessed. She had not worn her glasses during the trip to the CCC camp. Her identification of Carmine was a falsehood.

"Shoot," Temple said, kicking the file cabinet.

"I should have noticed right off, when she first climbed in the car," Ed said glumly. "I'll type up my resignation right now."

"Hold it," Temple said. "I don't think we need to go that far."

Ed swallowed audibly.

Temple studied the air. When he spoke, his words were clipped: "I think I'm a fair man and I believe in second chances. You already got a pass when you went out to the camp to investigate on your own. But I can't afford another slip-up. Got it?"

"Yes sir."

"I've got too much on my plate right now to be losing my deputy. You're going to have to work harder, be more careful to earn back my trust, though."

"No question."

"Good." The sheriff's tone was brusque. "Get going on that paperwork for releasing DiNapoli. I'll be back."

Temple was surprised to find Etha in the living room at this hour of the day, without a darning egg or even a book in her lap. She was sitting still as a bird on a nest.

"Everything all right?" he asked.

She started, as if she hadn't known he was there. "I'm afraid."

"What about?"

"People are saying you might lose to Doll. And I started to think about our home here and how much I would miss it. And what if you can't find work?"

Scrubbing his jaw with his hand, he said, "I don't think any of that's going to happen. And if it does, we'll get by. And here's something to feel good about: you got your boy out of a fix. Maxine has admitted she lied about the DiNapoli identification. He'll be out by afternoon."

Etha jumped to her feet. "Thank you, I—"

Temple held up a hand. "This is not a favor for you or anybody else."

Within an hour, the paperwork complete, Temple unlocked DiNapoli's cell and told him he was being released.

"But don't get too cocky," the sheriff said. "You're still under suspicion. This just means I don't have enough evidence to hold you for now. I'm going be keeping a close eye on you while we continue to investigate. You're still at the top of the list. Gather up your belongings."

Carmine snatched up the book, harmonica, and toothbrush. "All set, sir."

Temple snorted. "I'm not happy about this."

As the two left the cellblock, Etha emerged.

"I can't thank you enough, ma'am," Carmine said, his voice hoarse.

She flapped her hands at him as if to say, *No need.*

He caught another glimpse of her face, far up at the kitchen window, as he climbed into the county car.

As the sedan jolted along the road to Camp Briscoe, Carmine sat silently, his head turned to the monotonous rhythm of the fence posts. They passed a sign reading, *No Substitute*—the lone survivor of a Burma Shave roadside jingle, the remainder having been blown off by various dusters. Temple observed his passenger. The kid's hands hung limp between his knees. He seemed a different person from the one who'd punched Coombs in the bar. Etha saw this side, it seemed. Even knowing he was accused of killing a man hadn't deterred her. She passed out second chances as if they were sugar cookies, Temple thought, forgetting that he himself had done the same with Ed not an hour before.

When the sedan approached the camp turnoff, Carmine broke the silence: "Could you pull off a minute? There's something you need to know."

Here it comes, Temple thought. "Now don't tell me—"

"No, it's not that. I didn't kill Coombs and that's the truth. It's something else."

Temple drove onto the shoulder and cut the ignition. "You've got three minutes."

Carmine told him about rigging the electric boxes and the building fire. "I should've told you before. That's why I ran when I saw you. I've been scared stiff for all these years. On the move. I thought when I got accepted into the CCC it was finally my chance to turn things around."

Temple massaged his chin. "You were thirteen?"

"Yep."

Nothing was said for a few moments.

"I'll have to notify the Kansas City police, but given the amount of time since the fire and the impossibility of mounting an investigation, I doubt anything will come of it. And you were a minor."

"Thank you, sir." Carmine extended his hand but Temple ignored it.

"You're still my top suspect in the Coombs killing. Commander Baker will have someone watching you around the clock, so don't even think of running away."

Five minutes later they pulled into Camp Briscoe.

Baker emerged from his office. "We'll take over for now," he said to Temple. "But I'll be honest with you. I hope this isn't your man."

The kid's face softened at Baker's words and Temple caught an echo of Jack there. Etha had sworn she saw it yet he hadn't . . . until now. But he shook it off. This roughneck was nothing like their boy. When he had time, he'd call the KC police, but that could wait. More pressing matters brewed.

When Temple got back to the office, he took a long drink of water from the jug kept for such purposes, and then collapsed in his chair, beating the dust off his Stetson. "Pull your chair over here, Ed. We need to powwow."

For the next hour, the two lawmen picked through the shreds of their investigation. Coombs was still dead, but for what reason and by whose hand was unknown.

"What we *really* need to do is talk with more folks at the detonation; see if anyone noticed anything," Temple said. "I tracked down a couple, but then when DiNapoli seemed to be our man, I put that on the back burner. And that Saturday-matinee crowd needs going over too. Find out if anyone remembers seeing someone follow Coombs when he slipped out the side door."

Ed pulled a folder from a side drawer. "I've got the list of the Jewel patrons."

"Terrific. I'll hone in on those. You call on Attorney Hodge."

"About?"

"About a couple of things. First, we gotta take care of his Peeping Tom as best we can. Get a detailed description from Hodge and his wife. Times, dates, what the prowler looked like. Tell Hodge I'm hiring a civilian to patrol his block for the next three nights. In the meantime, Mrs. Hodge needs to keep the doors and windows locked. That's number one."

Temple shook a cigarette out of his packet, lit it, and took a draw. "Second, talk to him about the Coombs case. Seems to me Hodge has some connection with it. Not that I'm thinking he's a suspect, but he does seem to be turning up like a bad penny—at the explosives show, at the Maid-Rite when Coombs told anyone who would listen he was going to the movies, then later at the Jewel. And Hodge bought one of those shovels. I want to know if he still has it. Think you can handle him?"

Ed patted the notebook in the shirt pocket of his uniform. "I'm your man."

On his way out, Ed paused at the open door of the county offices. Viviane was threading a ribbon into the typewriter, her brows drawn together in a pretty frown. Since he'd taken her to the Maid-Rite, the county offices had acquired a new allure. She turned to him and her frown bloomed into a wide-open smile. He said hello, and after a moment went on his way.

As it turned out, Hodge was not in his office when Ed swung through the frosted-glass door of the reception room. In a stern voice, the secretary informed Ed, "He always lunches at home. You can wait here if you like." She pointed to one of two red-leather chairs embellished with borders of brass nail heads.

"No thanks. I'll catch him at his house."

"He hates to be disturbed at home. His time with the missus is sacrosanct."

Ed, mindful of wanting to get back into Temple's good graces as fast as possible, pushed on: "This involves a murder case so he'll have to accommodate me."

A wilted geranium provided the only bit of color on the Hodges' front porch. The lawyer answered the door, and when the man's eyes lit on Ed, a smirk stretched across his face.

"You finally here about the down-and-outer skulking around my house? Took you long enough." Hodge gestured for Ed to take a seat, then closed his front door and lowered himself into the porch swing. "Guess your boss heard from the governor. I called Marland this morning. The governor and I go way back. It's a shame strings have to be pulled to get protection for upright—"

"Excuse me," Ed cut in, "but Governor Marland didn't telephone. The sheriff apologizes it has taken so long to get on this but the murder case has taken up a lot of time." He filled Hodge in on the plan for a nightly patrol, adding, "But we also could use more specifics from you and Mrs. Hodge on times and dates." The deputy pulled out his notebook and looked attentive.

"Well, this is more like it. But your boss will still have to answer to the governor on why it took so long to get on this."

"Yes sir."

Hodge seemed to relax. He ticked off the four nights, mostly around nine or ten, when he or Mrs. Hodge had spotted someone peering around the edge of the kitchen window. Each time the lawyer had run outside, the prowler dissolved into darkness. Hodge hadn't gotten a clear look at the face. Certainly it was a man, not too tall, judging by the window frame. The face was dark. "Not a coon," he hastened to add, "but like the fellow hadn't shaved in a while."

Ed made a note. "When was the last time you saw him?"

"Friday, after Coombs's demonstration. Mrs. Hodge and I got home late, after ten. She went into the kitchen to make a cup of tea before bed and started screaming."

"I'll need to talk to her."

"She was too hysterical to get a good look."

"Well, maybe now she could—"

"I'm not involving my wife in this," Hodge interrupted.

"I need a couple more minutes of your time," Ed said slowly, but with force. "About the Coombs case."

Hodge paused. "I thought an arrest was made."

"Didn't hold."

Hodge shook his head. "Jennings can't leave office fast enough for me." He walked toward the door dismissively.

Ed swallowed his anger. "As of now, he is still sheriff and this is still an active murder investigation. Five minutes is all I need."

From down the street came a *thump, thump, thump,* as a small kid, listing under a heavy canvas bag, lobbed the *Gazetteer* against front doors. Both men watched him approach, and after the boy politely handed the rolled paper to Hodge, the lawyer said, "Five minutes."

Ed silently reviewed the questions he had jotted down in his notebook and decided to try to throw the lawyer off his mark. "How's the garden coming along?"

Hodge reared back. "What are you talking about? I don't have time for this foolishness." He reached for the doorknob.

"I understand you bought a shovel recently and it happens to be the type used as the murder weapon. I'm tracking them all down."

"Gave it away. It wasn't suited to my use," Hodge said curtly.

"Really?"

"I bequeathed it to one of those tramps always showing up at the back door. That all?" Again the fleshy hand gripped the doorknob, and again Ed stood his ground.

"All right. I'm making a note of that. Could you describe this fellow?"

"Ragged trousers and shirt, slouch hat. Standard vagrant attire. Tall and skinny. A real beanpole."

"All right. Also, we're asking folks who were at the Jewel on Saturday if they noticed anybody in particular sitting near Coombs."

"I don't know! This is enough. I barely know what the man looked like. I only saw him once, at the detonation. And that was from a distance."

Ed's antenna, which he had begun to doubt since the slip-up with Maxine, quivered. According to Ernie, Hodge had been at the Maid-Rite at the same time as Coombs on Saturday morning. A place so cramped that you couldn't bring the fork up to your mouth without elbowing other patrons.

"Maybe you've forgotten. Weren't you, in fact, at the Maid-Rite when Coombs was—"

"Are you calling me a liar? I won't stand for it. If the sheriff wants to pursue this, he'll have to bring me in for questioning. You tell him that. I don't have to tolerate this nonsense. And I better see someone patrolling tonight or I'm going straight to the *Gazetteer* offices to make this negligence public."

The oak door slammed hard behind Ed. What made Hodge so sore? he wondered. And how can I make that happen again?

CHAPTER TWENTY

"HE'S COVERING UP SOMETHING. I KNOW IT," Ed declared the moment he returned to the sheriff's office. "That Hodge isn't near as smooth as he thinks."

Temple thrust back a flop of hair. "I hope you didn't accuse him of lying. Hodge is a bigshot around here. We've got to tread carefully."

Ed snorted. "He's not voting for you anyways. He said so. And he threatened to go to the *Gazetteer*. Said he already called the governor, but I don't believe him."

"We can't let the primary influence this investigation either way. Whether someone votes for me or not has no bearing on the law."

"I know, I know. But he claims to only have seen Coombs once and from a distance. When I brought up his Saturday-morning breakfast at the Maid-Rite, he shut down. Heck, I'd bet money he could tell us the number of hairs in Coombs's snoot."

Temple grunted. "Probably so. But that's not close to making him a suspect."

"How about this?" Ed relayed Hodge's account of giving his new shovel to a bum who showed up at the back door.

"Smells sour, but if we arrested people on that count, the jail would be tighter than a can of sardines."

"But—"

"But with two probable fibs, I agree that Hodge is worth further study. Plus, one of the folks I called who'd been at the matinee said Hodge practically came in on Coombs's heels and sat not far from the man." Temple stood, gripped his hips and bent back. "I've been settin' too long. You hold down the fort. Here's the list the reverend gave me of those he recalled at the rainmaker's demonstration. Start calling to see if anyone in particular talked to Coombs." He tossed the paper to

Ed. "I'm going out to do some patrolling, get some fresh air."

Maybe it was by chance, but when Temple found himself coming up on
the turnoff to the hobo jungle, he dialed the steering wheel to the right.
Wouldn't hurt to ask about that shovel Hodge claimed he gave away,
Temple told himself. As he pulled in, he noted that the rough encampment
wasn't as populated as the last time he'd dropped by. That was the nature
of these bivouacs: the lodgers waxed and waned with the tidal pull of
the freights. A couple of teenagers catnapped near the darkened fire ring,
heads on logs and legs sprawled out unself-consciously, as if snoozing on
their mothers' sofas.

Murph and three of his deacons were playing cards. Another fellow
stood at a mirror hung from a branch, scraping a straight razor across
his cheek.

"Boys, put your cards away. Sheriff's in town," Murph said with a
chuckle.

A half-smile broke across Temple's face. "No need to panic. Nothing
illegal about a friendly game of cards in my book. Just asking for help.
I'm chasing down some information connected with the murder on
Saturday."

Murph gestured at a crate. "Make yourself at home."

Settling on the low box, Temple's knees pressed against his chest. Not
the most comfortable of positions, but the cottonwood's shade made up
for that. "What I'm hoping to find out is if anyone out here, or passing
through, got a shovel from someone in town. It wasn't stolen, so don't
stiffen up on me. And no one is wanting it back. I'm just trying to confirm
that the exchange occurred. Sound familiar?"

The three poker players shook their heads, their eyes steadfast on the
cards.

Murph said, "Should have brought the missus with you. She was a
big hit the other night."

The jab hit the target but Temple kept his tone level: "So I heard.
Etha's good heart sometimes overtakes her judgment. But what about
this shovel?"

"Seems I did see one of the youngsters come back from town with
a hoe or something. That kid moved on a couple of days ago, though."

"A hoe? Sure it wasn't a shovel?"

"Could have been. Out here no one looks too close into one another's business. You can wait a bit. A bunch are fishing but will be back in not too long."

While he waited, Temple surveyed the lean-tos and jerry-rigged clothesline. He thought of the days right after the great flood in Johnstown, when folks foraged among their smashed and sodden belongings. Drug out planks and doors and hammered them into shanties. Unearthed battered cooking pots with squeals of joy. And luck was with the mother who came upon a washboard. He'd been amazed at how fast the women managed to set up housekeeping among the splintered wood, the knee-deep mud, and the stink of corpses. Many Johnstown folks stayed and rebuilt. Within three years, he'd heard, most of the shops and offices were resurrected, the streets repaved with bricks, and 777 of the unknown flood victims were laid to rest in pristine rows with marble headboards at Grandview Cemetery. But not all survivors stayed. Some, including Temple's family, moved out quick, wanting, as his father said, "to be shut of the place." Not so different, Temple thought, from these times with young men and boys packing up and heading west in untold numbers. If I didn't have work here, I'd do the same, he mused. Some head out when things go bad, others dig in. Etha was a digger for sure. Prying her out of Peoria after Jack drowned had ignited the biggest dust-up of their marriage. But it was for the best. It was the kind of thing you just had to put behind you. Like his father said.

Lost in his thoughts, Temple didn't note a small band of young tramps approaching until they emerged from the tall grasses skirting the campsite. Most had crude fishing poles over their narrow shoulders and a few hoisted strings of glimmering sunfish. Despite the coolness of the shade and the promise of fried fish, most wore the hardened gazes of grown men. As Temple's glance flicked over their limp shirts and cinched belts, he began to understand Etha's urge to feed these young drifters and restore their boyhoods, even if only for a few hours.

When questioned, none knew anything about Hodge or his shovel. Temple checked his watch, saw he'd been gone too long from the office, and climbed back into the sedan. He motored back to town, believing that he was none the wiser for the trip. He was still angry at Etha but it seemed that the stone lodged in his heart had loosened a speck.

Back at the office, Temple sent Ed home for the day and then spent another hour with the receiver pressed to one ear, quizzing Vermillion's moving-picture devotees. Most declared it was too dark, even with kerosene lamps, to see much of anything, as the air was thick and murky. "It was no different from going down to the cellar and closing the door. The world was blotted out," one lady said.

When he got to the end of the list with no solid information, Temple stood up, stretched his legs, and rubbed his ear. A beer at the Idle Hour was in order.

Hinchie's rounded back occupied the short end of the bar. His stethoscope, its surface nicked with the hieroglyphics of constant use, was tossed over his right shoulder—the signal everyone in town recognized as, *The doctor is out.*

Temple swung a leg over a stool. Ike, the barkeep, delivered a glass of beer.

Hinchie studied Temple's face. "You look wore in. Getting enough sleep?"

Temple sipped the beer's foamy surface. "I am, and nope."

Hinchie studied his own topped-off shot glass. "Me neither. Three new cases of dust pneumonia just today. All three Fitzgerald tots. Fevers, coughing, the works. Not sure one of the babies is going to make it. When Minnie raises cane about what the dust is doing to her curtains, I say, *You should see what it does to the lungs*, and she clams right up." Hinchie laughed grimly and tossed back his whiskey.

The two men sat in silence, staring at the mounted elk head hanging above the door to the kitchen. Long ago someone had tossed a derby onto one of its antlers, giving the animal a jaunty air.

After a bit, Temple said, "The Coombs case has me stumped, I can tell you that."

"That so? Thought you had the fox locked up."

"Turned out might be the wrong fox."

"Don't say?"

"And here's the kicker: my most promising new suspect is John Hodge, Esquire."

Hinchie almost choked. "You're joking."

"Nope." Temple sipped thoughtfully. "The leads pointing to him are weak. He's acting dodgy, but I'm not sure if it's connected to Coombs."

Within Hinchie's mind, a nasty purple bruise bloomed. Over the years, Florence Hodge had come to him with a parade of shiners, lacerations, and poorly healed welts. One morning he found her sitting on his porch step cradling a broken wrist that had knit crookedly and had to be reset. The bones made a sickening crack as he snapped them apart. Most patients would have screamed, but Florence bit her lip and took it. Slippery stairs, cooking mishaps, and general clumsiness were always to blame. Sickened, but unable to shake her explanations, he had bound up her wounds and kept quiet despite his suspicions. But it didn't sit easy.

He was brought back to the moment with a nudge from Temple's elbow and a query: "Sound far-fetched? I mean, do you think the man is capable of murder? I've got to say that I don't. Full of hot air but not much else."

Two farmers moseyed into the bar, pulling the hats off their heads; bib overalls hanging loose as sacks over their haunches.

"Evening," one of them said, to which Temple answered, "Gentlemen." The two men slipped into a booth.

Temple turned back to Hinchie. "My impression, anyways."

The doctor screwed and unscrewed his empty shot glass. Now was the time to speak up. To lay out his suspicions about what Hodge's fists and belt had done. But to do so meant opening himself to the possibility of Hodge's retribution. I can't afford to pick a fight with the man or his cronies, he thought. Those cronies included Darnell the banker. Hinchie was deeply in debt to the bank after losing almost every penny he and Minnie had saved for old age on a land scheme that went bust. So far, Darnell had not pressed him about late or missed payments, but that could change in a snap. If that happened, the county poor farm loomed. Minnie knew none of this.

Hinchie considered the glassy eyes of the mounted elk. During the many hours he'd warmed this particular stool, he'd given the animal the name of Walt, after the poet Whitman. A bit of poetry came to him: *The courage of present times and all times.* "My impression," he said at last, "is that Hodge is a mean son of a bitch and is capable of killing a man, or a woman."

Temple jerked his head back in surprise. "Really?"

Back home, Temple and Etha fell into their usual dinner habit of complaining about the weather and sharing news of the day. It was just the two of them as the kitchen lockup was empty. Afterward, Temple turned the radio on and both let the comfort of routine soften, at least temporarily, the strains of disagreement.

CHAPTER TWENTY-ONE

THE NEXT MORNING, as Etha dried the breakfast dishes, the telephone rang. When she picked it up, Lottie was sobbing, ". . . not since Thursday. I don't even know . . ."

Etha jammed the receiver between her head and shoulder. "Lottie, dear, what's happened?"

A huge sniffle filled Etha's head. "Can you come over to the store? Now?"

"Is someone sick?"

"No."

There was a pause. Another sniffle told Etha all she needed to know. "Chester."

"Uh-huh," Lottie squeaked.

Hurrying up Main, Etha noticed the banner stretched across the street: *Rabbit Drive Today! Vince Doll For Sheriff! Join The Fun!* Her mouth turned down in distaste, not only at what would be a bloody spectacle but also at the glad-handing Doll, who was pulling out all the stops to win votes. Worry, like a cloud of gnats, was suddenly upon her. She tried to shake it off but a nub of anxiety remained even as she stepped inside Klein's Model Apparel and inhaled the pleasant starchy scent of new shirts and dresses. She caught sight of Mr. Klein's well-tailored bottom as he bent to extract a tray of men's handkerchiefs from below the counter for Reverend Coxey's approval. Mr. Klein straightened and both men exchanged greetings with Etha. Mr. Klein hooked his thumb toward the ladies' section in the connecting storefront, saying to Etha, "Over there."

A woman and her teenage daughter, fingering the fabric of a collared dress on a rack, appeared to be the department's only occupants. Then Etha heard sniffles from one of the curtained dressing cubicles and her own worries about the election fell away. Inside, Lottie sat on a small stool, her red-rimmed eyes and dripping nose replicated dozens of times in the three-sided mirror. She wore a rather dowdy skirt and blouse.

"He's cut me off!" she wailed the moment Etha parted the curtains. "Won't even take my calls."

"What happened?" Etha asked, offering a fresh hankie.

"It was Thursday. He'd made an appointment with the china salesman to sign up for Dish Night promotions. You know how he feels about those *abominations*. But ticket sales are way down and he thought he didn't have a choice. He asked me to help pick out the pattern. He always says I have such good taste." She broke into fresh sobs. "And it was going swell. Chester and I were working together—how I'd always dreamed. But then, after the paperwork was signed and the salesman and I were chatting, he just snapped. Said I didn't understand how hard it's been for him, a blind man and all, and that he's on the verge of losing the business. As if the drought is my fault! Then he ordered me out; the salesman too. Told me to leave! I'm crushed. I can't believe he'd think such—"

"Why don't you tell your father that you and I need to step out back for a minute. Then we can talk in private," Etha suggested.

This time of day, shade darkened the alley running behind the store. The two plopped down on the splintered loading dock, their legs dangling. They smoked silently for a while and, as Lottie's father called it, "contemplated the overhead."

Etha stubbed out her cigarette. "You must confront Chester. Today. Whatever got him lathered up has surely cooled off. Now it is a question of his pride. He's too embarrassed to admit he was in the wrong."

"He *is* a prideful man. Takes offense at the slightest things."

"That's just it! You have been nothing but loyal for how many years? You should be given the benefit of the doubt even if he believes you slipped up. Which you didn't." As she spoke, it occurred to Etha that the same applied to Temple and herself in a way, although pride was not his Achilles' heel. It was stubbornness.

Lottie looked doubtful. "Tonight's the Dish Night premiere. He'll be hepped up to beat the band."

"All the better. Get there early. He will be so relieved to have you there to lend a hand, he'll let down his guard."

A stray dog with patches of mange loped past, stopping to sniff a can of garbage.

"You're right!"

Etha nodded. "You run off home and make yourself presentable."

Back inside, Lottie asked her father for the afternoon off.

"No customers to speak of anyway. Go. Go!" He made a shooing motion. After Lottie had gathered her things, gave her father a peck on the cheek and her friend a hug, she was out the door.

Etha had been hoping to talk to Lottie about Florence Hodge. She'd had an uneasy feeling about the woman since stopping by her house. Now that Lottie had galloped off, she turned to Meyer. "I'd appreciate your opinion," she said.

"Of course," he said, "if you don't mind that I work on the front display as we talk." He opened the low wooden gate that separated the shop from the window area and stepped inside.

"In your line of business, you must know the temperament of your steady customers," Etha began.

Meyer, who was gathering up a wagon-wheel arrangement of neckties, paused. "Oh, yes. That is essential to establishing a strong relationship between customer and merchant."

"Why I'm asking is that I'm worried about Florence Hodge. Do you think she would welcome a woman-to-woman chat about—"

"My advice?" Meyer interrupted. "Waste of breath. A more timid woman I've never seen. Scared of her own shadow on the best days. She was here in the shop when the storm hit. Slunk into a corner with Nudnick at the first gust. They both shook and shivered the whole time. I suppose where she came from the weather was more tame."

"She's not from here? I had assumed—"

"She is not. Mr. Hodge went up to Kansas for some legal conference maybe fifteen years ago as a single man. Returned with a wife. But honestly, Kansas weather is the same."

"That must have been just before Temple and I moved here."

"Might be. Anyway, she twitched and shook the whole time until the blow passed by and her mister showed up."

"He was here? I thought Lottie said he missed the fitting."

"He did. But ten minutes after the storm passed, he was banging on the door. I had to clear a path with the broom to let him in. But nothing is done fast enough for that man. He was tapping his foot out there, pant legs rolled up, worried about getting his white suit dirty."

"Really?"

"For a big man, he has those bandy rooster legs. You know the kind? Bow out, white as his jacket. Forever I regret selling that suit to him. He insisted. Listen to me? No! Didn't I point out that the air here is so thick with dirt you could plant seeds in it? But a white suit he had to have."

Etha thanked Meyer and started for home. It was almost noon and, in the heat, her once crisp crepe wilted against her back. Fretting about the unreachable Mrs. Hodge and obstinate Chester, she walked home in a bleak mood.

While Etha was counseling Lottie, Ed had spent the morning on the horn, picking up where he'd left off the night before. Ticking off Reverend Coxey's list of the spectators at the rainmaker's display was nothing but drudgery. After a couple of hours, Ed's notepad was ornamented with doodles and not much else. No one had witnessed a fractious exchange between the rainmaker and anyone in the crowd. No one had heard any heckling or catcalls. In fact, Coombs had apparently made a sterling impression. He was the aces. So far, the only bright spot had been a small wave from Viviane, along with a glimpse of her calves, as she passed by.

The deputy was more than three-quarters of the way through his list and discouraged as all get-out when a glimmer of something promising emerged. Mr. Lovell, a teacher in the crossroad community of Sterling Grove, had answered the phone promptly. After Ed wearily recited his standard question, "Did you notice any harsh words exchanged?" the man had answered, "As a matter of fact, yes." It had happened at the end of the evening, as the crowd was dribbling back to town. He had overheard Coombs and Mr. Hodge in a brief but heated argument.

"*John* Hodge?" Ed asked excitedly.

"That'd be him."

"I'll be right over," Ed said. Leaving a note for Temple, who was due back from patrol any minute, he smashed his hat on his head and was dashing through the courthouse door before the telephone receiver cooled in its cradle.

Twenty minutes later, the deputy turned left at Sterling Grove's single intersection and, after a mile of nothing but empty sky, spotted a dirt-spattered school building on the left. Beyond the school was a trim four-room house. He nosed the county car through a gathering of tumbleweeds lingering in the lane and parked beside the house. On the porch, a fellow with sandy-colored hair and spectacles occupied a rocker, an open book filling his lap.

As Ed approached, the teacher tucked a ribbon between the pages and stood. He was a tall man in a too-small suit coat that pulled across his stomach and had only a nodding acquaintance with his wrists. "Harvey Lovell," he said, extending his hand and smiling broadly.

"Deputy McCance."

"Welcome to Thornfield, named after Rochester's manor house in *Jane Eyre*. Appropriate, don't you think?" He gestured at a second chair. "Have a seat. Can I get you something cold?"

"No thanks." Ed pulled out his notepad.

"Please indulge me. I've taken the trouble to chill a pitcher of buttermilk."

"All right, then."

"You won't be sorry."

Lovell ducked inside, the screen door bumping behind him. The view from the porch was as empty as Ed had ever taken note of. Besides the schoolhouse, there was nothing, not even a tree, to anchor the horizon. A tray with two glasses, a small pitcher, and a plate of soda crackers emerged from the doorway, followed by Lovell, who carefully placed his offerings on a small table. He poured the thick biscuit-colored milk into the glasses and handed one to Ed.

The deputy, not partial to buttermilk, sipped gingerly. Its slightly sour taste was surprisingly refreshing.

"Better than you thought, right?"

"Have to admit." Ed drained the glass and set it on the tray. "So, I just need a bit of your time. We're investigating the murder of the rainmaker."

Lovell spread his hands. "Got all the time in the world. It's the summer. School's out. Maybe for good, what with so many families leaving. As of yesterday, I'm down to eight pupils come September. If I lose one more the county has notified me it plans to consolidate. Load my students onto a bus and drive them over to Vermillion every day and put me out of a job."

Both men settled into their seats.

"So, if you could start with what brought you to Coombs's demonstration?"

Lovell held up the book he'd put aside when Ed pulled in. "Ever hear of this? *Tortilla Flat*?"

"No sir, but I—"

"It's about these roughnecks. Not bad fellows, just floating along without purpose. Of course, they get into trouble."

"Well, maybe I'll pick it up sometime. But I need to know what exactly you observed at the detonations."

Lovell took a swallow of buttermilk. "I understand that. But I need something too. I am a lonely man. It's awful quiet out this way. Sometimes I stroll over and ring the schoolhouse bell just for the heck of it. So I'm asking for ten minutes of your time. Ten minutes and then I'll tell you whatever you want." He swept his hand in a grand gesture. "We can discuss literature, music, baseball." He stabbed a finger at Ed. "I bet you're a baseball man. Right?"

Ed checked his watch; he could spare ten minutes. "All right. Sure. And yeah, I follow the Cubs."

"The Cubs is it? A Chicago man. Well, I'm Cards all the way."

The two men talked through two more glasses of buttermilk, arguing the merits of Leo Durocher's bat and Lon Warneke's overhand curveball.

Finally, Ed helped himself to the remaining soda cracker. "I have to say, you know your baseball."

Lovell saluted. "Books and baseball. If it weren't for them, I'd be a crazy man."

Ed brushed the crumbs off his pad. "Right then. Let's start when you got to town on Saturday."

"Glad to keep up my side of our bargain." Lovell cast his gaze to the horizon over Ed's shoulder, collecting his thoughts. "I drove into Vermillion at the dinner hour. I do have a car," he thumbed over his shoulder toward an outbuilding, "but not much money for gas. Anyway, I was treating myself to a ride, a sandwich at the Maid-Rite, and a show. The show being the rainmaker and his TNT."

"Big crowd?"

"Indeed. A couple of my older students were there. I'd introduced them to physics last winter. They took to it, I have to say. Other folks I recognized from coming to town for supplies. Shopkeepers and such."

"And John Hodge was familiar to you?"

"Oh yes. He fancies himself an amateur chemist. He invited me to speak a couple of times before the Vermillion Men's Club. But I didn't take note of him or Mrs. Hodge until after the show."

"And what did you see?"

"I happened to be standing close by." He laughed. "I'm one of those fellows who sits in the front pew at church. Don't want to miss anything. I heard Hodge asking Coombs about what chemicals he used in his explosives. Coombs started to answer, and then spotted Mrs. Hodge standing in back of her husband. He made a fuss over her, trying to kiss her hand. Coombs was a salesman, after all. She wasn't having any of it, though, yanked her hand away. It was then I saw Hodge grab Coombs's upper arm, jerk the rainmaker toward him, and say, quite loudly, *Don't you ever touch my wife again.*"

Ed looked up from his notepad. "Whoa!"

"Took me by surprise, I can tell you."

"And what did Coombs do?"

"Backed away saying, *Nothing intended,* or something of that nature. Hodge wasn't satisfied. He demanded an apology and Coombs couldn't get the words out fast enough."

Ed finished scribbling down the teacher's last few sentences, then raised his head. "Anything else?"

"Hodge seemed satisfied, asked a few questions, and then stomped off toward his auto dragging his wife with him. The man was making a stink over nothing, in my opinion."

CHAPTER TWENTY-TWO

TEMPLE CONTEMPLATED JACKRABBITS as he motored to the Campbell farmstead for the rabbit drive. Where herds of bison had once grazed, cropping the prairie grasses with their sensitive mouths, now jackrabbits overran the exhausted soil. They scoured the plains by the thousands—shearing off stalks and digging up the roots. Long and leggy, open-range jackrabbits could outrun hawks and coyotes. At dusk, as they zigzagged frantically across the prairie, the setting sun infused the orange membranes of their long ears—flames dancing and skittering over the dying ground.

An hour before the roundup, the Campbell place was crowded as a carnival midway. Kiddies brandished snapped-off broom handles as they dove and swooped around their elders. There were a fair number of women, some cradling babies, and men in overalls with wagon spokes propped on their shoulders. A river of barnyard dogs whipped through the throng.

From a farm wagon decorated with Vince Doll posters, jugs of corn whiskey were passed, while the candidate himself handed out blue *Doll For Sheriff* buttons. Temple skirted the hubbub, driving a half-mile beyond the farm and onto the hardpan. There, a dozen men pounded wooden stakes and unrolled chicken wire, knocking together a pen a couple of farm fields wide. Darting throngs of jackrabbits rippled across the ground, bounding over the bundles of wire and snaking between the fellows' legs. Unfolding himself from the Packard, Temple settled his hat on his head and ventured out to inspect the doings. A couple of fellows he recognized stopped to wave or tug on the brims of their hats. Temple knew they were happy to have real work after months of squatting in the shade of Vermillion's storefronts, spitting and ruminating. The men shouted directions to one another all the while. A couple of jugs of corn whiskey sat off to one side, giving Temple pause since he was out here to keep the peace and it was always dicey when men got liquored up. One of the fellows by the name of Ray Flynn paused from hammering in a stake to take a swallow.

"Got a project here," Temple said.

"Been at it since daybreak." Ray raised the spout to his lips a second time, wincing with pleasure.

"How do these things go anyways?"

Ray blotted the sweat from his forehead with a cuff. "My understanding is that we all form a big old square way out." He circled an arm as if spinning a lasso. "Way out. Standing apart to start, then, when the bell rings, walking slow toward the pen, tightening up the lines, and driving the jacks. Close off the pen and the fun begins. You brought a club, didn't you?"

Temple, though not a hunting man, respected those who were. "Nah. I'm here in the line of duty. When do you expect things will start up?"

Shading his eyes, Ray surveyed the men bent over the acreage and ignoring the skittish jacks. "Should be set in an hour or so."

Temple motored back to the farm, which from a distance had taken on the look of an anthill someone had driven a stick into. He parked across the road and ambled over. Mrs. Campbell, a twig of a woman, was selling slices of sugar milk pie. Temple dropped two bits into the jar and the farmwife shoveled a piece onto his palm to eat barehanded. It was not quite up to Etha's, but close.

Doll, now standing on the wagon bed with his suit coat off and sleeves rolled up, was reminding listeners that as a young man, he had all but birthed Jackson County. "I contend it is high time that the sheriff's office be run again by someone who knows and appreciates the pioneer stock. Who will weed out the charity cases and bums so that honest, hardworking folks can reap the rewards they deserve. Who will pursue thieves, debtors, and panhandlers with vigor."

This was met with a burst of clapping and finger whistles. Spurred on, Doll swore he would hire four local men as deputies. They would work on commission, getting paid when arrests were made, warrants were served, stills were raided. Temple knew Doll was taking a shot at his own hiring of Ed, who was not a local. The sheriff also disapproved of deputies working on commission, an arrangement common in other counties, but he kept his lips buttoned. He believed in running on his own record, not sullying his opponent.

Doll yammered on: "'Nother thing. I vow to break up that jungle of bums out by the tracks and run off the tramps once and for all. Many of you farmers have told me those vagrants are stripping your orchards and vegetable gardens. And they surely are a nuisance in town. Housewives can't hardly fix supper without being interrupted by a tramp begging at their back doors."

A shot was also taken at the CCC camp which introduced bad elements from the city into the county, Doll said, citing Carmine's arrest as an example but also adding that the corps was making it unsafe for the womenfolk. "When I'm sheriff, I will be patrolling that gutter every day. I promise you that!"

After pausing for a drink, Doll seemed to take a moment to assess the crowd's reaction, which was uniformly positive. His gaze lit on Temple. "I see that Sheriff Jennings has joined us. Perhaps he will favor us with an update on the murder investigation. I heard he might have arrested the wrong fellow and had to let him go. Or maybe got the right fellow but not enough evidence? We deserve to know what's going on and who bashed in the skull of the rainmaker who committed no crime other than pledging to end this drought."

Cheers greeted Doll's suggestion.

Temple pulled out a handkerchief, wiping the remains of the sticky crust off his fingers. "Excuse me, but I was just enjoying a piece of Mrs. Campbell's pie, which I highly recommend." He got a few chuckles for that. "Mind if I join you up there? Want to make sure folks can hear me."

"Plenty of room," Doll said, grinning. "Make yourself at home."

Temple boosted himself up on the wagon bed. More people gathered when it was clear a show was underway.

"First, I want to thank Vince for this opportunity to fill you in on the case. I am here at the drive chiefly to keep the peace. That is my duty as the sheriff and that comes first. But part of ensuring order is also informing the citizenry. Rumors, falsehoods, and such make rash actions more probable. Why do I say this? Take the current investigation of the death of Mr. Coombs. My deputy Ed McCance and I have been pursuing this case every day. This type of work takes time and patience. Interviewing witnesses, sending samples to the crime lab in Oklahoma City, tracking the victim's last hours and days. Many of you may have heard that a CCC boy was arrested and, after a couple of days, set free. That is true. All signs pointed to his guilt but when we discovered that a witness had mistakenly given wrong information, we had to release him. That's the law. It is not shameful to make an arrest and then later, when new evidence is found, to drop the charges. That is what a dedicated lawman doing his job the right way does. As of now, Ed and I have several leads on possible suspects we are following and will keep you informed, with the help of Hank Stowe and his *Gazetteer*. In the meantime enjoy yourselves, and all I can say is I think you'll harvest a good crop today. Plenty of jacks out there for the taking."

Someone shouted from the back. "Seems our county is overrun with tramps! Maybe you should be cleaning out that bivouac by the tracks, like Doll is saying!"

Temple gathered his thoughts. "My belief is that a lot of the fellows passing through out there were once honest working folk, but lost their jobs through no fault of their own. And at least half are just kids, set loose by families that are wanting fewer mouths to feed. It don't seem right to give them another kick in the pants. Of course, if they're breaking the law, that's another matter." He scanned the crowd. "Anything else?"

There was muttering but no other questions.

"Thanks for listening." Temple hopped down and joined a cluster of men under the shade of Mrs. Campbell's sassafras.

"Just so's you know, I'm here to sample Doll's whiskey, but I'm voting for you," Cy Mitchem said to Temple in low tones. The hardware store owner was leaning against the tree sipping from a tin cup.

"Appreciate that."

"You might have a tough sell this time, though."

"I'm getting that feeling. How's the missus?"

"You know Ruthie-Jo. Not one for hubbubs."

Nor anything beyond the front and back doors of her small kingdom, Temple thought.

"I closed up this afternoon. Figured no one would be in town with the rabbit drive and then Dish Night," Cy said.

"Forgot all about Chester's big doings. Lot going on."

Cy sucked on his teeth, making a fizzing sound. "All the ladies are fired up, I can tell you. Even my Ruthie-Jo said she might go."

Temple reared his head back. "Wouldn't that be something? Hey, I heard the lawyer was in your place last week. Bought a shovel?"

"Hodge in my store? Don't remember. And I would because he hardly ever comes by and I can't think he'd buy a tool. He has a handyman

. . . Oh, wait," Cy snapped his fingers. "Your missus was asking about a shovel too. Musta been Hodge who Jimmy Clanton sold it to."

"You're surprised about Hodge's purchase?"

"Oh yes. Ruthie-Jo says that man never dirties his hands if he can help it."

Temple smiled inwardly. Ruthie-Jo's knowledge of everyone's quirks, despite her self-imposed quarantine, was legend.

"Now, if he'd come in for, say—" Cy's commentary was interrupted by Doll's voice booming through a megaphone.

"Ladies and gentlemen, it's time to get in place for the drive. Follow my men out yonder and they'll show you where to line up. You all got your noisemakers?"

A cacophony of pots and pans burst forth along with a fair number of jalopy horns and the Campbell's dinner bell.

"All right then, let's get to it!"

The multitude moved forward, flowing around the wagon bed and on toward the pen. Temple waited a bit until the crowd cleared and he found himself ambling alongside Trot, the fellow he'd driven home after the Fullers' auction.

"Aren't you afraid the action will be over by the time you get up there?" Temple asked.

"Nope. Ain't any advantage in being the first to go over the top that I can see. I'll get my share of jacks when the time comes." Trot's grin slipped to one side.

Tipsy, Temple surmised.

They tramped on as, up ahead, Doll's men shouted directions, wrangling the crowd into a rough square.

Trot shook a heavy stick over his head, slightly swaying toward Temple. "Those jacks won't know what's coming when I start swinging. Even though my best club went missing, this'll do."

"Be careful with that thing. Keep it aimed at the rabbits."

Temple and Trot stepped into gaps on the southernmost side where folks stood a couple of yards apart. Three long blasts from a car horn sounded and a hundred or more scared rabbits skittered past. Suddenly the dusty air was filled with hoots and shouts and the continuous clanging of pots and pans. The men to the left and right of Temple moved forward in a slow march and he matched their strides. Soon he spotted the other two sides of the square closing in and the river of rabbits trapped in the center flowed faster, breaking up into frantic rivulets and coming back together, fur packed into a tight weave, ears aflame. Now the people stood shoulder to shoulder, stooping and waving their arms in a drive toward the pen. The wind whipped up, stinging everyone's faces with grit, but no one stopped to pull on a bandanna or press a handkerchief to his face. The last few yards before the pen were dicey. Children tripped over the packed herd. Rabbits squealed. "Plug up that hole!" Doll's men were shouting. A stream of rabbits broke free and made a run for it, but were headed off by a swift pack of young men. Temple, who was near the open end of the pen, saw the last few dozen forced inside before a makeshift gate was slammed shut.

Inside the corral, the rabbits formed an undulating brown-and-white fur carpet as they swarmed atop one another. And now the clubs and wagon spokes came out. Some folks stayed outside the pen, bending over the chicken wire to strike and smash. Cy Mitchum, Temple noticed, attempted one or two ineffective swipes with a broom handle before stepping away, his brows contracted in pity. But a good number of men jumped the fencing and waded in, sticks raised. Jess Fuller was near the center, his sledgehammer pounding relentlessly, his jaw set in granite. Beside him, other farmers swung and cussed. Temple was surprised to see Trot in the thick of things administering crushing blows. As the rabbits died they emitted high-pitched screams, eerily mimicking the howl of newborns.

The air grew heavy with the dust of panicked animals, the crush of bones, the agonal shrieks. Temple, who had seen his fair share of mangled flesh both after the Johnstown flood and as sheriff, winced. Years of anger, loss, and hunger bubbled up in that bloody pen. A jackrabbit, its back legs crushed, crawled toward Temple's feet, mewling pitifully. He turned away. It took another twenty minutes before the last of the rabbits had the life beat out of it.

Then the drivers flung the limp bodies into a heap, to be carted off later and ground into livestock feed. The citizenry cheered. Men and young boys boasted. Someone brought out a camera. Folks clustered around the mangled remains to pose. After a bit, everyone started drifting back to the Campbell farm. Temple stepped inside the pen and squatted by the pile. Most of the rabbits had their skulls bashed in; concave wounds thick with clotted blood. Not so different from Coombs, he observed. The sheriff gazed back toward the farm. A lot of fury to unleash on a pitiful heap of fur and flesh.

Eventually, chores called most people home. Those who stayed proceeded to get liquored up. Temple's gut told him to hang around for a while to ward off a whiskey-fueled brawl. And who knew? He might get a lead on Hodge and the Coombs killing, although he couldn't think what that might be. He settled on the wagon bed with a stick and a whittling knife, tuned to the various conversations washing past his ears. There were the usual complaints about the drought, the *gov-mint*, about tick fever and screwworm. Temple was on his second stick, with a pile of shavings beneath his feet, when Doll, who had been powwowing with his cronies under the sassafras, approached.

"Best get yourself up. One of the fellows has had too much to drink."

Temple cocked his head, smiling lightly. "That was the idea, wasn't it?"

"And he's pissing alongside the barn over there, exposing himself to the ladies."

Temple looked over his shoulder and saw that, indeed, a fellow was watering the weeds. He tossed the stick and hopped down from the wagon. "I'll take care of it. But you need to cut off the source. Time this shindig is over anyway."

"Don't know if the men will go for that."

Temple wanted to say, *That's the way it is with being a lawman: telling people to do things they don't want to,* but thought better of it. By the time he reached the offender, the man was already zigzagging his way. It was Trot.

"All right, let's get you home," Temple said. "And jeez, man, close your fly."

As Trot bent to comply, he stumbled forward. The sheriff sighed. He doubted that if Doll were sheriff he'd stoop to nursemaiding drunks. Temple buttoned Trot up, grabbed him under the armpit, and steered him toward the Packard.

Trot's soddie was not more than three miles away, and as they bumped along, Trot commenced humming. After a bit, the humming became singing. He garbled the words and Temple didn't know the song. Only bits and pieces of the verses made it past the drunk's lips:

"Jesse James was a man that killed many a man,
He robbed the Danville train,
(Mumble, mumble, mumble) . . . and a brain."

But the chorus came through strong:

"Poor Jesse had a wife who mourned for his life
And three children, they were so brave.
But that dirty little coward that shot Mr. Howard
Laid poor Jesse in his grave."

Trot sang continuously until they pulled up to the soddie, where he abruptly nodded off. Temple carried him inside and laid him on the tick mattress. It was then he noticed that Trot had a *Vote For Doll* button pinned to the buckle of his overalls.

"I'll be damned." Temple shook his head and grinned.

Driving back to town, he found himself singing Trot's ballad, giving particular attention to a funereal baritone on *"Laid . . . poor . . . Jesse . . . in . . . his . . . GRAVE."*

C HAPTER TWENTY-THREE

CHESTER WAS BATTLING AGAINST THE CLOCK to ready the Jewel for Dish Night. A case of the jitters woke him before dawn and had stuck around all day—a pugnacious jockey whipping his flanks.

Now, in late afternoon, with doors set to open at seven sharp, the Jewel wasn't close to ready. Chester had, with trepidation, recruited two of Maxine's friends to help along with the cashier herself, and the same Jimmy Clanton who Mitchem's Hardware called on when extra hands were needed. Still, with all this help or maybe because of it, almost nothing had been accomplished. That night's giveaways, teacups, remained nestled in their excelsior nests. The podium from which Chester was to give introductory remarks was not on stage. Nor had the easel been found to display the illustrated poster. And the poster itself was missing. The banner welcoming ladies to Dish Night languished in the balcony.

Chester was drilling Jimmy on how to sling the bunting from the marquee when Maxine sprinted out, yelping that something was amiss with the place-setting display.

Suddenly Chester's nightmare that the Dish Night premiere might fizzle out seemed a real possibility. When the doors opened, the patrons would encounter not an elegant soiree but an amateurish effort not even rising to the level of a church potluck. On top of that, in the past several days it had become clear that, as more bills rolled in and receipts continued to spiral downward, this campaign was his last chance to save the Jewel.

All these terrible thoughts rushed in at once. Quickly he turned away, stumbling toward to his office stairs, leaving the girls to their paper chains and chewing gum. Halfway up, he sat down hard, head in hands. Tears dripped on his trousers. In his protracted scramble up through the darkness, he'd never admitted failure was possible. His entire life had been devoted to erecting and maintaining the illusion of sight. Every movement, from lighting a cigarette to counting out change, was drilled over and over until each could be executed without a false movement. And yet, none of it mattered a wit if he lost his livelihood. So what if he could make sure his socks matched if he didn't own any? If his feet were scraped raw inside busted shoes and he was nothing but a sightless beggar with a tin cup? He sat woodenly until the understated voice of a woman, mingling with adolescent chirps, touched his ears. It was Lottie. Lottie! His spirits lifted and, swabbing the tears from his face and blowing his nose, he sailed downstairs.

"Lottie, thank God you've come," he blurted out.

There came the moist sound of her lips parting in a smile. "I thought you might need help."

"Oh yes. I can't tell you . . ." Chester leaned toward her and she pressed her cheek against his mouth. For several moments they lingered, catching their breaths.

Finally, pulling away, she asked, "So, what needs doing?"

Forty minutes later, as Lottie and the girls admired their handiwork on the display, someone tapped on the lobby door. Lottie was surprised to see Etha's earnest face behind the panes. And then she made out the crush of women behind her friend and gasped. At least thirty ladies were crammed into the small space shaded by the marquee, and beyond that, many more hats pressed forward. As Lottie unlatched the door and Etha squeezed inside, several matrons tried to push their way in after her.

"Sorry, ladies, doors open at seven," Lottie said in a polite but firm tone. The shoulders of the eager crowd slumped. Lottie clicked the dead bolt into place.

"Goodness!" Etha exclaimed. "There are at least two hundred women out there. The line stretches past the Idle Hour. Can I help?"

Etha was assigned the chores of counting teacups and tracking down the errant poster. At six forty-five, Lottie marshalled everyone into place. Maxine was snug in the booth. Lottie herself stood erectly at the ticket canister ready to collect the stubs. She positioned Chester to her left where he would greet the ladies and present them with the teacups, passed to him by Etha. Maxine's pals June and Harriet stood at each doorway ready to escort the ladies to their seats.

Lottie gave Jimmy the signal to unlatch the doors.

The women pushed in, bringing with them excited chatter and the click of pumps on the lobby floor. Many were from town. Their faces fresh under Sunday hats. Some towed youngsters in short frocks. But most were from the farms. Their complexions tawny and tight from too much sun and too little food. Each, however, wore a freshly ironed dress and a fragrant coating of dusting powder.

Etha watched as the ladies handed their tickets to Lottie, who greeted them with a warm smile. Chester was at his best—suave and professional in a pinstripe suit. It was well known that a number of married women had secret crushes on the theater owner.

"Welcome to the Jewel," he said, handing each a glossy bone china cup.

Most of the patrons, after gushing their thanks, stopped to admire the pattern and had to be urged to move on by Etha. The lobby filled with exclamations of pleasure as more women pressed inside. Even Ruthie-Jo, Cy Mitchem's reclusive wife, was in attendance. She stood in line, pocketbook pressed against her sturdy body, her clever eyes alight with determination. Once she had a cup in hand, she pivoted abruptly and marched back out.

Several times Lottie glanced Etha's way and mouthed, *How many left?* The supply of china seemed limitless, but so did the patrons. About ten minutes into the crush Etha spotted Viviane approaching. "Nice to see you," Etha said.

Viviane smiled. "I brought my mother."

The woman was a wisp of a thing with limp pale hair and gray eyes bleached with fatigue. When Chester handed her a cup, she covered her mouth and broke into tears. No one noticed except Viviane and Etha. Etha guessed the china was the first pretty thing this woman had ever owned. Viviane gently guided her mother toward June, who smiled brightly and led them into the darkened theater. At last the long line dwindled. Only six cups remained and Harriet reported that there were no more seats. Etha had been watching for Mrs. Hodge but she must have stayed home.

Now it was time for Chester to address the audience and he turned to Lottie. "Please do me the honor," he said, crooking his arm so that hers could slide inside. Together they marched down the aisle, mounted the steps, and took the stage. Everything was waltzing along perfectly and he didn't want a single clumsy movement to spoil it. With this crowd, he'd be able to pay the bills and keep the Jewel open for at least another month. Why had he fought against Dish Night for so long?

He stood behind the podium, Lottie at his side. "Thank you all for making our premiere an unqualified success. Each week that you attend on promotional night, you will receive another piece of fine china to add to your collection. So you won't want to miss a single show!"

The audience enthusiastically beat their gloved hands.

"And I want to also thank Lottie Klein for helping me prepare the Jewel for opening night." Chester nodded to Lottie, who stepped forward, smiling and bowing to applause, before returning to his side. "And now, without further ado, on with the show!" He waved to Jimmy, who threw the switch on the newsreel.

After retreating to the lobby, Chester closed the quilted doors. He and Lottie immediately slumped against them.

"My God," Chester said. "Without a hitch. If I were a betting man, I'd have never thought we could pull it off."

Lottie squeezed his hand. "But we did."

Etha joined them. "I just talked to Maxine. Two hundred and twenty-five tickets sold! And Chester, I wish you could have seen the faces on those women. Especially the farm wives. Having those sorts of niceties in their homes means the world to them. I know you were against the dish promotion, but I'm glad you went ahead. You did a lot of good tonight."

Chester laughed. "An unexpected bonus, to be a do-gooder *and* pay my bills! Now, if you ladies will excuse me, I must take over the projectionist duties from Mr. Clanton."

Lottie turned to Etha. "I need a cigarette."

"Me too."

They stepped into the sultry evening. In her cage, Maxine was wrestling nickels into paper tubes.

Lottie said, "Did you hear that? Chester said *we* pulled it off. We! I've got goose bumps. Feel." She extended her arm. Then she glanced at Maxine, who might be eavesdropping. "Guess we should find a private place for our smoke."

Etha chuckled. "Who's to see us? They're all inside."

"True. But I'd feel funny."

The women strolled around the side of the building and into the alley. They lit up and leaned against the brick wall. Lottie continued, "It's just as I dreamed—Chester and I working together."

"You must be relieved. Back to the way things were before he blew up."

"After today? He'll be proposing within the next couple of weeks. I know it."

Etha had her doubts but didn't want to dampen Lottie's spirits when her friend had been so low earlier in the day.

"I've been meaning to tell you," Lottie said, "when the Dish Night pitchman was here he mentioned being up in St. Joe. Described a salesman he ran into who sounded like it could have been Coombs. Seems the fellow got into an argument with another boarder and a gun was involved. Might be something for Temple to check out?"

Etha perked up. "I've been trying to get him to cast the net wider."

"Also, if Temple . . ." Lottie paused, biting her lower lip. "If he loses, I could ask Papa about hiring you part-time. It wouldn't pay much, but it would be a help."

Etha squeezed her eyes shut. "I'm hoping I won't need to take you up on that. But thanks."

That night, after the last of the patrons had drifted out into the quiet streets, Chester and Lottie plopped down in the back row and toed off their shoes.

"A magical evening, don't you think?" Lottie said. She laid her head on his shoulder.

"Yes, in that I will be able to pay my rent and electric bills. If that's magic, I'm all for it." He scrubbed his face with a palm. "I'm exhausted."

"But also in how we worked together. A team."

Chester grunted.

"And standing beside you on the stage and having all the ladies in town seeing us together."

"As I said, there is no way the premiere could have happened without you."

"I've missed you so much these last few days. Did you miss me?"

There was a pause. Lottie thought he might be drifting off. Then he said, "I did."

She sat up. "I've thought a lot about what you said the other day. You always seem self-assured. I didn't understand why you were angry at first. But now I see that, to get dressed every morning, run the business, all without knowing each time you take a step if there's a hole waiting to trip you up, it takes a lot of gumption."

He smiled, his hand finding her shoulder. "And I regret losing my temper. I'm sorry for that. I tend to be closemouthed about a lot of things. I want you to know that I am pleased that you and I have set things right. There is nothing I want more than to forget that outburst happened and to go on as we were."

Lottie frowned. "As we were?"

"Yes, lunches, dinners. I don't know if I can afford the out-of-town trips for a while—"

"But I thought, after all this, we'd be running the theater side by side. I was a huge help. You said so yourself."

Chester yawned. "And you were. I couldn't have pulled off the premiere without you."

"But what?"

He shrugged. "But there's only one premiere. Why change our arrangement?"

"Our arrangement? Is that what this is? I thought we were building something together—a life together."

Chester stiffened. "My dear, that is . . . Well, it seems we have a slightly different perspective on what—"

Lottie jumped up. "Are you saying it never crossed your mind to marry me?"

There was silence.

"It didn't, did it? You never even thought about it."

Chester reached for her arm and tried to pull her back down. "Let's talk reasonably here. Two adults. Sit down."

Lottie suddenly saw her ten years with Chester. Understood that those years had been nothing more than the desolate existence she'd thought she'd been taking steps to escape. Her future with him had always been barren. The air thickened, as if another suffocating duster was bearing down. Lottie slowly turned to Chester. "Not on your life, mister." Her voice rose in anger: "My uncle who owns that store in Oklahoma City? He's been begging me to come work for him for at least five years. You didn't know that, did you? I kept putting him off, thinking that there was something here for me. But now I see there never was." She gathered up her shoes and purse. "You've got my pity, but it's not for the reason you think," she said before marching up the aisle and out the lobby doors.

Behind her, Chester sat alone, stunned at this rapid fall from the day's triumphs. His throat thickened with tears. He tried to swallow them but realized it didn't matter. No one was there to hear anyway.

* * *

After smoking a second cigarette with Lottie in the alley, Etha had hustled home, where she'd left a plate of cold boiled ham and cheese, covered with a tea towel, for Temple's supper. Scurrying in, she saw that he had already set out the coffee cups. From the living room, a clarinet tootled on the radio.

"How do?" she called out. "Do you want coffee in there?"

"Sure." There was a rustle as, Etha imagined, Temple folded the newspaper and set it aside.

She carried in the tray and her husband helped her unload it onto the coffee table.

"No pie?" he asked disappointedly.

Etha sighed. "Actually, Carmine stopped by before I left for Dish Night. He'd hiked all the way here from the camp. He wanted to thank me for—you know."

"Etha, you got to remember that DiNapoli is still a suspect. The only reason he still isn't in jail is that a thirteen-year-old girl lied to us."

"But you are considering other leads, right?"

"Yes, but he has not been ruled out. What about the pie?"

"Carmine finished it off."

"The whole thing? An entire pie?"

"I had a piece too. A pretty big piece, but yes, it's all gone. I'll make another first thing in the morning."

Temple closed his eyes.

Etha's voice was tentative: "Rabbit drive went okay?"

"Yep. Had to deliver a fellow home after too much corn liquor, but other than that it was fine. Same old-timer I gave a ride to after the auction. He's in a soddie outside of town. I think he's squatting there. These times are tough on the old folks. I think this Trot might have a son somewhere, but he seems pretty much on his lonesome."

"That's so sad!"

"Anyway, Doll was in his glory. Cornered me into saying a few words to the crowd. I think I held my own. Who knows?"

"Big turnout?"

"Never seen bigger, even at an auction. Not my cup of tea, clubbing jackrabbits. But then again, they're destructive pests."

Etha wrinkled her nose. "They didn't just shoot them?"

Temple laughed grimly. "Let folks wade into a crowded pen with guns? You're asking for trouble."

The conversation turned to other matters and eventually came around again to the murder.

Etha tapped her front tooth. Something was lodged at the back of her mind. Something she'd heard that day. Meyer Klein's round face suddenly surfaced. "You know, I was talking to Meyer about the storm. He said Hodge showed up at the store to escort Florence home within minutes of its passing."

"So? Coombs was killed in the middle of the thing. Hodge could have done the deed, slipped back into the theater, and easily been at Klein's afterward."

"But Meyer said Hodge showed up in a practically spotless white suit. If he'd been out in that alley in the middle of the blizzard, his clothes would have been black as night."

Temple sighed heavily. "Can't catch a break. I'll send Ed over to interview Meyer."

"What if Hodge doesn't pan out? Maybe it's worth going up to St. Joe where Coombs was from. Could be the killer knew Coombs from way back."

"That again?"

"Lottie did mention something," Etha pressed on.

"That so?"

Etha relayed the china salesman's story. "It might be nothing, but when Lottie said it happened in St. Joe, that caught my ear."

Temple tipped his head. "I'm not sure an argument between two drunks in Missouri, even if one was Coombs and someone was threatening to shoot him, is connected to his murder down here. It still feels local to me. Someone from around here developed an aversion to the man."

"Someone like John Hodge?"

Temple sipped noisily. "He clearly has a short fuse. Had access to one of those shovels. Was at the Jewel when Coombs was killed."

"Hmm . . . It seems to me the killing was not a spur-of-the-moment thing. Someone trailed Coombs to the movies, brought along a weapon, then followed him outside in the middle of the worst dust storm we've seen and bashed his head in. Coombs was in town less than twenty-four hours. Hard to anger someone enough in that short a time to plan a murder."

Temple stretched out in the chair—lanky legs crossed at the ankles, hands folded across his belly, head cocked against the back cushion. "I can't think straight on any of this tonight. It's been a long day. How about ten minutes of Tommy Dorsey and then bed?"

Etha carried the tray to the kitchen, knowing not to press the point. But tomorrow she'd bring it up again, and if he did decide to drive to St. Joe, she intended to ride along.

CHAPTER TWENTY-FOUR

THE NEXT EVENING, as Temple and Etha sauntered home from weekly Bible class and Etha contemplated the state of her pantry, Temple broke into her thoughts: "You know, I've been turning over what you said about Coombs's past."

Although she wanted to jump in with her opinion on the matter, she held her tongue. It didn't pay to rush him. Temple's voice moseyed on.

"It *is* possible that the killer knew him from way back. So it might be worth poking around further out. Find out more about the man. About his business dealings. Did he have a sweetheart or even a wife?"

"Good idea," Etha said.

"This is all by way of saying I'm cogitating a drive north on Saturday."

"To St. Joe?"

"Yep. But first I want see what Ed comes up with about Hodge and that white suit."

They'd reached the courthouse and Temple pulled the heavy oak door open for her.

"If you go, I want to come along," Etha said.

His brows lifted.

"I want to see how this turns out. I've been a help on the case. You can't deny that."

"No, I can't. But this all could be a wild goose chase and it's a long hot ride up to Missouri."

"I know."

"The roads are bad."

She tipped her head to the side.

"And the springs on the Packard are shot to hell."

When she didn't respond, Temple sighed. "You're set on this?"

"Yes."

"All right then."

As they reached the third floor, they found Carmine sitting on the top step. Temple frowned. "What are you doing here?"

"Returning the library book Mrs. Jennings loaned me, sir. I bummed a ride."

Temple snorted, yanked the door, and headed inside the apartment.

Etha lingered in the hallway. Carmine handed her the Hammett.

"What did you think?" she asked. "Good one?"

"Heck yeah. If you haven't read it, you should."

"Maybe I will. It was nice of you to bring it by, but I could have driven out and picked it up."

Carmine flushed. "I know. Had the time and wanted to. You've been so swell. Anyway, I'll be going."

"Okay." Etha was aware of Temple's presence just beyond the apartment door.

"So, yeah, you really should read it," Carmine said, still rooted to the top step.

Then he wheeled and abruptly clattered down the staircase. Etha watched him descend and waited to hear the big doors shut behind him before going inside.

The next day, while Temple grumbled over a stack of paperwork, Ed interviewed Meyer, who repeated what he'd told Etha: that, while not spotless, Hodge's suit had most certainly not borne the full force of the Brown Blizzard. Next the deputy approached Maxine in the cashier's booth. She meekly confirmed that yes, Mr. Hodge had attended the previous Saturday's show and that he was wearing a white suit. Finally, Ed took it upon himself to question Hodge one more time. As he turned the block, he spied the lawyer bent over the open hood of his Ford.

"Mind if I interrupt?" Ed asked.

Hodge straightened with a grunt, delicately wiped his fingers on a rag, and rolled down his shirtsleeves. "If you are here expecting my gratitude for setting up the nightly patrols, you are not going to get it. The Peeping Tom situation should have been taken care of long ago. Shame I had to get the governor's office involved, but so be it."

Ed kept his face smooth. "Actually, I'm here about the murder investigation."

Tendons in Hodge's neck strained above his collar. "I'm not answering any more questions. If you want to talk to me, you'll have to bring me down to the courthouse."

"I am within my rights as a public servant to question you at your place of residence," Ed said, hoping this was true. "New information has come to light."

Hodge turned his back on Ed and fooled with the motor.

"We have a witness who heard you arguing with Coombs on Friday night."

The lawyer, still bent over the car, stopped tinkering. "Who says?"

"A very credible witness. And we have also learned you were at the movies on Saturday, seated directly behind the victim. Do you have an explanation?"

Hodge straightened up and pushed his chest inches from the deputy's. "I don't have to explain anything to anyone. That two-bit hustler was attempting to seduce my wife. Had the gall to do it right in front of me! Insisting that she looked familiar. Tried to kiss her hand. I let him know straight out that he was to stay away from Florence."

Ed wrote in his notebook. "And the next day at the movies?"

"When I was having breakfast at the Maid-Rite, I heard him asking about the movies. I needed to know he hadn't arranged to sneak off with her. Get her in the back row in the dark. So I followed him inside the theater, settled in, and made sure nothing happened."

Flipping over a new page, Ed asked, "What were you were wearing when you attended the picture show?"

"What I was wearing? What does that have to do with anything?"

"If you could just answer the question." Ed planted his legs apart.

"Don't think I won't remember you harassing an upstanding citizen. I never forget anything. For your information, I wore a blue shirt, brown socks, brown shoes, black leather belt, white jacket, and white trousers. That enough? Or do you need to know what drawers I had on?"

"Got it. Thank you, sir." Ed made another note and turned, forcing himself into a slow and dignified gait.

Back at the courthouse, after Ed reported his findings to Temple, the two agreed there wasn't enough to make a case against Hodge. Regardless of how odious the man was, his clean white suit and the general lack of anything but circumstantial evidence against him ruled him out as a primary suspect. That tent had collapsed. Time to turn their attention elsewhere, Temple decided. It seemed a trip to Missouri was indeed the next logical step.

When Etha brought sandwiches down to the office a little while later, Temple announced, "Pack your bags. We're going to St. Joe."

"Hot dog!" she cried, clapping her hands.

Ed chuckled. "I never heard anyone get so excited about spending twelve hours bumping across lousy roads."

"Never dismiss the need of a woman—or a man, for that matter— to get out into the wider world every so often. Besides, I've dropped a healthy number of coins into this particular collection plate. Better watch it or I'll be taking your job."

After she left, the two men were quiet for half a tick.

"Guess I got told," Ed said.

"Keep on your toes, boy. I wouldn't put it past her."

That evening, Temple got called away after dinner on a report of a fight at Mayo's. Etha was packing for St. Joe when there was a knock on the door. It was Carmine, standing self-consciously in the doorframe.

"You again," she said jokingly.

Carmine shrugged. "I couldn't get the taste of your pie off my mind. Wondered if you had a spare piece I could take back to camp."

Etha laughed. "How can I turn that request down? Come on in. You can eat it here."

When he finished, she wrapped another piece in wax paper for him to take on the road.

It was late when Temple returned. Etha was already in bed reading. He unbuttoned his shirt, stepped out of his trousers, and wearily threw them over the back of a chair. Etha had promised herself there would be no more secrets between them and so she told Temple that Carmine had stopped by for pie. Maybe the fatigue worked in her favor because Temple didn't raise much of a squawk, just reminded her as he fell into bed that DiNapoli was not completely off the hook.

The next morning, as the sun inched above the horizon, slowly tinting the clouds lilac and pink, the Packard had already been on the road for several hours. So far, it had rumbled across nothing but dirt roads. But now, sixty miles east of Vermillion, the tires jounced onto a stretch of concrete highway. Etha sighed in relief.

"Well then," she said.

"Don't get too comfortable. The roads are hit and miss until we get on 40, north of Wichita. Then it's smooth sailing. But that'll be late afternoon at best. Having regrets?"

"Not a one. And do you think I'd admit it?"

"Not for an instant."

During the remainder of the morning, the conversation meandered. Will Rogers's dispatches from Alaska were on Temple's mind.

"You know, he says they are flying right over herds of caribou and polar bears? What a sight that must be. Boy, I'd love to be along on that ride. Landing on water with those floats? What a thrill."

"Not my idea of fun."

Talk drifted to Etha's sister Nance, who lived in Arkansas with a dedicated drinker and his ailing mother. Near Ponca City Temple turned the radio knob and the plinky-plink of a banjo came through from station WBBZ. They listened to a solid hour of music before the car jerked out of range, heading north into Kansas.

Outside of Wichita, Temple pulled off under a spreading hackberry. They stretched their legs. Etha unstuck her dress where it was pinned to her skin with sweat.

"You get the hamper and I'll bring the cloth," she said.

They settled under the stubby tree; Temple unscrewed the thermos of lemonade while Etha unpacked the egg salad sandwiches, apples, and oatmeal cookies. Not a single car passed.

Eyeing the road sign indicating that it was twelve miles to Wichita, Etha raised her sandwich in its direction and said, "Did you know John Hodge met and married Florence there? That she's not from Vermillion?"

"Nope."

As there was nothing more to say on that topic, Etha continued, "Driving by all the empty farms made me think of the folks moving on. But others, you can't blast them out with dynamite. Why is that, do you think?"

"Circumstance. Some farmers were already edging into bankruptcy before the hard times set in, or owed money to bankers not willing to wait. Others lost babies to dust pneumonia or an entire crop of wheat three years straight and the spirit was kicked out of them."

Etha bit her bottom lip. "I also think some people are born with the jitters in their legs and will pick up and move at a moment's notice."

"I'm guessing that's directed at me?"

They exchanged smiles as people long married do, even when they're fussing at one another.

"We've been in Vermillion fifteen years now and I'm running for reelection. I intend to stay."

"Do you still have a chance? I mean, it looks bad with the unsolved case and Hodge calling the governor and all the grumblings among the townsfolk."

Temple laughed grimly. "The farmers aren't too happy with me neither."

There was a quiver in Etha's voice: "What will happen to us?"

Temple reached across the remains of their picnic and patted her hand. "Don't worry, my sweetie. We'll be fine."

But within themselves, both Temple and Etha were skittish and recognized that the other was too.

Trying to lighten the mood, Temple said teasingly, "We could move up to Alaska. Will Rogers is making it sound mighty attractive."

Etha jumped to her feet with a grin and threw a crumpled ball of wax paper at his head. "You'll be going up there by your lonesome."

They spent the night just north of Kansas City in a spick-and-span tourist court with a sign promising, *All The Comforts Of Home.* Temple carried their suitcase inside and opened it on the foldout rack. The bathroom had a small tablet of soap and two drinking glasses. The couple collapsed on the twin beds, pushed off their shoes, and promptly fell asleep on top of the chenille spreads.

The next morning, they finished the drive northward along rolling bluffs above the Missouri River to St. Joe, a city that had been circled on many a map besides the one spread in Etha's lap. In the 1800s, it had been a starting point for those heading west. First came the gold prospectors traveling to California. Later pioneers outfitted there before hitting the Oregon Trail. Eventually St. Joe evolved into a cow town. The odor of manure and hay hung over the pens thick as fog when they drove past and into town. Blodgett's Boarding House, their first stop of the day, was within sniffing distance of the stockyards.

The usual lodgers, unshaven and wary, had arranged themselves on the front porch. Yes, Mr. Blodgett was in. However, after no answer came to Temple's repeated jingling of the call bell, he and Etha stepped inside. Following a heavy clanging from above their heads, they took the stairs to the second floor. There they found Mr. Blodgett in a hall bathroom, balanced on a stepladder. Wielding a wrench, he was smacking the pipes of an old-fashioned toilet tank mounted high on the wall. Spotting Temple and Etha in the doorway, he paused.

"Either of you know how to fix a commode?"

After a surprised pause, Temple said, "I'm pretty handy. Willing to take a look."

Mr. Blodgett, a man in his thirties with dark brown hair, descended the ladder.

Temple rolled up his sleeves. "What's the problem?"

"It's dripping down through the kitchen ceiling."

Temple mounted the ladder and peered inside the tank. "By the way, I'm Sheriff Jennings from Jackson County, Oklahoma. This is my wife."

Blodgett backed up. "Whoa there. I'm not responsible for any illegal activities my lodgers may or may not partake in."

Temple said dryly, "I'm not sure that is truly the case. You got a screwdriver?"

"Think so." Mr. Blodgett scrabbled around in a toolbox sitting inside the bathtub which, Etha noted, was thickly circled with grime. "Here."

"Those are pliers," she said calmly. "That with the yellow handle is the screwdriver."

"Jesus, but I hate this place and the son of a b, pardon me, I bought it from. Nothing works, the furniture isn't even up to junk-shop standards, and it's in a nasty part of town. If I had any other place to go, if I still owned my properties in Kansas City, I'd be long gone."

Etha passed the screwdriver up to Temple. "How long have you been running the place?"

"Six months. Six months of hell. Pardon me. I bought it as an investment, oh, maybe eight years ago, when times were good. Adding to my string of, er . . ." he glanced up at Temple who was elbow deep in the tank, "social clubs in KC."

"You mean speakeasies," Etha said.

"Anyways, after Prohibition ended and the Depression set in, all I had left was this dump. So, here I am in Nowheresville waiting for better times and cursing Arthur Blodgett."

Temple yanked on the pull chain. The toilet tank emptied with a vigorous cascade. He climbed down the ladder. "So you aren't Mr. Blodgett?" he asked, tossing the screwdriver and wrench into the box.

"I go by that. Makes it easier. But the name is Joe Curtis."

"Okay, Mr. Curtis, I don't think you're going to have any more trouble with your tank. I'll wash up here, and then is there someplace we could talk?"

Curtis's desk was jammed into the kitchen's narrow pantry because, as he explained, "If I can let out the back room to a boarder, I'd rather have the money than an office." He offered Etha the guest chair, next to a shelf of canned corn.

Temple slouched in the doorway. "I believe a secretary at the courthouse called you about a Roland Coombs?"

Curtis snapped his fingers. "I knew there was something familiar about where you were from. Just couldn't place it. Yeah, that freeloader. Did he leave any money? Because if he did, it's mine. He owes—owed—me two weeks rent plus storage on the trunk."

"Let's back up a minute. How long did he board here?"

"Came with the property, same as all the other junk."

"So he lodged here a while?"

"Yep. Couple of years, I think he said. Born here in St. Joe. Guess you know that. Salesman of some sort. Always coming and going. Last time he stayed here was about three weeks back. Kept the same room and mostly paid for it even when he was away."

"Did you notice any hard feelings between Coombs and anyone?"

"Not in particular. Well, he was sort of a big mouth. Braggart. Actually, I think the last time he was here he got in a fistfight."

Temple straightened. "With who?"

Curtis waved his hand dismissively. "Bud Hitchcock. Pulled an empty pistol on Coombs. Hitchcock's been bunking here longer than Coombs, I'm told. Picks a fight with someone every other week."

"Has this Hitchcock been away in the last week or two?"

Curtis tapped his finger, outlining Hitchcock's daily routine: "Here, stockyards, saloon, back here. That's it."

"You sure?"

"Who do you think bangs on his door every morning to get him to the yards on time?"

"Okay. This last time, did Coombs happen to say how long he expected to be gone? Where he was going?"

Curtis traced his mustache, no thicker than the fine print in a pocket Bible, with the tip of his tongue. "Now as I think on it, he did. I had just come back from the post office and he was holding court on the porch. Talking about driving down to Oklahoma, naming off a bunch of burgs no one had heard of."

Temple scratched his chin. "I'd appreciate glancing at your register. See if any of the names look familiar."

From atop a row of Mason jars at his back, Curtis pulled down a canvas-bound ledger.

Etha stirred. "While you men finish up, could I have a look at his trunk? It might save some time."

"Okay by me." Curtis looked at the sheriff, who nodded. "It's not locked, as I remember. I'll take you out to the trunk room."

The trunk room was nothing but a stack of suitcases piled behind a partition in the stable. Coombs's baggage was neatly labeled. Etha made herself comfortable on the wide plank floor, snapped open the trunk, and caught the chemical scent of moth balls. A plaid winter jacket had been carefully folded on top. It was probably ten years old, Etha thought, judging from the style and the frayed cuffs. But someone had carefully stitched up tears in the lining. The sweaters, wool trousers, and a knitted cap underneath were also worn but respectable. Farther down was a jumble of keepsakes: a lumpy and deflated football with *1916 City Champs* painted on one side, a Brownie camera, a dented Kewpie doll of the sort given out as carnival prizes, and a framed certificate from a sewing machine repair correspondence course.

"Now here's something," Etha said aloud as she pulled out *The Crescent—1917*, a yearbook from St. Joseph Central High School. Flipping through the pages, she soon found Coombs among the thirty or so seniors. Printed under his name and list of activities, which included football and glee club, was the observation, *Three-fifths genius, two-fifths sheer fudge.* Sounded about right. Etha idly glanced at his classmates. They all had nicknames: *Pudge, Watso, Spuds, Sparky* . . . and *Floss.* Something in Floss, who was a slight girl with sorrowful eyes and a narrow chin, caught Etha's attention. She pulled the yearbook closer.

My God, it's Florence Hodge! The spitting image. Etha, her hands shaking, quickly read the brief words beside the photo:

Well-Versed in Household Arts Is She. Clionian Literary Society, 3, 4. —Florence Case

Her name was Florence Case. Etha's mind jumped all over the place, like a needle bouncing across a scratched phonograph record. Coombs and Florence knew each other. Had grown up in the same town. Had they been sweethearts? Had Florence recognized him when he'd turned up in Vermillion? Bursting with questions, Etha shoved everything back into the trunk except the yearbook. Clutching it to her chest, she raced inside.

In the pantry, Temple was saying, ". . . the uncle is the one to talk to about Coombs's debt. And if you think of or hear anything else about Coombs that might be relevant, call me. Remember, you owe me one after I fixed your toilet. So think on it real hard."

Curtis slowly escorted them to the front door, still lamenting his bad fortune in getting stuck in a cow town. He kept them at the front door for a couple of minutes listing all the things that needed repair in the kitchen and outbuildings. Etha thought he'd never shut up. Her insides fluttered, wanting to tell Temple what she'd found.

At last they were alone on the sidewalk and she blurted out her discovery: "See. Right here." She tapped on Florence Case's photograph.

Temple, lower lip pushed out, nodded in a way that Etha recognized as conveying, *I'm impressed.*

"So what now? The connection between these two must have something to do with the murder. It's too much of a coincidence, don't you think?"

"I do." Temple said. "And Ed tracked down a lead from a teacher at the explosives who overheard Coombs talking to Hodge and his wife. Seemed Coombs thought he knew her. Sounds like he did." He bent over and kissed his wife on the cheek. "Good eyes, my dear. And now I think we need to go talk to Coombs's uncle. Fill in some more puzzle pieces."

Bert Coombs, the closest living relative of the murdered man, was a ticket clerk at the train station. When they strolled into the brick building, a long line of travelers was crawling toward the window, toeing their picnic baskets forward an inch at a time. There was a general air of noise and confusion. All the tall-backed benches were packed with weary fathers and mothers watching as their children chased one another around the aisles. Several small boys played on the penny scale.

"Goodness!" Etha exclaimed.

"Wait here. I'll see if Mr. Coombs is around." Temple moved toward the counter, bypassing the line with a show of his badge.

Etha asked a harried mother where everyone was headed and learned that the state fair in Sedalia was underway. She wandered to a metal postcard rack and flipped through its offerings. Mostly buildings and statues from other parts of the state, but one St. Joe attraction caught her eye. She dropped three pennies in the honor box and slipped the postcard into her pocketbook.

"We apparently showed up on one of the station's busiest days," Temple said, returning to her side. "Coombs gets a break at three."

Etha brightened. "So why don't we grab a bite and poke around? I found a place that might be worth a peek."

At a lunch counter one block from the station, they ordered roast beef and mashed. Temple asked the waitress if she knew Roland Coombs or Florence Hodge, née Case.

"Only got here last week. On my way west."

The food arrived on thick plates. After two strong cups of coffee, they felt revived. Etha pulled out the postcard which depicted an old-fashioned frame house with splintered shutters.

"You want to see this?" Temple asked, frowning at the tiny lettering on the back.

Etha returned the postcard to her pocketbook. "It's where Jesse James was killed."

"Don't say?"

"I knew you'd be curious."

After motoring up and down the hilly thoroughfares overlooking town, Temple fussing about the clutch the whole while, they found Lafayette Street and the sorry little house. *Tours By Appointment Only,* a hand-painted sign announced.

"Shoot," Etha said, "let's peek in anyway."

"You know this man was a cold-blooded killer? Got what he deserved?" Temple replied.

"Yes, but he is a legend after all."

They waded into the weedy yard. Tourists had tattooed initials on the clapboard and torn away pieces of the spongy wood for souvenirs. Behind the panes of the single shutterless window, swarms of dust motes threatened to smother the dingy parlor.

"Why, there's a pump organ!" Etha declared. "Just like my granny's."

Temple starting crooning, "*Jesse James was a man who killed many a man . . .*"

"What?"

"Something I picked up from a drunk." Temple hummed a few bars, interjecting words when they came to him.

"It is a shame to let a good pump organ go to rot." Etha turned from the window and headed back to their car.

When they returned to the train station, they found Bert Coombs leaning in the main entrance, tamping tobacco into the bowl of a pipe. He was slightly built with watery blue eyes, and thin ribbons of hair raked across a pink scalp.

"My wife Etha and I offer our condolences on the death of your nephew," Temple said, extending his hand.

Bert nodded. "Appreciate it. Why don't we go around back to talk. There's an old caboose we use for breaks."

The dilapidated car that once housed train crews now sat on a stretch of sidetrack thick with Queen Anne's lace and blue chicory.

"I've always wanted to see inside one of these," Etha whispered to Temple.

Bert swung up on the ladder and reached down to help Etha. She had brought along Roland's yearbook and tucked it under one arm as Bert pulled her up by the other.

The car smelled of pipe smoke and linseed oil. There was an antiquated potbelly stove, a snug desk, and, beyond the hatchway, a tiny kitchen. The three settled onto the narrow padded bench lining one wall.

Temple began: "My deputy and I are working the case hard, but so far no leads have panned out. I came up here because, frankly, Etha convinced me that maybe your nephew's death is somehow connected to St. Joe."

Bert studied his hands. "I don't know how much help I'll be. He was my sister Trudy's son. One of those kids who palled around with older boys. Got in a fair amount of scrapes, but nothing serious. Bloody noses, tardy at school, that sort of thing."

Temple said, "Fair enough. What about high school?"

"Oh, he was the big man on campus. Captain of the football and baseball teams. Very athletic. Took after his dad. My side of the family are skinny minnies."

Pipe smoke eddied toward the ceiling.

"And after high school?" Etha asked. She noticed Temple raising his brows as if to say, *Whose interview is this?* but she went on: "Did he join up?"

"According to my sister, he was deferred due to a bad heart. Although, to be honest, I sort of found that hard to believe, being that he played sports and all. Of course, many young men in town did go overseas. Lots of sweethearts got left behind. Matter of fact, I believe Roland got engaged right after graduation and it seems to me it was to a girl that one of his classmates was sweet on. A fellow who got the patriotic fever and signed up before even finishing high school."

Etha's breath quickened. She pulled a stool opposite Bert and sat down. "So he stole a soldier's girl? That seems to me a reason for revenge."

"But that was seventeen years ago. Long time to hold a grudge," Temple said.

Etha ignored him. "Did your nephew and this young lady marry?"

Bert shook his head. "Roland wasn't the marrying kind, even though he pretended he was. I believe he had a number of lady friends after that one."

"And what happened to her? Do you remember her name?" Etha's eyes danced excitedly.

"Not really."

Opening the yearbook to the pages of the senior class, Etha passed it to Bert. "Could you take a look at these girls? See if one looks familiar?"

Bert pulled a pair of folded spectacles from his shirt pocket, settled them on his face, and drew the book toward him. "Um, none of these," he said, slowly turning the pages. "There's Roland, of course." He prodded the page with a finger. "Hey! I believe it was her. Yes, Floss Case. She was the one."

Etha was practically jumping out of her skin. "Do you know if they stayed in touch?"

"No idea. Doubt it. He and she ran off, then he left her high and dry. Somewhere in Kansas, I think."

"Wichita?" Temple asked.

"Maybe."

"And what about her soldier?" Etha asked. "Do you see him? What was his name?"

Bert flipped the pages. "He left before finishing school. His name was Frank something." He studied the window abstractly, then abruptly said, "Turnball. Frank Turnball."

Etha drew the yearbook into her lap. "Did he did make it home after the war?"

"Oh, yeah. But he didn't stick around. Likely because of Floss. He'd turn up every once in a while to see his mom and for funerals, but that was it. Matter of fact, he was just in town a month and a half ago. I spotted him here at the station. Life has been hard on him, from the looks of it. Could have passed for sixty or more. Heard he got gassed in the war."

Temple exchanged glances with Etha. "He was here, in St. Joe?"

"Yep. Sitting right inside," Bert thumbed toward the station house, "for a couple of hours, waiting for a train. Heard him jawing with a couple of different folks about how he hadn't been back in town for ten years or more." Bert snapped his fingers. "And hey, one of the ladies was kin to Floss. A second cousin or something. She must have recognized Frank too, because I heard her telling him Floss was married to a lawyer and had been living down in Oklahoma. Some town. I don't remember the name."

"Vermillion?" Etha said quietly.

"That could be it. Not sure."

Etha leaned forward. "So, this young man came back from the trenches to find that the girl he had a crush on had been romanced by your nephew and then cast aside?"

"Seems that way."

"He must have been terribly angry."

"I would be," Bert said. "But I can't remember hearing of a showdown, if that's what you're getting at."

From up the rails came a screech of brakes, the soar and dip of a train whistle. Bert checked his pocket watch. "It's the 3:17 out of Kansas City."

"One last thing," Temple said. "Besides this Frank, was there anyone else who might hold a grudge against your nephew?"

"Not that I know of. But he had a way with the ladies and I wouldn't be surprised if he had an angry husband or two on his tail. Sorry I can't be of more help."

Temple stood and extended his hand. "Appreciate you taking the time. I'll be in touch when we find who did it."

Etha nodded her thanks.

As they slid into the car, Etha said, "Do you think it's possible that this Frank came to Vermillion to track down Florence?"

"If so, that's something I've got to work on back home. I haven't heard of a Frank Turnball rattling around the county, but there are a lot of tramps floating through, so maybe."

Etha pulled out the postcard and scribbled some notes on the back. "Got to be someone who was a veteran, who was Roland's age—what, thirty-seven?—but looks older, like the uncle said. Someone who showed up in Vermillion about six weeks ago."

Temple absently tapped his fingers on the steering wheel. "I'll put Ed on that. And I'll speak with Florence Hodge. Bad luck that Frank quit school before he could get his photo in the yearbook."

They drove until early evening, spending the night in a tourist camp near Lawrence, Kansas. The next day, they were on the road before sunrise, reckoning to get home by midafternoon. But they hadn't calculated on another duster.

CHAPTER TWENTY-FIVE

TEN MILES WEST OF VERMILLION, Temple spotted the wall of dust, as massive and imposing as the Rockies, abruptly taking shape in the rearview mirror. His first impulse was to stomp on the accelerator and try to beat the roiling mass to town. It would be a gamble, though, because you never knew how fast the towering clouds of grit and sand were traveling or, without a single landmark to gauge their size, how big they really were. He glanced at Etha dozing beside him and changed his mind. Her earnest face, even as she slept, moved him deeply. No, better to find shelter now before the sightlines were reduced to zilch.

Temple slowed the Packard to a crawl and kept a lookout for a barn, shanty, or even a clump of trees. After fifteen years out here, you would think I'd know this stretch of road by heart, he thought. Dirt roads intersected the asphalt in a couple of places. Some might end up at a homestead but others could just be shortcuts to remote wheat fields. Best to keep heading east. Then it came to him that Trot, the fellow he'd ferried home from the auction and rabbit drive, lived down one of these roads. Temple recalled a spindly cottonwood near the turnoff.

The advancing steamroller of topsoil was closing in. Temple guessed the turnoff was not more than three miles away. Another five minutes passed. Not a cottonwood in sight. Fear boiled up in Temple's throat. He jiggled Etha's shoulder.

"What?" Her eyes opened wide and unfocused.

"Duster."

She squinted through the rear window. "Oh Lord."

"I'm looking for a place to shelter. When I pull off, get ready to make a run for it."

Etha reached into the backseat and snapped open the suitcase. After some scrambling, she unearthed two bandannas. She tied one around

Temple's neck as they jounced along and another around hers. She clamped her pocketbook to her stomach.

The towering storm closed in. The wind pushed against them, rattling every screw and nut in the sedan's frame.

"Just pull into that gulley!" Etha hollered.

Temple gritted his teeth. They were close to Trot's. He knew it. Sand clotted the windshield like a stirred-up river bottom. Was that a tree? He wasn't sure. Maybe. Yes! And beside it a dirt track. Temple yanked the steering wheel to the right and they bumped off the asphalt just as the full force of the duster slammed into them.

"Get down!" Temple shouted, pushing Etha's head into the footwell. The Packard jolted and swayed. Through the heavy curtains of dirt, Temple thought he spotted the soddie. They'd have to chance it. He braked hard and yelled at Etha to stay put. Smashing his shoulder into the door, he forced it open. Grit filled his eyes and mouth. Jerking up the bandanna and bent double, he lurched around to the passenger door. With the wind plowing into the side of the car, he yanked on the handle but it wouldn't budge. Through the window, he made out Etha's pale face. She pushed against the door while he wrenched the handle, and she finally tumbled out. They staggered toward the fluid dark shape that Temple hoped was Trot's soddie. When his fingers touched the door's rough planks, he was weak with relief. He turned the knob. They fell inside.

Trot, for it was indeed his soddie, jumped away from the kerosene lamp he had been in the act of lighting. The burning match dropped to the dirt floor.

Hurrying over to Temple, he shouted over the wail of the wind, "You all right?"

Temple nodded and helped Etha to her feet. Trot rushed back to the lamp and got it lit this time. Only then did he seem to recognize who had burst into his house.

"Sheriff! What you doing way out here in this?" The air in the soddie was thick with dirt, silt raining from the porous roof. Etha was coughing heavily.

"Get her some water!" Temple bellowed above the noise, and Trot hurried to the kitchen pump. Etha's cheeks were smudged, nostrils blackened. Temple gently pushed the hair, stiff and gray with dust, away from her forehead.

Trot returned with a cracked drinking glass. A squatter's china cupboard, Temple thought. Etha took the glass and drained it.

For twenty minutes, the howling duster made talk impossible. Several times the kerosene wick wavered, but it held. As dust storm veterans, the three knew how to wait it out. Trot wet down their bandannas and a rag for himself. They crouched, heads down, taking shallow breaths through the sodden fabric. Then, mercifully, the whipping sand and soil moved on, leaving behind a murky fog of dust.

Temple untied his bandanna and blew his nose. "Trot, you are a sight for sore eyes. Etha, this is the fellow I gave a ride to after the auction and then the rabbit drive."

"Oh yes." She extended her hand. "Sorry to bust in."

"Glad to be able to return the favor." Trot's seamed face broke into a toothless smile.

"We were heading home and didn't quite make it," Temple explained.

Etha took in the surroundings. She'd been in many a soddie but this one was in particularly poor shape. No one had bothered to change the newspapers covering the ceiling in several years, she judged. The walls were pocked with snake holes. The air smelled of earth and the stale odor of unwashed skin. Poor soul, she thought.

"Where were you at?" Trot asked.

"St. Joe."

"Really?"

"Investigating that murder. Got a promising suspect. Now just need to flush him out," Temple said.

Trot's laugh was brittle. "Not another kid, is it? I have to say, I don't think a young'un would do something like that. Bash a man's head in. It plagued me when you had the other one under arrest. Didn't seem right."

"No, this fellow's older."

Trot reached for Etha's tumbler. "Let me refill that, ma'am."

Temple peered out the window. "I think the worst has passed. Etha, I'm going to see if the road is clear enough and dig out the car. Then we'll be on our way."

Rising, Etha said, "My, I'm stiff." She moved around the cramped room, shaking out her legs. There was an illustration torn from a children's magazine tacked low on the raw wall where a child's bed had undoubtedly stood before the last family moved out. She bent for a closer look. The magazine was dated July 5. Six weeks ago. Straightening, she gazed at Trot. So the soddie had only been abandoned a short while. A spout of dirt suddenly opened above her head as the little house settled itself.

"Gracious," Etha said, bending to shake out her hair. She continued her tour. She came to a photo of a soldier, propped on a rough shelf. This must be the son that Temple had mentioned. She studied the picture. The doughboy stood stiffly with his hands behind his back and legs apart. Taking it off the shelf, Etha noticed that *Camp Funston* was scrawled on the back. They had driven past the former camp in Fort Riley, Kansas, just that day. It was not quite 150 miles from St. Joe.

Trot brought her the glass, dribbling water across the floor. She noticed his hands. They were smooth, the veins hidden beneath the flesh. The skin was nut brown, but not spotted by age. She considered his face. With its wrinkles and missing teeth, it might be that of an old man. But Etha knew that hands were a better judge of age.

Etha pointed to the photo. "That's you, isn't it?"

"Is."

"You were in the war?"

"Yes ma'am."

There was a bang from outside as Temple dropped the hood in place. The sky and grasses were still, as if the blow had drained the prairie of movement.

Temple tucked the oil rag he kept for cleaning the pistons under the seat. As he did so, he took note that he was once again humming the tune about Jesse James. He rested his gaze on the soddie. Trot had never said where he'd come from. But the man had mentioned stockyards. And Jesse James.

Temple strode toward the house, yanking open the door. Etha and Trot were facing one another by the far wall.

She was saying, "You were sweet on Floss, weren't you?"

Temple froze.

Trot mumbled, "I was." He jerked his head up, his voice louder. "I was, and that bastard used her and threw her away. And I couldn't protect her. She was the purdiest little thing. Nice as can be." His face distorted by grief, Trot pressed his palms into his cheekbones, covered his eyes.

In two steps Temple was across the room, gripping Trot's upper arm. "We need to talk. Sit down." Trot tried to pull away but the sheriff, keeping a tight grip on the man's arm, pushed him into a chair.

"Let's start with your name."

"I didn't do nothing wrong."

"Your name."

"All right. It's Frank Turnball. But I've been Trot for a long while."

"From St. Joe?"

"Born and raised."

"And since then?"

"Over there with the army. That's where I got the gas. When I got back home and found out that Floss was gone, it didn't matter where I was. I bummed all around, mostly in the south. Working as a hired hand. Painting houses. That sort of thing."

Temple rotated the other chair and straddled it; his face was inches from Frank's. "So you never went back to St. Joe?"

"Never said that. But only swung through every now and then. Was there in early July for a funeral."

"And how long have you been squatting here?"

"Six weeks."

"So you came down here right after your trip to St. Joe?"

"So?"

"Why here?"

Frank shrugged.

"Most folks are leaving Jackson County, not moving in."

"Wasn't really thinking of settling. Just riding the freights; jumped off here and thought to stay for a bit."

Etha, who had been standing in the shadows, approached, and said softly, "You came because someone told you Floss was here. Isn't that so?"

Frank studied his hands. After a moment he muttered, "No law against it."

"But there is a law against peering into folks' windows. That was you at the Hodge house, wasn't it?" Temple said.

Frank thrust his jaw out stubbornly. "I just wanted to get a look at her. Me being not much more than a broken-down bum and her married to a lawyer and all, I couldn't just go knocking at her door, could I? I didn't mean no harm."

Temple leaned toward the man. "But you *did* mean harm to Roland Coombs, didn't you? After all, he ran away with Floss while you were off soldiering."

Frank's eyes narrowed. When he spoke his voice was bitter as bile. "Roland was never nothing but a no-count. He deserved what he got.

Floss and I had an understanding that she would wait for me until after the war. But then, while I was overseas, he took advantage of her sweet nature and afterward tossed her away like a piece of trash."

"You must have been mighty surprised, and angry, when you saw Coombs pulling into town not long after you."

Frank's toothless mouth contorted into a grimace. "Yeah. Heard about the explosive show and thought, *Sounds like fun!* Got there just in time to see Roland boasting and preening as if he was still some big man. Talking about his time in the army when he'd never served a day. Every vein in my body swoll up like a balloon set to explode. And my poor little Floss was there in the crowd, listening to his guff. I decided right there I wasn't going to let him near her ever again."

"How did you plan to do that?"

"Follow him. Keep him within my sights and clobber him but good if he stepped out of line."

"But it didn't quite work out like that, did it?"

"After the explosive show my jalopy wouldn't start. So I tucked a busted shovel handle that I kept in the car for protection inside my overalls and started marching back to town. Roland passed me in his truck with some young fellows riding in the back." Frank huffed. "Asked if I wanted a ride."

"Go on."

"I couldn't risk him recognizing me so I turned him down. But I can tell you I hoofed it fast."

"And when you got there?" Etha prodded.

"When I got there, first place I looked was in the bar. Saw him from a distance and slunk back outside and waited. After a bit he staggered to Mayo's. I bunked up in the empty stable across the street. The next morning he stepped out, chipper even with a swollen nose some fellow had pasted on him. I followed him to the diner, keeping my hat pulled down, and then on to the movie house. I snuck in after the show started. The ticket taker was bent over a magazine and didn't even look up."

"When the duster started up and he slipped out the Jewel's side door, what did you do?" Temple asked.

Frank glanced at Etha, then at Temple. "I followed him."

"And then?"

Frank's head dropped. "Came up behind him. The wind was howling like a freight train. It was so loud I couldn't think clear anymore. I'd started out just wanting to keep him away from her, but now that wasn't enough. I had to make him pay. I raised the stick. He went down like a stone. Dropped just that quick. I still couldn't make out nothing but shapes in all that dust. When I kicked my toe into his side and he didn't move, I hightailed it out of there."

"So as far as you knew, he was still alive?"

"Yep. But then I heard that he was kilt. And later when you arrested that poor kid, I felt down as dirt. Kept hoping you'd figure out he didn't do it. And you did! But then, just now when you said you were chasing down someone else, I figured the time to step up was coming soon. Guess it did."

Temple stood, slowly tucking the chair in its place at the table. He gestured for Frank to stand. "I'm placing you under arrest for the murder of Roland Coombs."

Frank pressed his hands into his thighs and pushed himself up, his head bowed in surrender.

CHAPTER TWENTY-SIX

THE THREE RODE TO TOWN IN SILENCE. Dust motes, lit by the setting sun, hung in the air, heavy as embers. At the courthouse, Temple took Frank to the cellblock while Etha put on the coffee pot. The kitchen smelled stale, as if she and Temple had been traveling for weeks rather than two days. Despite the churning dust beyond the panes, she yanked up the windows. Temple shouldered open the door and lugged their suitcase inside.

For a time, they sat silently in the living room, sipping coffee.

Temple said, "Your thinking that the case was rooted in Coombs's past was right on the mark. You understood that better than me."

Etha smiled sadly. "I pity Frank. And poor Florence."

"You gotta remember that Frank took a man's life."

"So sad."

"Sadness all around."

"What about the primary?"

Temple shrugged.

They looked away from one another, her words falling across the carpets, the lamps, the piano with its fringed shawl, and all that was home. Etha busied herself with stacking their coffee cups, not wanting Temple to see her tears.

"I think I'll go see if Hinchie is holding down a stool at the Idle Hour." Temple rose and shook his legs.

"You've earned a glass or two." Etha smiled weakly.

Temple settled his hat on his head, its band still clammy from the day's sweat. "If that DiNapoli stops by for pie, don't tell him about Trot's arrest. I'll need to officially notify the boy he's in the clear. I'll do it first thing in the morning."

* * *

A thick cloud of cigarette smoke engulfed Temple as he loped into the bar. All the booths were crammed. A cluster of men and women hovered over a table of card players in the back. Hinchie's rear was firmly planted on his customary stool. When Temple laid his hand on the doctor's shoulder, Hinchie turned and grinned. "Saved you a place just in case." He patted the empty seat beside him.

"You know me well." Temple threw a leg over and signaled to Ike.

"Did you hear the news?" Hinchie asked.

"What news?"

"That plane Will Rogers and Wiley Post were flying around Alaska?"

"Yep."

"It went down."

Temple blanched. "And?"

"Gone."

"Both?"

Hinchie nodded.

Temple's face drained of expression.

Hinchie signaled Ike to bring whiskey. The barkeep poured two shots and started to walk away with the bottle. "Leave it," Hinchie said.

After knocking back three shots, Temple shook his head. "Can't believe it."

"Minnie says that you and Etha have been on the road," Hinchie said after a moment.

Temple studied the ceiling. "Crossed the county line right along with that duster. But I made an arrest."

Hinchie reared back, a little too far, and grabbed the edge of the bar. "That so? Good for you! Will this one hold up?"

"Got a confession. I'll fill you in if you swear not to tell Minnie until the *Gazetteer* comes out tomorrow afternoon."

Solemnly, Hinchie raised a palm.

"All right, then," Temple said, launching into a detailed account of the trip to St. Joe, the confrontation in the soddie, Frank's admission and arrest. "And you could have knocked me over with a feather to find out that Mrs. Hodge was the cause of it all."

Hinchie shook his head. "I am privy to a lot of misery but Florence has been through the wringer."

"You told me a couple of days ago you thought John was capable of murder. Something else you need to say on that?"

Hinchie stared into his glass. "She's never admitted it, but I believe John beats the daylights out of her on a regular basis. I can't tell you how many times I've patched her up for household accidents that don't match up with the damage to her body."

Temple dropped his head. "Christ."

Behind them, Doll and his cronies pushed into the narrow saloon, laughing and snorting. A few of the fellows broke off from the herd and shoved up to the bar. One, a store clerk by the name of Smith, spotted Temple and shouted, "Look who it is!"

Temple nodded in acknowledgment and turned toward Hinchie. "My turn to—" he began, but was interrupted by Smith.

"Making the most of your last months as sheriff?"

Temple struggled to keep his tone light: "As far as I know, voting's not until tomorrow."

Smith leaned in, but his voice was loud: "You should know that we just came from a rally at the grange hall. Seems that the farmers are none too happy with your performance these past few months. The thinking is you should've done more about the bad elements in the county—those that are stealing and begging. And they are wanting a man who has personal relationships with the top officials in the statehouse. Who can get what's due Jackson County."

The noisy crowd, sensing a flap, hushed up.

Temple labored to still his face.

Smith poked him in the shoulder. "And without the farmers, your vote count will be mighty low." The clerk turned and shouted to the crowd, "Right, boys?"

At the rabbit drive, Temple had wanted to swat down Doll's barbs, but he had pulled back. It wasn't his way. He had wanted to point out that hiring deputies on commission, like Doll planned, was a bad idea. But between the whiskey and the misery over Will Rogers, there was nothing holding him back. The angry words rose in his throat like a wave. Sure, he wanted to win, but just as much he wanted to set the record straight on the specious ideas that Doll was propagating like bindweed.

Standing, Temple gazed across the faces of the crowd, many toughened by sun and wind, their high cheekbones carved out from months of short rations. Doll leaned against the wall by the door. He raised a glass to the sheriff.

Temple steadied himself. "Look here. I've been sheriff of Jackson

County fifteen years. I've done my honest best to keep the peace and
enforce the laws fair and square. I am mindful of circumstances, especially
in these hard times, and willing to bend when I know someone is trying
to right a wrong." He cleared his throat. "It is true. I don't have pals in
the highest offices of the capital, as Doll says he does. I am not on a first-
name basis with the governor and such. But I am known among sheriffs
and judges across the state. And I'd like to think that I have their respect."

He paused, searching for some nods of affirmation. The crowd was
stone still. "I was hoping to stand on my record, my reputation. I am not
one to attack my opponent. But let me ask you, Vince. What exactly have
you done for the people of Jackson County?"

Doll grinned and shrugged elaborately. "I'm not sheriff."

"No, but you are a town founder, as you constantly remind us. A
businessman. You own the grain elevator. What is more important to a
farming county than that? These are tough times. Drought. No work.
Hungry kids. Foreclosures. You benefitted from the sweat of the farmer
in the good times. What have you done to help in the bad? You are in
a position, so you say, to speak to state officials. To make sure Jackson
County is not forgotten. Gets its share of farm aid. To date, none of that
has happened. The farms are shriveling up, the children are crying from
hunger, the man who wants to do an honest day's work is reduced to
asking for handouts."

There was silence. But Temple was too pie-eyed to tell if that was
because the crowd was ruminating on what he'd said or gathering itself
for an attack.

Doll, who also might have been uncertain, quickly stepped into the
pause. "Mr. Jennings, you well know that I have dedicated my life to
Jackson County. Have done everything possible to see that it grows and
thrives. Yes, this drought is an unfortunate setback, but I am confident
that the rains will return soon. It is a matter of waiting it out."

Temple studied his hands. "I also want to say that I think your plan
to hire deputies to work on commission is ill-founded. I have seen other
counties go this route. And I have seen the number of unwarranted
arrests go up. I myself have attended funerals downstate which were
patrolled by commissioned deputies hovering like vultures, waiting for
the grieving to get liquored up and take a swing at someone. I even saw
one such lawman provoke a fight so he could make an arrest. This is
not the kind of person we want protecting the peace. We want someone

like Ed McCance, my deputy. Yes, he is not local, but he is the best man for the job. I've never seen a harder-working young fellow. Honest and dedicated."

He sensed that beside him, Hinchie was fidgeting in his seat, maybe trying to get him to sit down. But Temple went on. This all had to be said. "And as far as the tramps go, I just want to say that most all of those fellows, to a man, would rather be earning their own bread and living at home with their families. Hardly a one is a no-count or criminal. Most are just men and boys down on their luck. I'm not inclined to clear out the only place that gives them some shelter before they hop the next freight." He stopped abruptly. "I've said my piece. Thanks for listening." He sat down hard on the stool.

After a minute, the hum and chatter of the Idle Hour resumed. No one approached the sheriff to shake his hand or pledge support. Hinchie patted his shoulder. "You're a good man."

"That doesn't put food on the table," Temple responded grimly.

Soon after, Hinchie headed home and Temple stayed on, ruminating on where a fellow of fifty-four years might get work in hard times.

After Temple left for the Idle Hour, Etha had burst into tears. The sadness of Frank's story, of poor misused Florence, cast a pall over her heart. But there was something else. Minnie's warnings, the murmurings in town, and Temple's own countenance told Etha that by tomorrow evening, he might very well lose. And a few months after that, she would be relinquishing the house keys. Turned out like so many others these days.

There was a knock at the door. It was Carmine.

"Stopping by to hear how your trip went."

Etha sniffled and blew her nose. "Aren't you a sight for sore eyes. Come on in."

Carmine ambled into the kitchen, beating his dusty hat against his leg.

"You should know," she said, "that I haven't had time to bake a pie seeing as we were on the road for the past three days."

Carmine chuckled. "Shoot."

"But I might have some oatmeal cookies in the jar."

"Milk?"

"Check if it's still good."

Carmine opened the icebox and took a sniff from the bottle. As Etha arranged cookies on a plate, he grabbed a tumbler and poured himself a glass.

They sat at the kitchen table, Etha burning to tell him about Frank's arrest. If she swore Carmine to secrecy, Temple might never know. She opened her mouth to begin but the young man was shoving a package wrapped in brown paper across the oilcloth. "For you."

Etha straightened. "Really?"

It was a copy of *Cimarron* with a worn khaki cover and a cracked binding.

Carmine bit into his second cookie. "Read it?"

She shook her head.

"The guys were passing it around and I thought you might like it."

"Thank you."

Busily pressing the crumbs off the plate with his index finger, Carmine said, "Like to read it when you're done."

"Of course," Etha said. But then the thought came soon that she might no longer be living in this place, with Carmine just up the road. Watching him finish off the milk, her throat swelled.

He continued to chatter about goings-on among the fellows and then, after goodbyes were said, Etha sat alone, pressing her hands against her eyes, feeling her palms grow slippery. An advertising jingle blared from the radio. Slowly she rose and fished an old *Gazetteer* out of the trash. In the parlor she approached the knickknack shelf and her eyes fell on the green-glazed vase. The miniature tea set. The celluloid cowboy that Temple had won for Jack at the Illinois State Fair. She kneeled and slowly wrapped each piece in newsprint. Later she'd find a cardboard box. And then other boxes. Until by November, all their belongings were packed and they headed out for parts unknown.

Primary day emerged hot and hazy. Temple spent most of the morning filling Ed in on the events leading up to Frank's arrest and preparing for the arraignment before Judge Layton, which was scheduled for that afternoon. He telephoned the CCC camp. Carmine was out on a planting brigade. Temple asked Commander Baker to let the boy know an arrest had been made and that he was cleared.

As Etha dressed to run errands, Lottie called. Her first words were: "I know I should be upset about this, but strangely I'm not."

Etha, in her slip and one stocking, frowned into the mouthpiece. "What's going on?"

"Chester. After the premiere I expected . . . well, you know. And when I brought up how well we worked together, he agreed, and when I pushed further, he all but admitted he never intended to marry me."

Etha sucked in her breath. "Oh dear."

"No, it's all right. I was crushed but then my eyes opened. I saw our ten years together for what they were—a long road going nowhere. So I walked out. Walked out and this morning called my uncle who has been pleading with me to take a buyer's position in his department store out in Oklahoma City. I start next month."

Etha, who had been leaning against the wall with the receiver pressed to her ear, slid down to the floor with a thump. "I can't believe it. Are you sure?"

"Never more so."

Etha sighed. "I think this is the right decision. But I'm going to miss you terrible."

Lottie's voice was determined: "We'll make it a point to get together regular. And when we do, you won't have to listen to my laments about Chester."

"Well, that's a relief," Etha said, and then they were laughing.

On her way to the butcher's, still struggling with a lump in her throat after Lottie's call, Etha crossed through a line of voters snaking through the courthouse foyer, making their way to the basement where ballots were cast. Most hung their heads or looked away when they saw her. Earlier that morning she had urged Temple to call Hank Stone at the *Gazetteer* about the arrest and he promised to make time. Yet seeing the steady line, it seemed likely that many votes would be recorded before the afternoon newspaper was out.

But the fact was that the *Gazetteer* had just completed an early press run. The front page announced, "RAINMAKER KILLER CAUGHT," in the tallest, thickest font the linotype had in its arsenal.

A fresh stack was already front and center on the customer counter when Florence Hodge stepped up to pay her past-due bill. She'd been too twitchy and anxious to answer the door when the delivery boy rang last week. Now she stood at the counter, waiting for the office clerk to look up. He was counting a pile of coins dumped from a dirty canvas collection bag. Most were pennies. How long would it take for him to finish and notice her? Florence stared at her fingers, bloody and raw around the nail beds from constant nibbling, and quickly curled them under. She felt the press of time. In not too long, John would be coming up the front sidewalk and she had yet to run laundry through the wringer and get dinner underway. *Count faster,* Florence silently begged the clerk. Then her eyes fell on the stack of newspapers, on the cacophonous headline. The blood in her veins seemed to empty. Timidly, she plucked up the top issue, still damp from the press. Below the headline was the same photo of Roland that had run the day after he was murdered. Two weeks ago, seeing that image had set her nerves twanging and jumping all over the place. But not as badly as the night before, when she and John had driven out to the TNT demonstration and she had first caught sight of Roland standing smugly beside the pastor. Everyone's head was bowed. Except his. Except hers. Their eyes had briefly met. Florence thought she would collapse right then and there. The one thing that had gotten her through these years with John was that she would never see Roland again. Vomit had pushed into her mouth. She squeezed her eyes shut and swallowed it. The smothering shame that she'd endured every day since she had run off with the no-count all those years back was choking off her breath. Roland did not seem to recognize her. John had never met the man who had, as he described it, "soiled her." But later, at the end of the explosions, John had insisted on talking to the rainmaker. Florence had asked to wait in the car but John said, "Oh, no, I don't want any men sniffing around when I'm not there." So it was then that Roland took her in. He glanced casually at the pale face and shapeless dress and looked away in . . . what? Indifference? Disgust?

Now he cast the same look at her from the front page of the *Gazetteer*. Florence began reading. A man had been arrested. One who had known Roland Coombs in St. Joe. One who had shipped out as a doughboy and returned to find Roland had run off with the girl he was sweet on. The killer's name was Frank Turnball. Florence froze. That nice quiet boy? Frank? He'd had a crush on her, she knew that, but they'd never gone on a single date. It didn't make a bit of sense that he had killed Roland, killed anyone. And because of her? Her head throbbed. She sat down hard on a chair at the end of the counter.

The clerk must have heard her. "You all right?" His spotty face, aflame with adolescence, swam into focus.

"Just a little faint."

"I'll get some water."

When he returned, she drained the glass and paid her bill. Then she sat down and finished the article.

The prisoner had been arrested in a soddie five miles from town and was housed in the county cellblock. She peered out the window, trying to imagine Frank Turnball, the schoolboy, in jail. A wagon pulled by a lame mule passed down the street. Suddenly, she remembered Frank gimping across the playground at the end of recess. Frank had been marked out by a couple of older boys. Every day they stalked him, cornering him by the cellar stairs. There they kicked his scrawny shins with their heavy shoes until his legs bled. It all rushed back—the dark wet spots on his trouser legs and his stiff shuffle toward the schoolhouse door at the end of recess.

Florence pressed her hand against her mouth. The memory was as vivid as if it were yesterday. And that was not really surprising. She had felt the crack of John's brogans against her own shins many times. The fierce pain as if her bones were snapping. The sticky trickle of blood running down her stockings. The purple lumps. The shame. But she had never once thought of poor Frank Turnball's sufferings until now.

Temple was alone in the office, the telephone receiver pressed to his ear, when Florence walked in. He gestured to the chair beside his desk, holding up a finger to indicate he was almost through. She sat, pocketbook pressed tightly against her stomach.

"Sorry to keep you," he said after hanging up. "You here about Frank Turnball?"

She jerked as if someone had pierced her with a darning needle. Fumbling within herself, she said, "How did you know?"

"Frank told us about you and him," he said gently. "How you were sweethearts—"

"No, we weren't," Florence interrupted. "I don't know where he got that idea." She studied her hands. "I did know him from school, of course. He was always kind. A quiet boy. That is how I remember him. And that is why I can't believe . . ."

"That he killed a man?"

Florence nodded.

"The man you ran off with?"

She squeezed her eyes shut.

Temple leaned forward and laid a hand over hers. "Even if there was nothing between you two back then, you need to know that Turnball believes there was. And that is why he cracked Coombs over the head."

Florence crumbled. "Oh Lord."

Beyond the closed door a steady stream of chatter flowed from the line of voters. Her dress stuck to her skin and her mouth seemed filled with cotton.

Temple was talking: "It is not your fault Turnball got things twisted around. He might not be quite right in the head."

Florence's legs ached. She bent to rub them, then straightened abruptly. "I'd like to see him."

Temple paused. "You sure?"

"Yes."

And so Temple and Florence passed through the line of perspiring voters and mounted the stairs to the dim cellblock. Inside an office fan churned. The space smelled of bleach and sweat.

"Turnball, you've got a visitor," Temple said, swinging a chair in front of the cell.

Florence approached timidly and lowered herself. A thin figure gradually emerged from the dark cocoon of the bunk.

"And who might that—" Frank stopped. "Why Floss!"

"Hello, Frank," she said softly.

Both hesitated, seeking out their younger selves in the other's face.

"You were always the prettiest girl in school." Frank produced a crooked grin. "Still are."

Florence leaned forward. "I'm sorry to see you in such a state."

He quickly covered his mouth. "Lost most of them when I got gassed. Did you know the Huns gassed me?"

"No. But I meant sorry you are in jail and all."

Frank shrugged. "Roland? He deserved it. Boy, are you a sight for sore eyes!"

Florence said to Temple, "I'd like to stay a bit, if that's all right?"

The sheriff studied the set of her mouth. "I'm right downstairs if you need me."

The lukewarm breeze from the fan lifted the damp hair from her forehead. She became aware of an inner stillness. As if all her twitching anxieties, her shame and denigration, had sunk, silt-like, beneath a vast lake. Maybe it was because Frank, even in his deluded state, had sought to punish the man who had used and discarded her. No other man, certainly not her husband, had

tried to right that ancient wrong. Or perhaps the tight fists of her nerve fibers
had opened because she now beheld someone truly more pitiful than herself.
Someone to whom she had something to offer—comfort, friendship.

She turned to Frank. "You were in the war?"

"Saw action in Argonne Forest."

"Tell me. I want to hear it all."

The polls closed at six sharp. As was the tradition, most of the farm
folk who had come in to vote decamped to the courthouse lawn for
box suppers, to gab and eat for the couple of hours it took to count
the ballots. Then they'd come back into the courthouse foyer to hear
the results. Townsfolk made their way to the Maid-Rite or the Idle
Hour with similar intentions. Wagering in general was not acceptable in
churchgoing circles, and so did not figure in on the courthouse lawn or at
the Maid-Rite counter. However, it was a different story at the Idle Hour
where bets were placed with the odds favoring Doll.

Stomach twisted with worry, Etha could hardly think about cooking
supper and she supposed Temple wouldn't be hungry anyway. Still,
she decided to prepare some chicken for frying, figuring if it didn't get
eaten that night, it would be good tomorrow. As she dipped the second
drumstick in buttermilk, she heard the shouts of two men reverberating
up the staircase and getting louder. One was Temple. Etha opened the
door and saw a red-faced John Hodge puffing up the stairs toward her.
Her husband was right behind.

Hodge was yelling, "I demand to see my wife!"

Temple's face was stern. "If Mrs. Hodge wants to see you, that is her
decision."

"Of course she wants to see me, I'm her husband!"

The two men reached the top of the stairs and were now facing off in
front of the cellblock door.

Temple grabbed Hodge's arm. "Stop right there."

Hodge whipped around. "You've no right."

Temple brought his face close to the man. "You've no right to beat
the daylights out of her."

Hodge pulled back but Temple didn't loosen his grip.

"I promise you, no matter if I am sheriff or not, I will see that you are
locked up if you ever touch her again."

"How dare you talk to me like that when you've left her alone with a murderer?" Hodge was still blustering, but Temple's accusation seemed to have temporarily taken the wind out of him. He glanced at the heavy steel door and turned back, disgust crossing his face. "I'm not standing here begging like a dog for that poor flop of a woman. Tell her I'm going for a drink and will be home in an hour. And I expect dinner on the table."

After Hodge stomped down the steps, Temple turned to Etha. "Sorry you had to witness that."

She hurried over and hugged him hard about the waist, nestling her head in the bony valley of his sternum. Temple wrapped his arms around her, murmuring, "My old sweetie," into her soft hair.

She took his hand and led him inside. "It's been a long day."

As Etha had predicted, neither she nor Temple had any appetite. But when she brought Frank's tray over to the cell, he beamed and dug right in. Florence asked if she could come over and make a cup of tea.

"I'd be glad to bring you one," Etha offered.

"Thank you."

Etha dropped her voice: "I know the Hinchies have an extra room for patients who need watching overnight. I'm sure they'd let you stay as long as you need to. Should I call Minnie?"

Florence nodded. Then she turned to Frank. "May I come back tomorrow?"

"I'd be grateful."

Temple and Etha retired to the parlor to wait until it was time to go downstairs for the returns. For a while they listened glumly to a dull musical program, stalled a bit longer, and then Temple said, "Guess it's time."

The wide courthouse foyer was packed with party backers, clerks, farmers, teachers, and old-timers—all refreshed after time spent in their various watering holes. Doll was there along with his wife Carrie, who tottered along after him in high heels.

Within the next half hour, the lobby was swarming with bodies. Etha spoke briefly with Lottie but then her gut cinched up and she retreated outside. The night sky was still. Sitting on the top step of the courthouse, she drew in the slightly cooler air.

From the shadowy street, a slight figure approached at a trot. It was Carmine.

"Had to see how the election comes out," he said, dropping onto the step beside her. "Ran all the way here." He wiped his brow on his sleeve.

"Feeling pretty blue," Etha said. "I was just thinking that if Temple loses, I won't see you anymore after November."

Carmine blushed. "Ah, ma'am, I won't let that happen. After I finish with the CCC, I can hop a freight to visit you wherever you land just like that." He snapped his fingers.

Etha shook her head. "I don't want you hopping any more freights. You should settle someplace and build a life." She inhaled the grassy scent of a young boy that still clung to Carmine, despite his years. Then she abruptly slapped him on the thigh. "What about curfew?"

"This is more important. Besides, what are they going to do to me? I've already been arrested for murder. Can't get worse than that."

"There's my old sweetie." Temple's boots creaked as he sat down on Etha's right. "I've been a-looking for you." He tipped his hat toward her companion. "DiNapoli."

"Sir," Carmine replied respectfully. Then, rising, he said he'd wait for the announcement inside and dashed up the steps.

Etha pressed a hankie against her eyes and snuffled. Temple put his arm around her and drew her close. "You all right?"

Etha blurted, "I guess I didn't realize how attached I've become to everything here."

Temple tucked her hand in his. At that moment the door behind them was yanked open and Viviane stuck her head out. "They've got the results."

Inside, Judge Layton was standing beside the Great War memorial plaque, rapping a table with his gavel. "Quiet, please!" he shouted in the stony tone that had made many a bootlegger quiver. "We have the results of the five primaries. We will start with the post of county treasurer, which was uncontested . . ."

He droned on through the outcomes, meticulously reading each in measured tones and giving the vote count, even though the only contested office was that of sheriff. "And finally, the results of the primary election for sheriff," he announced. Etha squeezed her husband's hand. "The vote tallies are: 248 for Vince Doll, 270 for Temple Jennings."

There was stunned silence. Temple reared back in surprise, then swept Etha up in a huge embrace. The Doll camp was clearly in shock. "Had it all sewn up," more than one campaigner mumbled. Temple's supporters, for he must have had some, seemed almost as confounded.

Hank Stowe approached the sheriff and his wife with his reporter's notebook in one hand. With the other, he gave Temple a heavy pat on the back. "Any comments for the press?" he asked with a grin.

Temple guffawed. "Didn't expect this, that's for sure."

"I didn't either until early afternoon," Hank said." I stopped by the courthouse here to talk to the folks in line. A good many heard about your remarks last night at the Idle Hour. Either were there in the flesh or got the word from someone who was. Seems your argument against deputies working on commission hit home."

"I'm mighty grateful."

Hank said, "And you owe some gratitude to Commander Baker. Seems he was in the same regiment as Mac Williamson, the attorney general. Got him to endorse you at the last minute. My job shop printed up handbills with Williamson's testimonial."

"I'll be."

"Baker asked for volunteers among his CCC boys to pass them out. Any idea whose hand went up first?"

Temple shook his head.

"That kid you arrested."

Folks pressed around the sheriff to offer congratulations. Etha pushed her way through to Minnie and Lottie, who had settled on a hard wooden bench.

Lottie jumped up and kissed her on the cheek. "Here I was, sort of hoping you and Temple would be moving to Oklahoma City with me. But I'm happy for you."

Minnie issued a salute in agreement. "The first thing you need to do when you get there, Lottie, is buy me a new pair of shoes. I can't abide these a minute longer." Stooping, she drew off her pumps. Two pieces of cardboard flopped out. "I mean, really."

Eventually, the crowd trickled down to a couple of dozen folks quietly chatting. From the sheriff's office, Ed and Viviane emerged, holding hands. As they approached, Etha, who had rejoined Temple, whispered, "Something's up."

Ed, whose slicked-down hair was slightly ruffled, wore a dazzled expression. "Sir, I wanted you to be the first to know that I have asked Viviane to be my wife, and I can't believe it but she has accepted."

"Of course she did," Etha said stoutly.

Temple slapped the deputy on the back. "You lucky dog."

Viviane, who was hanging back shyly, was pulled forward by Ed.

"You must let me play at the service!" Etha said, hugging the young woman's narrow shoulders. "And I have fried chicken upstairs just waiting for a celebration dinner," she continued, taking in Temple and Ed. "We can toast your engagement and the primary."

"Fine with me," Temple said. They all trooped up the steps. Temple stopped halfway. "Is DiNapoli still here?"

"I believe he's talking to Hank," Etha replied.

Temple looked over the railing and saw the crop of dark hair, the denim uniform. From this angle, the kid looked less like Jack than ever. But Etha saw something there, and even if the kid was just his own self, Carmine and Etha were clearly devoted to one another. Temple realized that, for the first time in many years, he was not harboring, way in the back of his mind, the thought of uprooting and starting afresh yet again. It was a yearning from long ago when the flood came through Johnstown and his father decided to pack up the family and flee. Jack's death stirred it up harder. But now it seemed clear that staying put and rebuilding was better than running. He considered that always facing forward, like a horse pulling a plow, was not the only way or maybe not even the better way. What came before continued to color the present, even if you pretended it didn't. Look at Frank, for God's sake.

"I'd like him to join us," Temple said to Etha, and trotted back down the stairs.

Etha watched from above as her husband laid a hand on Carmine's shoulder.

And so the night ended with a string of toasts. To Ed and Viviane. To the election. To Etha's pie and to Carmine's exoneration. After the guests filed out, with handshakes and hugs and a restrained pat on Carmine's back by Temple, the sheriff and his wife decided the dirty dishes could wait until morning. As they lay side by side, the heat of the day finally lifting, Temple brought up their son.

"I know you've been wanting to get to Peoria to see the grave. Let's do it. I've earned a bit of time off."

Etha studied the ceiling. "You know, I don't need to do that now. Maybe later, but not now."

"All right. But whenever you say, I'm ready. My thinking's changed somewhat. I've come around to seeing there is nothing wrong with staying put or even looking backward every once in a while."

Etha scooted over, fitting herself against his long form. "I'm going to hold you to that."

The bedroom air thickened. Above them, the clock struck the hour, rattled the china cupboard, but neither stirred. And then, deep in the night, Etha suddenly awoke. Small splatters hit the window. Rain! She nudged Temple's back.

"It's raining," she whispered.

He continued to breathe the heavy air of sleep.

"Wake up!"

Temple sighed. "What?"

"I said it's raining."

"So?"

"So come on." She stripped the light sheet from his legs and pushed her feet against his back.

"Hey!" He twisted around, squinting. "I heard you. It's raining. Good. Go back to sleep."

"It hasn't rained a drop in eight months." She pushed harder. "Get up."

"Oh, Etha."

"Come on. You can get right back in bed. I promise."

"And I'm not going to get any more rest until I'm up?"

"That's right." She was out of bed, pulling on his arm.

"All right, all right. Hold your horses."

Etha was as excited as if it were Christmas morning. In the quiet darkness, they descended to the first floor, their bare feet slapping on the treads. Temple still groggy, Etha as alert as a chimney swift. The wide foyer was empty. Etha twisted the lock, yanking on the tall wooden doors. Drops of rain spattered the granite stairs.

As Jackson County slept, Etha took Temple's hand. They smiled gently at one another, turning their faces to the sky. Small drops splashed against their foreheads and eyelashes and ran down the sides of their faces and into their ears, as tears sometimes do.

From the third floor, Frank peered out the cell window. He watched the woman in a white slip twirling on the shadowy lawn. He watched the bare-chested man in pajama bottoms sweep her into a waltz. Why, that's me and Floss, he thought, smiling. Me and Floss.

Acknowledgments

This book was inspired by *The Worst Hard Time: The Untold Story of Those Who Survived the Great American Dustbowl* by Timothy Egan (Houghton Mifflin, 2006), in which he tells the stories of those who stubbornly stayed on the land during the 1930s, despite the devastating dust storms that stripped away the topsoil and, soon after, the farm fields, schools, churches, and entire communities. Many thanks to Egan for shining a light on these brave and enduring souls.

I am deeply indebted to the tireless, supportive, and whip-smart folks at Akashic Books: Johnny Temple, Ibrahim Ahmad, Johanna Ingalls, Susannah Lawrence, Alice Wertheimer, and Aaron Petrovich. None of this would be possible without you.

Thank you to the fearless imprint, Kaylie Jones Books—for humbling me, filling me with gratitude, and encouraging me to grow as a writer. Special thanks to KJB's irreplaceable Lauren Sharkey and to Jennifer Jenkins.

And no thanks are enough for the courageous Kaylie Jones—my teacher, publisher, and friend. Edith Wharton once wrote, *There is one friend in the life of each of us who seems not a separate person, however dear and beloved, but an expansion, an interpretation, of one's self, the very meaning of one's soul.*

And finally, I am lovingly grateful to my wonderful family that now stretches farther and wider than I ever imagined.